Nina Dufort spent her childhood split between the Kent countryside and The Lebanon. After spending many years employed in diverse travels and occupations and bringing up two daughters, she became a successful painter. At present, Nina Dufort lives with her husband on Romney Marsh and spends her time writing and painting.

Also by Nina Dufort

Defrosting Edmund

Painting Out Oscar

Nina Dufort

FLAME
Hodder & Stoughton

Copyright © 1999 by Nina Dufort

First published in 1999 by Hodder and Stoughton
A division of Hodder Headline PLC
First published in paperback in 1999 by Hodder and Stoughton
A Flame Paperback

The right of Nina Dufort to be identified as the Author of
the Work has been asserted by her in accordance with the
Copyright, Designs and Patents Act 1988.

10 9 8 7 6 5 4 3 2 1

A CIP catalogue record for this title is available
from the British Library

ISBN 0 340 71683 5

Typeset by Palimpsest Book Production Limited,
Polmont, Stirlingshire
Printed and bound in Great Britain by
Clays Ltd, St Ives PLC, Bungay, Suffolk

Hodder and Stoughton
A division of Hodder Headline PLC
338 Euston Road
London NW1 3BH

The sight of you is good for sore eyes.

Jonathan Swift,
*A Complete Collection of Polite and Ingenious Conversation
(dialogue 1)* 1738

Chapter One

An ivory face framed with sallow hair pressed close to the window and watched the morning. Mrs Lewis passed most of her long days just watching. Her eyes merely recorded, her brain filing the images to no great purpose since she rarely wondered about what she saw or imagined about what she had not. Even comparisons were an effort for her.

A white car pulled up outside the cottage next door and she was startled by the rare description that fluttered through her vacancy: that the car resembled an upturned bathtub.

The occupants of the car were the next-door neighbour Oscar Mitty and an unknown woman in a red jacket and they appeared to argue briefly before Oscar climbed from the car, dressed in the weather-beaten black leathers he wore for riding his motorbike. Mrs Lewis had heard him leave on the bike earlier that morning, not long after his wife had gone to work. He now strode up the damp brick path in the fine spring drizzle and out of her field of vision, a roll of plastic bin bags beneath his arm. She heard him let himself in and the door slam. The unknown woman stayed at the wheel of the car, pulling the rear-view mirror into a more convenient position for fluffing up her dark hair with her fingertips.

The woman was the only moving object in view so Mrs Lewis sipped instant coffee from a Charles and Diana mug and continued to watch. She was unsure how this piece of commemorative pottery had come into her ownership. On the mornings when she was conscious enough to notice its poor design, she intended to donate it to the Help the Aged shop but a fog came down upon her before she ever managed to get it outside the door and so it continued in her possession. A white cat joined her at the windowsill, staring with her. The woman in the car tapped her fingers on the wheel, perhaps with impatience or to music which Mrs Lewis could not hear, bent forward to retrieve something from the floor, leant her head back on the headrest and stretched her arms, shifting about irritably.

Half an hour elapsed before Mrs Lewis heard the latch click and she saw Oscar return down the path, laden with bags. The woman leapt out to help him, supervising the loading into the boot. They were hurrying, maladroitly knocking into each other, silent and eager to be gone. Oscar Mitty cracked his head on the hatch and stopped to rub his scalp, ruffling the straight blond hair, now rat's-tailed by the soft rain. The woman reached up to kiss him, but caught sight of the vigilant face framed between the threadbare curtain linings at the window of the larger house, thought better of it and glowered. She drove off fast, leaving Oscar to fetch more cardboard boxes from the house. He loaded these into his own car and then he too drove away. Mrs Lewis sighed. Their houses were at the bottom of a dead-end lane, on the outskirts of the small town of Bellhurst; it was unlikely there would be more movement till lunch time when Beatrice Mitty returned home.

Seen through the faulty panes of the kitchen window, the blackbird on the bird table outside appeared to four-year-old Seb as a monstrous, distorted fairground raven. Letting out a histrionic shriek, he threw himself beneath the table. Bea put down her pencil, exasperated; the free Friday afternoons away from the job at the Bellhurst Bookshop were sacrosanct and she'd hoped to salvage a morsel of that particular afternoon by drawing Seb. He'd been still for precious few seconds since his mother Agnes Spring, needing time for research into her psyche with a healer, had importunately deposited him on Bea, preventing her from getting on with the small painting she had in progress.

Bea, coming up to thirty-one, had no children of her own and was neither particularly regretful nor overjoyed by the fact, finding children very much as she found adults: interesting, loveable, cantankerous or boring and treated them accordingly, making few allowances for age. Seb was an energetic and intelligent child possessed of all these characteristics, displaying them in dizzying rotation, but his beautiful oval face, surrounded by chestnut curls, was disfigured by a perpetual expression of fury. Bea discerned real fear in the howls and came down to his level on the floor to give him a comforting hug and determine the cause of the uproar.

'Look! Look!' He pointed a shaking finger at the window. She followed the line of his eye, saw the distorted bird behind the wavering surface of the old glass and patiently explained to him what the problem was and how it came about.

'If you stand on the table, you'll be able to see through the top of the window, where the glass is new, that it's just any ordinary blackbird.'

Clutching her hand as he did so, an exaggerated expression of fear on his face, he ducked up and down, making the bird alternately shrink and swell till he was satisfied that she was right.

During the course of that afternoon, Agnes having left him at one o'clock and it was now nearly four, Bea had entertained Seb with painting, stories and letting him help her prepare a lamb stew for Oscar's supper. She had coated his hands with gouache and helped him make white hand prints in the centre of the black squares of the chequerboard floor tiles. It had the pleasing effect, not wasted on Seb, of a small person having walked on his hands from the door to the sink. The drizzle having stopped she then suggested he came with her to the end of the garden so they could hang out the washing and perhaps see a squirrel or two on the way.

'No!' he'd shouted vehemently, 'I'm frightened of squirrels! I get nightmares if I see squirrels!'

'Well, what shall we do then?'

'If you'd knowed I was coming, you'd have got me a video, wouldn't you?'

'No, I wouldn't have. The video machine is broken.'

Seb, having denied himself a tantrum so far that day, now threw a whopper.

'I'm 'sterical, I'm 'sterical!' he screamed, 'I *need* a video! I want *Dan Vard and the Children of Doom!*'

Bea weathered this by pretending exaggerated horror, as if watching a melodrama, impressed by the stage effects but ultimately dispassionate, knowing she could bring down the curtain when sufficiently stimulated. However, she was a kindly and quite patient person and having got him to giggle, made a house beneath the table as a distraction, draping it with a tartan blanket secured by a dictionary and a heavy cooking pot to provide some dark privacy for him. He played there for a while with a green rubber snake, hissing and snarling gutturally as he circled with it in an intricate Celtic lacework pattern, first clockwise then widdershins round each table leg. It was then that he had suddenly spotted the bird outside on the bird table and the screams began again.

Once comforted, Seb feigned exhaustion and curled up in front of the stove on the rush mat, apparently asleep. Bea had seized the moment and commenced a drawing. Seb was small for his age and with his eyes shut unrealistically tightly, he had looked almost feminine.

'Not one of the lads,' she thought as she explored the satisfying curve of his cheek, the roundness of his arm with a 3B pencil. She was reminded of her younger brother Patrick at the same age and the miseries of sharing a bedroom with him. Once, having stolen one of her precious drawing books of strange cartoon-like happenings, Patrick had scribbled a large 'P' in red wax crayon in the centre of each page. She could hear in her mind's ear his howls and recall his raspberry-coloured face as he shook the chair on which she had stood on tiptoe, punishing him for his misdeed by posting all his Lego pieces out of the bedroom window. The sense of outrage at the desecration was still faintly present more than twenty years later.

Theirs had been a childhood of constant disruptions as their father, Tom Kerepol, who had lost an eye in an accident in the Navy, sought to earn a post-naval living. They had accompanied him unwillingly among alien corn, moaning up silver ladders and groaning down unpromising snaky paths. He had worn a black eyepatch since the accident and the children saw him as a thinner but still hopelessly unreliable Captain Pugwash.

Bea had found the frequent upheavals of house moving deeply worrying. Melting away from the disordered rooms with which she had only recently become familiar, hating their denuded windows and wading knee-deep through scrumpled newspapers, she sought refuge in garden shed or attic where she sat on the floor and drew anything that came to hand, becoming absorbed in the fatly ridiculous curves of elderly teapot or the metallic intricacies of egg whisk. Brown-overalled men tramped past, her mother called distractedly for her to come and look after Patrick, and her father sang continuously – Zarastro's 'O Isis und Osiris' from the *Magic Flute*, nursery rhymes, the 'Ballad of Lucy Jordan' and 'Sweet Lass of Richmond Hill'. She ignored them all till it was time to close the door behind them and follow the van.

Memories of the family's earlier homes were defined by the bedrooms and whether or not she'd been forced to share them with Patrick: the first, a square attic in London, its window fitted with nursery bars from which she had gnawed all the chipped cream paint; the last the large dark room in the ancient

Canterbury house with a tilting, oak-planked floor down which marbles rolled into inaccessibility beneath the chest of drawers. There, aged ten, she had poked imploring letters through the cracks in the floorboards, addressed to her private, imaginary female deity Freda, pleading that she wouldn't have to share a room with Patrick again. Freda occupied the place taken in other children's lives by their teddy bears or their best friends. Bea had given up making best friends since they always stayed behind when she was moved on. The prayers to Freda had been answered almost immediately, for they moved yet again to a larger house with an ample amount of bedrooms, twice more in fact, before Bea had reached fourteen.

Her mother's Aunt Maude Cadwell then died ... it was a family dominated by aunts of several generations and in Bea's dreams, Aunt Maude's bulging greyish-ginger appearance had become confused with the large tan-coloured pigskin bag she habitually carried, bulging with leaflets and the agendas of feminist meetings. It was the feminism which decided her on leaving her nieces a sum of money and one house each from an eccentric portfolio of properties haphazardly sprinkled about Kent. The less fortunate male relations received a shelf of books each from her library to remember her by.

Jane Kerepol had come off slightly better than her sisters Nest and Isla. Aunt Maude had been worried by her marriage to such a particularly impecunious and erratic naval officer and her inheritance was a tall weather-boarded house in the High Street of Bellhurst. The ground floor was taken up by a rambling and chronically untidy ironmonger's shop and the garden was divided into two, half being taken up by a yard where lawn mowers were serviced and water butts, garden seats and a dispiriting collection of garden ornaments — sad grey concrete cats and lugubrious toads — were sold. In the half of the garden which went with the three-storey living quarters there was a quince tree, gloriously covered that afternoon when they first saw it, with furred, citrus yellow, bullet-hard fruit.

Here Jane Kerepol had at last assumed authority, as Aunt Maude had hoped she would. Jane had been extraordinarily patient with their wandering, penury-with-prospects existence but had at last become concerned by her offspring's continuously disrupted education. (Bea's confusion over the chronology of the Celtic, Roman, Saxon and Viking invasions of Britain and which of them had worn horned helmets had begun to irritate Tom.) Flushed with ownership and with a substantial improvement to her private bank balance, she felt it high time she called the tune.

'You can do what you like, Tom, but I'm going to live here with the children. This is the last move I ever intend to make.'

So they had moved out of a smelly chicken farm near Canterbury and into trim little Bellhurst. When the lease on the ironmonger's shop had run out some months later and old Jeremiah Hoad the ironmonger had retired, the family were not entirely surprised when Tom Kerepol announced his intention to buy up the remaining stock and continue the business. He had been distressed by the surreal arrangements of the store rooms and shop windows where moulting doormats and quivers of broom handles hobnobbed with seed trays containing incontinent bags of cat litter, mousetraps, gimlets and hatchets. He set about with naval precision to remove the extraneous without disturbing the charm and order was achieved. Although he had not been expected to stick at it, the business prospered when, at Jane's instigation, he started to sell French enamelled cooking pots and shining kitchen knives. Upstairs, the kitchen windows were perpetually steamed up by simmering cauldrons of plum chutney and quince cheese and Jane was happy, writing cookery articles for magazines aimed at the new young country-dwellers who had poured out of London in the eighties looking for farmhouses to do up and space to breed. Tom was possessed of a fine baritone voice and joined both the church and local amateur choirs, sang his heart out and encouraged his children to do the same.

Patrick and Bea's relationship grew less scratchy as they matured; he found her to be a reliable confidante and she discovered in him a variety of loopy humour which wonderfully defused the bouts of overintensity that so used to puzzle her mother. They escaped the incessant busyness upstairs by heading for the store rooms where, happily inhaling the delectable atmosphere of tarred string and paraffin, they played cribbage on an upturned packing case or went to the workshop where Patrick tinkered with a derelict lawn mower and Bea drew studies of Patrick tinkering.

Patrick was soon packed off to board while Bea attended the extant grammar school in the town, her seventh school, and after a while, discerning no imminent lapse in her father's enthusiasm for his new trade, decided this time they might possibly be staying put and cautiously bothered to make friends, the first of whom had been Agnes.

When they were younger, Bea had found the relationship a little claustrophobic. Agnes had found it difficult to accept diversification in friendships and had been apt to sulk possessively if Bea invited other people along on their jaunts up to London to shop in Camden Market or the cinema. There had been childish ruffles: Agnes had not turned up to Bea's fifteenth birthday party. She'd been unable to decide what to wear and had sat on the floor of the bathroom at home, damp with self-pitying tears. It never occurred to her that her non-arrival at the party mattered as much to Bea as it did to herself and that Bea would be hurt. Out of pique at a tactless remark of Bea's, she had let the cat out of the bag about underage drinking at one of the local pubs, with the result that both of them were put under a severe curfew; she'd also stolen Bea's first mascara and a tape of the Wonderstuff. Consequences were not her strong point.

So they had picked and poked at each other's half-fledged selves, then huddled close together again for comfort and somehow the rows smoothed themselves over, their relationship swinging from the ecstatic to the petulant and back again throughout their schooldays, continuing on the same footing even now.

They made an odd, contrary pair: Agnes with inky black hair, slate grey eyes and the demeanour of a wayward china doll, was small and giggle-prone, a clothes-twitcher, a fidget. Bea was tallish and fair, that's how she saw herself, no more. She was unhappy about her feet (too big) and sad about the nose (not straight) but had the common sense to realise that the sum of the whole was generally not unpleasing. To others, her enviably slim, high-breasted figure resembled a gilded gothic effigy, or maybe a cathedral saint stepped down recently from its niche. The narrow nose, only a trifle long and due to an accident with a hockey stick, just very slightly crooked, had the effect of emphasising the strong regularity of the rest of her features. The clear blue gaze was considering, amused, sometimes apt to narrow in deep isolating concentration but just as frequently widened into sudden all-embracing eiderdowns of laughter. Beneath the apparent dreamy self-containment ran a deep rift of artfully concealed timidity and a will, which whenever put to the test, proved to be of iron.

Agnes had swirled off gleefully to London for a course in design and illustration. She'd married in her third year, and then after a short time, unmarried. Seb had arrived eighteen months later, cramping her style somewhat; finding it impossible to make ends meet as a single mother/freelance illustrator, she had been forced into an ignominious return to her mother and a year or so before, she and Bea had resumed their edgy friendship.

Agnes seemed unchanged, still attractive, flirty and untidy, still balancing chronic unreliability with apparent good humour and spontaneity and whose sexuality was all she thought she had to offer to the world. After a hectic bout of activity with the available local talent, during the course of which she caused two fights and a suicide bid, she surprised everyone by a further attempt at domesticity and mystifyingly married plain Phil Spring, works manager of the small ironworks owned by Bea's husband, Oscar.

Bea put her pencil down and yawned. Seb had woken up and disappeared beneath the table again, muttering dark things to himself. He was aware of the closeness of Bea's long, black Lycra-covered legs invading his private space and was intrigued by the shoeless feet, the tiny hole showing white flesh at the side of the rounded black calf. Forgetting that the legs were attached to a sentient being somewhere up above he was overcome by an urgent need to sink his teeth, experimentally, into the ankle. Bea shrieked and was jerked most painfully into the present.

'You little beast, Seb! How would you like it if I bit you that hard?' Wondering what the hell had happened to Agnes, she limped exaggeratedly across to the radio, fiddling till she found a Mozart concerto, hoping that flute and harp would soothe both herself and the little savage sulking silently in embarrassment beneath the table, aware that he had gone too far but unable to apologise. The back door crashed open and Agnes blew into the kitchen with a blast of cold air, her skirts all prancy-pouncy and apologies flying from her lips like confetti but with less substance.

'So calm in here, Bea! I'm parched with so much talking. Are you making tea? Such an interesting session with Ludmilla.' She threw a couple of plastic carriers and a shoulder bag down in the middle of the table, as if claiming territory, and rubbed her hands. 'I've been regressing. You should try it sometime. Do you know, I never realised what an unhappy childhood I had – but you're looking a bit boot-faced – I really am sorry I was so long. Where's Seb?'

'Under the table. If I'm boot-faced it's because he's bitten my ankle.' Bea stuck her foot up on the table and stretching the patch of tights around the offending area, indignantly pointed out a little semicircle of baby tooth marks. 'Should I get a tetanus injection, do you think? Does he do that sort of thing often?'

Agnes looked mortified for no more than a second, then became defiant.

'Well, yes, he did bite someone at nursery school, but it was pure frustration, you see. He had such a difficult birth and is so very intelligent, but he can't always explain what he needs.'

'He needs a good smack.'

Agnes ignored this and sipped her tea. 'Ludmilla wants me to take him to her for a session. She thinks she ought to meet him.'

There were times when Bea found it hard to take Agnes seriously and she now had an unguarded attack of censoriousness.

'Agnes! I'm sure he's forgotten being born by now ... and do you think you should muddle children up with those sorts of people? Has she any qualifications, this Ludmilla?'

'She doesn't need qualifications – she's psychic!'

'That's what I mean. Oh, never mind! Perhaps one *can* remember one's birth – I used to get nightmares when I had a temperature, of trying to get out of the inside of this very tightly wound ball of red knitting wool. Have a biscuit?' Bea's voice had an edge of impatience to it which Agnes picked up immediately.

'But you don't understand! You're calm and ordered, and *evaluating*! I'm so muddled all the time. Don't be ratty with me – you sound just like Phil!' Seb emerged from his hiding place and she picked him up and hauled him onto her lap, smoothing the curls and twitching the collar out of his jumper. He snuggled into her, casting petulant sideways glances at Bea from beneath his frowning eyebrows.

'No, I'm not ratty, Agnes. It's just that I don't think other people are much good at helping unravel oneself; I feel it's something that's got to be done alone. Does Ludmilla charge a lot?'

'Only twenty pounds a session.'

'Good grief! That sounds rather expensive just to be told you had an unhappy childhood. Couldn't you remember on your own whether you had an unhappy childhood or not? I can remember nearly everything about mine.'

'Lucky old you! I have great voids in my memory. I can't remember why I married Phil. All I'm doing is trying to get some of *your* order into *my* life. I had a double session actually, then I had to buy a new bra in Parden. Look! Matching knicks as well!' She produced a tiny handful of crunchy black lace and wafted it about. 'But you did get time to do some drawing, I see. I know you like to sit and draw.' She rarely saw any of the secretive Bea's work and peering critically at the sketch book, open at the firm and unfaltering outlines of the drawing of Seb asleep on the floor, felt forced to acknowledge the truth: 'Oh Bea! It's so very, very good! I still don't understand why you didn't come to art school with me, when you'd got the place and everything. Couldn't you have waited to marry Oscar till afterwards? It seems such a waste.'

Bea considered this while making a fresh pot of tea. She was unsure why she had spun off the track so suddenly but had an inkling that it was due to lack of confidence. She'd had a shy resistance to being taught and from the beginning the art lessons at the various schools she had attended had seemed a form of sadism. At primary school she had been required to paint pictures with titles such as 'A Windy Day' or 'My Family' on vast sheets of coloured paper, with big stiff brushes in the garish poster paints supposedly beloved by children but which to her were anathema. Wistfully wishing the subject could have been 'In the Hall of the Demon King', she used to fold the intimidating sheet into a more manageable size, eventually producing with great trouble some small drawing in the corner. Pig-headed obstinacy and sheer ability were eventually harnessed to produce the required portfolio of work to gain a place at art school.

But then she met Oscar. Beautiful, amiable Oscar. Oscar who

had come to visit Tom in the shop one morning with a new range of iron door fittings copied from eighteenth-century originals. Bea, luminous, lissom and seventeen, had entered the shop as they were discussing prices and had been violently smitten. Oscar, then aged twenty-two, self-confident and charming and already showing signs of the good businessman he was to become, had similarly been attracted. He had an agreeably childish streak in him and she had enjoyed this and besottedly mothered him, long past the time when he should have grown up.

They had, Bea eventually came to admit, been attracted like Narcissus, look to look, in love with being in love and also revelling in the attention they received as a pretty couple riding about the countryside on Oscar's motorbike, a princess and her matching child-knight errant. Tom had been alarmed by Bea's sudden awakening and the sight of her searching her mother's cupboards for unwanted pots and pans rang warning bells. Informed by an excited Jane of their intention to marry, he had been disappointed and gruff.

'Oh God! I always knew it was pointless educating women!'

They had married the autumn after Bea had at least taken her A levels – Art, English and History – that much she had conceded to her unhappy father, but once the excitement of getting married was over, she appeared to her family to have happily gone to sleep. She continued to paint and draw in private, never sure that what she achieved had any point other than her own satisfaction, but rather expecting that one day everything would fall into place. What she did was a habit of consuming interest, a near-obsessive necessity. Oscar was encouraging about her abilities in the early days, although he initially found it disturbing that she had any serious interests other than himself. His own mother had not been so distracted. He had jealously watched the perimeter of the area of what she called her 'work', looking for a gap through which to pour himself. When he found that she wouldn't even try to exhibit or sell anything, he began to lose interest, unable to understand that she was either shy of the opinions of other people, or uninterested in them and that to her the drawings and paintings were never more than preparatory work.

Agnes, catching the delicate bay-leaf-and-garlic waft from the lamb stew simmering in Bea's oven, remembered that she had forgotten to buy the sausages for Phil's supper and setting Seb on his feet rather abruptly, downed her second cup of tea in a hurry. Seb set up a howl. He had enjoyed the afternoon spent manipulating Bea's attention and he had to be manhandled into the child seat in Agnes's scraped red Citroën.

'I wish I had a pair of handcuffs!' his mother moaned, dodging a flailing foot as she attempted to strap him in. 'Leg-irons, even. 'Bye, dearest Bea, and thanks a million for looking after him. I honestly don't know what I'd do without you.'

Once the turbulent pair had departed, the kitchen assumed a disappointed air, as if a party had been cancelled at short notice. Bea cursed herself for mean-spiritedness in having wished to be by herself that afternoon. She really rather enjoyed the friction that Agnes's visits caused and clearing away the pencils and paper, she felt a prickle of guilt at her earlier snappiness.

She hovered over the table and picked at the succulent pot plant in its centre, sharply digging a fingernail into one of its fleshy leaves, leaving a little crescent tattoo which would survive for years. She was thinking about Agnes's phrase 'calm and ordered'. If she was, it was due to a massive effort of will, not a natural instinct, it being something of a battle to keep things running smoothly in order to fit in the drawing. She couldn't tap her disturbing visual imagination unless at least one room in the house was in perfect order and if Oscar was about and unoccupied, he wouldn't stand for her shutting herself away for long. She was amazed at his ingenuity in finding new methods of disruption, never realising she been made to believe over the years that she was at fault in wanting to continue painting.

She pulled down the yellow blinds and laid the table for their supper, using the remaining plates of her Great Aunt Maude's green-and-black Art Deco dinner service and placing a fat green glass bowl of primroses in the centre. It was Friday night, when she and Oscar usually ate early before going out for a drink at a local wine bar or in the summer rode off on Oscar's old motorbike to some more distant place to meet friends and chat. Black oily hand prints in the kitchen and pieces of engine soaking in petrol in the washing-up bowl were tolerable inconveniences, fair exchange for the few hours of peace she gained in which to paint while he took the bike to pieces in the garden. The friends who shared his interest in the more elegant older machines, the classic Triumphs, Nortons and BSAs, were scornful of the gross, modern Japanese bikes, snobbishly calling them 'fitted-kitchens'.

Bea checked the stew and opened a bottle of white wine, poured out a glassful and carried it upstairs with her. Their house, Fleming Cottage, on the outer edge of Bellhurst, was a two-up, two-down with a bathroom added downstairs, but the rooms were quite large and she had made it very comfortable, revelling in its permanence.

The bedroom seemed unnaturally tidy. She had left before Oscar that morning, leaving him humped beneath the bedclothes mumbling that he didn't have to be in at work till ten. Bea grinned to see that the bed had been made and that there was no sign of dirty socks or shirts. Was it possible that he had discovered the true use of the laundry basket after all these years? She changed her paint-smeared jersey for a short blue-green sweater – she liked strong, bright colours – dabbed foundation on a small spot on her chin and made up her eyes, light-heartedly humming 'Waltzing Matilda', one of her father's favourites. She brushed her shoulder-length hair and twisted it up into a blonde tortoiseshell clip, turning her head this way and that and deciding that her nose looked less crooked from three-quarters right before returning to the kitchen still humming happily, to read and wait.

Immersed in Angela Carter's *The Bloody Chamber*, Bea did not at first notice that it was getting late. She enjoyed reading almost as much as drawing but as a child had found it difficult to progress from fairy stories with their 'and so she married the prince' endings to seek more sophisticated denouements. Why should 'lived happily ever after' be considered a cop-out? Surely the suspension of disbelief was the whole point of fiction? Anyway, it stood to reason that happy endings occurred in reality with the same frequency as sad ones, didn't it? Oscar read mainly SAS memoirs whose covers all depicted the same black chin-jutting silhouette of a man behind whom a flash of lightning lit up a scene of destruction. He would quite happily have bought a copy of *Barchester Towers* had it had an explosion on the cover.

Oscar was usually home by seven-thirty and it was now eight-fifteen. He might be held up at the ironworks, or the smithy as he liked to call it, though it had expanded way beyond being just a smithy since he had taken it over. By nine-thirty a narrow cinch of unease settled around her waist, tightening gradually till at ten o'clock she telephoned Agnes and enquired whether Phil knew if Oscar was held up somewhere.

'Phil says Oscar booked himself out of the office all day today,' said Agnes. 'He's probably gone to visit a client in London and forgotten to tell you.' She paused and relayed another message from Phil. 'He hasn't been in all day. Apparently he often visits clients on Fridays.'

'Does he? I didn't know.' But then Bea heard what she thought was Oscar's bike humming along the lane. 'Panic over! He's coming now. Agnes, I'm sorry I was so bad-tempered this afternoon.'

'Oh, don't think about it! You were rather controlled under the circumstances! See you soon, Bea. 'Bye.'

The anxiety dissipated, she hurried to put on the stew again, heard strangely uncertain footsteps coming up the path followed by a fumbling sound at the door and before she could get there to open it, the squeak and flop of something being thrust through the letter box. The letter, with 'Bea' scrawled on the envelope, lay on the coconut matting of the passage. She flung open the door and called out 'Oscar! Oscar?' but the rider was already astride the bike and off into the dark.

Back in the kitchen, heart thumping and wondering why she had not noticed that neither his car nor his bike had been outside the house when she returned from work at lunch time, she laid the letter down on the table in the place she had laid for Oscar's supper, lining up its upper and lower edges with the grain of the wood and the sides with the knife and fork and staring at it transfixed, as if expecting it to open itself. She knocked back another glass of wine then, fumble-fingered, ripped open the envelope.

'Dearest Bea, I know this is the cowardly way out, but . . .' Her eyes blurred and odd words leapt out like jeering sprites from the bramble-patch of writing: sorry, selfishness, children, art, Andrea. Art? He had always patronisingly referred to her drawing as 'your *Art*', with a capital A, as if it were a tiresome hobby. The letter was half diatribe against herself, half *mea culpa*, and ran on, and on. Selfishness? It seemed unclear whether he referred to her or himself. She was disbelieving and indignant. Had she not spent the early years of their marriage working for him, helping as best she could with his new but wavering enterprise? And later the tedious years in the book shop to provide a backup to his fluctuating income? They had never spoken of children, that she could recall. At least he had never, in any way, indicated that he wanted any or that they should address the situation and she had always felt relieved, knowing that he wouldn't have been able to cope with competing for her attention with a baby. As for herself, she'd been frightened of the idea – frightened that she would never again have a moment to herself in which to paint. Yes, she supposed that amounted to selfishness. Andrea? It appeared he had left her for someone called Andrea. She combed her mind for Andreas but

could only think of one. 'Andreary Bullshit', the name she and
Agnes had coined for the suffocatingly over-feminine woman for
whom Oscar had made a pair of wrought-iron gates. Agnes had
designed them, with elegant greyhound forms loping across the
tops, and she, Oscar, Phil and Agnes, had gone over to Sussex
together to see them hung in place at the entrance to Andrea
Bullingden's rambling Victorian house. 'Actually,' Andrea had
announced in her strange, falling little voice, 'it's not Victorian,
it's William the Fourth.' Andrea Bullingden, who had totally
ignored Agnes's part in the work and who had lavished praise
and cow eyes on Oscar. Andrea who had left them drinking mugs
of tea in the kitchen while she led away Oscar, by the arm, to
inspect a further small gate she wished to replace. They had got
bored waiting and nosed into the cupboards, finding in one of
them a neatly stacked green glass wall of empty gin bottles.

Bea's first reaction, after the shock, was the uncorking of
several years' worth of vintage rage which until that moment
she had been unaware had been stored in her cellar. It seethed
about her till she felt imminent suffocation. She picked up the
fork from Oscar's place at the table and jabbed it through all
three sheets of the letter with such force that she pinned it to
the kitchen table; she clasped the rage tight and would not let
it go again. The air began to fill with greasy smoke as the
stew scorched, but she drank another glass of wine before
turning off the gas and opening the window. She cleared the
table, putting away Oscar's untouched knife and methodically
tidying the kitchen. She took the shed key down from its place
above the door and went outside, carrying the burnt and cooling
stew pot.

In the shed lay a wooden tool chest which had belonged to
Oscar's father. She switched on the light, lifted its lid and with
difficulty shook the dead, stiffening stew onto the gleaming,
greased and lovingly cared-for contents. Small gobbets of burnt
meat stuck to the saw teeth and the handles of the graded sets
of screwdrivers. Thick and glutinous tomato dripped into the

motor of the electric drill. Caramelised carrot and barley clung about the interior, bejewelling the tobacco tins of nails and screws. The dusty light bulb popped and in the darkness Bea shut the lid, locked up the shed and returned down the garden path, sobbing.

'After revenge, what is there?' she wondered, and went to bed where the tears came faster; loss, hurt, regret, self-pity, but, oddly enough, no despair, merely a terrible sense of time wasted. 'What has happened to Bea?' she imagined people asking in the months to come. 'Oh, she's bravely soldiering on alone,' she heard the answer. 'I will *not* bravely soldier on alone. I will not become a cliché. I will not be just another discarded wife,' she promised herself, through clenched teeth. She had accepted the fact, if not the reasons of his going, with a strange rapidity.

By the early hours of the morning she slept, a little, and dreamt in chasing clouds of colours and shapes, that she was part of a prayer meeting, evangelical in mode, out on a shingle beach. She wore, as did the other worshippers, a white sailcloth robe which billowed stiffly about her.

'Allelujah!' they all cried, raising their arms to the hot blue sky. 'Allelujah!' Out of the lapping waves arose her own particular goddess, wearing a straw hat trimmed with poppies and cornflowers, resembling a garden statue of a nubile nymph with folds of muslin carved discreetly about her hips.

'What is my name?' called the goddess and it seemed to Bea that she was being personally addressed, so she replied:

'Freda. Your name is Freda!'

The goddess grinned, showing sharp stone teeth and sank back beneath the water, her hat floating off, twirling round and round in the scummy foam.

Oscar lolled exhausted on the large leather sofa, his boots off, his pale blond hair being fondly smoothed by Andrea of the man-drowning eyes. The room about him, Andrea's drawing room, was decorated in film director chic. Each item in it was large, but spare and singular. Space echoed about a wooden horse placed by the long windows, a fairground relic whose hectic colouring had been tastefully burnished back to leave a ghostly pink, green and blue-stained grain. The heavy coffee table, carved and silver-leafed, was placed just too far from the sofa to be of use in serving coffee. Pale polished floors shuddered away from contact with Oscar's cast-off leather jacket. The dark green walls were almost hidden behind gargantuan paintings in distressed gilt frames; poor, old copies of indifferent seventeenth-century paintings, perhaps even copies of copies, in which Brobdingnagian nymphs lumbered through their painted woodland, heavy brocade draperies floating impossibly lightly about the flaking acres of their flat, cracked and uncleaned flesh. Andrea's ex-husband, a film producer, had, she mournfully complained, '. . . left her with all the tat.' Oscar was past taking notice of the decor, was in any case more familiar with the blue-and-white striped silk tent that was Andrea's bedroom upstairs.

All day he had been in an agony of fluctuating guilt and excitement. After Bea's departure for work that morning he had biked over to Andrea's house near Battle, returning in her car to collect his possessions and refused, out of some misplaced delicacy which Andrea did not pretend to understand, to let her come inside and help. Bewildered by his own decision to leave Bea, he felt half penitentially that her home should not be violated by Andrea's presence in it, however brief; he was unused to complicated emotions and his feeling that Andrea should not come inside made him angry and confused.

His life with Bea, all twelve years of it, had been so stable, so still. She had made so few demands on him that he had at times felt perhaps it was because she had thought him incapable of fulfilling them. It was this general tolerance that had annoyed him most. He'd tidied the bed and just to show her that he was capable of it, unthinkingly rammed his dirty socks, pants and yesterday's shirt into the laundry basket. All that he was certain of at that moment was his inability to resist Andrea.

One last look and out he came, seen by no one except the pale, incurious eyes of Mrs Lewis at the window of the house next door. They had driven back to Sussex in their respective cars, heading, for the time being, in the same emotional direction.

It wasn't until later in the afternoon that Oscar had become so unflatteringly silent, white-faced and haunted that Andrea had had to tease out of him that he had as yet made no attempt to tell Bea either that he was having an affair or that he intended to leave her. Becoming whimperingly tearful, she insisted that he should do it at once and he had eventually ridden off into the evening's slight drizzle to do the impossible deed.

'You've done the right thing. You know you've done the right thing,' she whispered in his ear, 'for you and me. How brave you were to go and tell her now. How did she take it? Was she hysterical?' She rubbed his cheek with hers, painfully entangling her dangling silver earring with his small gold one, not knowing that he had floundered, panicked and instead of telling Bea in person, had gone to his office desk in the ironworks to write the lame and infamous letter, trying desperately to dredge up slights and injuries he knew he had not felt at the time, to find faults in her that he had never previously imagined were important. He knew, as he lay on the sofa with Andrea, that he had behaved appallingly, but also, rather smugly, that he could not on that particular day have done otherwise. He turned to Andrea's drooping eyelids, inhaled her civet scent and sank, choking only weakly, to the bottom of the well.

Chapter Two

It was April Fools' Day, in the early pearl of the morning with the sun not yet risen when Bea awoke. Nauseous with tiredness, eyes gummed together with rubbery sleep and dried tears, her vision was hazy but her mind painfully clear. She washed her face and opening the window, flung Oscar's blue, duck-shaped sponge as far as she could into the back garden. She dressed in the first garment that came to hand out of the wardrobe – a long scarlet evening dress, a plain tube of stretchy satin that she had last worn for their tenth-wedding-anniversary dinner in London. She draped an old gardening jacket across her shoulders; its pockets held bits of string and crumbs of earth, a half-empty packet of perpetual spinach seed and one of the ubiquitous bits of broken blue-and-white china that litter old gardens, which she'd saved because there was a transfer print of a pheasant's head on it.

Downstairs, barefoot, she put on the kettle and set about washing the floor on her hands and knees, expunging with vigour yesterday's splash of stew, a smear of jam and Seb's hopeful white hand prints. Yesterday was March, today was April. Ritually dressed, she ritualised the unnecessary housework in order to pass through the time, hoping to hold disorder at arm's length. Naming the months, the days, the hours and minutes would keep everything in proportion. It was now a quarter to seven and moving with slow dignity she emptied the bucket down the sink and ceremoniously made tea. She did not care for China tea, but the occasion demanded it. She ate a knobbly Lincoln biscuit while staring blankly out through the undulating glass to the garden, childishly scraping the moulded nodules off the top of the biscuit with her teeth.

The sun was up now. The stealthy frosts had started to retreat northwards like vandals on the run and the sprouting tips of shallots and the young leaves of pink fir-apple potatoes were bursting through their earthy pie-crust in the vegetable patch. Out of habit she wandered outside to inspect them, kneeling to loosen a minute feathery seedling from beneath a cramping stone and gently pushing it upright to face its future. 'I don't want to be here to help them,' she muttered. 'I don't want to hoe, water or weed the sodding things and I don't want to harvest them on my own.' It was impossible to stay here, waiting. She'd been waiting for years. It was time to leave for another place, time for something quite different.

Mrs Lewis opened her back door with a rattle and enfolded in a stook of shawls and dressing gowns, tapped hesitantly with a spoon against a tin plate, calling her cat in a faded voice which lacked any sense of urgency:

'Here, Pig. Pig. Piggy.'

The white cat arose from his spot beneath Bea's yew tree, stretched his smooth front legs, then his fat, fluffed-up hams, yawned and gathering speed, cleared the fence in one bound. Mrs Lewis saw Bea in her scarlet dress, but if she was surprised at the choice of clothes for dawn gardening, her impassive face did not show it.

'A very nice morning, Mrs Mitty,' she called formally, feeling that since their eyes had met she ought to speak to her neighbour. Bea forced the muscles of her face to produce a spasm of a smile and managed a careless wave of the hand. Mrs Lewis's appearance was as normal; untidy but not unkempt, scrubbed out rather than unclean. A small cloud passed over, abruptly switching off the yellow sun.

Indoors the clock ticked out the morning and Bea commenced a frenzied cleaning, blocking out all thoughts of Oscar's
whereabouts, of his disloyalty, of his indigestible letter which
still lay skewered to the table. Only ideas of the future were
allowed to percolate through the sieve of practicalities and these
she developed furiously. While polishing lime-encrusted taps,
wiping old fly spots from windowsills and even dusting Oscar's
empty desk, a plan began to form, inspired in part by the night's
disordered dreaming.

At ten o'clock she telephoned her mother's younger sister,
Nest, who ran a plant nursery and who had inherited, as her
share of old Aunt Maude's will, a small Victorian villa near the
coast, just outside the town of Fingle.

'Hello? Nest's Nursery here. Could you speak up a bit, the
line seems very faint.'

'Aunt Nest? It's Bea. I need to ask you something, a favour.
I'm surrounded by mega-catastrophe.'

There was a pause at the other end.

'Is that an herbaceous perennial?' enquired Nest cautiously,
finding it hard to imagine that anyone should telephone her
about any other subject.

'No! Aunt Nest!' Bea tried to raise her voice, but her throat
contracted and cold sweat gathered on her neck at the thought
of all the explaining she would have to undertake over the next
few days. 'I said "catastrophe". Oscar's left me. I can't, don't
want to stay here in this house. I wondered if you had rented
out the Fingle house this year? If you haven't, do you think I
might? I'd pay proper rent, of course.'

Nest's response was generous and immediate.

'Darling Bea! How dreadful! The sod! The unspeakable
bugger!' Nest curbed herself. 'Oh my poor love! Of course
you can have it. It's quite empty. It's usually advertised in the
birdwatching magazine in February, but we had the deep snow
then and fearful frosts and my mind was taken off it, trying
to keep all the greenhouse heaters going. I only remembered

25

yesterday, as a matter of fact. It's free for as long as you want it. I could take some time off at lunch, and take you there to have a look, to see what needs to be got in?'

Alone among the family, Nest had never been concerned or impatient with Bea's lengthy nursing of her draughtsmanship and apparent lack of progress in the art field. If the child was slow to make use of her undoubted talent, then it was because she was not yet ready to do so. She had no doubts that Bea would one day astonish them all. She was reminded rather bitterly that her own husband Ivor had left her some years before, unwilling to compete for her attention with pots of *Meconopsis horridula* and *Polemonium carneum*. Bea, to Nest, was a sleeping princess, put to sleep not by the prick of a spindle but by that prick of an Oscar. Her mind shot off tangentially, exploring the possibility of the spindle being a phallic symbol – she had attended university in an era when any object longer than it was wide was granted this doubtful Freudian smear. Perhaps the princess had encountered something nasty in the attic which had enforced her being locked away for a time ... say nine months? A gestation period of one hundred years seemed a little excessive; she needed to re-read the story in all its versions ...

'Aunt Nest? Are you still there?'

'Yes, Bea darling. I do so hate to think of you on your own at a time like this. You've told Jane, of course?'

'Not yet, but I will have to very soon. I need to borrow her car.' She was aware this sounded as if this was the sole reason for informing her mother and that her voice was tired and diminished. 'Oscar has taken ours as well as the motorbike. If I can borrow the car, I'll be over at lunch time.'

'*Au revoir* then, dearest.'

Bea slipped a long green mackintosh over the red dress and walked the half mile into the centre of Bellhurst where, shaking a little with shock at the simplicity of the start of the enterprise, she withdrew £4,000 from their joint building society account, leaving behind £15.90. 'Not enough for him to take bitch

Andreary out to dinner,' she thought, pocketing the cheque and heading with some trepidation for T. Kerepol, Ironmongers.

The remainder of the morning was filled with expressions of indignant solicitude and fist-shaking, exotic naval threats from her father peppered with offers 'to go and sort the bastard out', viciously strong coffee, hugging, general bewilderment and mud-slinging from her mother. This left Bea comforted and encouraged since it was very much the way things had forever been expressed at home, where sound and fury often took the place of significance. It was her own disaster and it would be dealt with in her own reflexive way but she felt like a dead weight on wheels, spinning off after Oscar's violent shove. 'Mum would have been happier if I'd been hysterical,' she reflected sombrely as, exhausted by their emotion, she left in the borrowed car for her aunt's house. 'She never could cope with anyone trying to contain their feelings.'

Nest stood at the end of a long glasshouse, bending over a bench repotting cuttings of a particularly dark mauve-flowered *Abutilon vitifolium*, easing them gently into larger pots and firming them down with long bony fingers. Beside her was a half-eaten ham sandwich, lightly peppered with dark specks of compost, and a half-empty glass of white wine in which a small insect floundered in its death throes. Nest, not unlike Bea in features and slim but shorter, looked up and her sharp violet-blue eyes (better than Elizabeth Taylor's, she'd been told in her youth) softened as she took in the dishevelled and woebegone appearance of her niece. She at once gave her a muddy hug but Bea felt that she would be unable to survive much more hugging and drifted unhappily up and down the central concrete path while Nest dealt with the last pot, drained the wine, and finished up her horticultural sandwich.

'There, now that's done. Shall I get Blue to get you something to eat?'

Bea thought of Blue's perpetually soil-filled fingernails and declined the offer.

'I'm not really hungry. I did eat breakfast and I've had a gallon or so of Mum's coffee.' She forced her voice into a conversational tone as her Aunt rinsed her hands beneath a standpipe and wiped them on her faded pink shirt, 'How is Blue?'

Blue, dark and earthy, was Nest's lover. It was accepted that he was a good few years younger than Nest. He had relinquished his earlier job as a shepherd in order to look after her, deciding that there was little difference in the jobs. He could just as well see that she ate proper meals, didn't get footrot and had her hair shorn occasionally as he could deal with a flock of sheep. Sheep also were fussed at being interrupted about their business to be dosed, dipped and clipped. He had discovered to his delight that Nest had surprisingly catholic views on sexual matters and they suited each other very well indeed, sharing also a love of fairy stories, which Nest would read to him at night after supper. He called her, affectionately, Cuckoo.

'Blue,' answered Nest fondly, 'is pricing-up pots of *Perovskia* and has quite got over his bronchitis. I'll just go round the back and tell him we're off, but we mustn't take too long ... I've got a new girl – Lucinda – on her own at the till this lunch time. She seems to be rather too chatty and is trying to gain recruits for some ecological group she's involved with. I found it quite riveting but I hope she doesn't start on the customers.'

Bea followed her, threading through the narrow paths around gravel beds tightly packed with container plants, past handwritten signs illuminating the prices, virtues and vices of the stock. The entire front garden was taken up in this way and on busy days in spring, such as today, Nest had found it necessary to introduce a one-way system round the maze to prevent the more ardent plant collectors from overflowing into the beds. Nest ignored her own warning signs and strode ruthlessly through the browsers, leaving Bea awkwardly leaping across roundabouts of ferns in her wake, dodging bamboo stakes and oncoming traffic.

Nest's house and nursery garden were on the high ground of land that some hundreds of years past had been an island but which was now merely trammelled by a tamed river and various dykes, sewers and channels. Bea's spirits lifted as they drove off in Nest's yellow van down a lane running with rivulets of water, its deeply cut banks singing with primroses. She glimpsed the expanse of marsh lying below them and the varying greens of the fields of wheat, rape and grazing dotted with sheep and lambs. The road dropped sharply down to the levels, heading for the coast and Fingle where they stopped briefly to satisfy Nest's sudden need of a Mars bar.

Driving out the other side of Fingle and taking a narrow pot-holed track across pebble-strewn fields barely coated with grass, they came first to a group of bungalows, then after half a mile of emptiness, to a small brown farmhouse, its window frames painted alternately red and yellow and surrounded by rotting sheds of corrugated iron and rusting machinery.

'That's Rumm's Farm,' Nest informed her. 'Jerry Rumm lives there. He's a nice old boy and will happily help you out if you have any difficulties. It was his grandfather who built the house I've now got, for his second wife who thought she was a cut above him, but Jerry's father hated it, sold it off and moved back into the old one. His father also refused to have electricity put in when Aunt Maude bought the new house and had it installed. The line goes right past his farm, but he wouldn't pay the extra to bring it in. Jerry has a generator. Here we are.'

A few hundred yards further still stood Nest's surprising white Victorian villa. Bearing no relation whatsoever to its surroundings, it resembled a child's drawing of a house: a weather-beaten central blue door with a square window on either side and two more symmetrically placed above, a slate roof and single central chimney from which one expected to see issuing a curling of woodsmoke. A wooden board propped against the stone wall was inscribed in dribbled green paint, 'Little Rumm'.

Bea got out of the van and stood in the scrubby, square walled garden, taking in the windswept tamarisk bushes, the pink rusting child's bicycle abandoned by a previous summer's tenants. A line of pylons, grey against the spring-blue sky, loped bleakly across the flatness, but the sky itself seemingly came down to one's feet in every direction, a broad and sweeping compensation for the lack of what most people would have called an attractive landscape and an agoraphobic's nightmare. 'As near as one can get to flying while staying earthbound,' thought Bea, gazing up at the white streak behind a toy silver airliner thousands of feet up. The area was short on trees of any height and even the telegraph poles leant drunkenly with the prevailing south-westerly wind. While she stood and stared about, suddenly alarmed by the thought of being here on her own, Nest was wrestling with the door handle.

'It seems to have jammed. I shall have to put the boot in,' said Nest, standing back to give it a hefty blow with her stout, mud-encrusted boot.

It swung open unwillingly on the third kick and Bea followed her aunt into the hall. A long, sparsely furnished sitting room lay on one side, white, rush-matted and sunny, with a pile of dusty bus timetables, local newspapers and badly folded footpath maps on the window seat. A collection of large grey-and-white pebbles stood along the upper shelf of an ornate Art Nouveau iron fireplace, along with odd bits of seaside flotsam, a gull's feather, and sea-smoothed fragments of green bottle. Cockle shells and empty sweet wrappers filled a glass bowl on the gate-legged table. On the other side of the hall there was a smaller room with the kitchen lurking dimly behind it. Nest's ideas of what was necessary for a holiday let seemed a bit odd. Bea pulled open a drawer in the mildewed post-war utility dresser and discovered eight miscellaneous corkscrews, a tin-opener, an apostle teaspoon and a lot of silverfish.

'Don't worry,' said Nest, briskly shooting up the kitchen blind and flooding the room with startling light. 'I take out all the small bits and bobs when it's empty in the winter.'

'Can I bring some of my own things?' asked Bea hopefully, hating the stained and matted rag-rug on the floor and the blackened aluminium saucepans hanging above the stove. There was grubby cream paint on the walls and a lot of chipped grey Formica.

'Of course you can. Anything you like. It's all got a bit tatty, I suppose. But quite suitable for bird-watchers.' Bea, wondering at what degree of discomfort the house would become unsuitable for the poor bird-watchers, gave a watery giggle.

Upstairs the sunniness and comparative modernity of the bathroom were cheering as was the stark but comfortable bedroom with a large iron, brass-knobbed bedstead, its castors sunk into the floorboards as if it had stood there for ever. The feeling of permanence was comforting.

'This room has a good light,' said Nest opening the other door off the landing. It gave into a square white room, with two windows hung with floor-length striped black-and-white curtains, rough pine floorboards painted black and a bed covered with a red counterpane. White wardrobe, white chair and a white painted dressing table. 'It'll do very well as a studio for you – that is, I'm presuming that the plan is to come here to paint, not sit and keen? If you *are* going to paint, then I won't charge you any rent.' She stared at her niece, the violet eyes challenging.

A room with a sense of purpose, Bea thought, standing at the sash window and staring out across the pancake land to Fingle where the church's peg-tiled roof lay long and low among the houses, like a lizard warming itself in the spring sunshine.

'No, no keening,' she agreed, turning back to re-examine the space. 'I'll work and then there won't be time to mope. And anyway, I'm more enraged than sad.' There'd been a sickening little knot in her stomach which had untied a little as Nest spoke; not having been quite aware of the idea of coming here to paint till Nest so confidently put it into words, that of course was what she'd do and this was where she would do it, living through all the mess as one lives through lunch, cutting one's toenails or any other necessity. It would end. Eventually another set of circumstances would take over, something would be achieved here and Nest's generosity was a wonderful bonus. Bea's imagination began to fly.

Outside again, the practicalities of electricity and gas bottles dealt with, the necessity of a mobile phone insisted on, Nest sat down on a low brick wall in the garden and lit a cigarette.

'I'd like to come and live here myself one day, when I've made enough money to retire. There are days when I ache to get away from all the lush and feathery greenery inland. It's so dry and hard here. Wind-blown clean and so little mud. It's quite surprising what'll grow. I'll look out some seeds for you to brighten up the garden during the summer. There's a well-sheltered spot out at the back.' Nest leant sideways and picked some young leaflets from a thorny stem, crumpling them between her fingers and holding them out for Bea to sniff. 'What does that remind you of?'

Bea obediently sniffed. 'It smells of apples! Granny Smiths in particular, slightly fake – an apple scented bubble bath or something. What is it?'

'I'm not a rose-fancier myself and the flowers are insignificant, bright pink and very tiny, but it was growing here when I came. I'm not sure what it is ... *Rosa eglanteria*, or a *villosa* seedling perhaps? The scent is twice as strong as any I've ever come across before or since. It smells even stronger when it rains. I can't remember the name of the rose on the wall, either. Lady something ... but there's a nice old horticultural joke about it – it's a difficult rose to please and they say it's lousy in bed but great up against the wall.' Nest watched Bea snort with laughter and nodded approvingly, chuckled herself and put out her cigarette half finished, hiding the butt beneath a stone and stood up, eager to get back to work.

Bea could smell the invisible sea behind the high-banked shingle of the sea wall in the distance, see the black silhouettes of a man and a prancing dog moving along its top, heading for the great wen of the nuclear power station. She was grateful for the pause in the day's frenetic movement and could have sat there for a while longer.

'We must get going,' urged Nest, 'much as I'd like to go for a walk. Blue and I'll pop down tomorrow evening with the things you'll need, clean sheets and blankets and such. When do you want to come over here?'

Bea gulped, breathless with the speed with which things were falling into place while Oscar's side of the bed was still virtually warm. She found it difficult to think about him, the unpalatable *fact* that he had gone off with someone else, like one of those gelatine capsules of cod-liver oil which disgustingly burst in the mouth before one can swallow them down. It was his failure to tell her in person that had been more devastating than the actual departure.

'I thought next Friday? I've got things to settle, things I need to buy.'

'Fine. You take these keys; I've got others. I must say I envy your capacity for putting aside the irrelevant,' said Nest, glancing at the tense little face beside her as they sat in the van and remembering the child's unbending determination once she had put her mind to marrying Oscar. 'It means you're thinking extremely straight, in spite of what's just happened.'

'How do you mean?'

'Well, for the time being at least, your errant Oscar is an irrelevance. You seem to be accepting without any argument that he's gone? Perhaps he was a hindrance to your creativity, which, by the way, I also envy.'

'I am still operating on reflex,' Bea admitted. She tried to turn the conversation away from her aunt's blunt and worrying percipience. 'You're creative too. You're a gardener.'

'No, I'm a manufacturer,' said Nest, forcing the gear stick

into reverse and jerking backwards in the first manoeuvre of a six-point turn. 'I produce plants for gardeners to use in *their* creations. Like a paint-maker grinding colours for artists to use. Only gardening is such a variable thing.' She grunted as she scraped the garden wall. 'There's no exact formula as there is with paints . . .' Nest took the turn out into the main road too fast, straightening up with difficulty, barely pausing in her talk but Bea's mind was elsewhere, thinking about Oscar, absently nodding her head to Nest's lecture on the differences between gardening and painting but hearing none of it. 'I should be sadder, madder, badder about it all. Why do I feel so . . . so little?'

'. . . However talented one is one can't rely on one's materials in the way you can predict what will be squeezed out of a tube of Winsor and Newton's Cadmium Red,' continued Nest, slowing behind a Land-Rover and trembling trailer-full of nervous sheep. Bea clutched at the dashboard, shutting her eyes as her Aunt, at last managing to find second gear, overtook the sheep on a blind corner.

'Damn Blue,' said Nest, 'I always have trouble with it after he's been driving it. How are Jane and Tom taking all this?'

'Mum and Dad seem to think I'm bent on suicide,' Bea said, 'at least that seems to be the only way Mum can imagine how I feel.'

'And you're definitely not?'

'No . . . I'm angry,' then sadly, 'It hasn't really sunk in, I suppose, what his leaving means. Perhaps he thought things had ground to a halt between us and I didn't notice . . . there weren't any signs that he was having an affair.'

'No not-quite-hidden incriminating photographs in his sock drawer? No unexplained phone calls, or unknown knickers in his pocket? How very unpredictable of him. If men are having an affair, they seem unconsciously to want to let one know about it.' Nest spoke from experience. 'But perhaps it's not unconscious?

'There was nothing, but I wasn't looking for anything, you see. I'm not a jealous person. I was quite happy, being at the book shop and painting in my spare time and supposed Oscar was happy too. He never said anything to the contrary and I always thought we got on so well. I thought he loved me. I certainly loved ...' she paused uncomfortably unfinished, knowing that what she had been about to say was possibly not as true as she'd imagined it to be.

Bea's predicament and her apparently extraordinary fortitude were remarked on by relatives and friends during the following week. Agnes remained agog at the suddenness of it all and came hurrying the next week to the Kerepols, full of aggravating sympathy, to help Bea sort out some belongings from her old bedroom in the attic. Later, as they sat with coffee at the Kerepols' overcrowded kitchen table, the day before Bea's planned move, Agnes was at first a little overawed by her air of furious calm and was inclined to mournful personal reminiscing which Bea found more tolerable than the continual regurgitation of the reasons for and the events leading up to the Flight of Oscar, which was all she'd heard for the past few days.

'I used to love coming here in the days before I went to London. It was so much more comfortable than at home. Here it didn't matter where you left your coat, or where you put down your tea cup.'

'You were lucky to find a space to put down anything. It was always so cluttered.' Bea remembered the contrast between Agnes's mother's house and her own very well; Agnes's mother smoked cigars and was an interior decorator. Every year a new look was ruthlessly imposed; Agnes would return from school to find her friendly green velvet curtains had been changed for sophisticated, crisp grey-and-white *toile de Jouy*, or that her paintings had been taken down from the walls and hidden behind the wardrobe because they didn't accord with the current look. This unnerving chopping and changing had had a dire effect on Agnes and she had taken to secreting precious possessions in boxes, bringing them to a sympathetic Bea for safety in case they were to be the objects of the next ransacking of her bedroom.

'Do you remember Minimalism,' demanded Agnes, 'where one daren't leave even a hairbrush anywhere or the entire effect was spoilt?'

Bea nodded and gave a small sigh. It all seemed impossibly long ago, another life.

'There didn't seem to be any space to actually live in,' carried on Agnes. 'I once caught her scooping up that pink-and-green nylon satchel I had, do you remember, from the kitchen table and hiding it in the cupboard under the sink. She said it looked out of place.' She groaned theatrically. 'It was a relief when "Decaying Country Gentry" came in and she went off and bought some broken fishing rods and a box of old riding boots in a sale, because she thought they looked good in the hall. It was OK to be untidy then, as long as it was the right kind of untidiness. You know, antique patchwork flung carelessly across a chair was all right, but tartan Doc Martens left on the stairs were a no-no. Your mother achieved it without even trying so mine used to come and take notes to see how it ought to look. She never quite got the hang of it – it had to be explained to her that it wasn't something you could arrange convincingly, more something that grew organically.'

'I always wondered,' said Bea slowly, 'if she might have been trying to control you by causing as much uncertainty as possible.' She wished Agnes would shut up.

Agnes looked startled, then dubious. 'Yes, I suppose it's possible – although I'm sure she wasn't aware she was doing it. Anyway, her current craze is *still* feng shui. She shudders whenever she comes into our house – last week she wouldn't come past the door and said she wasn't feeling strong enough to cope with all the negative aspects.'

Agnes then returned to worry at the subject which Bea had hoped had been laid aside: Oscar, and her own imminent removal.

'You and Oscar always seemed to me to be the perfect pair — I was jealous of you. He's so stunningly attractive, so interested in everything.' Here Bea wondered briefly if they were talking about the same Oscar, but Agnes flew on. 'It's hard to believe he's gone off to that cow-woman with the mooing voice. She had a bad skin, I thought, as if she might have had bad spots in her teens and I thought her legs were a little short.' Agnes's porcelain skin had never known the indignities of acne, but she was on less solid ground with legs.

'You won't shut yourself away completely, will you? I can come and visit, can't I?' Agnes sounded plaintive.

'Of course you can come. Fingle's not abroad.'

'But it won't be the same, not being able to pop in to see you at the book shop, or meeting you at lunch time for a glass of wine and a moan. What did they say when you gave in your notice?'

'Bill thought I was being overdramatic. He told me he'd keep the job open for me so that I could come back when my forty days in the wilderness were up. He's going to get someone in temporarily, imagining that Oscar and I have just had a little tiff, as he put it. I couldn't explain to him that I hadn't even been given the chance to have a tiff . . .' There was a tickling at the back of her nose and a prickling in her eyes. 'I don't want to be thinking about it. I want to be "doing".'

She leant her chin on her hand and drew circles in a splash of coffee on the table. Things had been achieved at such high speed over the past few days that there blessedly had been no time to think: a fourth-hand pick-up truck had been bought, ancient and rattling, but with six-months' MOT and a good starter. Stretchers and canvas had been ordered from London, entailing a drive up there to collect them and to replenish stocks of paints, wrestling all the way with the unfamiliar mechanical foibles of the truck. Then there had been the selective packing up of belongings loved or needed in the self-imposed exile.

The artists' suppliers, which she had visited on Agnes's advice, had lifted her spirits. There had been a magical feel to the premises just off the Holloway Road, a dusty cave guarded by an amicable dragon, filled with the tantalising jewel-sheen of tubes of oil paints, water-colours and gouaches in colour order, the very names of which induced a delinquent chemical hunger. The ultramarine, cobalt, cerulean, monestial, Prussian and indigo, the alizarin crimsons and scarlet lakes, the cadmium reds, chrome oranges and yellows, the earthy ochres and Havannah lakes. Passing up and down the collections of shining coloured crayons and dusty rainbows of pastels in their black pigeon holes, Bea, like a child in a sweet shop, almost salivated at the satisfying sight but put herself on a diet and bought only what was strictly needed.

She looked up and saw Agnes was staring at her, head on one side, a speculative jackdaw.

'Do you think *I* should open up communications, make some sort of effort to speak to him?' Bea asked, dipping her finger in the cold coffee and adding a few dots to the pattern she had made.

'I think you should at least give it a try,' Agnes replied, self-conscious at giving advice, the reasons for and advisability of which she was uncertain, to the Bea who had never previously seemed in need of any, 'you won't be happy if you don't. Till death do you part and all that. Personally, I'd never, ever speak to him again.'

Bea did not answer. Agnes had not read that self-pitying letter and there were a large number of people in the south-east of England whom Agnes no longer spoke to. From the store rooms beneath the kitchen came the sound of Tom singing.

Agnes felt that Bea had retreated deep inside her head and was unreachable. Both of them dissolved into tears; Bea because she was exhausted and Agnes because it seemed, well, suitable to keep Bea company in her sorrows.

Tom Kerepol mounted the stairs with heavy tread, still singing:

> *'Dies irae, dies illa,*
> *Solvet saeclum in favilla ...'*

He wanted to find out what had happened to the cup of coffee he had been promised earlier, but broke off, embarrassed and alarmed by the two lachrymose women and uncertain how to proceed. It hurt him dreadfully to see Bea cry. When she was small he'd made her laugh by waggling his false tooth but he could no longer very well try that, since being deserted by one's husband was a bit more serious than a grazed knee. He adjusted his eyepatch, cleared his throat and looked around hopefully for Jane before remembering she had gone to London that morning to consult a specialist in eighteenth-century handwriting, seeking help in the decipherment of the Cadwell family commonplace book which had resurfaced after a miraculous escape from a garden bonfire. Jane hoped to have it printed in tandem with a quantity of pictures and updated versions of the receipts plus a copious commentary of her own.

'As if there was a need for more cookery books,' Tom thought, looking balefully at the stuffed bookshelves around the kitchen. 'If she thinks I'm going to put up with folksy food while she experiments, she'd better think again.' The month before he had broken a tooth on a candied violet during the testing of a range of mediaeval marchpanes and scented custards.

Bea solved his emotional inadequacies by regaining control of herself, going to the stove and pouring the coffee. Tom imagined that crying was not such a bad thing for her; didn't Jane always swear that it made her feel better? Best not to say anything.

*　　*　　*

Agnes sat that evening with arms crossed, warming her feet on the fender at the coal fire, which wasn't burning as well as it might since the cinders hadn't been raked out for several days.

The only sounds were the occasional footsteps along the narrow Cuckold's Lane as people passed close by the sitting room window on their way to the fish and chip shop. As gentrification had taken its stultifying grasp on the town and the business rates rose inexorably higher, the fish and chip shop had been moved from Bellhurst High Street into their mediaeval alley. There was little natural daylight in the sitting room because of the oppressive closeness of the overhanging jetties of the opposite houses and there was only a small courtyard out at the back for Seb to play in. She envied Bea's flowerbeds and vegetable patch at the back, with only the fields behind her and the ineffectual and uncomplaining Mrs Lewis next door.

Initially guiltily aroused by Bea's predicament, her spirits had plummeted, for other rather selfish reasons, on hearing of Bea's planned emigration. It was, however, most interesting to her that Oscar was on the loose again, even if temporarily he was holed up with Andreary. But his timing had been poor. If Oscar had left Bea for anyone, Agnes felt it should have been her; she'd delighted in flirting with Oscar at parties when Bea was in the kitchen, had always been certain that her attraction was reciprocated and that she knew how to manage him better than Bea did; she was able to compose her features into a wonderfully fascinated expression as he spoke and yet be thinking of something else entirely – an effect Bea had never mastered – and he used to flash her understanding, commiserating looks when Phil decided autocratically that it was time that they went home.

Seb had gone to sleep at an unusually early hour, exhausted by his acts of terrorism at nursery school and in the unaccustomed quiet she contemplated the viruses of marriage, her own as much as Bea's, without finding any remedies. The bacteria of boredom were beginning to multiply. She was prone to sudden bouts of dissatisfaction and these had led her into a circular therapy syndrome, a peripheral exploration for answers, employing practitioners of fringe alternatives about whom she was ecstatic, briefly, until a crisis of a different colour fell upon her. She often switched treatments before she could possibly have had time to find out the positive or negative effects of the previous one.

Agnes yearned for a soul mate, frequently imagining she'd found this quality in some man or other but when eventually disappointed, never realised she'd wilfully confused intellectual compatibility with physical attraction, continually overestimating the former in order to put the latter in a more attractive setting. Thinking of Phil, she started to describe him to herself, to see if she still fancied him. Five feet ten, wide shouldered and strong. Large feet and rough hands with fingernails so stout that he broke scissors trying to cut them. His face was pleasantly cast and surrounded disquieting eyes, one hazel, one clear green. The small, neat nose had once been broken playing rugger and was now a little flattened ... Hair fair and thick, prone to curl. A chipped front tooth. Cheeks pink, freckled ... an adult but still boyish version of Just William, which had made the idea of sleeping with him seem oddly illicit; after a year the charm of this had worn away and she could no longer convince herself that it had been an adequate reason for marrying him, but he'd seemed to want to look after her and Seb and opportunities like that didn't come along too often. She liked boyish faces. Bea's brother Patrick's, for instance. He'd had the same look when at fifteen and she was eighteen, she had joyfully seduced him in a prickly field of barley and then again, she smiled smugly at the memory, on several more comfortable occasions before the summer holidays ended; it had been difficult to get him to understand that it was their secret and that being under age, he must not under any circumstances tell his family. Patrick was in the Navy now and they hadn't met for several years.

When Phil had come home that evening Agnes had been busy catching up on the work she should have done that afternoon instead of comforting Bea – another set of illustrations for the children's *Charlie Chooch* series. There had been no signs of preparations being made for anything in the kitchen so Phil had volunteered himself to fetch a fish supper, which annoyed him a little since he was tired out.

He now strode back in purposefully and went straight to the kitchen, ostentatiously rustling paper and clattering plates and she hurried to the drawing desk at the end of the room, switching off the Anglepoise, guiltily tidying paints and swishing brushes in the dirty paint water. She cleared a place to eat at the dining table among the thick grey strata of accumulated newspapers and magazines before Phil returned to the sitting room with two warmed plates of plaice and chips decorated with half a lemon.

As they ate, Bea's troubles were naturally uppermost in their conversation. Phil indignantly denied that he had known that anything was afoot although Oscar's secretary Sheila had mentioned that there had been a flurry of calls for Oscar from Mrs Bullingden recently, but they'd both innocently assumed that these concerned the garden gates that were being made for her.

'Bea says she never noticed anything about his behaviour to warn her either. But then, she *wouldn't* notice. She didn't notice any of the others. She's intolerably vague. I'm sure Oscar found it irritating.' Agnes polished off the last chip and sucked her fingers.

'Not half as vague as you,' replied Phil, good-naturedly surveying the innocent doll's face. 'I'm starving when I get home from the ironworks.'

Phil's green eye was disconcerting; it appeared to a sometimes unquiet soul to interrogate, to criticise, even if its owner hadn't intended to do so.

'But it's all a bit *sad*, isn't it?' she demanded. 'I always thought

Oscar was the perfect husband, so tolerant.' She reached out and stole one of Phil's chips and added with light sarcasm: 'She *always* had his supper on the table like a good little slave.'

'God! You do wolf your food down. Do you mean sad that he's left her, or sad that you misjudged him? In any case, I definitely don't understand him. I'd die for a woman who had supper waiting for me.' Phil hastily reached out, put his arm round her waist and tickled her ribs. 'Don't glare at me. I was only teasing – I know you've been busy working too. Can't we drop the Mitty scandal and get on with our own lives? The Koreans I told you about? They're bringing the architect for the new offices in the City over tomorrow and there should be a commission coming through.'

'Any chance of design work for me? I really enjoyed doing those gates for Andreary Bullshit although,' she added loyally, 'now I wish they'd clang shut on her neck and decapitate her.'

'If there's a chance available I'll make sure you get a crack at it. You didn't get enough praise for the Bullingden gates.'

'The money more than made up for the lack of praise. Anyway, I've got some title illustrations to do next week for a new glossy gardening magazine. Very upmarket. Lots of little green watering cans and hanks of raffia. That'll make a welcome break. It's more satisfying doing that type of work than yomping through these repetitive *Charlie Chooch* books. If I have to draw his smug little face again, I'll be sick. I'm just praying that the author doesn't take it into his head to do a fourth series.'

'You invented his face in the first place. That's the reason they're so successful.' Phil went over to the fireplace and rattled the poker half-heartedly among the smouldering coals, setting himself down with a sigh of tiredness on a sagging, knobbly chair whose cover consisted of an overambitious patchwork of cobbled-together pieces of Indian bedspread.

'Any danger you might make some coffee?' he asked, unlacing his boots, levering them off against the edge of the iron fender and wriggling his toes in their red socks in relief at being home, fed and safe from the worrying world outside.

Things had been difficult enough this week, trying to lay the flying sneers and rumours at work. It would have been better if Oscar had come in and carried on as if nothing had happened. Not having himself found Andrea Bullingden particularly attractive, he was puzzled by the man's behaviour; Andrea, he'd thought, was a sly, catty woman, the type who rub themselves up against one, pleading all manner of hardships while their whiskers quiver with acquisitiveness and challenge. He was fond of Bea ... the beautiful, faithful Bea. Agnes had told him once, with amazement, that she didn't think Bea had ever even looked at another man since meeting Oscar.

He'd first seen her almost dancing down the street, mouthing the words of a song on a Walkman plugged into her neatly-modelled little ears, but there was something about her that gave the impression of a girl merely paying lip service to the common concerns of her age group. She couldn't have been much more than sixteen then and he had for some time fantasised about her. There'd been glimpses of her at pubs and parties that year where, with an attractive otherworldliness, she had appeared to be thinking of something other than what was going on around her but he had been too shy to approach. By the time he'd gained enough courage to ask her out, it was too late; the bolder Oscar had scored a bullseye. Now that he had Agnes, he thought of Bea only occasionally ... but still experienced a little jolt of unrequited love every single time he saw her. He was distressed for her and disgusted with Oscar, but talking about it would achieve nothing. He was too tired that evening to have an opinion and shut his eyes for a moment, waking an hour and a half later to find that the fire had gone out, that a cup of coffee stood cold on the fender and that Agnes had gone up to bed without him.

Chapter Three

During the weekend Bea swept away the accumulated dusty clutter of Little Rumm's previous tenants – she would find her own shells, stones and feathers for different aesthetic and sentimental reasons. The acts of cleaning away the house's winter mildew, of nesting and rearranging only partially dimmed the sense of loneliness. She squirted the last remaining drops of a bottle of Poême on the backboards of the wardrobe to mask the mustiness and snuffed appreciatively before unpacking the single suitcase of clothes. The precious collection of blue glass was displayed on little shelves hastily fitted-up across a narrow window at the side of the sitting room. Now the early morning sun glittered through Bristol finger bowls, a turquoise wine glass and a Victorian sapphire poison bottle, throwing a stained-glass pattern across the rush matting. Books were on the bookshelves, a monograph on the paintings of Samuel Palmer and her grandmother's copy of *Grimm's Fairytales* among them, and *Gulliver's Travels* which she'd always meant to read but never managed. The painting room upstairs was cleared for action and waiting, like a person meeting an unknown visitor off a train. Anything was possible.

The immediate area around the house was treeless and the need for kindling for the fire drove her further afield to search the ness for driftwood, driving back into Fingle and out again on the road to the point with its lighthouses, shacks and bungalows. These were dwarfed, even the massive disused brick lighthouse, by the elephantine outlines of the nuclear power stations squatting in gross intimacy together beside the sea. She found them so invasive a feature that it was strangely possible to ignore them – in the way in which it is possible to ignore distant atrocities – by simply suspending belief in the evidence of eyes and ears.

She'd been to the area before as a child, when she and Patrick had climbed the echoing white interior of the old lighthouse and stood beside the polished latticed glass containing its giant lamps, staring out over the windswept shingle ridges scattered with broom. A ghostly grey tanker sailed far out past the point, almost hidden in soft mist. Jane was a vertigo sufferer and had leant stiff as a doll against their toy car far below while the children sickeningly waved and screamed from above. Half way down the lighthouse stairs, on a window ledge, they'd seen a kestrel's nest; it had been one of those days when Bea had caught and held a feeling of buoyant happiness, right there at the moment rather than looking backwards and remembering it at bedtime.

The fishing boats perched on top of the shingle bank were tough, squat shapes against the sky, their upper outlines a confusion of ropes, wires, aerials and quivers of flapping black and red marker flags, the purposes of which were unknown to Bea. They loomed above her as she walked along below the deeply shelving shore towards the lifeboat station; her pockets were full of rattling cockle shells and a canvas bag of driftwood was on her shoulder. The wind was in her ears and salt on her lips and the night before, the third at Little Rumm, she had at last slept well, unstirred by dreams. Nest had been right; life was cleaner and simpler out here and the untidy limbo of the week before was at least physically behind her.

As Bea scaled the bank, moving crabwise up the steep incline of shifting stones to the flat-topped storm beach above, a tractor came into view, nosing a fishing boat down to the sea. There was a steady-paced activity as men moved back and forth with planks, rotating them from behind the boat's transporter to place them beneath the wheels at the front, inching it across the gentle slope from where it would undoubtedly tilt and slide smoothly into the high water. The boat was new and blue, its paint unstained and its cabin shiny white. Although it was only eight o'clock in the morning, several groups of interested spectators stood placidly about with loose children and joyful mongrels galloping dangerously about among them. It dawned on Bea that she was witnessing the launch of a virgin fishing boat and being secretly a little superstitious, felt in need of good omens. This looked like a most auspicious one and she squatted down optimistically in a dip in the shingle to get out of the wind and watch the technicalities.

It became fast apparent that the launch was not proceeding according to the rule book. The boat became stuck fast with its conveyor's wheels pressing ever deeper into the shingle, the weight too great for the straining sea tractor to shift forwards. The prospective skipper, navy sweatered and rubber booted, stood on the deck leaning over the rail, his grey hair flapping in the breeze as he engaged in strained discussions with the launchers below.

Bea took out her pencil and pocket-book and drew, leaning her back into the bag of lumpy driftwood, absorbed by the tubby boat and awesome rotundity of a new arrival, a white-bearded man also in navy sweater, who carried red-and-green flags beneath his arm and who gesticulated towards the lifeboat house as if indicating that help would soon be at hand. A very tall, energetic-looking man with a short thick plait of red hair hanging down the back of a faded green jersey was consulting with two dark, deep-chested men with hefty forearms who ambled off to fetch more planks to place beneath the wheels. Erik the Red, she thought, swiftly sketching him in, and Castor and Pollux.

The sky grew dreary and a spatter of rain forced her to put away the sketch pad and patiently wait but in spite of this it seemed to Bea miraculous to be away from Bellhurst and the claustrophobic book shop and out of reach of those people who *would* keep wringing their hands, unkindly reminding her of the fact that she had been deserted.

After a while, as the watchers were beginning to disperse disappointedly, the lifeboat made a swift entrance stage left, and shot down its ramp past the stationary fishing boat, slapping satisfactorily into the grey-green water and bringing fresh orange, blue and scarlet drama to the scene. The launchers were re-animated and rushed about attaching a turquoise nylon line to the transporter; the lifeboat with its yellow-oilskinned crew moved further out and at a signal from the fat flagman, went engines full ahead into the slight swell. The rope drew taut but still the boat stayed put. The signaller waved the red flag vigorously, and then frantically the green. Bea got up from her hollow and crept closer to watch. It was beginning to drizzle in earnest.

Nothing budged although the lifeboat was straining ahead again and pungent blue smoke from its roaring engine was floating out across the water. At that moment Bea, perhaps hearing a change of pitch in the singing sound from the vibrating rope, had a flashing premonition of danger and stepped back, tripping on an abandoned plastic fish box. Erik the Red leapt back too, yelling a warning as the towrope snapped apart and flew like a striking snake, whip-lashing backwards towards the fishing boat and missed slicing into Bea only by inches.

There were some red faces about, pinked by embarrassment and the freshening wind but Erik the Red turned white-faced to Bea as if she had no place there at all and was in some way to blame for their mortification and in a surly fashion, gave her a hand up.

'You all right?' he asked, kicking the fish box out of the way.

'I'm fine,' she bent to take off her boot which seemed to have collected half the beach inside it when she fell, 'I shouldn't have got so close.'

'No. There are problems enough without looking out for sightseers.' To Bea's English ears the tenseness of voice and the faint Ulster accent instantly brought to mind TV news interviews with other recalcitrant and self-justifying men and she momentarily stiffened; but by now she felt quite desperate for them to succeed with the launch and asked timidly if they were going to try again.

'Once more, perhaps,' then seeing her genuine interest, his voice softened and became less churlish. 'The water's getting too low. We'll get a new line attached but if they can't make it this time, we'll have to leave it till next high tide, this evening.' Perhaps feeling he had explained enough, he smiled briefly, turned his back on her and with a squaring of broad shoulders went back to his mates.

She found the shoulder-squaring amusing, rather poignant, a male reminder that she had come perilously close to getting in the way of men's work and shamingly witnessed its failure. There were other women among the quiet onlookers, wives and girlfriends perhaps; one of them in white high-heeled shoes and black leggings, the visible bare skin between the two unattractively blue with cold. She tottered when she moved, inappropriate feet sinking deep in the stones and forcing her to clutch, helpless and tittering, at the leather-jacketed arm of the patient man beside her.

Bea rather weepily wished she hadn't turned the launch into an augury for herself and when the final attempt also came to nothing, moved off to carry the driftwood back to the pick-up, deeply disappointed. Erik the Red turned from his rope-coiling or whatever it was he was doing and waved as she left, and she raised a hand only tentatively to acknowledge it.

'I must not waste working time,' she muttered to herself, stumbling along on the wet and slippery sleepers of what looked like old railway track, before remembering that her hours were no longer circumscribed. She would like to have seen the boat on the water, but perhaps they would be able to get it afloat tonight.

Back in the house, she laid out the kindling to dry by the fireplace and went up to the painting room with a cup of strong coffee to stand in the middle of the floor, day-dreaming for a moment, vividly imagining the room overflowing with paintings, zooming in on them in turn, inspecting aspects, details, shapes, colours. Then she laid out the components and started to assemble the stretchers for two canvases, larger than anything she had so far attempted or indeed had room for before. She measured, cut and tacked on the canvas and primed it. Nest was right too about this room; it had a positive, workman-like air about it and with the red-sheeted divan bed pushed up against the far wall and the white-painted wardrobe shifted into a corner, was spacious. Intending that the first attempt at such a scale would be a trial run, she primed a large piece of hardboard. There was a play on the radio, set in urban Yorkshire, but it was heavy-handed amusement with an irritating overload of surrealist touches of the '... me wife's mother went off with an entomologist who had a deep regard for kippers ...' variety. She switched stations and with Berlioz's *Symphonie Fantastique* as background, roughed out on paper the picture loitering in her brain.

The morning passed and suddenly starving she foraged for a bowl of tinned pea-and-ham soup and a couple of squashed fly biscuits. The sunshine came and went. Isolated, coping, working. Contentment hovered shyly above but although aware of its presence she refused to allow it to settle before setting down the outlines of her theme.

By mid afternoon the blank white surface of the hardboard was dry; the great space was sufficiently daunting to make her pause, inhaling deeply as if about to leap over rather than paint on it. There had never seemed to be enough time before – it had always been measured by Oscar's needs. Now it all appeared delightfully open-ended and she could carry on painting till circumstances dictated otherwise. She took off her watch and laid it face down on the chair and began, jabbing at first anxiously with the brush, only to be stopped when the light began to fade and it was urgently time for more food.

The composition was in soft grey outline, with some sky blocked in and trial patches of colour, more or less as she had seen it in the dream. A group of robed figures stood on a beach, their arms raised and behind them the fishing boat was being towed out to sea by a large wading figure of the goddess Freda, draperies tucked up above the knee and on her head the poppy and cornflower-trimmed hat. Bea grinned the first grin she had grinned since Oscar had left and started to clean the paintbrushes, humming again. Unburdened or unblessed by children, unless you counted Oscar, she'd squandered the years. She *could* have gone to art school, or even university, *could* have started painting properly years before. Well, she was going to make up for it now. Was it conceivable that the rage and hurt felt at the manner of his leaving were already undergoing transformation, into something like relief? She was too tired that evening to think of going back to watch the second attempt to launch the boat and after supper, lay on the lumpy sofa beside the crackling blue-flamed driftwood fire and started on *Gulliver's Travels*, falling asleep at page four and dreaming. 'You must paint on these,' said an overseer, handing her a blank perforated sheet of second-class stamps; however when she returned with pictures of the fishing boat painted neatly on each stamp, he snorted and tore them up, saying 'Not nearly big enough! Try some first-class ones. They use a better class of glue for those.'

Two days later the first visitor arrived. A solicitous mother stood beaming on the doorstep with a bulging carrier bag in one hand and a bunch of narcissi in the other.

'Beatrice! Darling! You didn't telephone to say everything was all right as you promised! You don't mind me coming unannounced, do you? Look, I've brought some vegetables and two goose eggs and a bottle of wine. Oh, and a sharp knife! Nest wouldn't know the importance of a sharp knife for cooking. I thought we could have a little lunch and a drink together? I couldn't bear to think of you being lonely and miserable.'

Bea had been working confidently since seven o'clock that morning and having just eaten a large cheese-and-onion sandwich, was both touched and irritated by the assumptions that she was miserable and couldn't be anywhere else but in.

'I haven't had time to be miserable,' she tried to reassure. 'I'm trying to put it off and there hasn't been time to be lonely either, I promise you,' and added, uselessly, 'Please, you mustn't worry about me.'

A visit from one or other of her parents had been inevitable, but she had hoped they might have allowed her a week to herself first. A routine was still being established. No longer having to fight for time, the concept of total freedom was troubling; doing what she wanted, when she wanted, didn't come easily. There was a need for some type of framework to the days and having been freed so abruptly from the self-imposed domestic courtyard, she was constructing a much longer and more interesting perimeter to pace.

Tom had already seen the inside of the house when he'd helped Bea move in but Jane had been worried by the vagueness of his description of its comforts or possible lack of them and couldn't restrain herself from hurtling over as soon as she had got rid of ancient Uncle Perry whose arrival on a long-promised stay she'd been unable to avert.

She strode into Bea's kitchen and arranged the flowers in a child's tin seaside bucket which she found beneath the sink and looked about, recognising various vital items imported from her daughter's kitchen but in the main the dreadful inadequacies of the catering arrangements were confirmed. She whipped out a red notebook and scribbled down 'colander, grater, chopping board'. Bea heard her rattling swiftly through the drawers and smiled. Jane had been in the forefront of a generation of relatively impoverished upper-class women whose own mothers' helplessness when faced with the loss of their cooks during the war and whose hopeless struggles with limited and poor-quality ingredients had led their daughters to pray that there might be more interesting things to eat than potato-and-onion pie. Jane had loathed the way the lead shot clattered out on to the plate as the thin rabbit stew gravy was served, the indigestibly undercooked potatoes and the monotony of the brown, pink or white packet cornflower puddings. In her teens she discovered Elizabeth David and had taken over the family's feeding, at least during the school holidays. There had been unkind rumours among the family that her father's early death had been induced by gorging himself on her chocolate pie. It was in the house at Bellhurst that she'd written her first cookery article on the delights of rediscovered suety puddings such as Humpy Locktooth, Figgy Hoggin and Flabby John.

Bea had inherited her mother's talent for cooking, when it was necessary, but not the obsessional approach. Having already eaten a sandwich, she refused to be moved on the subject of lunch, but happily opened the wine and made her mother a deep yellow and thickly frothy goose-egg omelette, under unnecessary shouted instruction from the sitting room.

Jane, suddenly unsure how to start on the substance of the visit, nudged with her foot at the books which lay on the floor by the fire.

'What's this you're reading? *Gulliver's Travels*? And what's this — what a horrible title!' She picked up the Angela Carter. Its cover was curled and its pages were stained. Bea had been reading it in the bath the night before and had dozed off, to wake with a jerk as her head and the book slid beneath the soapy water. She'd tried to dry it out in front of the fire but it was seriously spoiled and smelt of Badedas.

'Adult versions of fairy stories, Mum,' Bea said. 'You wouldn't care for them.'

'Yes, I can see. Not about my sort of people,' Jane happily agreed and Bea smothered a giggle. Jane would have dismissed *Crime and Punishment* or *Nana* in the same fashion, seldom having time for more than cookery books and when consulting these, marking errors of method, punctuation or typography in fine red pen in the margins. In one book by an over-celebrated television cook, she'd indignantly scrawled across a recipe for stuffed courgettes: 'Tastes like sea-slug stuffed with sick.' Patrick had once unfairly remarked that she was the sort of literal-minded woman who might check love letters for temperature and quantities.

'Now,' said Jane brightly, having eaten the omelette fast without more than a surprised 'Not bad at all!' and, having firmly re-corked the wine bottle although Bea would have liked another glass, 'you must tell me what your plans are. You haven't told me anything at all about what you intend to do about the cottage, or what you are going to do about Oscar.'

'Firstly, I've changed the locks, so Oscar can't take Andreary there, although I can't imagine he would, really. I'm sure he's safely tucked up in her mansion. I just couldn't bear the thought of her looking at my things. The cottage is being looked after by Mrs Lewis – she's got a key but won't tell Oscar. I was a bit worried about asking at first, since she appears half witted at times, but she seemed pleased to be asked and said it wouldn't be any trouble. She'll send on any post for me, and all the bills to Oscar. Anything valuable I've put for safe keeping in my old room at home, as you know. I don't see that there's anything else to worry about, is there?' Pleased with her own practicality, she looked hopefully at her mother to see if she was satisfied.

'But who's going to mow the lawn? And finances? You *must* get in touch with a solicitor'. Jane wailed. 'And what about Oscar?' The poor child was being most impractical.

'What about him?' said Bea edgily, removing her mother's plate and trying to evade things by taking it out to the kitchen.

'Don't wander off like that, and don't be difficult.' Jane got up and followed her, protesting. 'You can't let things slide, like this. You *must* get in touch with him, for money, till things are sorted out. How long do you propose to stay here in this isolated shack?'

'I don't see why *I* have to get in touch with *him*. I need to be isolated, to work things out on my own. And this is not a shack. It's got everything one could possibly need and I mean to stay here for the moment ...' How long could one extend a moment? Why was it so hard to accept the look of distress on her mother's face? '... Indefinitely. As long as Nest will let me. As long as the money will last.'

'I see.' Jane excelled at sounding just slightly hurt and she stared at her daughter's smooth, still insolently young and closed, self-protective face. 'Golden' was the word that jumped into her mind whenever she saw her daughter and a clear image of the new-born Bea slid before her eyes; nervously holding the child for the first time, she'd feverishly searched the squashed pink face for resemblances and signals. The fragile head with its still encrusted strands of hair had nuzzled sideways then raised a near-invisible and cynical eyebrow in a miniature query, as if to wonder whether she had been deposited with the right parent. Jane had just then caught that look as Bea was speaking. She had turned out to be an attractive but wilful child, a little oddball, difficult for Jane to fathom. Although she had had her doubts about the advisability of such a youthful marriage, she had breathed a cautious sigh of relief when Bea was safely ensconced in her cottage with Oscar and had been secretly amazed that Bea had settled down so peacefully for so long.

'Well, let's talk about something else then, as you're obviously going to be intransigent. Patrick is home on leave for three days in July so I hope you'll come out of your cocoon of self-containment and see him?'

'Of course I will.' Impatiently. July was a long way off. 'He's written to me with the dates.' It would be a pleasant relief to see the still unmarried Patrick whose leaves seemed to be less often spent at home; he at least would not lob unreturnable questions at her all the time.

'And what do you do with yourself all day?' Jane asked, rather desperately, feeling herself unfairly being forced into the role of interfering mother yet unable to resist the pressure, and the pleasure.

'But I'm working of course. Painting.' She misjudged Jane's tenacity if she thought that any mention of art would send her off on another track. Jane felt called upon to ask, as eagerly as she could manage, if she could see and Bea prevaricated, knowing that although her mother might be wonderfully adventurous in the area of taste buds, had a good sense of colour and three-dimensional form, she was bizarrely inadequately equipped in the two-dimensional visual sense, being slow to unravel the subject from the lines of a drawing and finding any distortions hopelessly puzzling and tedious. Bea had once been reduced to asking her, when she'd expressed a lack of understanding on being confronted with one of the simplest of figurative paintings, whether if it had been a plate of food, she would have been tempted to eat it? Her mother, forced to pretend to study it in depth, had replied that it seemed to be a bit heavy on the cabbage side.

'Not yet. It won't be finished for ages, the thing I'm working on. But I will show it to you, and the other things I've planned, if they work out all right,' and she added, 'I'm quite all right, you know. I will keep in touch. I'm not going to become an anchoress.' And more desperately, seeing Jane's expression of forlorn concern, almost as if *she* had been the one to have been deserted, 'I was thinking of going out for a drink, to try a pub in Fingle.' This was a faux pas. Jane's mouth tightened, the tiny lines above the top lip deepening. Her mother had imagined her to be pining, felt that she *should* be pining and had needed to be able to console her.

The visit ended. Gathered up in Jane's arms and fiercely hugged once more, Bea wished she had been less childishly defensive, but that involved comforting the would-be comforter and she hadn't the strength for it and she so very much wanted to get back to work.

'Well, you *must* be careful. I seem to remember hearing Nest saying the pubs were rather rough. I hate you being sequestered out here. Anything might happen. You must keep the door bolted at all times, particularly when you're working upstairs. Anyway, I must sally forth, although I've no idea how one sallies — where does that expression come from? It sounds as if it should be used for gays coming out, doesn't it? I have to run through a Turkey *à la Normande* and a honey ice cream for an article and it's your father's final rehearsal of the Verdi *Requiem* tonight. He'll need feeding up beforehand.'

Bea expressed a hope that all would go smoothly with the Verdi, and remembered to ask whether the commonplace book had proved to be interesting.

'Oh, yes! Very, very interesting. I'm certain there's going to be money in it. There's an awful lot of tiresome research to be done first but I'm getting the hang of it at last.'

Bea kissed her good-bye and waved from the doorstep then taking the bucket of narcissi with her, she skipped upstairs to try to catch the painting unawares, to see it as it might be seen for the first time and check that the composition was really working out as she hoped, before she had been interrupted.

She gave it a stern stare, stepping back to the opposite wall for a better view, then mixing the colours on a dinner plate, began to fill in the schematic head of the figure on the boat with Jane's face, ruefully remembering a childhood episode when she had shown her mother a drawing of an acrobat perched on the back of a donkey.

Jane had been leaning up against the kitchen dresser, writing business letters. She rarely sat to do anything and even sewed standing by the window.

'That's a lovely drawing,' Jane had said absently after giving it the merest glance. 'What book did you copy it from?'

'I didn't copy it,' Bea answered, puzzled and annoyed, 'not from a book. I thought it.' She'd removed the drawing and later that afternoon presented Jane with another one, in bright crayons. Her mother was now scribbling in a notebook with a marbled cover, standing by the stove while keeping an eye on a chicken carcase boiling in the stockpot.

'Oh God!' she'd said, putting down the pen and staring hard. Even to her it had been a recognisable portrait of Patrick in his scarlet-and-black striped Dennis the Menace jersey, apparently being eaten alive by chickens. Quite gory. 'Darling! It's quite horrible!' Then hastily: 'Whatever gave you such an idea?' She had looked anxiously down at Bea's narrow, obstinate little face beneath the fair pudding basin haircut. Bea did not know where her ideas came from. She deliberated.

'I thought this one too, in my own head. You couldn't say I copied it.'

'No, I can see now that you didn't. I'm sorry that I thought you had copied the other one. I'm sure they're both very good drawings indeed. Poor Patrick though. I wouldn't show it to him – it would give him dreadful dreams.'

'I don't mean it to happen, or anything like that,' Bea had said anxiously. 'I just thought it.'

Bea was too young still and had lived too continuously close to her parents seriously to have examined her relationship with them.

Oscar sat uncomfortably at the bar that evening, waiting for Phil. The new trousers which Andrea had bought him were too tight around his waist. Was it possible that in spite of all the worry he could have put on weight in the two weeks he'd spent with Andrea? The atmosphere at work had become miasmic with disapproval since he'd gone to live with her and hoping to clear the air, he'd invited Phil to come for a drink to discuss events in general. Sheila had been casting him basilisk glances from behind the screen of her word processor and he was certain he'd heard the foreman Ernie Fletcher call him a prat behind his back when the Koreans were being shown round the works. There had been a resentful silence from Phil, which had to be broken.

He'd cautiously returned to Fleming Cottage, early in the evening a week after his decampment, steeling himself to cope with a distraught and hysterical Bea and unreasonably, he could see now, expecting to be able to make her understand how deeply sorry he was that he had let her down by falling in love with someone else. Knowing her normal rationality he had not expected a major campaign and imagined that they would be able, not all at once of course but gently, in time, to come to an understanding and make sensible arrangements about their possessions and the future.

He had encountered only Mrs Lewis, who had trailed him like a pale slug up the path while ineptly explaining that Bea had gone away. He was angered to find that the front door lock had been changed. However he had the spare key to the tool shed on his key-ring and opened that up, intending to remove the chainsaw.

Inside he had been assaulted by a powerful smell of decomposition. Snuffing about like a dog in the dark, his heart pounding with foreboding, he eventually traced it, throwing open the lid of the tool chest and staring in disbelief at the encrusted tools inside and the ruined electric drill. It looked to him as if someone had been voluminously sick into the chest and it dawned that he didn't know Bea at all, had been unable to imagine how she might behave, and that it was possible that things were not going to be so simple to finalise as he'd hoped.

The sun had set and he peered through a window into the darkening kitchen. All was neat and tidy apart from the fork piercing the pages of a letter on the table. He knew even at a distance that it *was* his letter. He felt foolish and turned sharply away, straight into the wretched Mrs Lewis standing silently just behind him.

Unable to get any sense out of her, he'd apprehensively tried Tom on the telephone but had received an emotional and imaginatively abusive ear-bashing, Tom refusing to tell him if Bea was in the house and only grudgingly agreeing to pass on messages. Oscar thought she must be staying with her parents though, since first Phil then Agnes had denied knowledge of her whereabouts. Andrea had suggested frostily that morning that it would be best to write to her to organise a discussion about the separation with a solicitor at hand and he was now inclined to agree with her.

It had been foolish not to have foreseen that there might be some partisanship among his acquaintances and staff. It appeared that Bea had taken time off work at the book shop and disappeared and no one was prepared to tell him where she was hiding, which seemed to him unnecessarily obstructive since he wasn't a wife-batterer or anything like that, merely ... he paused to think for the first time what he was in other people's eyes ... an adulterer, a deserter, a prat? He found it hard to acknowledge that he was any of those things, particularly after spending time with Andrea who thought him a gleaming white knight, her rescuer from solitary confinement in the country. But it wasn't as if he and Bea had children to worry about – in fact if they had had children ... he tried to justify himself and failed. Andrea had a child, a little boy now at preparatory school, and perhaps, in the not too distant future, he might have one of his own too.

Where the hell was Phil? He'd chosen the Eeldyke Inn particularly as being remote enough from the town to make it unlikely that he would encounter any more baleful stares or knowing whispers. It was a quiet old place with no music, but the landlord didn't seem inclined to make conversation and the only other customers, a middle-aged man and woman laughing and chattering in the corner by the window, seemed more than content with their own company. Quickly glancing in their direction he saw that the woman was pretty, in fact she was very attractive but although all her bits seemed still in the right places, she was obviously quite old, at least fifty.

He wished he had Andrea with him, although this was hardly the sort of place she'd be used to. Judging by the reception he'd had so far, it would take time before they would be able to be seen in Bellhurst together but people surely had other things to think about and it would all soon be forgotten?

He began to feel sleepy. Although it was a warm, wet evening, willow logs snapped and sparkled on the fire. The clock on the wall suddenly struck the half hour, making him jump. The door flew open and six or seven men came in, stamping their mud-spattered seven-league boots and shaking out work-stained raggedy jackets, for it had started to rain heavily. They were obviously regular customers. Noisily pulling out stools and chairs and teasing the landlord, they settled near to Oscar, taking up a great deal of room with elbows and splayed out legs, setting up a wide and intangibly fenced area about them. Oscar read the proprietorial signs and moved along the bar. There was much passing about of tobacco pouches, borrowing of Rizlas and careless slopping of pints of real ale. They appeared to be celebrating something for they were impossibly jolly. After a while one of them leant over the bar and in a penetrating stage whisper, offered to sell the landlord something.

'Here, Seth, fancy a bit of wild boar? Got a nice leg out in back of the van.' Seth looked interested and stopped polishing the glasses.

'Phylly's partial to a nice bit of pig, wild or not.' He whispered back. 'Where did you shoot it?'

'Cade's Wood. Charlie and I split it down the middle, so to speak. Come outside and have a look.'

Seth disappeared into the wet dark outside and re-appeared a little later with a grin on his face and a large bundle loosely wrapped in dirty sacking which he carried out through the back room and into his private quarters. The pub began to fill up, but still no sign of Phil. Oscar studied the wall behind the boar-seller's head. It was covered in notices, some handwritten offering washing machines or lurcher pups for sale, others small posters advising the advent of past point-to-point races or sponsored beard-shaving for Balkan orphans. There was also a pink poster, computer-written by someone with such an eclectic eye for typography that it took him some while to decipher, advertising 'Dwyle Flunking on Easter Monday at the Eeldyke Inn. 3 p.m.' Whatever dwyle-flunking was, it had already taken place.

The wild-boar man slipped over to the couple in the corner, had words with them and the woman got up eagerly and followed him outside with a backward conspiratorial smile at her companion, so glowing that Oscar felt quite lonely. They obviously fancied a nice bit of boar as well.

Phil slammed through the door, obviously in a foul mood and Oscar nervously bought him a pint.

'This is a hell of a long way to come for a drink, it's pouring out there and I still haven't caught up with my sleep after your little flit for freedom – you might have left it till we'd got the fire-backs order out.' Phil sat down heavily on the stool beside Oscar. 'Ernie was off work that week with a bruised foot and I've done my back in helping load up the lorry.' Phil sank a third of the pint and waited, aggressively. 'Come on. Spit it out.'

'Look, I know you – everyone – thinks I'm a bastard to have left Bea so suddenly like that. I've tried to get in touch with her to apologise but she's gone to ground somewhere.'

'Apologise?' Phil, recalling again how obsessed he'd been with Bea all those years ago, suddenly felt a flush of pure anger.

'I wouldn't have thought you could round off ten – twelve is it? – years of marriage with just an apology.'

'No, of course it isn't possible. But there are things about our marriage that you don't know about. She's never treated me as if ... as if I were an adult. More as if I were her child. And we haven't got any children ...' he added, very lamely.

'The sperm count a bit low, is it?' said Phil, nastily.

'Um ... No ... why should it be?' Oscar shrugged his shoulders carelessly. 'It's Bea. Women's problems, odd periods, that sort of thing. But she never seemed interested enough to get checked over by a doctor.' It had not occurred to Oscar that it might in any way be his problem. But if it had occurred to Bea ... and she had not said anything ... 'Anyway, she'd be useless with babies – they'd probably have to make their own bottles while she carried on daubing away. Bugger everything! I know there's no excuse, Phil. I just fancied Andrea rotten, I fell for her. End of story.' Oscar's handsome face bore an expression of self-conscious complacency. Phil loathed his straight nose and even white teeth.

'Being honest doesn't help either,' he said slowly. 'Open, but still amoral. What about Bea?'

'She's still young; she'll get over it and she can have Fleming Cottage.'

Phil stood up, and hit him.

Chapter Four

Agnes stared moodily down from a bedroom window into the damp little yard where Seb stood in a puddle in his socks, bumping a toy car up and down in a tray of double daisies. After yelling at him she clumped grumpily downstairs, dreary with the lack of stimulating happenings in her current domestic life. Perhaps it was time she visited Bea and poached a share of hers? Her rampageous London days sparkled still in her memory; she was wasting away, drowning in small-town mundanity. The idea of having a chat with Bea was instantly cheering – she at least had managed to kick Bellhurst in the behind and get away – quite romantic really and besides there was one morsel of news she could justifiably impart; Phil's bruised hand had not gone unnoticed. She had been accustomed in the past to people fighting over her and although to have her husband punching Oscar on Bea's behalf wasn't exactly ego-boosting, it was at least an event and she was aching to see where Bea had secreted herself. Bea's mobile seemed to be permanently switched off but undeterred Agnes abandoned work for the morning and set out with Seb, knowing it was only about fifteen miles away but with only the haziest idea of how to get to the house. Bea had described its appearance in detail but on leaving Fingle Agnes took several wrong turnings before happening on the right God-forsaken, unmarked track.

Drawn away from her work by the need to cope with maniacal clankings inside Nest's diluvial washing machine, Bea had mopped up the floor for the second time that morning and then discovered a snail trying to force an entry into the bread bin. A further search and some tracking on hands and knees of viscid trails discovered a veritable gastropod's doss-house beneath the piece of slate covering the outside drain so she fetched a bucket and piled in all the snails, intending at first to fling them over a far corner of a foreign field.

'I wonder if *all* snails are edible?' she thought, pausing with the bucket and leaning on the wall at the front, enjoying the piercing brilliance of the spring morning. Earlier that day there had been brief visitations of dark squalls flashing across the windows of the painting room. There had been an unimpeded view of the whole dazzling one hundred and eighty degrees of rainbow, the arc framing a thunderous sky above the miraculously sunlit line of orange and yellow thumb prints – polled willows decorating the dykes in the distance. Pots of gold doubtless lay buried at both ends.

Her relationship with the new surroundings had grown ever warmer with the weather. In the first damp days of the move there she'd walked disconsolately across the fields around the house and the air had pressed crushingly on her skull. Now with the heat of the sun striking through her shirt, the deep, clear sky appeared to draw her up into itself, breathe and suck her own breath in and out and cause a sense of giddy levitation.

Another noise was competing with the muffled but now despairing clattering of the washing machine. Agnes's car was proceeding erratically up the track to the house, diapasons of tuneful twanging emanating from its suspension as it bounced along, swerving to avoid the pot-holes. Bea sighed, abandoned the bucket of snails and thoughts of garlic butter and hurried to welcome Agnes and also Seb, who glowered in the back. Releasing himself from the imprisoning car seat he rushed for the pink bicycle, leaving Bea to show Agnes round the house.

Agnes was near speechless with envy.

'But Bea, it's magic!' How fortunate Bea was with all this space to herself and how interesting she'd made it, bringing the yellow sitting room curtains from Fleming Cottage and the favourite little soft blue armchair sitting in the sun by the window. The room had a cool, uncluttered look that was very different from the cushioned cosiness of Fleming Cottage and the walls reflected back the sunlight in a myriad of different shades of grey and translucent creams. A neat stack of bleached driftwood lay beside the fireplace log basket and the fire itself was already laid against the evening chills. Bea had the knack for that sort of thing, apparently effortlessly turning the most unpromising place into something that looked suitable to be photographed for *Country Living*. She looked amazingly good too in spite of the recent emotional upheaval: hair clean and windblown, no bags beneath the long, cool blue eyes. How like Bea to turn a disaster into a asset.

'I tried to phone you but you must have switched it off,' said Agnes as they sat in peace on the warm stone steps in the sunshine and drank coffee. 'Anyway, you might have put me off if I telephoned first.' She bent forward to roll up the bottoms of her jeans and kick off her shoes, offering up pale legs and grubby feet to the ultraviolet rays.

'I would have called you, quite soon, anyway,' said Bea. 'I tried to explain to Mum that I didn't intend to become a recluse, but she doesn't believe it. She seems to have given my phone number to almost everyone. It never stops ringing. I have to turn it off sometimes to get any peace. She's always been able to work with seventy thousand people around her all demanding different things and not turn a hair. I don't think she understands at all what I'm doing here.'

'What *are* you doing here?'

'I'm working. I've never worked so hard. It started out as a means of blocking out things but already there's more to it. It's what's been put off since I was eighteen – a score that needs to be settled. I owe it to Aunt Nest, too, not to disappoint her and waste the time here.' She paused and cleared her throat, tried to sound matter-of-fact but came across rather dryly; not surprisingly it had not been entirely possible to expunge thoughts of Oscar and Andreary from her mind. 'Anyway, a change of scene seemed sensible. The least of it is that it's extremely embarrassing, being dumped.'

Agnes hesitated, chewing her fingernails, then said: 'Talking of settling scores, Phil met Oscar the other evening, after work. I think they had a bit of a barney. I mean, I *know* they had a row. Phil hit him.'

'God! Whatever for?'

'Don't be naïve, Bea. Phil always had the softest of soft spots for you. You must've known? No? Well, he did. Phil thought, afterwards, that he would have to leave his job. However, Oscar seems to have taken it on the chin.' She giggled and Bea could hear the relief in her voice. 'They were both thrown out of the pub and the fact of them both being ejected seemed to have brought out a smidgen of male fellow feeling. Cleared the air a bit. I expect Oscar was hoping to be punished, secretly. Now Phil's landed him one, he'll feel his conscience salved, a little anyway.'

Bea gave a snort of disbelief. 'You think Phil's hitting him makes Oscar feel less guilty about what he did to me? What sad dogs men are.' She found her hand shaking a little as she raised her mug to her lips, which had suddenly become tight and dry. 'Don't worry about the job, though. Oscar's usually pretty practical. He couldn't do without Phil, not at the moment certainly.'

'Would you go back to him if he left Andrea and came home?'

Bea shook her head. 'No. Absolutely not. Well, yes, I suppose it's possible. But not yet, certainly. I haven't thought it through. First I've got to see if the painting works out. But he won't come back. I'm sure of that.' She got up from the steps and stood with her head down and hands tucked defensively into her armpits, thinking that a little time spent away from the painting wouldn't do any harm, but she wasn't going to spend it discussing Oscar, having him and the so-recent past dragged out to this pleasantly anonymous place, polluting it by forcing her to think, undermining the too rapidly acquired disregard for the future.

Perhaps because inlanders automatically think of going to the coast as an occasion for a picnic, Agnes had happily stopped off at a supermarket and bought food on the way: a selection of fine-cut salamis, *pain rustique*, a decadent treacle tart and an odoriferous goat's cheese.

'Let's take the food you've brought out to the sandy beach,' Bea suggested. 'It's so warm today and Seb would love it. It's too far to walk from here but we could go in the pick-up to save your car's poor springs?'

'That sounds perfect. What's in that bucket?' Agnes peered in and drew back in disgust. 'Whatever are you doing with those?'

'I thought they might be nice, cooked properly. I think you have to feed them lettuce, or bran, perhaps, to clean them out in case they've eaten hemlock in the night, and put on a lid to stop them escaping. I was going to telephone Mum and ask her how to cook them.' She saw Agnes's wrinkled nose. 'You could stay and have some for tea.'

'How repellent! Don't tease. You've gone native already. I bet the locals eat frogs?'

'No, I don't think so, but they could if they wanted.' Bea laughed. 'Aunt Nest says the frogs make a terrible noise as the nights get warmer.' She poked some air holes in tinfoil and sealed up the bucket. 'Right, let's be off.'

As they got to the top of the narrow track a blue van came along the road from the left and paused as if about to turn in. The driver was the red-haired man she had met a few days before, Erik the Red. The track was too narrow for two and he smiled in recognition, making a graceful gesture as if to ask them to pull out first and she waved back a thank-you.

'And *who* was that?' asked Agnes, craning round, goggling.

'I don't know his name. I just watched him launching a fishing boat a few days back. I suppose he's a fisherman.'

'He's rather yummy-looking, isn't he, for a red-haired man and in spite of the pigtail?' It appeared to Agnes that there was life after death on the marsh.

Seb enjoyed the beach, wildly. They sat with their backs against a wooden groyne out of the breeze and Bea, having dodged further enquiries about her state of mind, when questioned about her painting, explained some of her doubts.

'Do you remember the malevolent Mrs Morgan, who taught us in fourth year?'

'Of course. It was free-expression time and she hated you because you refused to express yourself. She used to have it in for me too, for the opposite reason.'

'It was having the means of expression forced on me that I didn't care for. Anyway, I'm doing the kind of thing that she would have simply hated. She once asked me which artist I liked most at the moment, and I said Stanley Spencer, at the moment, and she said in her most spiteful voice that that was just what she would have expected. "Your work is so idiosyncratic, Beatrice,"' Bea mimicked. 'I've been a bit haunted by it ever since.'

Agnes thought she shouldn't worry about that now. 'I think its all the rage. Think how successful whatsisname, Damian Dewhurst the artful butcher is – if those displays of surgical dissection and ambitious pickling weren't idiosyncratic, I don't know what was – perhaps he became unhealthily interested in the contents of all those disgusting bottles they have on biology lab windowsills, at school – *Seb! Seb!* You're not to paddle in the sea on your own . . . Come back where I can see you. Look there's a lovely shallow pool just by the end of the groyne – Do you remember when we went to see that silly sheep? Pass me a bit more of that salami, would you? The one with curly edges?'

'Here you are. I thought you'd become a vegetarian? Yes, I do remember. Was it important to him that it was a *pickled* sheep, rather than a stuffed one, do you think? It was too clean by half compared to any sheep that I've since met round here.'

'I'm a vegetarian four days a week, except for bacon at breakfast. I visited a food therapist the other day who said people of my blood group shouldn't eat meat more than three times a week, and then it should only be game. I couldn't afford to eat pheasant for breakfast though.' Agnes chuckled. 'Yes, wasn't it a clean sheep! Bum hand-washed in Dreft, and the way its fleece stood out about the body in the liquid, as if it had been electrocuted.'

'. . . And we couldn't afford the catalogue to see if there were any clues as to how we were supposed to think about it. Perhaps he meant to insinuate it's cruel to eat fluffy food. The only thing it made me think of at the time was Nelson's body being brought back to England on board ship, preserved in rum.' Bea took a bite of salami sandwich and watched Seb for a minute as he filled his little plastic beaker with sea water and tasted it. 'Talking of fluffy food . . . you could always eat rabbit . . . that's game and very cheap. Jerry Rumm told me about a game dealer who sells them, dressed and everything, for one pound apiece.'

'I hate rabbit.' Agnes cut another thick slice of bread. 'I suppose what you were getting at is rather like those "artists' statements" one sees pinned up beside the pictures in art galleries,' she said, folding the last of the salami into a monster doorstep sandwich, 'you get dragged back to the perpetrator as if it was them that was the artwork.'

'But does it matter?' persisted Bea, 'I do wish I'd been to art school, then I'd know if I was talking nonsense or not.'

Agnes snorted with laughter. 'I don't think you missed much on that score. I found most of it great nonsense. The fine art lot were always rather precious.' She lay flat out and patted her stomach. 'I've eaten too much, as usual. I'll have to have a rest before the treacle tart.'

Although she was genuinely pleased to see Agnes, and the sound of the incoming sea rustling in over the sand was very soporific, Bea began to feel a certain amount of angst at the time slipping away and after a while, a feeling of longing for the safety of the painting room came over her. She was relieved when it clouded over and a niggling wind reminded them it was still only April. They suffered the usual screeching from Seb when they decided to leave, Agnes holding him under one arm and trying to push him into the cab head first, while he clung to the doorframe. Eventually they achieved it but then Bea felt she couldn't drive till he'd calmed down. He was throwing his arms about and thrashing, kicking the dashboard and, by now desperate to get on with her work, Bea lost her temper and smacked his knee, just hard enough for him to take notice.

'You've damaged me! You've damaged me!' he screamed.

'Well, you shouldn't have damaged the dashboard!' She held out a sizeable piece of broken plastic. 'I'm sorry, Agnes, but I must get on.' Seb stopped screaming and looked at his mother in surprise, having expected support, but Agnes looked straight ahead, trying not to laugh. 'Oh well, whatever does the trick,' she said, settling back comfortably. She'd enjoyed the outing.

Agnes had to stop at the supermarket on the way back to Bellhurst. During her raid on its shelves earlier that day she'd again forgotten poor Phil's supper. With Seb sitting in the trolley she went and had a look at the frozen game; there were imported rabbits there, miserable skinny little things in plastic wrappings priced at two pounds seventy-five each. She was looking at them doubtfully when someone tapped her on the shoulder.

'Hello, Agnes!'

Mary Dunnock, a friend from school days, stood behind her with three of her children clinging stickily to the trolley, their faces gaudily smeared with orange ice-lolly. Seb immediately crossed his eyes and stuck his tongue out at them and made the youngest howl. Mary herself looked annoyingly trim and un-marked either by lolly or the wearinesses of motherhood.

'Hello, Mary. Just look at the price of these rabbits! My game dealer sells much better ones for only a pound each.'

'Ssh! You'll frighten the children. They think all rabbits are called Benjamin Bunny and can talk.' She lowered her own voice. 'I heard that Oscar Mitty's done a runner – it can't be true?'

Agnes had no sympathy with anthropomorphism but replaced the frozen bunny hastily. 'It is, I'm afraid. I've just been to see poor Bea – she's in a dreadful state and gone into hiding. Oscar ran off with a Sussex cow from somewhere near Battle, Andrea Bullingden. Isn't it sad, after such a long marriage?'

'How extraordinary!' Mary patted the howler on the head, none too gently and looked at Agnes, curiosity laced with suspicion. Mary's husband had once confessed to a passing affair with Agnes some years before she had married him and he had told her some strange stories. She could never quite understand why Agnes and Bea appeared so friendly but put it down to the attraction of a goody-two-shoes for a reprobate and vice versa.

'I've met Andrea. Actually, I met her when I had that little trouble and had to go for a short stay at Saint Cecilia's Rest Home-cum-clinic, at Hatton Hoo, if you remember? Andrea was being detoxed.' She raised her hand and rapidly made the delicate repeated unscrewing motion before her mouth generally used to indicate a drink problem. 'She said it was her fourth time. I thought she was rather charming but her husband had left her because of it so perhaps Oscar won't stick it out very long either.'

Agnes stared back at Mary, noting with satisfaction the rather large pores in her nose but greedy for further information and remembering the massive kitchen in the 'William the IVth' house, remembered also the stash of gin bottles in the cupboard.

'Isn't she cured this time?'

'I don't know, we didn't meet again. She used to get supplies of miniature vodkas smuggled in, so probably not. Well, I must get on. I've got to collect the baby from my mother's, and we've got eight for dinner tonight. I'll call on Bea myself soon.'

After Agnes had left Little Rumm, Bea hurriedly hung up the abandoned washing and went back to work. Messianic wafts of scent from her mother's narcissi hung in the air above the lower notes of paint and white spirit. It was hard to get into a rhythm knowing that all too soon the light would begin to fade, expecting any minute that there might be another interruption but she made good progress during what was left of the afternoon and after clearing up, decided to brave a Fingle pub, have a glass of cider and a bowl of chips, watch the world go by and stop trying to make sense of her present mode of existence. Being on a voyage of discovery and constantly having to return to port and report progress, which was what it felt like when people called, destroyed her concentration for hours afterwards but she was ashamed of her tetchiness with Seb. 'I mustn't be so quick-tempered,' she thought, scrubbing yellow paint from her nails, 'I'm lucky that Agnes cares, and everyone else. But it's such a paradoxical situation ... I've got to be alone to work, but can't help feeling lonely. Perhaps it would be better to get in first and arrange the visits, in the evenings, then they would come when I was pleased to see them and they would go away happy.' At least Agnes had stopped suffocating her with sympathy and advice. Bea had never found it easy to receive either gracefully.

There was a tinny, crackling sound in the kitchen coming from the snail bucket left by the sink. A mass escape had been effected but two or three had become institutionalised and were rattling about on the underside of the tinfoil, as if trampolining in reverse. It was nearly eight o'clock by the time they'd all been recaptured and saying farewell to the impractical idea of a solitary snail-*fest* she tipped them up outside again, whereupon they slick-footed it back to their previous crannies.

She changed into a freshly-ironed blue shirt, clean trousers and, as it was still cold in the evenings, a black quilted cotton jacket. She glanced at herself in the mirror and lifted her chin, wiping the frown lines from her forehead. Once seated behind the steering wheel however, confidence began to ebb and she fought an impulse to run back into the house.

'Perhaps I only exist on paper,' she thought uncomfortably, 'like a novel. I'm nothing more than the sum of my paintings; but Going Out should restore a measure of reality – it'll be quiet and boring – but I will have been Out. I'll feel less like a statistic.' On the front seat of the pick-up was a plastic bag full of the shells and smelly weed that Seb had wanted to take home. There was also a dear little pair of wet and sandy red socks rolled up and hidden in the bottom. They could be dropped in on Agnes on Saturday when visiting Bookshop Bill, Mrs Lewis and making pre-emptive calls on Tom and Jane. 'Stop prevaricating, get going. You *will* get used to being uncoupled.' She started up the truck.

The Bell and Hatchet had a strong nautical theme, was crowded with brass binnacles, bells, rudders and ships' wheels, the walls hidden by browning photographs of gnarled fishermen in sou'westers, posing by their boats, hauling on ropes and doing embroidery. Blue was perched on a stool against the wall, round the corner of the L-shaped bar, drinking with his friend Nut and talking about that wide range of things which men discuss in bars. Their conversation did not dwell on their work or private lives in any detail, but covered the fact that the rust on Nut's van was sufficient to stop it getting through its MOT and which of them should go out fishing on Sunday afternoon with Big John, since there was only room for one more in the boat. Nest's great approval of the rabbit terrine Blue had made for her the night before was mentioned, as was Nut's useful discovery on the beach of a small wooden table, drifted up in the spring tide last night, relatively undamaged and complete with drawer. They went from beaches to the sea, from sea to sailing ships, from ships to triremes and ancient Greece. Their conversation sometimes veered in unlikely directions.

'What was this golden fleece, d'you reckon, that Jason went out after?' enquired Blue.

'Ah. There's a theory it might be the way the Greeks used to pan for gold. Weight sheep fleeces down on the river bed with stones, then take them up after a couple of days and find the little bits of gold caught up in the fleece along with the silt. It sounds possible.' Nut enjoyed Blue's discursiveness and Blue liked the way Nut told him interesting things, without ever putting on the appearance of being surprised by his ignorance. Though virtually illiterate, Blue was highly intelligent and like many illiterates, had an amazing memory.

'I see. Very clever. It was a good story. All them brazen bulls and dragon's teeth.'

'Is that what you've been reading with Nest?' Although Nut had known Blue for the best part of a year and they got on famously, he had not yet met Nest, and would very much like to.

'Yes — *Tanglewood Tales*, the book's called. I didn't know they were Greeks though. She's teaching me poetry too,' he said, proudly. 'She says I often speak poetically. What *are* iambics?'

'What was it you just said, when you asked about Jason just now? "What *was* this *golden fleece* ..." Speaking of golden, the girl that's just walked in ... she's the one I told you about, that I met on the beach.'

'Ah! And that's the one I told you about too. Nest's niece, Bea. We'll go over in a while and I'll introduce you. But go careful. She's been a bit upset recently. What a racket — things seem to be getting a bit rough round the other side. Yes, her husband walked out on her and she's come down to live in Nest's place, to get away from everyone. Hey, it's getting way out of order over there . . .'

It was dark and what little room was left seemed to Bea to be taken up by couples, chomping fish, chips and peas, or pies, or indeterminate pieces of something in orange breadcrumbs with floppy lettuce. She sidled up to the bar, bought a cider, ordered chips and finding an inconspicuous small table in a corner, began to watch. Being tall, fair and on her own, she had not gone unnoticed.

The customers at the bar seemed to fall into two groups: one, a noisy bunch of young men with aggressive haircuts and manners, were clustered round the end of the bar nearest to her, and another group round the corner of the L, who seemed to be mostly locals.

The division between the two groups was not only marked by the geography of the bar; their clothes as well as their behaviour and motley collection of regional accents set the young men apart. Apparently celebrating a birthday, they were spruced up, well-shaved and wearing fairly uniform, pointedly casual trousers with loose pastel-coloured shirts and polished loafers, not trainers or boots. The locals that she could see from her corner appeared scruffier, but were quietly sober and watchful.

Bea sensed a mounting, muttering irritation with the celebrators emanating from a grey-haired man and wife sitting at the next table. The man, dressed in several shades of brown, was of the opinion that squaddies shouldn't be allowed in while there were decent people eating. His wife, in a silver-sequinned T-shirt and black jersey tracksuit trousers worn with high heeled red sandals kept repeating, 'Go on, Les! They're only young once.' There were cheers as one of the boys spilled a pint of lager down himself. As he wavered through the bar on his way to the gents he spotted Bea and her heart sank as he lurched over to her table. Oh no, not over here! Please not over here.

'What 'ave we 'ere? A spot of loveliness in with all the grey shit.' He stared, unfocused but heavily meaningful, at the man in brown, then put his hands on Bea's table and leant over to her, rocking slightly and slopping her drink. He was not bad-looking, Bea thought, but rather short and about to be sick at any minute. She leant as far back into the corner as possible.

'Gi' us a kiss then, sweet'art.'

'Perhaps another time,' said Bea, smiling at him in a placatory way, hoping to defuse him, her clear-cut and well-educated voice echoing unfortunately in her own ears. He swung unsteadily round to his mates, seeking reassurance.

'I'm not drunk, am I?' Then back to Bea, suddenly vicious, 'No need to get upset, you little slapper ... just passing the time of day.' His breath was noisome with beer and curry.

Bea was saved from further annoyance by the delivery of the bowl of chips by a woman of considerable breadth and height.

'Push off now, and leave the young lady alone.' She towered over him, and Bea also stood up, adding further height to the confrontation. She was suddenly angrily prepared to douse him in cider if he didn't leave her alone. He only came up to her shoulder.

'Oooh! Young lady, is it? You watch it, Pete!' jeered his friends, 'They're bigger than you!'

Pete's bravado was overcome by his need to get to the lavatory fast and he disappeared. The waitress looked at Bea apologetically:

'Don't worry. They're all mouth, this lot,' and she disappeared. Bea sat down and started to pick at the chips. The atmosphere was getting a little tense. Sequins leant over and patted her knee consolingly. 'That's right. Don't worry, dear. We'll keep them in order.'

At that moment Pete re-appeared, and in passing, removed Sequins' plate of chicken nuggets from before her and carrying it high up in the air, danced towards the bar, shouting,

'She's too fat already. She don't need these!'

Sequins sat back, her plump thighs splayed out on the Dralon-covered bench, her jaw agape, knife and fork poised uselessly in mid-air. Her brown-trousered husband leapt to his feet and set off, bent on rescuing his wife's supper. No easy matter, since the plate was being passed around from man to man above his head while he leapt and grabbed ineffectually, a piggy-in-the-middle, a rainstorm of peas cascading on his head. The group of locals put down their pints and moved in. The landlord behind the bar was frantically telephoning.

Then they were instantly brawling and Sequins' remaining chicken and chips were ground into the worn floral carpet. The juke box was playing 'Love Me Tender, Love me Do' from its golden oldie section but as Elvis faded and Brown was decked, it switched to pre-selected jungle music. Sequins started to squeal in short breathless bursts. A tiny grey-faced old woman in a bright pink nylon shell-suit stood by the flashing fruit machine, unconcernedly poking money into it and nudging buttons. Bea shrank disbelieving back into the darkness of her corner, wondering how to escape and was considering diving under the very inadequate cover of the table. She heard for the first time in her life the agonising crunch of fist against cheekbone, and thought miserably of Phil and Oscar. People were trying to leave through a side door, but it appeared to be locked. A beer mug flew across the room.

'Come on. Move. This way!' Erik the Red urgently put a hand on her arm and hauled her to her feet. 'Come on! The red-caps'll be here in a minute.' He ducked as a bunch of plastic daffodils, still wedged in their vase, sailed past him and shattered on the wall. He almost dragged her through the door marked Toilets just as a whistle blew and the front door burst open. There was a frenzied barking and a sudden lessening of the din but also the sound of a pumping cascade of coins as the old lady in pink won the jackpot.

There was a long stone passage lying behind both bar and

kitchens and she followed Erik out into a dark and greasy backyard.

'You *must* have been hungry,' he said, grinning with no trace now of his previous surliness. She was still carrying the half-empty bowl of chips.

'I hadn't finished my drink either.'

'Well, we'll have to get you another one then, won't we?' said another voice behind her, and there was a dishevelled Blue, his shirt hanging out, sucking his knuckles. He had an attractive gap between his front teeth when he smiled, and looked remarkably pleased with himself. Bea knew why Nest found him so compelling. 'The police have taken the dogs in to sort them out. They only bite squaddies – they can smell their aftershave. I don't think Nest'd approve of you being in the Bell and Hatchet.' He wrung his wrist as if to re-arrange the bones in his hand. 'We'll take you somewhere a bit quieter, if you'd like? Bugger! I've left me jacket behind in the bar – I'll just pop back into the kitchens and get Susie to fetch it out.' He disappeared again.

'But where do they come from, the squaddies?' Bea offered the Viking a chip and together they finished them, leaving the bowl on the doorstep where a fat, blue-chinned member of the kitchen staff in a stained white apron was leaning against the door jamb, unconcernedly rolling up a cigarette.

'There's army firing ranges not far away. Didn't you know? You've not noticed the MoD signs? There's only occasionally a bit of a bother. It used to be a good pub before the brewery changed its name, tarted it up, and put in a manager.'

Bea had never before seen grown men fighting. The build up to the affair and the subsequent violence had been both subtly fascinating and frightening – it was all a long way from evening drinks parties on the neatly mown lawns of Bellhurst. She asked him if he thought the fighting had been territorial or punitive.

'A bit of both, I expect. Protective even, for poor Lally's supper. But the fact that a woman on her own, a friend of Blue's, was being bothered might have had something to do with it!' He was scrutinising her, now so close, with an eye for the fine detail of her face. The so-almost-straight nose. Eyes like delphiniums. A couple of tiny lines at one corner of the mouth, as if she often smiled lopsidedly, up one side more than the other.

'But how did they know so quickly, the locals, that Blue knows me?'

'The people round here are very private about their own doings but not so pernickety about outsiders and aren't above a good gossip. I'm an outsider too. You can probably tell by the accent? It's known that you've moved into Little Rumm and there is a bit of speculation about it.'

Bea digested this somewhat uneasily while covertly listening for the colour in the voice beneath the Northern Irish accent, and found it a pleasantly crunchy chestnut brown.

Blue reappeared, wriggling into a patched army-surplus combat jacket. It had been the locals, not the soldiers, who had been wearing the odd piece of army uniform.

They were escorting her through an alleyway out into a small square green and over to another less threatening drinking place. Bea, heart still pumping with adrenalin, was much comforted by Blue's presence and more than a little interested in the now friendly Erik striding along beside her in his flapping ancient Dryzabone waterproof.

'I spotted you earlier and would have come over anyway, before the trouble started,' said Blue, standing back for her at the door, 'but Nut said he'd met you already and fetched you away while I sorted the one in the blue shirt.'

She turned to Nut. 'Nut? That can't be your real name?' It couldn't, of course, have been Erik the Red.

'Francis Nutmeg,' said the re-baptised Erik, somewhat defensively. He wandered off to fetch their drinks and she noticed Blue's expression had passed from smug to positively demure.

'Here we are there then, Blue — none but the brave

deserve the beer. How's your knuckles? Bea, your cider.' Nut folded himself up on the chair opposite her and grinned a companionable, even, white-toothed grin

'What happened to the fishing boat?' she asked. 'Was it launched eventually?'

'Oh yes. That night. A bit more drama to the story though. Shall I tell you about it? Well, its engine, a reconditioned engine, mind you, cut out on the way along to Rye, and there was a stiffish onshore wind. They got it tied up snug up against a wreck marker and had to radio for help, so the lifeboat had to be launched again, for real this time, to tow them into harbour.' Nut chuckled unmaliciously at the skipper's continuing misfortunes, pulled tobacco from his pocket and started to roll a cigarette, fingers deftly tidying the brown threads into the skinny white roll of fine paper.

'It seems,' said Bea, 'to be rather a reluctant boat.' She noticed that in the lapel of his long coat there was a little loop of very pale green ribbon fastened with a pin, like the red Aids ribbons or the pink ones for breast cancer, or the bright green for Sinn Fein. Curious, she asked him what cause it represented.

'That? Lettuce Awareness Week.'

'No, be serious! What is it for?'

'I haven't a clue. I got caught by a pretty girl outside the Boots in Parden. She had a tray of them, so I gave her twenty pence and she pinned one on. I must admit I can't remember what the charity was. Where were you off to this morning?'

'Taking a friend and her little boy down to the beach for a picnic. And where were you going, down the little track?'

'On a visit to Jerry Rumm.'

There was an exceptional something about Nut's cheek-bones. High and sharply jutting, they gave his face, which when resting had a certain fine severity of line, an attractive, almost elfin look. Concerned that she was staring too obviously she turned to her drink and pondered the source of the attraction. Too obsessed with Oscar's face for so many years, she truthfully hadn't often had fancies for other men, nor had she ever slept with anyone apart from him. She imagined now, probably rightly, that she was the only person among her contemporaries with such a limited sexual history and wondered what it might be like with someone else; with Nut, for instance?

Sex with Oscar had been, at first, a curious journey inside herself. It had taken time to discover what destination was intended and though there had been moments when she spotted it in the distance and swam desperately towards it, each time it seemed if not a mirage, then further off. She had put down the descriptions of sex in the teen magazines to fanciful imaginations, although she'd discovered from them what innovations to their private rituals kept Oscar happy and although vaguely disappointed, she settled for that level of pleasurable fun she had attained. There had been times when Oscar had quite suddenly gone off sex for two or three months and she'd felt lonely and crossly deprived. Then gradually things had picked up and he too tried unfamiliar things, but she was still aware that something vital was eluding her. There was something finicky, she now realised, about his delicate lovemaking. She had no idea how to discuss it. The large and immediate presence of Nut across the table had aroused pink-inducing thoughts of further research but she was interrupted in mid-blush by the sound of a siren.

'Do you think someone was seriously hurt?' she asked, thinking the wailing might be an ambulance.

'Doubt it,' said Blue, 'but here's more Bell and Hatchet evacuees. What's the score, John?'

'The birthday boys have all been carted off in a truck and the police are taking a statement from Lally. They've sent an ambulance for her Les. He's got a plastic daffodil embedded in his left buttock. The manager's trying to keep things low key and is offering everyone free drinks.' John was undoubtedly one of the two dark brothers Bea had seen at the beach talking to Erik/Nut and was now accompanied by a girl in tiny black top and jeans decorated with a red splash of tomato ketchup down one leg.

'This,' said Blue, with a vague introductory gesture in Bea's direction,' is my Nest's niece, Bea Mitty.'

'Pleased to meet you, Bea,' said John, 'This is Lucinda. She works for Nest.' Lucinda smiled rather fetchingly at Nut, more curiously at Bea and sat down beside her on the bench, dabbing at the ketchup with a paper napkin. She looked a bit young to be going out with John, who had greying sideburns, the promising beginnings of a paunch and monstrous blurred red and blue tattoos from wrist to elbow, and as far as Bea could see, more starting just above the neck of his T-shirt and working downwards. He asked Lucinda hopefully whether she hadn't been just a bit scared back at the Bell and Hatchet. She replied she hadn't been, but it had all happened so fast, hadn't it, and she did think it was a shame whoever it was had had their birthday spoilt, 'you're all as bad as pikies ... it was only a bit of fun, taking Lally's plate; I'm sure they'd have given it back, given the chance, and just look at the mess on my jeans ... someone shoved me and I sat right in Ernie Thompson's supper ... I only got them in the market on Thursday ... they were ever so cheap ...' she turned to Bea, 'Have you found the clothes stall between the man with the urns and flowerpots and the old girl with the cheeses and the wraparound Indian skirts? Those flowerpots are good value too, much cheaper than the ones your Auntie sells ... you look just like her, doesn't she, Blue?' She rambled on unchecked, till Nut caught Bea's eye — she'd been trying not to laugh — and smiled.

'Time I was off. I'll see you, John, and Blue.' He nodded pleasantly to Lucinda who nodded back without ceasing the flow of chat and then he bent down and asked Bea, very quietly close to her ear, where her car was parked and if she would care to be escorted back to it? Bea, having finished her drink, did rather. She certainly couldn't face much more of the loquacious Lucinda, nor did she want another drink. Blue looked up at her with a gap-toothed grin of irritating benediction.

'See you soon, Bea.'

A police car was leaving as they turned into the street where stood the infamous Bell and Hatchet; they could hear sounds of sweeping and the tinkle of broken glass being emptied into bins as they passed the closed doors. It was starting to drizzle.

'Is this yours? It's held together with baler twine! It's worse than mine!' He held the loose-hinged door for her while she climbed up into the cab. 'I'll see you around then?' he said, standing back with his hands in his deep pockets.

'I expect so,' she said, 'and thanks, for hauling me out of that mess,' and seeing from his expression that he was just about to say something else, waited.

'Would you like to come out for a drink with me one day?' He looked momentarily uncertain of himself.

She was also uncertain, but found the idea of saying untruthfully, 'No, thank you' quite impossible.

'I'd like to, yes. But not here, though? Not at the Bell and Hatchet?'

'Lord, no. Plenty of better places, round and about. I'll call for you, where you're staying. How about this Saturday, at eight?' Pin-heads of fine rain glistened in the street light on the caped shoulders of his coat and in the red hair. The street was now empty and silent.

Bea smiled; it was twelve years since she'd been asked out on a date. 'I'll see you, then,' she said, starting up the engine.

Nut watched the truck's tail lights till it turned the corner and then exhaled deeply. He'd been holding his breath, rooted to the spot, with knowledge in his leaves and branches. He hunched his shoulders as the rain became heavier and a sudden wind got up, drifting the spray across the road in the light of the single street lamp as he walked, softly whistling, to the blue van and sat inside rolling another cigarette. 'Jesus,' he said, aloud, 'I think that might be my woman.' He was a great optimist.

Nut had discovered early in his teens that he was attractive to a good section of the female population and had, at first, been terrified. Though his good fortune had been impressed upon him by envious friends who'd noticed that within fifteen minutes of him walking in to the JCR at Liverpool (where he was reading geography) that over half of the females present had gravitated down to his end of the bar, he'd gradually realised that those who could abide red hair in the first place, which certainly wasn't all of them, were very definitely overinterested and he'd had to unhook a few of them from his shirt like burdock seeds and rein in the ebullient, sociable nature. Friends had put it down to an unfair share of pheromones and found his reluctance to take advantage of the unlikely allure quite incomprehensible. Eventually he'd begun to enjoy himself, but carefully, learning to sift very politely through the women who were unaware why they stood so close that they almost drowned in his drink.

Twice he'd made mistakes and been seriously outplayed. Pretty, impatient, loquacious Mel, Mel the raven-haired Australian social anthropologist. They had not intended their relationship at university to become permanent and it had initially, on his part, been a means of holding off the hordes, but through a growing and genuine affection they'd stayed together for four years, until she decided she wanted a child, became pregnant, changed her mind and had an abortion all in three months and all without, for once, telling him a word of it. On discovering the scrunched-up antenatal card while searching desperately in her pocket for some small change to pay the milkman, he'd been gobsmacked by the unnecessary duplicity.

Nut leant his head on his arms on the steering wheel, remembering how it had been the secrecy which had been unhinging, since he wouldn't have tried to impede her, whatever she'd decided. He had not known that feelings could change with such drastic, tearing swiftness; tenderness to repulsion in minutes. Unbeknownst to him she'd been offered a well-funded job in Finland studying some social foible of the Lapps, who had surely already been seriously studied from every possible angle till they were in a state of nervous self-consciousness. She admitted that was at least part of the reason for aborting the baby (perhaps a baby daughter? – he'd thought about it a lot). It seemed incredible that he'd lost his child for the sake of some poxy, magic mushroom-munching Father Christmases, all tinkling bells and red-and-blue skirts. It hadn't made sense; he'd happily have looked after and loved it while she was charming shamans or researching the impact of TV on little Lapps.

Mel had also spent time in the States and been convinced that being Irish in England, he was a badly treated underdog and she would keep fighting his corner for him when there was no need. He'd explained about dual nationality, told her how she of all people should know how mixed and mongrelled the inhabitants of the British Isles were, but she'd sigh and look at him and say 'But, Fraz, I know that deep down inside you're culturally Irish. You must find it difficult, living in the land of past oppressors.' Well, perhaps she was right about the Irishness; it is the earliest years which count and still, after seventeen years here, the English picked up on his accent. However, whenever he went over to visit his Uncle Charlie, it was always commented a little mockingly, that he was 'quite the Englishman now'. He wasn't one thing or the other, sod it, and it was the English father who'd had red hair, but he was comfortable with being an inhabitant of the British Isles – he felt no urgent need to belong or conform to any particular ethnic group. Geographer was his nationality, and religion, well, that was merely one way of making sense of the world, but it was not his way.

There had been a period of globe-trotting after the separation from Mel, supporting himself by arranging temporary teaching posts along the way in Hong Kong and Singapore and after a brief stint in Sydney, returning to Europe for a glorious six months rounding the rim of the Mediterranean from Morocco to Spain, stopping for longer than was strictly necessary in Turkey where he'd met the ethereal, silent Annie and returned to England with her. It was during this odyssey that he regained his child's eye for landscape, had seen once more the emotional content of the earth rather than its physical consituents, taken pleasure in the shape of a hill without immediately analysing its provenance.

Happily indigent, he and Annie had shared cramped flats in a variety of places while he completed his PhD but his constant absences due to the nature of his work eventually irked her and she had given up on him while he was only half way through, embarked on a circumnavigation of the world with an over-charming and equally silent Swede. Not broken-hearted for long, more briefly melancholic, he'd nevertheless played hard to get till coming South, where there had naturally been the occasional hunting forays and once after a party, unfortunately, Lucinda. Sadly there'd been no one who'd held his interest for long and anyway, he'd been kept busy in his particular palaeogeographical bent, for the Siegfried McKay-Tart Trust's grand survey of the marsh.

But Bea. There was a rare grace and a deliciously gullible, half-bewildered innocence about her, a little out of keeping with her age, perhaps, but hers was surely an unusually gorgeous body. On one of their recent evenings out together at the Eeldyke Inn Blue had described Bea, unoriginally but with a dreamy sigh, as heaven on long legs and a bit shy. Certainly there was a great deal more to her than the legs and she was not shy but he had gained the impression of tension behind the eyes, a sense of purpose. He sensed competition.

Ironically it had been footloose Annie who had told him that he didn't take life seriously enough. He took work seriously though and thoroughly enjoyed it, but life – too short, too long, too unpredictable. When did you examine it? Give it an MOT? At what period did you begin to feel this is a life I'm living – I'd better poke about in it a bit and see if it's still pink inside, or getting burnt on top? If you're unaware of its beginning, how to judge the moment to take stock? The years had zipped past, but then, that was the payment for enjoying yourself. He was thirty-four. He felt the need for a different pace and a change in direction. Now Bea; he re-explored her golden oval face which disconcertingly faded as he thought about it, and what she'd said and the sound of the clear, bell-metal voice . . .

There was a firm tap-tap on the window. He nearly leapt out of his skin and glancing up saw through the rivulets of rain on the glass, the face of a constable peering in suspiciously. He swatted away the sensation of instant but unnecessary guilt.

'Are you all right there?'

'Yes. I wasn't asleep. I was thinking,' and seeing the doubt in the man's eyes, 'I'm not over the limit, I'm not smoking crack. I'm just thinking.'

'Might I see your licence please?'

He felt in his inside jacket pocket and produced it.

'*Doctor* Francis Nutmeg?'

'Yes, that's me.'

'Thank you, sir. Sorry to have bothered you. Mind how you go. Good night.'

Chapter Five

Bea sat outside Fleming Cottage, rain drumming on the roof of the truck and dripping through a gap in the windscreen seal, splattering her knee. Postponing the moment of entering her own house, she decided to visit Mrs Lewis first. She threw her green mac over her head and made a dash for it, shaking herself like a Saluki on the doorstep and ringing the bell. There was a lengthy pause followed by scuffling from inside as Mrs Lewis unchained, unbolted and finally escaped from her jail. Standing there clad in a long, drooping cardigan she blinked in the gloom as if confronted by a bright light. The cardigan was parrot green, with scarlet buttons. Bea had never seen her wear anything but grey before and the originality of her dress was astonishing.

'Hello, Mrs Lewis. I came to thank you and see if it was still all right, if you minded carrying on seeing that everything's OK next door?'

'Come in, dear.' said Mrs Lewis, surprisingly. 'You seem very wet.' She stood aside to let Bea in. 'Everything is quite in order next door. I've checked it every morning and every night. Here's your post.' Her voice retained its thick crackled glaze but there was something definitely different about Mrs Lewis, an awareness, almost a cheeriness that was difficult to comprehend. The faded grey-blue eyes, instead of sliding down and to one side now looked straight into Bea's, alert, pleading even? The semi-catatonic trance that had prevailed ever since Bea and Oscar had moved in next door seemed to have lifted; certainly so many sentences had never crossed her lips during their previous encounters.

Bea followed Mrs Lewis, for the first time, into the drawing room and was again surprised. It was a faded place but the colours had lightened into an exquisitely soft fruitiness. Palest lemon cushions lay on a sofa now unevenly bleached by the sun to pomegranate pinky cream. The curtains were of aged apricot and lime-green stripes, long since stripped of their chintzy glaze, the only patterned fabric in the room. Everything else was plain; the carpet a plain ripe melon, the worn armchair by the window plain grape-purple tweed. Even in the gloomy light it was a delicious fruit salad of a room.

'Would you care for some coffee?'

Bea nodded, speechless. On the walls hung black ink drawings in grey frames with yellow mounts and it was these that attracted Bea like magnets while Mrs Lewis rattled in the kitchen. A young man in a striped Breton jersey and rolled-up trousers lounged laughing on a stone wall, surrounded by fruit and fish. Another in boots, corduroys and waistcoat leant upon a spade, surveying a trophy of vegetables. They looked familiar to Bea — there was a similarity to the frontispieces of one or two of her mother's library of cookery books. There were others to do with food and cooking and a water-colour of derelict machinery in a farmyard by Eric Ravilious. The style of the room — the teak coffee table with its tapering pin-like legs stuck out at angles, the shapes of the jugs on the wide windowsill and the asymmetrical yellow fruit bowl on the side table — was the unchanged, unadulterated late nineteen-fifties. Agnes's mother, now on a new retro tack, would at present give her front teeth for the things in this room.

Mrs Lewis returned, moving steadily and with little sign of her previous shakiness, carrying bi-coloured cups of coffee, pink on the outside and green on the inside, on a smoky glass tray. She sat stiffly down by the window in the grape-coloured chair, gesturing Bea over to the sofa.

'Now tell me, how are you getting along?' Two direct questions in five minutes. Having decided not to dissemble when she'd asked for Mrs Lewis's help in keeping an eye on the cottage, and having told her briefly the facts of what had happened, Bea now found herself summing up.

'I've settled in very well. I'm ... I'm painting a lot. I was scared of being lonely, but I'm getting used to it. And people keep coming to visit. It's different.'

'Yes. People your age, so young, you need changes now and then, I expect. Although I don't mean for a moment that the sort of change you have undergone was in any way the sort you needed.' Mrs Lewis paused, her veined hands clasping and unclasping in her lap. 'I've seen your husband.' Her eyes gleamed briefly and Bea detected a little flicker of malice in the pale eyes now fixed on her again. 'He came to get a chainsaw. But I *didn't* tell him I had the new keys to the house, so he couldn't get in. Was that the right thing to do?' Her face had a hint of colour to the cheeks and Bea saw she was very pleased to be participating, however peripherally, in an undercover operation.

How sad it was that she had not made more strenuous attempts to be friendly in the years gone by, but Mrs Lewis then had appeared inert, dementedly dull and unresponsive; but this was not the room of someone dull, however long ago it had been arranged.

'Yes, you did the right thing. If he wants to get in touch with me he can, via my parents. I can't face speaking to him directly, at least, not yet ... That water-colour ... it's very interesting isn't it? The arrangement of the machinery shapes into a believable order and the clean hills behind, so round and fat? Are those the South Downs, do you know ...? I've only ever seen his work in the Imperial War Museum. We went there on a school trip once, years ago ...' Bea halted since further signs of animation were flowering on Mrs Lewis's face.

'That was my mother's. She was at the Royal College of Art with Ravilious,' Mrs Lewis's eyes, so nearly always cast aside or down when she was speaking, now looked with hope straight into Bea's, 'and the John Mintons as well. I hope you won't be cross with me ... I found a sketch book of yours, on your kitchen windowsill when I went inside to check, and had a little peep.' She cleared her throat and sipped at her coffee, peering shyly up at Bea over the rim of the cup. 'They were beautiful drawings, quite exceptional. I saw you often, drawing in the garden ... I wanted to see what you were doing, but couldn't make myself ask. Silly of me, I know.'

'Why did you feel you couldn't ask?'

'Because ... I ... I get frightened of people. Not all the time – just on and off. But since you came round, and asked me to look after the house, I felt I could talk to you, perhaps. But it was too late. You were leaving. And you were so distressed. I think it was the coming in contact with your distress that made me stop.'

'Stop what?' asked Bea, her sense of sins of omission nearly reducing her to tears.

'Stop taking the pills – I've been taking them for such an age – they'd become a habit you see. They stopped me thinking, and that was very pleasant, easy. I took sleeping pills, too. For quite a while after stopping them, I felt rather ill, been tempted back, but I've been feeling so much better over the last three days. I wanted to apologise to you, for being such a bad neighbour.'

'It's us, we who've been such bad neighbours, Mrs Lewis.'

It was extraordinary, she explained to Agnes later on that morning after she had cursorily visited her own cottage, which had a moribund air and seemed already to belong to the past, quite extraordinary how one could see Mrs Lewis returning to life, stretching her cramped faculties like a cat let out of a basket. '... and the black-and-white illustrations on the walls were John Mintons, and she had her mother's paintings upstairs, and her own – amazing still lives of fungi. Her name is Geraldine and she's been suffering from depression, on tranquillisers and Mogadon since her husband died. I think it's criminal, locking up a woman's personality for all those years. I feel so guilty. We, I, *could* have helped her before, at least we could have tried. If *only* I'd known.'

Agnes looked at her doubtfully. Bea rarely sounded so impassioned; how was it that she managed to unearth such interesting people in such unpromising surroundings? She appeared to be growing wings since moving and seemed to be getting to grips with life without Oscar rather too fast. Her cheerfulness was out of place. Having asked Bea if she would like to meet Phil and herself for a meal out that night and been told that no, she couldn't as she was being taken out for a drink by a fisherman, Agnes could see that her own caring role might be short lived. She had imagined herself as the loyal friend providing interesting succour for the grieving, lonely Bea and finding she was not needed for the part, well it put her out, just a bit. One relies on one's friends to need one now and then.

'Tell me more about this Nut, then.'

'There's not much to tell. I don't know him yet. But he seems very pleasant and pulled me out of the pub when there was a fight.' It was quite enjoyable, teasing Agnes.

'Fight? What fight? Tell me about it!' Agnes squawked, gratifyingly agog and Bea obliged, ending up irritatingly with '... so, anyway, he asked me out for a drink. I'm finding it quite exciting living on my own. What does he look like? But you saw him in the blue van, just as we were pulling out of our lane, do you remember? That one. He's big and rangy, a good six foot four, and has astounding bones. I badly want to draw him.'

'So you're going round picking up fishermen as models then?'

'Of course not. Actually I don't think he is a fisherman, but it's nice to find some tottie on the marsh. I've got to be going. Here's Seb's shell collection and his little pair of socks. I've washed them. I'm sorry the shells are a bit noisome; something must have died in one of them.'

Agnes was quite stunned by Bea's insouciance and was left feeling unreasonably acid, taking it out on Phil when he came home with the food shopping.

It had been a carefully produced show of bravado. Bea had been determined to give Agnes no space to start Oscar-ing, almost as if she were mourning his loss herself. By the time she got to the Bellhurst supermarket, she was feeling very nervous indeed of being alone with Francis Nutmeg. Although Blue knew him, and she had some trust in Blue, it had occurred to her that perhaps Blue had had an ulterior motive in sending him over to rescue her. Perhaps they had even discussed her as they sat out of sight round the bend of the bar? She watched a tall man and woman in well-bred jeans and identical Guernsey sweaters meet by the kitchen towels; they both wore spectacles which clashed like stags locking antlers as they kissed, totally unself-consciously, once, twice, thrice. They seemed so pleased to see each other that Bea felt a little pang of envy. Then she bumped into Phil in the Pet and Baby-food aisle.

'Hello Bea,' said Phil, awkwardly. There was an unnatural expression, combining complicity and guilt, on his normally guileless schoolboy face. '. . . Agnes says you're bearing up well, under the circumstances. I am so sorry . . .'

'Does she? Well, yes, I hope I am.' Tensely.

'If there's anything I can do for you, you know, chopping firewood or lifting anything heavy?' The startling green eye looked wistfully at her.

She wanted to tell him, but did not, that there was a faint crust of breakfast egg yolk gilding his upper lip. He was a kind man, Phil. This, however, was the man who had thumped her husband. How rough everyone seemed to be becoming; she hoped Nut didn't go in for that sort of thing.

'That's sweet of you, Phil, but there are logs there already, a great heap of them, cherry and apple, piled up against the wall and I shouldn't think I'll be needing fires for much longer. But thank you, for offering.'

She must get back to the marsh as fast as possible; it was too exposed in the supermarket and she was dreading running into other acquaintances. They made their farewells, locked the wheels of their shopping trolleys, sorted themselves out, flustered and apologising and said good-bye again. She got as far as Fingle before remembering she'd forgotten to buy a chicken.

The rain clouds had passed over and there was a carrion crow in the garden, tearing with its horny beak at the sodden remains of a rabbit. It flew off as Bea heaved her shopping up the path to the blue door and she side-tracked across the damp garden with the bag of food, to stand and stare curiously down at the little corpse. It had died of myxomatosis, blind, its eyelids grossly swollen and weeping. The crow watched her from the field, pacing up and down like a shoulder-padded, small-town crook, waiting to resume its meal. With revulsion gagging her throat, she gingerly picked up the rabbit by a hind leg and flung it over the wall towards the crow, who flapped upwards a foot or two then pounced again on its interrupted lunch.

She went in and washed her hands, deciding not to eat anything. The sight of the diseased rabbit had been off-putting. Upstairs in the painting room, she watched the bird from the window; it had now been joined by two other circling undertakers, their black plumage dull even in the brief bursts of afternoon sunshine. She stood drawing them while thinking about the revelation of Mrs Lewis that morning and about the possibly revelatory meeting with Nut that evening. This was flustering but she calmed herself by adding a crow to the prow of the fishing boat in the painting before restlessly returning to the wet garden to draw. The child's bicycle still lay, dying, where Seb had left it half-crushing a rosemary bush. One of the pedals had fallen off and the leprous chrome was peeling from the handlebars. She was saved from becoming further oppressed by the obviousness of the image of decay by Nest's arrival bearing gifts of chocolate biscuits and little brown envelopes of seed.

'Hello, my darling! Am I interrupting anything? You look very gothic sitting on the wall. May I show you where the windproof patch is? We should scatter these seeds about, now.'

Bea looked curiously at the labels on the packets, hand-written in Nest's awesomely irregular writing and read them aloud, rolling the words around in her mouth: 'Opium, single, dk. purple/scarlet fringe. *Papaver rhoeas*, claret and smoked pink doubles ... Opium, v. double, dusty-mauve ...' Smoked pink doubles sounded exciting, like a salmon sandwich. Nest's 'should' emphatically signified 'must'. Now was the time, so now they would do it.

'All right, Aunt Nest. Let's find this windproof patch.'

When they returned to the front of the house, seeds sown and carrying mugs of tea and biscuits, to sit damply on cushions on the steps, one of the carrion crows was sitting on the handlebars of the bicycle. He did not fly away but sat there beady-eyed, patiently waiting for something. Nest ate the chocolate off the top of a biscuit and threw it the remains, remarking that he seemed too tame for his own good.

'Perhaps he's someone's pet?' suggested Bea. 'What about the farm back down the track. Perhaps it's Jerry Rumm's.'

'Not very likely – most farmers are convinced that crows peck out lambs' eyes while they're still alive and I wouldn't put it past them. Jeremiah Rumm would be more likely to shoot it.' Nest finished her tea, and got up to go. 'Right, I must get back at once. The nursery's open all day tomorrow as well.'

'I met your Lucinda the other night, in a pub.'

'Blue said. I bet she gave you earache. She doesn't draw breath, does she? I have to rescue customers from her sometimes, standing there with heavy pots in their hands, their eyes glazing over while she tells them about what she wore to last year's New Year's Eve party at the Alcatraz in Parden. But she's gentle with the plants, seems to know quite a bit and is resolutely cheerful. She's still nagging me to join that ecological movement she's involved with, but I haven't really got the time for anything formalised like that. It all sounds a bit strange and I couldn't get from her who exactly the organisers of this group are. I might pop along to one of their meetings but I'll stick to writing letters to the papers, I think. Glad you're getting out and about, though. See you soon, my sweet.'

Nest swung nimbly up into the yellow van and rattled off, leaving Bea even more restless and wondering what to do to fill in the time — it was impossible to concentrate on painting with the evening's outing hanging over her head. She thought of ringing Blue to get Nut's phone number, calling him to say she didn't feel well, or perhaps hide upstairs and leave a note on the door saying she'd unavoidably had to go out to look after a sick granny, but knew she couldn't.

'For goodness' sake,' she told herself, 'stop making such a big deal out of going out for a drink! Other women do it every day, I believe. We'll have a beer, tell each other lies about ourselves, rub noses and then he'll bring me home. There's no need to get involved. The fact that I *think* it's going to be so difficult probably means it'll be perfectly easy. It'll be a positive step — good to have a friend in the area. I won't change my clothes — I'll go as I am. This is me. Take it or leave it.'

At seven o'clock she bathed and washed her hair, spending some time at the mirror plucking her eyebrows before changing into a thick cotton, indigo blue skirt, long and narrow and a matching long-sleeved top. She thought she looked too dressy, changed back into her jeans, then almost weeping with annoyance, back into the skirt again, cursing her neurotic indecision. *Had* Blue suggested to Nut that he take her out to cheer her up? She didn't need cheering up; she wanted to work without these nagging interruptions. What had Blue said about her, if anything? 'Go on, Nut! have a crack at the ice-maiden . . . ?' She could hear the round Kentish intonation of Blue's voice in her head, imagine the suggestive grin . . . one couldn't go out with someone attached to such a ridiculous name. However, when Francis Nutmeg rat-tatted firmly on the door at eight o'clock, out she went.

He had been leaning gracefully against the garden wall, resting back on his elbows, the great long legs encased in black trousers. The sun was setting behind the fiery head and he wore a black shirt and dark jacket which emphasised the eerie paleness of his skin. If she had been in the mood to allow herself to consider such a thing, she would have fallen for him on the spot. His startled appraisement of her as she came through the front door was first pleasing, then annoying and he smiled broadly, which was annoying then pleasing since he had a smile that started deep under the skin and fairly zipped across his face, around the short, straight, sharp nose and up along the wondrous cheekbones.

Bea awoke to a mighty noise, and fell out of bed. On hands and knees, head throbbing with thunder, she peered about in the gloom and found she was still fully dressed and had not been in bed, but lying on it. There was a flash of lightning, pink, another rip of thunder and she crawled shakily back onto the bed and clutched the duvet round her. With mouth parched, her head a football being kicked about the room, she fumbled for the bedside glass of water and knocked back the dusty contents. What time was it? What day? Why did she feel so ill? Oscar was good at tea and hot-water bottles. Why wasn't he looking after her? She had been dreaming that patches of gelatinous green mosses and liverwort had been growing round her hairline and peering frantically at her reflection in a dark, spotted mirror, had been trying to pull them off, but as fast as the green pads and cushions were peeled away they grew back again.

Wincing at each movement, she put fragile feet to the floor and stood, swaying. There was paracetamol somewhere, but where, where was she? Little Rumm, that much came back to her. She must be ill, have typhoid, yellow fever or marsh ague ... what had happened yesterday? Bill at the bookshop, parents, Mrs Lewis, Agnes ... not in that order but it was a start. Nest with her poppy seeds in the afternoon ... she opened a drawer of the dressing table, found the pills and tottered to the bathroom, downing two with great throat-stretching gulps of water. In the mirror the face was white, eyes ringed with black and what at first she took for shaming bruises on her neck turned out to be stains from the indigo dye of her shirt. She was grateful however, that the expected creeping growth of moss around her face was not a reality.

The thunder still grumbled and it was the sky itself which was bruise-purple, the light an angry bronze. The sound of a fire engine in the distance brought to mind a previous evening, of a fight, of Blue, and of Nut and she sank down on the damp bath mat on the floor with a moan of mortification. She must have become ill and he had brought her home. She stood up again and holding both temples tight in case they flew apart, returned to the bedroom at the front and looked down into the lane. The pick-up was there, and so was Nut's dark blue van; a carrion crow, *the* crow, was lurching up and down, sliding on the roof's wet surface. There was a lumpen burden on her head. Remember, remember.

First they'd gone to friends of Nut's who'd lived, where? A place called Rhee? No, it was Eeldyke. She remembered the lettering on a signpost. But where was Nut now? At least she had not woken with him in her bed. Asleep on the sofa downstairs? There was no sound of a soul about the house. It was all too much effort and she returned to bed, slithering down beneath the bedclothes feeling pitifully grim and dozing fitfully, the noise of the circling storm and occasional monsoon-like downpours invading her unconsciousness.

She regained her senses two hours later and feeling infinitely better though still amnesiac, had a bath. The door of the painting room was half-open and still towelling her hair, she went fearfully in to check on the painting.

Nut lay asleep on the bed, an alien presence sprawled out in a patch of watery sunlight, still fully dressed in black but with the flaming hair unplaited, wildly at odds with the half-covering, crumpled scarlet poppy sheet. A starkly uninhabited dark jacket hung over the chair, empty sleeves still echoing the curve of his arms. She tiptoed forward and felt the warmth rising up from the long, unstrung-puppet body, caught the definitive male scent and the beer and tobacco of the night before.

A feeling of wicked power overcame her, a smirking Delilah examining Samson as he slept and itching for the scissors, or the paintbrush? A stealthy professionalism insinuated itself: 'Why not? I've done things I can't remember. Perhaps said things I shouldn't have? I shall steal a portrait without him knowing and get my own back. How stupid it is to be so seduced by the shape of a cheekbone. Just bone, that's all it is, a form caused by a gene. *Mere* bone, like bones from the butchers.'

Nut woke later to the sound of a paintbrush tinkling against a glass of water and found Bea sitting nearby in the sunlight on a white chair, frowning in concentration over the drawing board on her knees, a black water-colour box in hand. Dressed in a small green jersey and long skirt, with bare feet, pretty feet, tucked up on the rung of the chair, she sat there with clean gold hair swinging round her face, quietly considering what she'd done. He stared, unsure whether he were awake or not. That had been quite a session, last night. She'd seemed so cool when he first met her, but had turned out to be surprising, talkative and funny, although the drink didn't seem to have agreed with her.

They had hilariously broken all the pub taboos with religion, sex and politics, continuing with manifestations and miracles and their own belief in them or lack of it. She'd said that she didn't understand why Jesus's turning water into wine was a miracle, since if Jesus was divine and it was accepted that God could perform miracles, what was miraculous about His son being able to do them as well? Or words to that effect. But then, becoming gradually more irrational as the evening progressed, answered herself that she supposed that if you wanted proof that Jesus was divine, then the fact that he performed miracles would be that proof and that was the whole point, and whether or not miracles could actually occur was not the point and did he like monkey nuts or dry-roasted peanuts because she was about to buy some?

Confused, but interesting that someone with no ascertainable religious background had even thought about it. But then the most unlikely things seemed interesting when drink was being taken. He smiled and stretched.

Bea looked up intently, straight into his open eyes, jumped nervously and dropped her paintbrush, hastily getting up to lean the board face to the wall. There were dark shadows beneath her eyes and a small smudge of scarlet lake beside the upper lip, as though she'd been caught out eating some rare forbidden fruit. It would have looked almost charming on someone less good-looking but on her it was delightfully risible.

All Sunday afternoon Bea spurned her headache and worked furiously on the boat picture while running over the events of the night before as they had been amplified by Nut and touched up, here and there, by recollections of her own. Sitting at first a little edgily together over toast and tea in the sitting room that morning, he'd obligingly filled in the voids.

It appeared that they had called on friends of his, Amelia and Edmund. They were considerably older than himself; Amelia, a pretty, gregarious woman in her forties, was a jeweller and Edmund a book-dealer. Bea regained a clear memory of a soft yellow lamplit room, with shelves of books and a bottle of wine, or two.

From there they had all visited a nearby pub and with a flash of recognition, Bea saw the four of them sitting talking round a candle-lit table in a low-ceilinged room. They'd played a game of darts and she'd felt more at ease. It had turned out Nut was neither a fisherman nor a professional boat-launcher and had only been helping out a friend at the launch for fun. He was engaged in some long-term scientific research project on the area. Geographical, or was it geological? She remembered geomorphology. She had imagined geographers to wear brogues and khaki jerseys with leather patches on the shoulders as had the geography master at school but things had obviously moved on since then. After the departure of Edmund and Amelia, whatever conversations had taken place alone with Nut had sunk down into the dark and spongy peat-bed level of her mind.

'Then what happened?' Bea asked anxiously, resigned to hearing that she'd pranced on a table with a rose between her teeth, although all she could recall was talking too much. It was humiliating enough to know that Nut had had to search in her pocket for the key and carry her indoors flopped over his shoulder. It was important to find out the precise degree of her imbecility so she could be properly repentant. Mercifully he hadn't so far shown a propensity to mockery.

Nut, thickly waterproofing another slice of toast with butter before spreading it with Jane's runny raspberry jam, had been teasingly comforting.

'We just talked. I think we covered most of the usual subjects last night: overpopulation, the murder in Rhee, the greenhouse effect, the Four Horsemen of the Apocalypse and when they might be calling.' He paused, the muscles in his jaw smoothly working beneath the skin as he munched his toast. 'Then we hit some of the high spots: the creative impulse, muses, visions. By the way, who's Freda?' He stared at her with long, clear sea-water eyes, emphatic eyebrows lifted enquiringly, as expressive and illustrative as a pair of Italian hands.

'I can't explain. Not now, it would take too long. And what happened then?'

'You hadn't had a great deal to drink, but the cider at the Eeldyke Inn is very strong, been known to make big men cry. I should have warned you off it; you were squinting a bit, like a Siamese cat.'

She laughed uneasily and recalling retreating and advancing out-of-focus candle flames, wandering planets in the dark back room of the pub, again insisted, 'What next?' Politely factual, he told her. She'd stood up and thrown some more darts, with startling accuracy, more than she'd shown when they were playing Edmund and Amelia, suddenly unburdened herself of the last few weeks' worth of fears and humiliations, punctuating sentences with enviable and previously unattainable double and treble twenties. A lifetime's private insecurities had been dumped in his lap and she'd been as angry with him for listening as if he had been eavesdropping.

She covered her scarlet face with her hands but Nut gently removed them, denied it had been boring, said he knew she was under a lot of stress and reassured her that before the volcanic eruption, she'd been excellent company, asking him his views on this and that, what his work was and telling him about her mother the single-minded cook and her one-eyed naval father, singing in the ironmonger's shop. He left out the bit about the miracles.

'You muttered that you shouldn't be out drinking, you should be at home working and told me that you were painting a picture about letting go of childhood. I'm glad you told me what it was about. I'd never have guessed when I saw it this morning. Then you passed out with your head in a dish of peanut shells and fag ends. I brought you home and sat with you for a while, in case you were sick. It was late so I dossed down in the first bed I found. I didn't know I was in your holy of holies.'

'You must think me a complete idiot.'

'Why should I think any such thing?' He embarked on yet another slice of toast. 'May I have some more tea? And am I allowed to be pedantic when you're feeling rough? I once looked up idiot in the dictionary, probably because someone had called me one. It comes from the Greek *idiotes* which means a person who doesn't hold any public position and who has no professional knowledge. I know, before you leap at me, that just because an idiot is defined as such a type of person, it doesn't follow that all persons of that type are idiots, but it's a tad ironic, isn't it? I mean, think of the vast amount of people with professional knowledge in public positions who appear to be the most complete idiots, in the English sense of the word. Particularly politicians.'

'Yes, but I suppose it's their being elected or promoted by us idiots that has something to do with it. Oh God! My head does ache.'

'Did you mind me looking at your painting before you'd finished it?'

'Yes. No. I'm realising it's ridiculous to mind. I would be more confident if I'd been to art school. It's my own fault that I didn't go. I'm neither communicating anything nor amusing anyone with it all hidden. Sooner or later one must find out if anyone else can understand it, or cares.'

'I look forward to your first exhibition then.'

'Unimaginable! I'm terrified of people laughing, in the wrong sort of way.'

'So is everybody else. What I saw looked as if it should be on someone's wall, being admired. I liked it a lot. You're an arch-imaginist. Why is the term "exhibitionist" so derogatory, do you think? Someone who makes an embarrassing public scene, rather than just a person who exhibits their work? Is it English false modesty, perhaps?' He stared at her, interested in her predicament. 'Would it be that, that's worrying to you?'

'I don't know that it is, quite. I've a confession to make.'

'Go on. Confess.'

'I painted you, when you were asleep.'

'Oh shit! How scary. I wondered what you were doing. Can I see?'

'I can't very well refuse, after what I've said, can I?'

'No, you certainly can't. No one's painted me before and I think I'm entitled to see it.' He sat back, still munching, and although teasing, he was deeply intrigued.

'OK.'

She fetched it, still taped to its board and he sat and stared at it, dumbfounded.

'Well?'

'It's quite extraordinary! I mean, I know I do look like that – would suppose that that's what I look like when asleep. But the likeness isn't the only thing, is it? It's the pattern of reds and blacks – the elbow of the black shirt on the red sheet makes one think of poppy petals. It's so immediate. Did you think of the poppy because of the colours that were there, or because of Morpheus?'

Bea let out a little shriek of delight. She'd thought it was fortuitous, the connections between the sleeping man and *Papaver somniferum* – the opium poppy, dreams and Morpheus the Son of Sleep.

'You're too clever by half! I just painted what was there, and had to work in a rush, in case you woke up, but I saw it was quite Elizabethan, emblematic. Although it *doesn't* mean anything. It just tied up so neatly.' Bea stared at her own work, the shapes and colours blurring, then it became the picture also of Flanders poppies, red blood and ripped white skin and her own skin goose pimpled; the hangover was still lurking.

'Now you've seen it, and like it, I suppose it doesn't have to be hidden away.' She propped it up above the fireplace.

'It still seems disturbing, that I didn't know you were doing it. A bit like a native who feels a portion of his soul is stolen each time a photograph is taken.' He leant back in his chair, long fingers laced across the flat stomach. 'Taking a likeness, portrait painters say, don't they? Photographers *take* your picture.'

'I'm sorry.' She reddened again, remembered the feeling of theft as she painted him. 'If the photographer had said, "I'm going to *make* your picture," then perhaps no one would have thought of losing a snippet of their soul. Can you imagine what it might be like, to be shown a shiny flat black-and-white something and be told, "that's you," when you've never ever seen yourself before? How could one interpret it?'

'That could be it, the making or taking. And the photograph, a magic drawing of some sort.' He smiled at her, the same knock-out smile. 'Well, thank you for the breakfast. I've got some work to catch up on this morning, or is it the afternoon? We'll be meeting again, quite soon, I hope?' He gave her a quick, almost furtive kiss on the cheek as they stood on the doorstep. Then the crow flew straight at him, and thinking it was about to attack she screeched as it flapped about his head, but it settled on his shoulder and quickly wiped its beak on his jacket sleeve. So, it was a pet. 'But he's been grown-up and free for over a year,' said Nut. 'This is only the third time I've seen him. He just turns up occasionally, where I happen to be. They're quite bright, crows, but it's odd he doesn't seem to have found a mate.'

'Has he got a name?'

'Yes. Budgie.'

Budgie could not be persuaded to leave him alone and Nut swung into his van and drove off with the bird still aboard his shoulder, chuntering absurdly into his ear and leaving her, almost breathless, on the doorstep.

Bea scratched at her finger. A rash had developed beneath the wedding ring. She removed it and saw a narrow circle of irritated pinkened skin above the knuckle. She put the ring down on the chair beside her watch and the mobile phone, cleaned a paintbrush with white spirit and started on another canvas.

'At least I understand now what the subject of the boat painting is ... it wasn't at all that clear when I started. I've got a new friend, I think. Thank God I wasn't sick. He wouldn't have been so friendly if he'd had to mop me up.' Bea felt tenuously bonded to the person who'd neither taken advantage of her drunken state nor appeared in the least disgusted by it. She now knew more about him: he'd been born in Dublin, of an English Catholic father with an over-romantic view of Ireland and the Irish, and an Irish Protestant mother. They'd gone North to Ulster when he was three, before moving again to live in England when he was sixteen; he lived in a house made from a converted railway carriage near the lighthouse and was a lovely cheerful man, and quite strangely beautiful. Apart from the weak moment on awakening that morning, Oscar had been absent from her thoughts for twenty-four hours, which she counted as a triumph. The physical separation had been a stone breaking in half, the mental more like pulling dough apart into two separate rounds. Her half at least was rising. She stood beside the bed where Nut had slept, and then sat down on it, leaning forwards to sniff the indented pillow, to try to catch the lingering smell of him. A single long red hair lay there. She picked it up and gently dropped it out of the window.

Chapter Six

'Yes, Major Higgins, we did manufacture the gates to open outwards, as you specified, not inwards. Yes, we did check them before they left the works. No, the circular pattern should be at the bottom, not the top.' Oscar leant back in his chair and kicked up savagely at the underside of his desk in frustration.

'Well, perhaps if you'd let us hang them ourselves as we suggested, rather than allowing your Bagshaw do it ... No, no, I'm sure he's perfectly competent ... May I suggest you do the following? Lift the gates off their posts and turn them upside down, are you with me? Then turn them back to front, keeping the pattern at the bottom. OK? Then reverse them, left to right and right to left, re-hang them and you'll find they then open outwards and close properly. Oh, good. Yes. Right. Good-bye, Major Higgins.'

He put the receiver back and let out a groan of annoyance before turning back to the paperwork before him, running his pen down a column of figures with a frown. But his instruction to Major Higgins — was he right? He retrieved a couple of empty cigarette packets from the wastepaper basket and drew on them in felt tip pen, L and R with a wavy line along their tops, marked on the sides where they sat upon their pivots and followed out his own instructions. Ridiculous, of course it worked. He was going insane.

'Whatever are you doing, Oscar?' Sheila had ceased to type and eyeing him curiously as he fiddled with the cigarette-packet puzzle, was obviously thinking the same thing.

'Nothing, nothing.' He threw the packets back into the basket and returned to the figures. During the month since he and Bea had parted Sheila had gradually eased off the overcoat of chilly disapproval. Things were back to normal now, everything going smoothly. She no longer passed over calls from Andrea with the words, 'It's that woman,' and had stopped accidentally slopping his coffee as she put it down on his desk.

That woman was being a little strange, he thought, ever since he'd suggested that once he'd got Bea sorted, the divorce in progress, they might think about having a child of their own. She'd shown every appearance of shock, her mouth falling open showing her tiny white teeth, then she'd screeched with laughter and told him she wasn't going to go through all that nonsense again. 'You can't be serious? Once was quite enough.' Hiding his dismay he laughed sycophantically and changed the subject. He'd bring it up again, when she'd had time to think about it sensibly. The telephone rang.

'It's Major Higgins again,' said Sheila.

Oscar picked up the phone and cleared his throat.

'Good morning again, Major Higgins. How can I help?'

This time Major Higgins had achieved the left gate on the left-hand side with the circles at the bottom, but the right gate was still the wrong way up. Oscar suddenly felt that this might be a wind-up.

'I think it would be best if I popped round to sort it out in person, don't you? No, no extra charge. I'll be there in fifteen minutes. See you then.' It was nearly lunch time in any case. What unfortunate regiment had had to suffer Major Higgins' ministrations?

He left the office and drove out the few miles to Major Higgins' residence, a tile-hung farmhouse, the front garden of which was colour-banded with pink and yellow tulips standing nervously to attention. He heaved the gates into their correct position with the hindrance of Bagshaw, an elderly man with a yellowing, droopy moustache and a near total absence of logic. Having ascertained that everyone was at last happy and politely refusing the glass of sherry offered, he drove back into the town to get some lunch. Andrea had become worried about his waistline and no longer provided bacon and egg breakfasts, so he had for the last week been resorting to compensatory meals at the Mummers where they served large helpings of sub-Mexican food. With rumbling stomach he was eagerly spooning up a plate of chilli when Agnes walked over and plonked herself down in front of him, a glass of wine in her hand and a strangely complicitous grin on her face.

'Hello, Oscar. Let yourself out of the cupboard then?'

He was pleased to see her since it signified a return to some sort of Bellhurst normality. She seemed friendly enough and was looking summery and sexy in short skirt and tight pink cotton jersey. A very tight pink cotton jersey. He automatically glanced down at his stomach, and tried to rein it in. It was extraordinary how women changed shape with the fashions, first all loose baggy things so that you couldn't tell what shape they were beneath but had to guess, now everything a size too small so that their shapes were thrust upon one. Their meeting might lay a few ghosts, but on the other hand . . . but she didn't look as if she was about to follow in her husband's lead and try to damage his face.

'Would you like to join me, have something to eat?'

'No, thanks. I just came out for a drink to celebrate finishing a piece of work. Why are you crying?'

The pub chef had incorrectly assumed a correlation between degrees of hotness and authenticity and having bitten on a whole incendiary chilli pod, Oscar's eyes were starting to fill with tears.

'Chilli. Too hot!' He self-consciously fanned his glowing face. 'I *am* pleased to see you – it's all been so difficult since the bust-up with Bea. I imagined you wouldn't be speaking to me? Phil still seems a bit touchy about it.'

'That's because he fancies Bea himself, didn't you know?' Agnes's round grey eyes looked at him innocently and without any ascertainable malice. 'So, how are things? How's life with the cow-woman, Andreary?' Her tone was teasing, with no trace of hostility, but he could hardly answer her without a self-defensive touch of it in his.

'It's wonderful. And she's quite wonderful, a beautiful, intelligent, self-confident woman. Everything's wonderful. If you've come over to be rude about her, I wish you'd go away again.' He took a more cautious mouthful of his meal.

'I'm sorry. I've heard different, that's all and you know how much I love Bea.'

'Have you seen her at all? I am, contrary to what you think, seriously worried about her. It was very distressing for me too, after all this time together . . . but we have to sort out our affairs, and she won't answer the solicitor's letter, or mine. All I got was a message from Tom Kerepol saying that she was too preoccupied at the moment to deal with it. I want to know what it is she's preoccupied with, and *where* she is?'

Agnes sat back and wondered which information and how much of it she should impart to cause maximum annoyance.

'She's doing very nicely.' she said, infuriatingly. 'She's recovered from the appalling shock you gave her and having a fling with a fisherman. She seems quite happy.' She watched his reaction to her barbed reply, noticing the faintest shadow of discontent on the so-fanciable face and the slightest yellow tinge at the side of his nose, the faded remnant of a bruise. 'I just don't understand why you couldn't just poke the cow-woman and leave it at that, as you did when you had affairs before?'

Oscar looked stunned, for a second or two, then wisely chose to ignore the last bit of her remark, deciding that it was beneath his dignity to deny but wondering how the hell she knew.

'What do you mean, a fisherman? Where would she meet a fisherman?'

'*I* don't know.' she said airily. 'Sitting weeping inconsolably on the bank of a river? Or knocking back double rums at an Inn called "The Jolly Roger"?'

He leant forward as she spoke, suddenly uncomfortably aware that he had had a sneaking thought when he left Bea, that his leaving her would cause her to think a great deal more about him than had his continuing presence. He was obviously wrong. It hurt him a little, to find that she'd recovered so rapidly. Agnes discerned an anxious interest. Perhaps Andreary didn't have quite such a hold on him as she'd thought but he'd hardly be likely to tell her if he'd discovered she was an alcoholic.

'I need to see her, really I do. There are all sorts of practical matters that need to be sorted out.' It was awkward and disturbing, not being in control of the situation ... of Bea.

'But you've only just left. I'll tell her, next time I see her, that you need to speak to her. But don't hold your breath — she *is* very busy.'

'That's what Tom said. But doing what, exactly?'

Now he sounded worried. Superb, she thought. The more he wonders about what Bea's up to, the less time he'll have for Andrea. First things first. Get him away from Andrea.

'She says just busy. Anyway, I must fly. I have to collect Seb at twelve-thirty, and look, it's a quarter to one!

She left, collecting a wolf-whistle on the way out which caused her to turn and smile at the perpetrator in a way more reminiscent of a cheeky sixteen-year-old than a woman of thirty, Feminism was drearily incomprehensible to Agnes and she found it more uplifting to the spirits to be whistled at than asked for her opinion on the judging of the Booker prize.

Oscar got out of the car, opened the elegant iron gates, *his* elegant iron gates, and was unwelcomed by Andrea's whippet Passe-Partout, who barked neurotically and nearly got itself squashed as he drove into the drive. It nipped at him as he got out again to close them and he fended it off gently with his foot, sure that Andrea would be watching from the drawing-room window, gin and tonic in hand, as she did most evenings. He was looking forward to a drink, and the pre-supper snacks of nuts and Kalamata olives she always set out. He looked forward to dinner and watching her as she ate, to being melted by the femininity of her movements as with a tiny, plump and almost inadequate hand she lifted the overburdened fork up to her open mouth ... Bea never needed help to open jars, or move a chair. Andrea's hands were beautifully shaped, with varnished nails, hands which he could imagine smoothing, touching ... Bea's hands were narrow, with tapering, spiky fingers of quite extraordinary length and strength, the thumbnails, and the thumbnails only, bitten. Exploratory hands that weren't reluctant to dabble in mud or gut a fish, hands that drew and drew, with a callus on the second finger of the left hand ... he stopped and pushed open the door to the drawing room and stared, jaw-dropped, at the sight of Andrea. He had become accustomed to her early evening dress of beautifully-cut slit tunics of some silky stuff over swishy skirt, in chestnut brown, chic grey or black, to her carefully tended face and hair, to her very eager kisses and seductive looks.

Andrea lay on her back on the sofa, her legs unattractively splayed out in some sort of exercise outfit of red and fluorescent pink-patterned leotard and orange leggings, which looked unfortunate on her pretty but slightly pear-shaped figure. Her mouth was indeed open, but she snored. An empty gin bottle and unemptied ashtray lay beside her on the giant silver-leafed coffee table and there was a dog's mess on the polished floorboards. She looked impossibly, dreadfully, ridiculous. There was no sign of either nuts or olives.

It was May Eve and Bea was out in the garden of Little Rumm, sitting on the wall, basking in the warm air and in the process of dissecting her situation in the safety of the copper sunset, forcing an admission that in her particular circumstances, being a deserted wife wasn't as miserable as expected. She could also admit freely now that over the last few years the marriage had rolled quietly and gently down the slope to a standstill although she had also made quite sure that this was what *she* believed, that she was not accepting it just because it was what Oscar wanted her to believe. At the very back of her mind was the uncomfortable feeling that things could be, ought to be mended should the chance arise, but it was unlikely that he would leave Andreary and anyway alongside it sat the thought that not in any way did she wish to return to life in a cottage in Bellhurst.

At night, however, still unused to sleeping alone, she lay wide awake in the early hours of the morning. She waited for the increasingly earlier dawns, listing the minutiae of night noises in order to prevent, or at least stave off, the uncontrollable remembrances of Oscar and fearful imaginings concerning the future which loomed up like threatening swans emerging from dark rivers, hissing warnings that she was too close to the water's edge, too close to them. She listened to the sudden dry rustling as a bird on the roof shook its feathers, the dripping tap in the kitchen, the creaking release of tension in a floorboard, a clatter as a fox investigated the rubbish bin followed by the sound of its tongue, rasping along the goffered sides of the tinfoil case of a chocolate cup-cake.

Had she ever done more than scrape at the surface of her life, been too insecure to dig any deeper? There had recently been a loosening of the snarled-up thinking, allowing an exploration of those few thoughts which were not connected with the painting in progress, or increasingly, worryingly, of Francis Nutmeg. It was too soon to get involved, would inevitably divert from her purpose of proving herself to be a painter. First paint the pictures, then . . .

Nut had put in an appearance a couple of days after the debacle of their evening together, arriving with a present as if to reassure her everything was fine. He placed a fossil, a sea-urchin type of thing in her hand, warm because it had been in his trouser pocket, with the delicate star-burst marking of tiny points where its spines had once grown still clearly visible. Nut was a magpie, laying a stolen trinket before a potential mate; she could feel him searching her face for signs of approval as she examined the fossil.

'It's so beautifully *almost* regular,' she examined it with care, turning it over and looking at the central depression, like a neat umbilicus, feeling the ancient shape with her fingertips, 'just these tiny differences in distance, as if they'd been caught growing, fluid, that are so pleasing, aren't they? And sea-urchin shells look the same now, don't they? They've hardly changed a bit?'

'Not much.' Nut was thinking that the description she had given applied to her face just as well, so pleasing. 'A few hundred years ago there was a widespread belief that God made fossils, just as they are and scattered them about the earth to amuse us, like toys.'

'But that's a consoling idea and it must have been so easy to believe. How old would this be, how long since it was alive? Where did you find it?'

'I found it near Dover. They're common in chalk, so Cretaceous times, perhaps seventy million years ago at least?'

'There was a seventeenth-century bishop who believed he had got the age of the earth all sorted out by using the Old Testament, did you know? He counted all the begats, I suppose, and came to the conclusion that the world was created at nine o'clock in the morning on the twenty-sixth of October, four thousand and four BC. I remembered it because I liked the idea of someone with such utter faith in the Bible settling down at a desk by candlelight after a supper of toasted cheese one evening and working it all out, even if they were so horribly wrong. And it must have seemed a certainty to the un-educated, having been pronounced by a bishop.'

'It's been revised since then. It's more like three and a half to five billion years old.' Nut grinned. 'Yesterday's certainties — fairy tales today. You seem keen on certainties at the moment?'

'I'm still missing the ones I thought I had, yes. But fossils are certainties, even if people did once think they were toys. I'd like to find some for myself.' She put the fossil down in the centre of the table. 'It's eerie, to be handling something as old as that, unearthed from beneath all those layers of other life. Do you see time, I mean your own life, as layers one on top of the other, like blankets?'

'As chapters in a book, I think. Less digging. Personally I never seem to get past Chapter Three. And how are you enjoying *Gulliver's Travels*? He picked it up from the kitchen table and flipped through it, examining the illustrations intently. 'Lovely pictures!'

'They're lithographs by Edward Bawden. It's my father's copy. Have you ever read it?'

'I have not, but since we are having a most polite conversation, I know that it was Swift who wrote 'The sight of you is good for sore eyes.' He meant it as an example of a particularly well-used compliment, but I mean it particularly truthfully!'

It being endearingly given, she beamed at him. 'I'm finding Gulliver rather heavy going. It's difficult with satire, old, old satire and I'm not always certain what particular trait of the times he is making fun of, but one can feed off the invention and I've only fallen asleep reading it once. You weren't so chatty, that time we very first met.'

'No. It was rather early in the morning and I'll admit to a hangover and considerable embarrassment. Have you recovered now, from yours?'

She was very pleased with the present of the fossil but disconcertingly, since an interruption by him was very acceptable — did not count as an intrusion at all, Nut insisted that he didn't want to hinder her work and only stayed a few minutes more, just long enough to draw a neat sketch-map of exactly where his railway-carriage house was and to invite her to drop in on him sometime soon.

'I can see you're in the middle of something, there's paint on your ear and I've got a site-meeting in a field four miles away in fifteen minutes.' His eyebrows flicked upwards, anxiously. 'I've been to Nest's house; now it's your turn to visit Nut's nest.'

'I will. Is the crow still with you?'

'No. Budgie's buggered off again. He didn't seem to care for roast chicken, which was all I had to give him. It was corned beef that was always his favourite.' He touched her arm. 'I've got to go. I'll be late.' He'd turned and left so fast that if it hadn't been for the fossil and the map, his visit would have seemed an illusion.

An old estate car came lumbering up the track towards her, nearly grounding itself between the hardening ruts for it was heavily loaded with women. The car slowed down and then pulled up, the front passenger calling out of the window to ask for directions.

'Hi there! Sorry to interrupt your communications with the natural spirits, but could you tell me if we're on the right road for the power station?'

This seemed to Bea an odd request. The power station's Visitor Centre must be closed in the evenings. The five women, a mixed age group, had a semi-suppressed nervous excitement about them as if they were anticipating a party although Bea thought it a bizarre location for one. There was a grumbling chorus from the back seat. 'We thought you knew a special way, Emma.' 'I knew you'd get us effing lost.' 'After all, you're supposed to know the area.'

'This track just peters out near the shore,' said Bea, aware of five pairs of eyes trained upon her as she leant forwards to the enquirer, 'but you *could* park and walk along to it from there, it's less than a mile. If you want to drive right up close to it, you'd have to go back to Fingle and take the lower road. That'd be much easier.'

There was a discontented 'That's what I suggested, only no one would listen to me,' from the driver. Intrigued, Bea watched as they consulted urgently among themselves, three for the walk, the other two groaning that the shingle would be too tiring to walk on and that they would be late. The chastened navigator thanked Bea and said they would be late in any case, and may as well continue the way they'd come, that is, if Bea thought it would be safe to leave the car parked there?

'As long as you don't try to park it off the track and sink in stones. The only people who use the track are the men who fish from the beach at night. But no one's gone past this evening, so far.' There was more excited comment at this but the car bumped off in the direction of the shore, exhaust pipe scraping the infill of broken bricks. Bea felt sure she'd seen the driver before, but couldn't place her. The heavy dew was dampening her hair and was falling visibly in the half light, gleaming on the stones.

Frying two dabs for supper, making toast under the hissing grill, the odour of the bottled gas reminded her of camping stoves and tents on holiday in France and she chirruped a song as she flipped them over, anticipating the milky freshness of the dab's white buttered flesh, the crunchiness of the toast. Her eating times had become wildly erratic, but she bothered to make each meal a treat, however simple, and it was important to keep things simple, to save time, to get on with the job. After supper she sat in the little blue armchair by the open window in the dark, stomach pleasantly full but brain churning.

'How *do* I appear to other people? To Nut, for instance? I want to know. Can self-confidence only be achieved if one believes in one's own image of oneself, of one's physical and mental shape? Other people's perceptions of ourselves seem so drastically different from our own. Which view is real? Does Nut have a view of me? And if he does (surely he must have one – I do hope he has) does it coincide with mine at any point?

And the other way about. What did Oscar think I was, or am? How did I see Oscar? Perhaps we disappear in our own eyes, in a puff of smoke, when others refuse to see us as we think we are. Did Oscar see me at all, as anyone? He must have lost sight of the me he thought I was or he wouldn't have betrayed me like that. But betrayal's far too high-flown a word for what he's done. How long had he been seeing Andrea? Sneaky pig. I didn't think to betray him, did I? But perhaps the thought was there all the time waiting for me to think it. I bloody well should have thought it.'

She got up and restlessly started pacing up and down, worrying at the river of questions and then thinking up a few more.

'Is it only the totally self-confident people who are undisturbed by other people's views of themselves? Perhaps a lack of imagination is necessary for real self-confidence, or at least an ability to turn imagination off. In which case self-confidence can't always be the mega-blessing it's supposed to be, can it? Very imaginative people are so often secretive. They daren't court too many of other people's views of themselves, or their work, for fear of destruction; but one can't perform forever without an audience. No, I'm going mad and muddling imagination with sensitivity. Over-sensitivity is a symptom of an unhealthy interest in oneself,' she addressed herself severely, 'which is what you are very much in danger of.' A large house spider raced across the floor and she sat down on her chair again in a hurry with her feet tucked up.

'One can pretend, go on pretending past childhood. One can act out self-confidence – dash about saying "Take it or leave it, I don't care! I'm the greatest. In my view *this* is right." Lots of people must do that and have to live with knowing themselves to be con-artists. All that calm and ordered bit was pretended. I pretended being happy and contented so well that I believed myself. Did Oscar know it was a colossal porky? But was it pretended for him in the first place because I knew he wouldn't have liked the selfish cow inside? What a tortuous, shitty muddle!'

Not surprisingly having lost the train of thought she turned again to the window where her eye was caught by an orange flicker on the skyline, up on the shingle bank. Then another blossomed after it, and another, till there were five flames bobbing along the top at different heights towards the power station. The women in the car? With torches, firebrands? What could they be up to? It must be a beach party, but it shelved so sharply there was no beach to speak of at that point, even at low tide. Her curiosity was up but since there was no one there to make her feel shame faced about being nosy and overcome with a sudden sense of excitement, she slipped on a jacket and locked up the house, thinking she could drive round to the ness before they reached it, and find out. If it wasn't a party, never mind. It would be more bearable, being outside in the night.

The exterior darkness was less scary to Bea than the interior darkened rooms of houses, where perhaps memories of past events and people of unknown nastiness might have become trapped, concentrated and stored like stock cubes. Outside they were diluted and one could run amazingly fast, at least in the imagination, to escape from the murderers or lolloping corpses that chased one in dreams. It would, she thought, be poetic justice if murderers were plagued by the nightmares of their victims, forced into taking them on as punishment, to dream them as well as their own, every night, for ever.

As a child she had been convinced that to recall a nightmare during the day would mean that she would dream it again the next night and so forced herself into forgetfulness of the worst of them; those dreams where things touched became disgusting decaying messes, like rotting pumpkins that looked so firm but gave beneath the pressure of a finger to expose a softening mass of putrescent, pulpy flesh.

She shuddered and drove off down the track, nervously remembering her mother's story of being frightened when a child by the idea of German soldiers beneath her bed, lying there waiting to machine-gun her ankles as she crossed the room. Jane said she used to run upstairs to her bedroom door, burst it open and fling herself across the room in two great bounds, shouting to surprise them, and crash down on the bed, safe. She said Gran eventually took to coming upstairs with a broom at bedtime and rattling it about under the bed to prove there was nothing there. The soldiers in their hideous chamberpot helmets had gone away by morning so she could get *out* of bed quite safely in the daylight. It was just the getting *in* which caused problems.

It wasn't too late in the evening to take up Nut's invitation and drop in. The map was in her pocket now. Nut, chestnut, cobnut, hazelnut, ginger-nut, nutmeg Nut — all vegetable — perhaps he'd respond to Carrots instead? But it wouldn't suit, the hair not being curly carrotty orange; it was thick, smooth, wavy and a riotous maple-leaf red. A fox ran across in the headlights as she drove along the causewayed road between the deep gravel pits on either side. There was a second's flash of reflected light from its close-set petty-criminal eyes before it disappeared beneath the wire fencing to the left. Foxy-headed Nut. But his hair was brighter than a fox's fur.

Approaching the lighthouse and slowing down, she began to scan for signs of more torches, or a bonfire, and there it was, blazing out on the shingle. Pulling in and turning off the engine, she debated what to do. It was still some way off, she could walk a little closer, see what was going on. No one else seemed to be about. Although there was a spread-out settlement of small bungalows and weatherboarded houses along that stretch of road, they all seemed to be dark or empty or have their curtains tightly drawn.

There was an astonishing crowd around the bonfire, in long, red hooded cloaks and black masks, circling several circles deep and holding hands. They were singing and every now and then one of them threw back its hooded head and howled.

Bea thought it looked both creepy and atavistic, and serious fun and since one could hardly be accused of gate-crashing in a wide open space, wandered up closer to watch. A couple stood at the base of the new lighthouse's ammonite-like spiral ramp, the firelight catching the look of disbelief on their faces as the bobbing horde, now indulging in mass ululation, stamped their feet on the rattling pebbles. Bea tried to estimate their numbers, but gave up.

'Bea? This is very jolly, isn't it? I wish I'd brought my red cloak too,' said someone who had come up behind her. It was Nut's friend, the affable Edmund whom she'd met on that disgracing evening out with Nut, standing there stockily, smiling widely. 'Are you about to join them?'

Amelia also arrived, a little out of breath, and slipped her arm possessively through his.

'Hello, Bea! This looks just like a scene from John Masefield's *The Midnight Folk*, doesn't it, Edmund? Do you suppose they have broomsticks and will do a fly-past later on?' She turned back to Bea, fairly bubbling with amusement. 'This is how we first met, Edmund and I, at a bonfire. Not like this one though. That was only a pedestrian Guy Fawkes' night. A bacchanalia is much more exciting. Let's enjoy it before someone calls the police and spoils it all.' She grinned. 'I had an overwhelming urge to come out this evening and have some fish and chips at the pub up the road. We were going to call on Mr Nutmeg afterwards, but we've been deflected by the spectacle. I'm so glad Edmund was willing to indulge me, or I'd have missed it all. Oh look! They're breaking up and leading a procession up the road. Where are they going?'

'To the power station – I think it was some of them that passed my house and asked for directions earlier on, only they weren't dressed up then. Perhaps they're going to put a curse on it.'

'That sounds rather unwise. Anything might happen. Let's follow and see!' So they linked arms, with solid Edmund in the middle and followed in the dark.

Inside the floodlit perimeter fence, the buildings and their gleaming, steaming exterior pipework and bright lights became a science fiction stage set – a surreal Alphaville, or a Mayan temple besieged by a revolt of priestesses. The red-cloaked ones parted in a well-organised fashion and in two columns filed either side of the gate, as if to encircle the area. 'They're like ants out on a foray,' thought Bea, 'single-minded and programmed.' Chanting and holding long lengths of red ribbon between them they spaced themselves out widely. A group who stood apart from the encircling ones still brandished lighted torches and the air was heavy with the stink of paraffin. There was a glittering and clashing as a large number of them appeared to be handcuffing themselves to the fencing. Security guards were both outside and inside, remonstrating with them, but were being drowned out by chanting. Tiny dark faces appeared at the lighted windows above in the main building, peering down on the extraordinary theatrical performance below.

'What is it they're shouting?' asked Edmund, enraptured by the spectacle.

'I think it's "The Daughters of Nature invoke your departure," said Bea. Far away in the distance sirens were heard, and across the flatness from every inland direction, blue flashing lights could be seen approaching, converging on the site. There was now a growing group of silent, entranced spectators. The first police car drew up and disgorged three young constables who, advancing upon the tethered maenads, were stopped dead by a well-organised, one-handed ripping of Velcro fastenings and a casting aside of cloaks. The women who were being advanced upon stood abruptly naked in the flashing, flickering, reflected lights.

The policemen wavered, halted again and conferred, then backed off a little way to use their radios. More cars arrived, three fire engines and an ambulance or two. Bea now recognised the woman who'd asked the way earlier that evening – she worked in the Parden library. Her mask had slipped around her neck and her stiffly lacquered helmet of blonde hair and heavy make-up caused her startlingly well-built body to appear even more naked than it was already, like a Cranach nude in a hat and pearls. A van load of more senior officers drew up and megaphones were being deployed.

It was after midnight now and policewomen, one of them apparently quite overcome with giggles, advanced on the naked ones accompanied by helplessly smirking firemen with bolt-cutters. The policewomen tried to cover the nakedness while the firemen snipped; however as soon as one was freed from self-imprisonment, wrapped up and ushered away, others, still chanting, triumphantly disrobed themselves. A flashing of photographers rushed upon the scene, intent on getting pictures of police manhandling, but more particularly of tits. Two women still safe inside their cloaks, were handing out leaflets till a pair of constables tried to take them away and then the taller of the two let out a screech and tried to claw them back.

'I'm not disturbing the peace! I'm handing out leaflets — this is a religious movement. We're natural witches about our business. We're not damaging anything! It's you lot of pigs who are disturbing our peaceful demonstration of . . . let go, will you . . . our trust in nature . . . our abhorrence of nuclear pollution . . . Let go of my effing cloak! You tear it and I'll sue you for damages! It cost a lot of money that material, *and* I had to make it myself.' The voice was undoubtedly Lucinda's. The shorter of the two women became overheated and a policeman's cap went flying.

Some of the expanding crowd took Lucinda's side. 'Go on, let them go. They're not doing any harm!' She was firmly taken by the arm and led back towards the old lighthouse where a police van was parked, but she wriggled and abandoning the leaflets, in one eel-like movement fell out of the cloak. Finding himself clutching naked flesh, he let go, reluctantly but pink with embarrassment. The crowd hooted and cheered as Lucinda disappeared into the darkness, leaving her companion jumping up and down with fury. There was something familiar about her too. 'Bea, Bea! Tell them I'm only handing out leaflets!'

'Aunt Nest!' Bea leapt forward anticipating some sort of struggle but the policemen shrugged and gave in, returning to their more challenged companions at the gates and fruitlessly imploring the onlookers to go back home.

'Now I can die happy,' chortled Edmund, 'I've seen a streaking witch! It's most impressive, as demonstrations go.' He rescued one of the leaflets fluttering across the road and put it in his pocket to read later.

Aunt Nest was quivering with indignation and Bea was near hysterical with laughter. 'You weren't going to strip off too, were you, Aunt Nest?' she asked, wondering whether to introduce the witch-aunt to Edmund and Amelia who were impolitely staring at her with delighted incredulity.

'Good God, no! I'm only a lay-witch, and just for tonight, I think. There are limits to commitment. Look.' Aunt Nest, temper restored and now with her violet eyes sparkling through the eye-slits of her fetching mask, flashed open her cloak and Bea was reassured to see she was wearing extremely sensible long navy blue Damart underwear. Edmund appeared to be inconsolable.

'"Cast not a clout till May be out!"' Nest cried gaily. 'The twenty-somethings may think it's a warm night, but I think there's a distinct nip in the air. I'd better take Lucinda's cloak back to the car and see if I can find her. Here's a leaflet to read. I'll tell you all about it later on. I didn't think it would get quite so rough but I've never enjoyed myself so much!'

'Does Blue know?'

'Perish the thought! He'd have got far too emotional.'

Bea rather wished that she had been alone to see the demonstration; on reflection it was a bit embarrassing watching with other people whom she knew, let alone finding that one of them was her aunt.

'I don't want to spoil your fun, but I think you've probably seen enough pink bits,' said Amelia, taking Edmund's arm again, her face reflecting Bea's own quandary.

'But it was the navy-blue bits which were so devastating!' gurgled Edmund, 'However,' he appeared to be recovering himself, 'it is getting too late to see if we can find Nut, although I suspect he's out here somewhere — even if he was immersed in work he'd hardly fail to notice a Beltane bonfire on his doorstep. Were you on your way to see him, Bea?'

Bea admitted that she had intended to drop in on Nut. It was getting very late, or rather early, since now it was May Day, but he surely couldn't be asleep with all this racket going on. They were walking back to where they'd left their cars, occasionally overtaken by a fleeing witch, when she caught sight of him.

Nut stood at his ease with folded arms, leaning broad shoulders against a peeling wall emblazoned with the Trinity House coat of arms, chatting to a man in waders, down-filled jacket and a flat tweed cap.

'... there must have been over a hundred of them,' Nut was saying, '... or perhaps they came in covens, say thirteen thirteens? That's one hundred and sixty-nine little witches!'

'Some of them weren't too little, neither,' said the man, stubbing out his cigarette on the wall, 'a bit too much, straight after a big fish supper, all that flesh. Fair puts you off. Didn't know where to look. I wasn't going to come up off the beach, meself. Thought it was just a radioactive leak alarm and went on fishing, but George said he'd look after me line ...'

'One of them was Lucinda,' said Bea to Nut, 'and another was my aunt Nest.'

'One of them was a bloke,' said the man who was unworried by the contingency of radioactive leaks. 'Surprised the lady constable a bit. Lucky the fireman had control of his cutters.' He shook his head in disbelief and ambled back to his fishing.

The amusement being over, more or less, Edmund and Amelia made their good-byes and Bea stood alone in the dark with Nut.

'Was it the witches you came to see, or did you intend to visit me at last?' he asked, arms still folded and a very slightly foxy smile on his face.

They crunched across the shingle to the house, avoiding broken lengths of rusty iron hawser and crushing the woodsage growing in the stones, releasing its antiseptic smell into the salty warmth of the night air. The house was rented from a woman who lived in Blackpool, he said, opening the door into a world so self-contained and so obviously suited to his own purposes that Bea initially felt quite out of place. He removed a pile of books from a small armchair, invited her to sit down and after flicking on a tape that he had been listening to previously, made tea. Kurt Weill's *The Threepenny Opera* unexpectedly welled out into the room. This Bea associated with evenings up in the attic bedroom at home, listening to 'Pirate Jenny' floating up the stairs as Tom played old vinyls of Georgia Brown, whose voice he adored, sometimes urging her to come down and sing with him, which she nearly always did.

They were in a narrow, dark green room with an arched ceiling, a reminder of the fact that it was once a railway carriage, with a tiny kitchen at one end and a black, dormant woodstove at the other. The walls were shelved and so tightly packed with books that they leaked out around the floor in puddles, then seeped up voraciously to cover every available surface.

Nut watched her while the kettle boiled, as she got up and prowled about, inquisitive and tense as a cat in new surroundings, exploring his Lilliputian territory. Beyond the kitchen a bedroom could be seen through the doorway. An extension with wide windows on the seaward side ran the length of the carriage and contained lavatory and shower room and formed what passed for a conservatory in which were fishing rods, tomato plants growing in Sainsbury's plastic carrier bags, waders and binoculars hanging from a hook. It was clean, and tidy in a way. Her eyes raked the room for signs of past or present female companionship and found nothing. There was a balance to the room, things were aligned, papers laid straight on the desk beside the computer, 'Palaeoenvironmental Investigation ... Rickards Flats ...' she glanced further down the page but it was too technical to be immediately interesting, seemingly to do with diatom counts, frustules, pollen analysis and inter-tidal mudflats of which she knew nothing. Maps, charts and a square of four framed drawings of delicately interlaced seaweed-like plants hung on the walls.

Nut brought out a tray with two mugs of tea and a half-eaten packet of ginger biscuits and as he leant forward she caught sight of his neck, the strength in it, the whiteness of it, and the red-gold hairs at the base of it seen through the open neck of the dark blue shirt. Her whole interior being suddenly shifted vertiginously downwards, a deep sinking feeling in her stomach and hips. Lustless for a considerable time, it was a sensation of extraordinary strength and most disconcerting. She turned quickly back to the pictures on the wall and desperately pretended to be studying them while listening to the insinuating 'Mack the Knife', fighting off the violently physical twinges in the loins department and trying to recover her internal dignity.

'I'm sorry. I'm being intolerably nosy,' she said, as the sensation fluttered and protesting, slowly died away. 'Did you do these?'

'No, that's Amelia's work.' He was looking at her, a sudden surmise had come to him and the slightest of tremors shook his hand as he passed over a mug. 'She comes down here to draw sometimes. That's how I met her. She was drawing seaweed, and I stopped to look, tried to chat her up on the spot, even. I must admit I thought she was pretty exciting. She held me off so elegantly. What do you think of them both?'

'Very friendly. They must have been married as long as my parents; they seem so definitely paired, twinned. I liked to see them walking off, arms round each other. Their happiness seemed almost tangible.' She wished she was like Amelia, so confident and happily garrulous.

'Ah, yes. But they're not married, and they've only been together for a year or two. Amelia's first husband died, committed suicide. Edmund's divorced.'

'Have they got children?'

'There's Amelia's daughter, Josie. She's a sunbeam girl, about nineteen, and just like her mother. She was there tonight, handing out leaflets too. I recognised her voice. I bet Amelia didn't know.'

'You seem to know them very well?'

'Yes, they've become good friends. You could see Amelia loved the to-do this evening. She's the grand-daughter of the writer Connaught Marvel, incidentally, and is a connoisseur of strange happenings. So, what's the story about your aunt? Aunt Nest?' The image he had gained from Blue was of an eccentric horticultural houri.

'Well, she told me Lucinda was trying to get her to join some eco-organisation, but I don't think she knew it was to do with witches. Or perhaps she found out and that's why she did join. It's the sort of thing that might appeal to her for a while. And dressing up is irresistible to her.' Bea was still in turmoil and her body was deeply disappointed. 'It's peculiar, this business of dressing up. I suppose it enables one to behave in a way one wouldn't if one started out the evening in a flowery frock.'

'What's dressing up? Have a soggy biscuit? No? It's hard to tell if people are dressed up for fun or for some more esoteric reason. Most of the people you see wearing sports clothes, they're dressing up, pretending to be sporty, imagining they've a chance of winning gold, if only . . . They've never played a game in their lives, look as if they'd have apoplexy if you asked them to run out and post a letter.'

'Don't they just? But that's fashion, not dressing up and what about judges and bishops wearing antique clothes to lend them dignity, and soldiers and police? Are their uniforms meant to inspire respect or to make sure they all recognise each other and do the right salutes?'

Nut laughed. 'I suspect uniforms came about when fights between tribes got so big they had trouble knowing who to hit. No problems if it's family versus family, but town against town would be difficult. If one side wore wolf-skin trousers and the others polecat, it would have made it easier.'

'I did really mean fancy dress, like tonight. The long red cloaks and masks, although in spite of the different shapes and sizes, the nakedness looked more like uniform than the cloaks.'

'I felt a bit embarrassed at first,' Nut said 'that I shouldn't be watching, not in the way that a man *would* watch. It was hard, trying not to leer. One can't help oneself thinking and sizing up, as it were. All those different coloured beavers. I did *try* to drag my eyes away and think of it as necessary exhibitionism! Was it necessary, though, to strip off like that, to make the point?'

'It was a wildly successful delaying tactic, wasn't it? You've got to risk ridicule, I suppose, to get the point across. Will they be charged with indecent exposure? I'm so glad Lucinda got away.'

'Lucinda likes taking her clothes off. That's what you'll have to do when you exhibit your work, in a way. Put your ideas naked before the public.'

'Yes, I suppose.' So, Lucinda liked stripping off, did she? Was he speaking from personal experience? The idea of it brought her sharply out of her hypnosis. 'Since you've now seen a picture, I'm less neurotic about it. It isn't so threatening. Tell me more about what it is *you* do, and do you have to wear a uniform to do it?'

'Oh God, where do I start? Well, I've been working for an archaeological trust for the past eighteen months, on the geographical part of an inter-disciplinary survey of the area. It was commissioned and funded by them when they were left a huge bequest by a dilettante patron, the late and unlikely Siegfried McKay-Tart from Vancouver. He believed his ancestors came from around here; but what seemed a very substantial sum is dwindling fast and my part in it is nearly over, for the time being anyway.'

'But if you're a geographer, and it's an archaeological set-up, so where do you fit in?'

'Simply or in detail?'

'Very simply, please.'

'The coastline and the marsh behind it are constantly in the process of change. We need to find out how it evolved, when it changed, where and why. That sort of thing. We can assess the presence and influence of man on the area from prehistoric times; find out when different parts of the marsh were inned, how changes in sea level and storms changed river courses, silted up harbours or destroyed what had once been prosperous ports. A little land lost at this point, some gained further along. There were Roman salt-workings here, small settlements on higher ground there ... it all ties in.' He stopped. 'Please, you're not bored? The most interesting thing to me about the job is the collaboration with the other specialist researchers, the palaeobotanists, the hydrologists, the historians, the archaeologists.' All the while he talked he was moving, a mercurial Nut, thrumming with energy, but he glanced anxiously at her. 'I just love it – the land is everything, poetry even, to me. Are you sure you don't think it's boring? Most people doze off if I tell them what I do. The only thing that gets them going is digging up buried treasure. One hint of precious metal and they're out causing havoc with their little detectors.'

'I'm not in the slightest bored. It's rare to meet someone so enthusiastic about what they do instead of moaning all the time. Do you have to do a great deal of writing, reports and things?'

'Well yes, there is, but I don't mind although I'd naturally prefer to be out of doors. I like putting the final full stop on a conclusion.' He waved his hand in the air with a flourish. 'A conclusion is the white rabbit being hauled out of a top hat.

Then everyone pokes and prods at it to see if it's real, worried that their pet theory might be discredited by it. The only trouble is the scientific vocabulary becomes a bit predictable and boring. I'd love to be able to use words like "angst" and "arriviste".'

'I've never had reason to use "arriviste" either! You are the most unlikely geographer! What happens when your work here is finished?

'When the money runs out, you mean? The work itself is almost unfinishable. I'm hoping to get a post at either London or Kent University. I should get to hear fairly soon whether I've got one or other of them.'

She watched him prowling about, picking up a postcard from the desk, moving the red Anglepoise lamp, tapping out a word on the computer keyboard, now carefully not looking at her. In spite of his size and the smallness of the space, he never brushed against anything. More and more she was attracted to what she saw, but was very, very wary.

He was thinking that he would need a butterfly net to catch this inconsistently timorous angel. But then angels were only messengers and didn't feel desire and that was what he'd for certain seen, flashing across her face for that one instant. How to make the leap from palaeobotany to bed?

'How brave are you?' he asked, moving behind her and suddenly laying just a finger lightly against her neck. She jerked involuntarily and slammed a foot on the brakes.

'Not as brave as that.'

'Please, stay. Stay with me.'

Bea had a brief tussle with physical instincts, and won. If he could be bold, she could, in competition, be at least resolute, and pathetically plead internal imbroglio.

'No, Nut ... Not now. I've got to go home, quite soon.' Why had she said that? How sad and unnecessary it sounded.

'All right, then,' he said, as lightly as he'd touched; you great fool! He cursed himself. Too soon, too soon.

Momentarily affronted, as when an offer or request is

gratefully retracted on receiving a first polite refusal, she was then relieved. He could have thought he'd ask because it was expected of him? To Bea, the obstinate waverer, her curt 'No, not now' meant: 'OK I'm attracted, and you know it, but there are other things in life just at the moment that seem so desperately pressing and I'm not interested in *just* sex at all, not without being involved and I'm not *allowed* to get tied up with you, or anyone. Not until this lot of paintings is finished. But when does one say that's enough for the moment? I can't go on for ever saying just one more painting, like Penelope weaving her everlasting tapestry. But I'd like to be able to say yes, and might perhaps, later on . . . Shit, it's *frightening*. But I didn't expect to be understood at once. As what am I dressed up? A siren in sackcloth and ashes? And what's he? A fox in a rabbit's mask? I must go before he pretends to nibble and then takes a larger mouthful. It was insane to have come in the first place – I haven't escaped from Oscar so recently to be recaptured, even for a single night. But it wasn't an escape from Oscar, he escaped from me. I was jettisoned . . .' Not unnaturally she couldn't bring herself to say a syllable of this aloud.

'Nut?'

'Yes, Bea?' He had been extremely patient with the long silence but still looked friendly, if somewhat resigned, leaning back against his desk as if waiting for her to speak again.

'You will see me again? Won't you?'

'Oh yes, if you'd like to, absolutely yes.' He sounded relieved, she thought.

'I would like. I can't say what I mean because it sounds trite – and I often don't know what I mean till after I've heard myself say it.'

'Don't say anything more then, if you're feeling unintelligible. Best to leave it, if you're needing certainties. I'm sorry I leapt over the fence.' He couldn't bear not to touch her again and put an arm round her shoulder and gave her a little squeeze. She felt a clear and definite physical kickback from the feel of the flesh, bone and muscle in his arm, and a second, echoing, craven ache.

'Come on, Bewildered Beatrice. I'll walk with you back to that rat-trap of a truck of yours.'

The smell of bonfire lingered in the little house and Nut clapped shut the bedroom window on the black velvet night, cursing himself again. But she'd taken it as her fault, the poor pigeon. Why was that? Well, he'd wait. He'd wait because she had a beautiful walk, swaying and gliding with an occasional stammer – a skip, a hiccup, like her speech – fluent then held up by a liquid giggle. He'd wait because she was flustered and still too recently bereaved by the marriage breakdown. But was she bereaved? He wondered about that. Things happened about her, she did not seem an instigator or a participant. Was her entire energy being saved for her work? Was she an introverted soloist? No, he was being unfair. But the urges to change, to progress, to defeat and to possess were as strong in Nut as in any man. He'd have to wait because there was nothing else he could do.

That night Nest, safely back at home, lay back in bed and gazed with immense affection at Blue as he haphazardly removed bits of clothing while weaving clumsily about the room, dropping a sock by the dressing table before picking up a bottle of scent and idly sniffing at it. 'Phew! Is that called Eau de Nil?' He discarded the other sock on the floor beneath the window and leant forward to stare at the stars as he clumsily unbuttoned his shirt, abandoning it by a chair, not on it, and the leather belt he wound absent-mindedly round one of the brass finials at the foot of the bed.

'Don't draw the curtains, Blue. I like to be able to see the sky when I wake up. You can see Cassiopeia, just above the weeping ash tree.'

'Where? I can't see nothing. Is that the one shaped like a W?'

'Yes. You can see it from here, from this angle.' He caught his foot in his trouser leg and staggered, falling across the bed, his face close to hers on the pillow. 'Ah, I've got it now, just above that branch that looks like an angel's wing.' He put his hand on her breast, and heaved himself up into a sitting position without letting go. 'What are you going to read to me tonight, my Cuckoo?'

'It's far too late. I'm sorry the meeting with the horticultural society went on so long. You shouldn't have waited up for me. Oh, all right. Don't look at me like that! How about Lamb's *Tales from Shakespear?* I think you'd like *The Winter's Tale* – but it's a bit complicated for someone who's drunk a bottle of Chenin Blanc and two double brandies. Do you think, by the way, that your friend Nut is interested in Bea?' She imagined Oscar to be well out of the picture, for surely he'd never come back to Bea now, but Nut could be a complication, a distraction to Bea's burgeoning talent. She'd not actually seen any of the dear girl's work yet, but last time she'd called there'd been a satisfying smell of oils drifting about the house, and the odd paint-stained finger which meant she was at least doing something.

'Might be. He'd not tell me if he was.' He sounded cautious.

'Keep an eye out for me, would you, to see if anything develops?'

'No, Nest, it's none of your business, is it? Naughty, nosy little Nest. Come on, let's have the lamb's tail story, then. If you don't start at once, I'll start on you.' So Nest commenced their strange game of literary foreplay, reading aloud while he leant up on one elbow, listening with his eyes closed and softly stroking her thigh.

Chapter Seven

Honey-scented seakale, then scarlet poppies and brilliant blue viper's bugloss rampaged across the shingle and insects in their thousands hummed, buzzed, bit and bumbled as Bea continued to explore in the few spare day time segments she grudgingly allowed herself.

The trips into the world outside the painting room were rewards for work completed but a tooth-achingly cold early evening swim from a deserted beach near the firing ranges proved more of an of an endurance test than a prize. Holly and foxgloves grew in these unpromising surroundings and freshwater lakes lay hidden among the scrub of goat willows, marred a little by an ugly scattering of rusting beer tins and plastic bottles jettisoned by the angling fraternity. In addition to the recent rubbish, the land was still blighted by concrete detritus from the Second World War, but it was hard to mind such things while larks sang overhead and on one duck-egg-blue-and-primrose morning she stood and painted from the vantage point of a ruined, tip-tilted concrete gun emplacement. She was ignored by an absent-minded looking heron standing as if tranced at the water's edge, but was kept amused by the abrupt illusionist vanishings and reappearances of grebes on the little lake.

Further inland, she uncovered the open grave of a skeletal horse-drawn carriage in a shallow dip and drew its unintelligible iron suspension parts, fanned out like rusting angels' wings among possessive thistles. Frogs flopped into dykes, always just ahead of her footsteps and at night they put up a froggy chorus as deafening as the cicadas in a Corsican pine forest.

Low-growing dog roses and ground hugging blackthorn wove themselves across the stones, splashed with bright pink centaury and white and yellow stonecrops. She sat contemplatively eating an apple on an old railway sleeper, unsuccessfully trying to distract herself from Nut-thoughts by searching at her feet for the minute plants which Nest had pointed out, the lemon yellow mouse-eared hawkweed and pink dove's foot cranesbill. Since the night of the witches she'd kept a half-Nelson on her emotions, in fact had swaddled them so tightly that they couldn't breathe, let alone wail in the middle of the night but she was delighted when Nut visited and guiltily thought about him afterwards when she was alone, mentally warming up her hands in his hair.

To save money on petrol, she acquired a maidenly upright bicycle from Jerry Rumm for a tenner and relearnt the skill one evening in the dusk with him standing by his gate shouting encouragement as she rattled up and down the dusty track, the bike stuck dangerously in the dried-out groove of a tractor rut. He shook his head disbelievingly but applauded as she rode past him over-confidently, yelling out: 'Look! Look! No hands!' Next day he came and pulled her out when she went, shrieking with laughter, headfirst into a bank of sedges and when she swerved and banged her knee on his gate post, he kindly brought her out a compress of witch-hazel. She re-painted the bicycle in scarlet and green stripes.

Jerry Rumm, shading his eyes when he saw it, commented that at least it was now pretty certain no one would dare to make off with it.

Back in the painting room, time was measured only by the

soft sounds of the brush on canvas, the sharp scraping of pocket knife on pencil and the steady encroachment of shapes across surfaces. Working four hours, five hours at a stretch, the number of new canvases lined up against the walls slowly multiplied as her imagination expanded and filled the painting room with whispering stories and silly jokes. She sang and whistled, adding to and consulting stacks of old sketchbooks, re-working and rearranging drawings, careful not to lose their immediacy.

Round about the beginning of June she arranged a seaside picnic for Mrs Lewis, a happily self-inflicted break in routine. It was showery in the morning and a little breezy, not the best of days for an outing, but warm enough as they drove out through the prettier lanes till forced to travel along the incoherent ribbon strip of coastal bungalows, hilariously deflected from their invasive unloveliness by the coyness of their nautical names: Halyards, Hispaniola, Scuppers, Bilges, Chip's Plaice and with touching irony, Sea View – this last built on land so low that even from the new loft-conversion windows the sea must have been teasingly hidden by the height of the sea wall across the road. Chalked signboards advertised Fresh Fish and Bait, two London cabs stood washed and polished on the forecourt of one and a dusty hearse was drawn up before another, its glass sides advertising a band, predictably The Overtakers.

It was the hearse which reminded Mrs Lewis that there was a church in the area which she'd always wished to visit; the church had an ossuary, the bones of which were already centuries old when disinterred some five hundred years before, when building work was in progress in the town. The mask-like skulls were prettily arranged, upturned brain-bowls in tiers in the wall arches of the crypt, along with a veritable hedge of femurs decorated here and there by the insertion of more skulls. Both Bea and Mrs Lewis found the effect matter-of-fact and calming rather than macabre and the curator pointed out that as one progressed along the ash-dry bone hedge, the skulls became more and more polished and rubbed, due to the visitors gradually becoming brave enough to give them a little caress as they progressed into the dark. Perhaps prepared for disgusted shrieks and overdramatic shudders and fearing for its safety, he doubtfully handed Bea a skull to hold, a child's skull, the eggshell lightness of which was infinitely touching, as were the yet unknitted plates of bone, the little molars still cusped, unworn by years of eating gritty, stone-ground bread.

The sky cleared and having done enough yoricking, they sat on a wall in the steeply sloping churchyard to eat their sandwiches, near the gravestone of Lionel Lukin, who '... was the first who built a lifeboat and was the original inventor of that Principle of Safety ...' A fat black cat made love to them, undoubtedly attracted by scents of tuna and hard-boiled egg.

'Now I wonder what your name is?' said Mrs Lewis, rubbing his broad chest and admiring his thunderous purrs and mighty whiskers.

'Morgue?' suggested Bea, still preoccupied with the rows of empty-eye sockets in the crypt and the thoughts and desires of those soft, long-gone brains and bodies, their impulses switched off and finally earthed.

They drove back along the coast before stopping for a walk and Mrs Lewis shared Bea's pleasure in the absence of prettiness in the landscape – 'How Ravilious would have loved the gravel-works!' She seemed to be advancing in unexpected hops and skips since their last meeting, shaking off the last traces of the tranquilliser zombie. They traipsed happily across the muddy shoreline, Bea slowing her pace to that of Mrs Lewis. Prehistoric-looking, reptilian cormorants sat on posts. Smart black-and-white oystercatchers sped with clockwork energy in parallel with their reflections along the fitfully gleaming sand, bobbing over ruched and pin-tucked ridges. Far out in the shallows a solitary shrimper in waders pushed his wide net across the outgoing tide.

'So, what have you been doing since we last met?' Bea asked, 'Are you still feeling better, off the pills?'

'Much, much better, though I still have the occasional shaky day, but it's easier to concentrate now, and I've ordered lots of books, and taken out subscriptions to some art magazines. I'm finding out what's been happening in that world, since I slid out of it.'

'What name did you use, when you were still painting?' asked Bea, bending over to retrieve first a razor shell, then a half-full discarded pink plastic lighter, which she shook and tried to flick into life, but the cog was stiff and rusting, so she put it in her pocket.

'Geraldine O'Brien, my maiden name. My husband, Richard, was a bit cross about that, after we married. But I pointed out that it would only confuse people to change it, since I'd already started to sell work under the name of O'Brien. What about you?'

'I've never even signed a picture. I've not tried to sell anything, so it hasn't been necessary but I'd use Bea Kerepol, I think. Not Mitty.'

'No, it sounds a woolly, fingernail-catching sort of name. Kerepol is unusual – is it Breton, or Cornish perhaps?'

'My great-grandfather came from Brittany, from somewhere near Saint Brieuc. He fell in love with an English governess and followed her back to England. It seemed to be a very happy marriage; he became a partner in a publishers and they had two sons and four daughters. In the old brown photographs we've got left, they're both always looking at each other and smiling. None of that stern, glassy, eyes-front look that you normally see in Edwardian photographs.'

'Photographs can lie, you know. I've photos of my husband and myself, grinning like maniacs.'

'And you didn't feel like grinning? You were unhappy, even then?'

Mrs Lewis halted and stood still, her hands deep in her

pockets, the skirts of her thin fawn raincoat flapping in the light breeze, a bleb of moisture on the tip of her nose. She lifted her chin and stared out to sea, meditating on an answer, appearing taller, straighter. She was changing before Bea's eyes from being Mrs Lewis into Geraldine O'Brien.

'I've only just started to think about it. I'd forgotten so much, intended to forget, I believe. I worshipped him to start with. But I think now he had a streak of cruelty, and was intolerably possessive. He wanted, it seemed at times, to *be* me.'

She stared at Bea, the pale eyes watering. 'He turned me against my family, one by one, destroyed my trust in them, and theirs in me. Then he started on my friends, little sneers here, unkind remarks there. I was very young when I married, very immature and something of a fool. He managed my career, dealt with the art dealers, commissions, everything. I was hardly allowed to meet anyone and I did so love people and parties. Then there was Simon Greensand.' She paused again. 'Forgive me, at my age time's short – I can't be bothered to wait for you to find out things. I have to tell you all at once, now.'

'Yes?' said Bea, captivated by the emergent tragedy, and a little flattered by the confidence of the older woman. 'Simon Greensand?'

'He had a gallery in Chelsea; was well thought of by the artists who showed there. I think he saw how it was with Richard and me. He refused to deal with Richard, only with me directly. The amount of work I was doing was dwindling steadily throughout the nineteen sixties, and had become a little unfashionable, being figurative, painterly. The young things, op, pop, bop and flop and the hard edge crowd were all the rage.' She laughed, a little bitterly. 'However he had clients who still liked the kind of work I did, and I was, had been, quite well known. Simon gave me a couple of shows, quite surprisingly successful, and Richard ... Richard made my life hellish after that.'

'What, jealous of your success or of Simon Greensand?'

'Of Simon certainly, but perhaps of both. I fell for Simon, although I must have been over forty, but he was married, very bourgeois and proper, with children, and though it was reciprocated, there was nothing we could honestly do ... It's a terrible mistake to force people against their grain. Richard slowly destroyed my confidence, accurately planting doubts like darts, and I felt I had no one else to turn to, to gainsay him. He wanted to be *the* magician in our lives, to control all the tricks. I was a fool.' She looked away again, and became distracted by the sight of a vast block of concrete which lay abandoned in the sea, with wreck-marker posts at each corner. 'What *is* that great incongruous lump doing there?'

'I've been told it's a piece of the Mulberry Harbour which slipped its towline, I suppose as it was being moved to France for the D Day landings. It was obviously too big to move again, once it had sunk. I don't understand how it floated at all, unless it was on some sort of giant barge. You can almost walk out to it at low tide. But do go on, you were telling me about your husband?'

'Ah, yes, my cautionary tale. I had what he called a nervous breakdown. That was in nineteen seventy. We stayed together but I didn't paint much again. He looked after me like a china doll, took over my sadness, even made it *his* so much that I felt I had no right to grieve over either Simon or my inability to paint. He suffocated me with forgiveness. I'm sorry – I'm a boring old woman.' She sniffed and smiled a watery smile at Bea. 'I've only unearthed all this myself so recently, not had time to rearrange it to make it sound less self-pitying, and I haven't blamed myself enough.' Her face drooped a little. 'I'm a little tired, Bea. Perhaps you should take me home.' She was distressingly returning to being Mrs Lewis.

'Of course, if you want. But wouldn't you care to come to my house first, and have some tea?'

Mrs Lewis considered for a moment, 'Yes, that *would* be wonderful, to go to someone else's house, although you mustn't think I've been entirely absent from such places for ever. There were days when I felt quite well, and even got as far as London. Although I couldn't always remember what I'd gone there *for*, when I got there, I seemed to have quite a nice time. I did notice things in my pill-addicted days! It was just hard to think, to decide what they meant.' She turned in step with Bea and they started the walk back. 'There is still a Greensand gallery, though not in Chelsea any more. It's moved to Savile Row, alongside the pinstripe and grey flannel.'

'And is it still run by your Simon Greensand?'

'I didn't ask. I did go up to see him, quite some time after Richard died and found the old gallery was now a boutique. I tracked down the new one eventually, but when I arrived it was so awe-inspiringly modern and spacious, I merely stood outside the door, too frightened to go in. Too old, and changed, you see.'

Refreshed by the experience of being driven somewhere new and by the form of transport, traces of the more animated Geraldine O'Brien confusingly reappeared on reaching Nest's house. 'A real doll's house. Out here in the middle of nowhere! Now, how extraordinary! The sort of house one visits in dreams.'

'It is, isn't it? Just like that. Only now I'm inside it, turning it inside out and dreaming in it, not of it. At first each time I came down the track, I felt that it might not be there and that I'd imagined it existed.'

Geraldine sat down on the little sofa, staring about her.

'I can see which bits of it are yours already and which were here before.'

'Which bits are mine?' asked Bea, returning with a tea-tray, unfortunately printed with cartoon Dalmatian puppies.

'Well, not that tray, for a start. How ugly it is, but one is not allowed to make judgements like that any more, is one? Now everything has to be equally valid so that no one gets hurt, ever? It must be a terrible shock to the poor young things, being told at art school that whatever work they produce is of *importance*, so they have nothing to kick against, then getting out into the world and finding that there are still some old-fashioned critics lurking in the corners, waiting to come out and nip their self-important little ankles. But I expect their self-confidence is so high they take no notice.' She sounded surprisingly malicious. 'But I'm going off on a tangent. What's yours? That bunch of the black-and-white feathers in the grey jug. Are they from magpies, or plovers? The scarlet mugs? The blue glass. The saffron yellow Indian cushion by that awful fireplace? I never could get to grips with Art Nouveau; it reminds me of my mother – all those plants rearing up and twisting about as if they'd been formally poisoned. Thank you, yes. I'd like some sugar. Now that is your work, the red man painting on the mantelshelf. You've made it look like an altar, with the candlestick, and all those shells. Is he worthy of it? Bring it over here and let me see?' Bea did so, biting her thumbnail and apprehensively scrutinising Geraldine's face for clues. She became alarmed at the prolonged silence.

Geraldine put her red mug down on the floor and stood up.

'May I see what else you've done, while you've been here?' She looked almost shaken but at least it didn't appear to be with disappointment. Bea hadn't realised her own need to hear approval. It *did* matter what Geraldine thought because she most obviously knew what she was talking about and it would be sensible at last to find out what. Twisted up inside with nerves, she led the way upstairs and showed her to the painting room.

Geraldine fairly danced about in her green socks, stooping over and moving smaller canvases, asking for help in turning around those facing the walls, propping one up on the seat of the white chair, muttering and grunting.

'Dear girl!' She swung around, her face alert and interested, ten, twenty years younger. Even her flaccid hair seemed to spring out and brighten. 'This has quite made my afternoon. I can't think what you've been *hiding* this away for, for so long. Your observation is acute and the technique is good, very good. You've developed your own iconography but it is really quite accessible and most original. I do think you should be able to do well ...' she beamed, 'Carry on, like this, and never let anyone tell you otherwise. Good heavens, is this really only two months' work? You must have been sweating blood.' She gasped for breath and sat down on the red-covered bed and clasped her hands together. 'It *is* exciting, seeing something fresh. I suppose that comes from your *not* having been trained with other people – they can all come out like little sausages. I gather the sausage machine at the moment is, on the whole, still churning out "conceptual", and the concept of horror is highly rated. I've been catching up, you see. Not that I ever lost touch entirely.'

Bea's worst fears were assauged, but she still felt an awkwardness. She was outside, untouched by the unaccustomed flow of praise. Experiences at school, contrary to Mrs Lewis's beliefs, had taught her never to expect encomiums and she still gnawed doubtfully at a thumbnail.

'I needed an opinion, I can see that now, from someone who knew how to look and I'm so pleased you like them. Can we leave them, and finish tea?' The pictures were disturbing with all their fronts facing outwards into the room at once, an audience waiting for a play to start, rather than the reverse.

Once they were safely downstairs again, the now almost ebullient Geraldine continued chatting and asking questions.

'Tell me about this red-haired man so sound asleep across the paper. Is he a lover?' She was quite unabashed to ask the question and Bea curiously did not find it intrusive and laughed.

'No. Not yet; he's been held off till ... till I've got to grips with what I'm doing. But he may not wait that long. I'm sure he thinks I'm playing games with him, but I'm not. I can't just let go and jump in, somehow.'

'Remember my cautionary tale. It's so easy for misunderstandings to arise. Perhaps women artists shouldn't marry. Husbands so often either want your whole attention or swamp you with all theirs, which comes to the same thing. Either way it's impossibly difficult to concentrate, but I'm being flippant. It's never that simple.' Her pale eyes, now alight with interest and fixed on Bea, seemed to have assumed a deeper, greenish tint; they reminded Bea quite forcefully of Nut's and she felt a little spasm of longing. 'But no, *you* mustn't turn your back on loving,' said the paradoxical Geraldine, more gently for Bea had looked quite lost for a moment. Bea was compelled to change the subject.

'When you spoke of horror earlier on ... do you think it's because we've been brought up to see horror as an entertainment? She was thinking it out for the first time. 'It seems a perversion, an unclean fascination, but perhaps it's a *need*, or a way of preparing oneself?'

'Yes, I'm sure we've a need to rehearse our responses to fear at a distance, so that if it happens one knows one's lines. I think women particularly do that type of rehearsing, imagining terrible accidents to our husbands, running through our children's funerals, making ourselves quite ill with fear as a precaution against eventual loss. I was born between the wars, but obviously some of the generation on either side experienced unbelievably disgusting atrocities – no rehearsal, but for real. A very few of them were inebriated by the excitement and found peacetime impossibly dull, but most of them didn't care to talk about it; any bloodlust they may have had was quickly sated. Read Siegfried Sassoon, or Robert Graves.'

'I have read *Goodbye To All That*. I was appalled.'

'It *was* appalling. You must remember to stay appalled. Now, I should go home. I've taken up far too much of your precious time and it's been a great treat, seeing you and your work. You must come and have lunch with me soon; I could go into Parden by bus and get ready-made dishes from Marks and Spencer!'

'Mrs Lewis, Geraldine, I mean, how does one get started? How do I get someone to sell my pictures? I know I haven't enough work yet, to show anyone. But I do need to start thinking about what the next step is and it all seems so intimidating.'

'Let me think about it, my dear. I'm so out of touch with everyone but perhaps I can come up with a plan of action. I think it really is time I looked up some old acquaintances. From now on, I intend to grow old boldly.' This sounded like a threat.

Bea's confidence soared after Geraldine's visit. She continued to drive herself hard and there rarely seemed enough daylight. The dreamtime was over. She was fired up with an energy and a certainty only once before equalled in her unfortunate determination to marry Oscar. The painting had taken precedence over everything else and she was gaining more and more control, knowing the likely effect in advance of every patch of colour, of each line, of each brushstroke on the canvas.

It was clear that several themes were emerging. The marble Freda appeared in more pictures. In one she sat as decorously as her draperies would allow, on a bar stool in a recognisably gloomy Bell and Hatchet in conversation with Oscar and Agnes who loomed menacingly over her. She sported a nose ring and her plump stone arms had acquired graffiti: '*noli me tangere*' round one upper arm as if tattooed, and 'man the lifeboats' round the other. There hadn't been quite enough space on the curving surface of the arm for the final four letters of either inscription. The other customers in the bar were the fishermen, watching with the wide-eyed horror of Fuseli phantoms as a pair of scarlet witches danced a tango. In another, Freda floated over the roof of Little Rumm, scattering a benediction of poppy petals over Mrs Lewis who sat in a deckchair in the garden beneath, reading a newspaper. The other works were mercifully less arcane.

But it wasn't easy. The major problem was the volume of interruptions. It seemed that in seeking seclusion she'd found a greater degree of popularity than she'd known when in circulation and felt unable to turn away the visitors who were intrigued by exaggerated stories of her lonely life spread around by Agnes and had travelled out to relieve the unhappy solitude.

In order to curtail the invasions she went visiting herself but found that the visited were all dying to see where she lived and promised to drop in soon, which quite defeated the object of *her* visits. Anyway she did enjoy company, even if guilty afterwards.

Three days after the picnic with Geraldine, Mary Dunnock arrived unannounced with her four children under seven, one of whom was immediately sick in the wastepaper basket. Mary, slim in her sensible denims and spotless white blouse, wandered about erratically after the children as they each in turn endeavoured to escape; Bea wondered how she kept herself so pristine while the children were so thoroughly encrusted with chocolate and marmalade. Mary continually broke off her conversation to answer their questions and demands and murmured discontentedly when she saw the red painting of Nut, that Bea was so lucky to have such talent and that she'd often thought herself how she would like to paint, given the time.

'Of course, it must be *easy* for you with no other worries,' she said, unblushingly, 'but then I'd no idea you were so talented. No, Megan, the top of the bottle unscrews *this* way. How do you get started, Bea? Do you drift about the marsh ... that's right, Harry, oh dear, you've spilt it ... waiting for inspiration to strike?'

Bea gritted her teeth at the implication that having talent was an unfair short cut, meant one did not have to sweat at it or frustratedly rip up days of work because it was crap. There were frequent occasions, unseen by other people, when things did go spectacularly wrong and she was either in a state of frenzy or of despair. However, Mary was a cheerful person and her visit was refreshing, particularly so since she did not deign to even mention Oscar.

The painting of Nut had not gone unnoticed by Nest who'd popped in with Blue and a bottle of wine one evening and towards the end of her second glass, she exhorted Bea to concentrate on the work in hand and not be distracted by pretty faces.

'And how are the Daughters of Nature, Aunt Nest?' Nest looked fiercely at Bea and indicated with a violent jerking of eyebrows and other physical hintings that she was to shut up in front of Blue.

'Oh, not very interesting,' she said dismissively and rather hurriedly. 'A lot of unsound eco-babble, with very little scientific backup. I told them they must have facts at their fingertips, facts up their noses and coming out of their ears if they want to get anywhere with officialdom.' Bea resisted asking her if she could borrow the red cloak.

Jane telephoned frequently, reminding her gently that she was lucky to have friends and relations so interested in her wellbeing, not to forget that she still had a family nor that Patrick would be home soon and that a publisher had been found for the Cadwell Commonplace Book, work on which was proceeding apace.

'Congratulations, Mum, I think you're a star. You'll prob- ably outsell *Country Diary of an Edwardian Lady* and make millions in spin-offs. You can have Cadwell Egg Cosies, Cadwell Cooking Pots and Cadwell Lavatory Paper … It isn't really going to be called that, though, is it? Don't you need something a bit snappier? Mum, I love seeing you and Dad. I love seeing everybody. I just wish they would ring first, or at least come in the evening.'

'If they do telephone, you keep putting them off. You must be more sociable, darling. You can't be throwing paint about all the time.'

But the interruptions increased. She thought they might as well make themselves useful and asked the visitors to sit for lightning water-colour sketches, shutting her ears if they were inclined to Oscar-speak, talking effects while thinking causes.

And there was Nut. She noticed that she never counted him as an interruption and even sought him out herself or came across him about his business on occasions. Even if she had not seen him for several days, the idea that he was working in his railway carriage or travelling about the marsh somewhere was enormously comforting. Her regard and liking for him steadily increased and they had reached a stage of warm but still wary, teasing companionship with a pleasant, almost exhilarating tension between them – unfinished business. But, as Nest said, he was an impediment to concentration and confused her devices and desires merely by knowing what they were. To Nut, she was increasingly a frustrating and tantalising enigma.

Out on a foray late one afternoon on the exotic bicycle, she was intrigued by the looming silhouette of a Tudor castle lurking apparently untouristed and inaccessible in the distance of the flat land and rode joltingly among the sheep along a grassy track, towards its crumbling, golden biscuit-coloured, sandstone walls. Sadly it was barred against her. She leant the bike against a wall and on walking round it seeking an entry, she came slap up against the solidity of Nut as she rounded a bastion, startling him and almost winding herself.

'What are you doing here?' she asked, rather rudely because her heart had jumped at the contact and continued to racket about after they disentangled themselves.

'I was supervising the collection of some core samples about two miles away and thought I'd walk over for a private viewing. Did you want to get inside? I've spotted a way.' He guided her round to the other side.

'The whole pleasure in this place,' he said, giving her a leg up to a gap where a grating had been at some time illicitly removed and giving her a friendly shove through it, 'is its emptiness. No car parks, none of that intrusive heritage stuff, signposting, payment booths and bookstalls. It's only recently been opened up on occasions in the late summer. It's too far for most people to bother to walk.' He squeezed his shoulders through and leapt down to join her in the sunlit dereliction.

They poked about, Bea bewitched by it in spite of its clearly having been in use for many years as a secret place for teenage drinking and other exploratory pastimes. In one area the odd crisp packet was pushed into a crevice and a drink can thrust into a rabbit hole, for it was a rabbits' paradise with ankle-wrenching burrows in the sandy rubble. 'I love Jim B. 1956' and the inevitable 'Chris is a wanker '92' were scored into the walls and a couple of used condoms lay limply among the weeds. A russet dragonfly large enough to qualify for helicopter status roared past, its copper and gold-spangled cellophane wings clattering harshly.

'And have you finished *Gulliver's Travels?*' asked Nut, presenting her with a jackdaw's feather.

'No. I'm still working at it. He's just jumped off the flying island, arrived in Lagado and met the old man who spent eight years trying to extract sunbeams from cucumbers. I was feeling a touch irritable at the time and thought that it was a good description of painting.'

'And why aren't you extracting sunbeams today?' he enquired, gazing at her as they sat together on a stone block in the honey-coloured light.

'One has to have a break sometimes! I weakly decided that it was too beautiful an afternoon to stay indoors any longer.'

'Weak isn't a word I'd ever use about you. You appear to have a most steely self-control.'

'What? Me? You must be joking. I'm the world's worst procrastinator. Anyway, the steely look can be put on in a flash – it stops people nagging. You make your eyebrows go straight across and stare at the spot between the person's eyes.'

'Go on, do it. Oh I see! Horribly intimidating!' He chortled with laughter and then leant back on his elbows, looking at her more seriously. 'Procrastinator, certainly. I'll go along with that but once you *have* made up your mind, you seem to stick to a decision like bubble gum to hair.'

'Is there by any chance a column of smoke in the distance? Do I guess what this is leading up to?'

'Oh, I hope so, Bea.' He leant over and put a hand behind

her head and turned it towards him, cool sea eyes sparkling with intent but she leapt up and dashed off, laughing a little nervously. 'Absolutely not, not here.'

'I only thought I might try for a kiss. Or have I got to ask your father for your hand first?'

'I'm still married. I won't ever get married again. Been there, done that.'

'So, it's "not now", then it's "not here". I'll be frightened to try again in case the next one's "not ever". I'll crumble into dust shortly. Then you'll be sorry.' He lay down on top of a narrow wall and folded his long hands together as if praying, a figure on a tomb, his face caught in a shaft of late afternoon gold, his lids closed. The image was chilling.

'No! Please, don't!' she cried out. 'You look like a knight crusader lying there. Didn't they have their legs crossed on their tombs to show they had been to the Holy Land? And shouldn't you have a little dog, or a lion at your feet? But it's definitely not "not ever". It's time I got back. I'm on the bike and it's quite a way from here.'

'Time?' said Nut, opening his eyes again and turning his head towards her. 'Time? Time's a bugger. *At* nine o'clock, *by* six o'clock, *before* next Tuesday, *after* tea, *only* a minute, *just* a second – this time, sometime never. How I hate having to work to other people's schedules! Time is for other people. You've got as much time as you need, honeybee. Just grab it.'

Bea laughed helplessly, since as he lay on the wall, she had become aware of the size of his feet.

'What huge boots, absolutely vast boots!'

He suddenly rolled off the wall and sat on the dusty ground, looking down at them with pride. 'Yes, they're pretty impressive, aren't they? Size thirteen.' He strengthened the Ulster accent. 'My mother said I'd the most beautiful big feet in the whole of County Down.' He looked up at her and held out a hand. 'Help me up. You are good at turning the subject. I tell you, your body and soul are made of stainless steel, just like a carving knife.

Pitiless woman, *Belle Dame sans Merci*, Iron Maiden ... Status Quo ... I have to try now and again, to keep my hand in. At least a hug, then, to keep me going, if I'm not allowed to make love to you.'

'Oh, all right!' Chuckling she hugged him and her knees let her down by nearly giving way.

He whispered in her ear — 'It's always the legs that go first. Me too — I know, you know,' he was reluctant to let go, having to keep close to her, 'I saw it in your face, the first time you came to my house. It was the most amazingly erotic expression, a stunning turn-on ...' He stopped and looked about him as if not quite sure where he was. 'Oh, well. Now getting out of here might be a bit more difficult than getting in ...'

She rode off across the nibbled grass on her bicycle, wobbling because he was watching and acutely feeling his longing looping after her like a lasso, rang the bell in recognition. She dreamed of him that night, striding across the green land with a great measuring stick in each hand, a chalk outline against grass, the Long Man of Wilmington, the Long Man of the Marsh.

During these weeks of early summer Agnes visited with a frequency that bordered on harassment. She was often short tempered and arrived unannounced or phoned at least twice a week to talk at length about her 'treatments' with Ludmilla, who was, it seemed, enjoying a longer period of favour than was usual. Arriving earlier one Thursday morning than Bea had expected, she walked straight into the house and started up the narrow stairs.

'Bea? Are you all right? What's that horrendous racket?'

Bea came out of the painting room, looking vague and preoccupied and preventing her from coming up any further, like a schoolchild shielding its work from a fellow pupil in case they copied the answers.

'Oh, the radio. Hold on a second, I'll turn it off.' She nipped back up again. 'I kept hoping it would get better,' she shouted out, 'but it hasn't. The composer talked about it first and said he wanted to create organised chaos, but I couldn't detect any attempts at organisation.'

'It sounds like a someone banging a cat with a carpet beater,' said Agnes, crossly, thwarted again in her attempts to get into Bea's painting room. 'Are you ready to come out to lunch?'

'I thought as it was still so early, you could perhaps sit for me for a few minutes?' Bea now had paintbox and water-colour book in hand.

Agnes grudgingly agreed. Sitting on the sunny steps where they now habitually sat for Bea's enforced counselling sessions and now rather astonishingly attempting to arrange a reconciliation, Agnes rumoured that Oscar was cooling off Andreary, harping tiresomely on the subject while Bea patiently sat paintbrush in hand, watching Seb destroying the wounded pink bicycle. He appeared to have forgiven her for the Battle of Slapped Knee and gave her a sly grin as he unscrewed part of the bicycle bell and tossed it over the wall.

Agnes was a lousy sitter and needed short breaks every five minutes, getting up and drifting about, looking and poking at things, leaping from subject to subject but, a symphonic nuisance, returning too frequently to her theme.

'He's been seen drinking on his own, in the evenings. I'm sure he's miserable and it's all gone wrong. Do you think your aunt would mind if I took this large flowerpot? I've got a pink geranium that needs a bigger home.'

'He often used to have a drink on his own, in the evenings, and no, I'm sure she wouldn't mind about the pot. Do come and sit down for me again, I've so nearly finished.'

'But Sheila said he was mournful,' said Agnes broodingly, first shaking out a root-bound, pot-shaped clump of stony earth which burst in an untidy dark smudge across the flagstones, before replacing herself on the steps again, with her legs in yet another position. Bea rearranged her.

'Tough titty! I'm glad he's suffering.'

'Why don't you come round to us for supper?' asked Agnes artfully. 'I could arrange for Oscar to drop in afterwards. Then you could meet on neutral ground? I could ask Ludmilla, too.'

'Are you mad? Don't you ever give up? It sounds horrific. I don't want, at the moment, Agnes, to meet Ludmilla on any terrain at all. Nor Oscar. I mean it. Nor, obviously, does he. He left me. I'm not saying never, but I'm serious about what I'm doing for once in my life. Now is not the time. You've changed your tune a bit, haven't you? And I'm thinking of pouring the paint water over your head, if you don't sit still! There's a lovely green reflection just along your jawbone and under your nose. If Oscar was having second thoughts, he'd tell me through the solicitors. Why don't you go round and cheer him up yourself, if you're convinced he's so depressed?'

'Well, actually . . . I did go over one Saturday morning.'

'You did what?' Bea sharply raised an eyebrow.

'I just went to see them, him and Andrea, only she was out shopping, he said. Honestly Bea, he doesn't *look* happy. He pretended to be very jolly, but I could see through it.'

'Agnes, please! Just shut up! He's got no intention of coming back to me. He's still with her, isn't he? And I've just answered the last and bullying solicitor's letter written on his behalf, and sent a new key to the cottage. That was childish of me, getting the locks changed, I must admit. Anyway I've told the solicitor that he'll have to wait till I decide what to do about the cottage and things. It's all too soon.'

'It's over two months. I visited Ludmilla the other day, and told her all about it. She's so supportive. She thinks you're in deep grieving mode and need to rediscover your inner strengths.'

'Bugger Ludmilla and her modes. Why did you go to see him?' Bea asked aggressively. A lobotomy would be too minor an operation for Agnes.

'Just nosing about. He seemed quite pleased to see me. He

was wandering about the garden with a spanner in his hand, as if he was looking for something to unscrew, for a change. Why have you made my legs look so short?'

'Sit down, please? Partly it's because I've got too many long vertical lines already, and partly because, from this angle, they do look a trifle chubby. Aach!' A fly dragged its feet across a pink painted cheek.

'Oscar . . .'

Bea flicked a plantain head at her and abandoning the water-colour, got up from the mat where she'd been sitting. The more Agnes pushed Oscar at her, the more she felt inclined to go in the opposite direction. Agnes, however, was well pleased with the conversation. Seb gave a shrill scream of triumph as the bicycle chain broke and he pulled it off, waving it in the air and clouting himself around the cheek with it.

'I'll get him a flick knife for his fifth birthday, shall I?' Bea asked. 'Then he'll be all trained up for when teddy boys come back into fashion. Come on. The idea was to have sandwiches in the garden at the Eeldyke Inn, wasn't it? We'd better get going soon. I'm starting work again at two in the afternoon, without fail.'

'We're only late because you wanted to paint me. Fifteen minutes you said, and it's been half an hour. When can I see upstairs in your secret room? When can I meet the hunky Nutty?'

'When *I* know what I'm up to, and not making a fool of myself, that's the answer to both questions and it *has* only been fifteen minutes.' She hadn't told Agnes about Mrs Lewis's visit.

'You always were too worried about that. Unlike me, you never have made a fool of yourself in the past. Oh God! I do fancy a break from Phil. I've been quite faithful, you know, since we got married. That's nearly a year. He's really getting on my nerves at the moment – so critical, you wouldn't believe! Just because I'm having a break between jobs – well actually, I don't seem to have a job in the offing. I shall have to go and shake up my agent or do the rounds with a portfolio again. I hate that too. Showing all one's best work to some snotty art director, only to have him say 'We'll put you on file'. I hate being filed; I can imagine myself abandoned, sex-less, chocolate-less and wine-deprived, in some dark drawer for twenty years. Oh, poor Agnes. She does need some fun! You've always been too careful to have fun, Bea.' Bea wondered what she did with Seb, when she was out having fun. It must be difficult, being a baby-sitter short.

In the garden of the Eeldyke Inn they came across Nut poring over a notebook and a packet of monkey nuts, long legs in mega-boots stretched out along the bench in the sunshine with hens clucking and pock-pocking around him, searching for miscarried nuts. Bea wished strongly that they had chosen another pub, wanting to keep him to herself, particularly did not want him to be exposed to Agnes, not in the ranty-tanty mood she was in today.

He looked up, startled as Seb hurtled past him in hot pursuit of a cabbage white butterfly, straight through a flowerbed of scarlet and orange snapdragons, then he saw Bea and gave the beaming smile that so unnervingly disarmed her.

Agnes fielded the greeting and caught the little tremor in Bea as she responded. Had anyone ever smiled at her in such a way, she asked herself. No, truthfully, they had not; grievance settled round her head like an itchy blanket. She did not wait to be introduced but plumped herself down beside him, asked him to budge up a little and kicked off her shoes, wriggling her toes in the grass.

'Mm, that's nice and cool. Hello. I'm Agnes. You must be the famous Nut.'

Bea sat on the other side of the table and watched, at first fascinated, then gradually becoming more and more incredulous, embarrassed and suspicious as Agnes proceeded to complain of the sultry heat, blew down the front of her shirt and then tied the garment up in a knot above her midriff, exposing as much of herself as was possible to the sun and to Nut's rather bewildered gaze. She then talked across Bea, asking wincingly provocative questions, appearing deeply interested and laughing conspiratorially at the answers and generally behaving as if . . . as if what? The landlord came out with the sandwiches and asked Agnes if she wouldn't mind keeping control of her child. He had planted the snapdragons, he pointed out, for the pleasure of his customers, not to act as a playpen for hyperactive little boys. Agnes apologised prettily, said nothing to Seb, delicately picked at her ham sandwich and continued to expend a vast amount of energy on charming Nut. Annoyingly, he seemed to Bea to be quite amused. She shrank back from the conversation, trying not to sulk. The intended quiet snack lunch was brought to a noisy close by an attack on Seb by a cockerel who was mooching about with murder in his heart beneath some bushes and who had taken a dislike to Seb's scarlet shorts. Agnes did a good deal of screaming and flapping, during the course of which her shirt appeared to become both unbuttoned and untied and revealed the fact she wasn't wearing a bra. Nut averted his eyes and hastily grabbed the cockerel up by the legs, hefting it gently over the fence.

Driving back later, rather silently, Bea decided that Agnes had appeared much as she had when she was seventeen – using tactics not out of place in one of the old black-and-white classic films from the 1930s that appeared on TV in the afternoons. The bright repartee, the gales of laughter, the fake-scatty flirtatiousness and the occasional smoulder.

'So, what's he like in bed then?'

'Agnes! Mind your own business!'

'Aha! Don't tell me you haven't yet?'

'I keep telling you, I haven't got the strength to get involved at the moment.'

'Don't leave it too long. He'll get bored, go away and take up with someone more accommodating. He's enormously attractive. I've never met anyone with red hair that I fancied before.'

'You're not allowed to fancy him! We're ... we're ... (what were they?) Anyway, he won't go off.' She was hurt and panicked by the thought.

'They always do.'

Old rivalries had come back to mind and Bea thought, quite reasonably bitchily, that it appeared that in the greater number of cases it was the men Agnes *had* slept with who had always afterwards gone away. 'I will not rise to the bait,' she told herself. 'She's got an attack of the seductions – she used to have the odd try at Oscar now and then, like testing the twanginess of an elastic band, when she thought I wasn't looking – and sometimes when she knew I was. She's just practising. I just wish she wouldn't go over the top.' She was a little rattled.

'I've got seventy-five snapdragons in my pocket,' interrupted Seb the Destroyer.

A couple of days later, Oscar, finding Andrea in yet another of her of pre-supper alcoholic comas when he returned one afternoon early from work, sat shaking with indecision on the steps of the terrace in the still fierce sunshine, massaging the neck of the perpetually quivering whippet for whom he now felt nothing but sympathy and consideration.

'My God,' he thought, 'what a mess she's made of things.' 'Things' had been getting worse; most evenings Andrea awoke snivelling and moaning with a hangover at nine o'clock, and crashed about the kitchen attempting to make supper from increasingly unlikely ingredients – the preceding evening they had eaten flabby slices of ham rolled round cold spaghetti, with mango chutney dolloped erratically across the surface and sprinkled with some roughly chopped green stuff which she had taken for sorrel in the dark, but which being tough and chewy and lacking the acidity of sorrel, he eventually identified as dock leaves. It had been served with fried carrots and a bottle of Krug.

His erstwhile helpless passion had turned to present and powerful disgust and this afternoon he rebelled from carrying her upstairs to bed yet again. Sitting at her desk and sweating in the stuffy heat, he wrote another letter, left it on the silver table beside her as she snored away the rest of the afternoon and packed up most of his belongings. Regretfully he pushed the motorbike into the garage, to be collected at a later date, patted Passe-Partout commiseratingly and drove away through the wrought-iron gates and back to Bellhurst. He returned via the Mummers and stoked up on what passed for lasagne at that establishment: pasta interleaved with lunch time leftovers of chilli mince and beans, which left him feeling aggressive and near-nostalgic for one of Andrea's messes.

Mrs Lewis, or Agnes and if not them, Tom, would now have to give him Bea's address, although he quailed at the idea of asking Tom. He could not go on like this. It was a cock-up. He'd been misled, bewitched, and yearned to return to Bea's pastel calm rather than endure any more of Andrea's poster-paint hysterics. Andrea's ex-husband had cut her allowance since finding out that she had another man living with her. The dear little son to whom he'd looked forward to being a second father had some type of behavioural problem involving animals – at home for half-term, he'd been discovered in the kitchen dissecting a mole on the bread board; after being taken to the cinema in Hastings to see *Robin Hood*, the boy had tried to execute the whippet, hanging it from an apple tree with a length of clothes-line.

On leaving the pub he met a bright and cheerful Agnes hurrying towards him with a letter in her hand.

'Can't stop now, Oscar, I've left Seb on his own. Why don't you come and see me and Phil this evening before you go back to Battle? Any time after seven-thirty – I'll have Seb in bed by then!' And not waiting for an answer she dodged between the cars and ran across the road, dropped the letter in the postbox opposite and turned to wave before disappearing.

The freshly ground points and angles of the new key were stiff in the lock so Oscar jiggled it a little and it turned with an unwilling crunch. The hall smelt dusty and the rush matting squeaked dryly beneath his shoes. All seemed to be in order but once upstairs in the bedroom he detected a faint scent, of jasmine, or perhaps vanilla, at any rate a scent of Bea, hanging softly in the air.

There was an unopened pot of instant coffee on the shelf and some semi-solid brown sugar still in the chipped blue-and-white Spode bowl by the kettle. Bea would never have thrown it away, she was kind to cracked objects but they made him uneasy. He made a mugful of coffee and sat at the kitchen table staring remorsefully at the fading pages of his letter, still impaled by the murderous table fork. He casually tried to pull it out, but was surprised by the depth to which it had penetrated and had to stand and tug hard to remove it. The letter he scrumpled up and threw in the rubbish bin. He reckoned it to have been written under duress and didn't wish to be reminded of its sulphuric acid contents. He would go later to see Phil and Agnes, tell them the good news and he even briefly imagined basking in their approbation. It was time he had a word with Mrs Lewis, whom he imagined would be fairly easy to browbeat into revealing Bea's whereabouts.

He stared open-mouthed at her when she opened the door. In order to leave a free hand to tackle the locks, she held a paintbrush clenched in a grimace between her yellow teeth, and in the other hand was an old wooden artist's palette. Her pale face was enlivened by farcical red lipstick and her eyes were almost fierce. Her long body was encased in a paint-stained lab-technician's coat worn over a jazzy leopardskin print T-shirt. She removed the paintbrush from between her teeth.

'Ah, Oscar. What can I do for you?' Astonishingly self-assured and crisp.

'Mrs Lewis, it is vital I get hold of my wife, contact her, I mean. Would you please give me her address, at once.' Brusque and bullying.

'No.'

'What do you mean, no? I must get in touch. I've come back to her.' Even to Oscar, this sounded a little optimistic. He tried to be ingratiating. 'If I could just get to see her, I'm sure we could sort everything out.' It was ridiculous, pleading with her on the doorstep.

She thought so too, and invited him to come inside. The old-fashioned, scruffy drawing room was scented with cat, with top notes of turpentine. An easel stood beside the window of her sitting room and beside it a newspaper-covered table bore oily scraps of rag and an assortment of stained, ancient tubes of oil paint, the colours of which were unascertainable to the casual eye. On the windowsill, arranged beside a hideous purple Charles and Diana mug and an empty brown glass pill bottle, was the skull of some animal, the haunted hollows and powerful jaws of which were decidedly perturbing. She didn't ask him to sit down and he didn't like the unpromising tightness about her lips.

'You must apply to your father-in-law. She has not changed her instructions *not* to let you know where she is, and I have no intention of going against her wishes.'

The old witch, Oscar thought. She was enjoying this ... it was amazing what a little bit of power would do to a woman. It was demeaning enough that she knew so much about his personal affairs. He tried again, forcing his features into an expression of open-eyed honesty, which merely made him look surprised.

'Mrs Lewis, I'm sure you would not want to stand in the way of a reconciliation. I *must* see her.'

'No, I wouldn't want to stop you getting together again. But it has to come from her. I presume you'd rather not speak to her father − it would be embarrassing for you. I'll pass on the message, tell her you have returned and want to make amends. but I think you may find that she has other ideas.'

'I think that's for me to find out, don't you?' He was getting angry. The leaden pasta was behaving belligerently in his stomach.

'Perhaps. I will pass on your message but she is occupied, and . . .' she looked at him pitilessly and added, without licence, 'she's very happy as she is.'

He'd heard this before and was unable to accept it, nor his failure to obtain what he wanted and he was stunned by the flow of decided opinions. He stared about the room helplessly and his eyes rested on the easel. Keep talking, he told himself, and perhaps she'll relent.

'I didn't know you painted.'

'Yes. But not for some time. I'm doing this in order to get my hand in again. A *vanitas* painting, to remind myself that time is short and how much of it I've already wasted.'

Not understanding what she was talking about, Oscar returned to the subject of Bea.

'What *is* she doing?'

Mrs Lewis ignored his question, but pointed to the skull and said; 'Bea lent me that, the badger's skull. A friend of hers found it, and boiled it up. But the teeth fell out and the jaw came apart in two, see here, where the join is?' She pointed again with her paintbrush to the gruesome object. 'She stuck it all back together again with Uhu but she may have got some of the teeth in the wrong places. It doesn't matter, of course; only a zoologist would know the difference.'

Oscar gaped at her, and she thought what a foolish man he was, though heart-rendingly good-looking. Bea must not be distracted from her painting. She would do everything in her power to stop it.

'I must tidy up now. The light's quite gone.' She was put out by this visit; she could have finished that little bit of ivory cream in the inside of the eye-socket if he had not come. 'The sun's setting. Thank you for letting me know you are back in the cottage.' She walked quickly out into the hall and opened the door, so Oscar had no option but to leave.

He drearily finished unpacking the car then wandered disconsolately about the garden for a while in the twilight, looking at the lush jungle that had been the vegetable patch. How quickly weeds took over, hid the traces of human effort. An untidy row of poppies had appeared, not yet flowering and struggling for air between the lanky potatoes and the spinach; mixing up flowers with the vegetables was a habit of Bea's that had always annoyed him. What were flowerbeds for? What to do, what to do? His stomach was still twingeing but the worst was over. Agnes held the key. When Agnes had visited him over in Sussex she had seemed to be sympathetic to his problems; surely she'd be prepared to part with Bea's address, now that he'd come home again and needed so badly to be forgiven.

It was a warm evening but the town's streets were now empty apart from a few early tourists wandering hand in hand round the ancient streets in the half-light, marvelling at the quaintness but wondering where the action was. The spell of settled hot weather had induced a small hotel in the High Street cautiously to place a few potted bay trees and white plastic chairs and tables outside on the pavement and a group of teenagers had commandeered these and were shrieking and laughing exaggeratedly, their noise echoing against the stolid Georgian brick frontages of the buildings. Oscar approached them feeling old. 'Ooh!' said a girl aged about fifteen, in a voice intended to be heard by the boy sitting opposite her, 'I fancy *him*,' and giggled. Oscar straightened up and held in his stomach as he walked past. 'Go on!' jeered another, sensing blood. 'He's old enough to be your Dad!' Oscar turned thankfully out of sight into Cuckold's Lane, and rang the doorbell of No 8.

'Oscar! How good to see you! I was feeling so bored. Do come in – I'm so sorry, but I forgot that Phil had arranged a drink with a couple of old school friends, a boys' night out.' Agnes was dressed in a small blue cotton dress with tiny straps, not much more than a petticoat and her hair was tied up in a pink towel-turban, dark curlicues escaping, dripping onto her brown shoulders. She led him through the kitchen and out on to the pocket-sized terrace where sat two chairs and a tiny table crowded with glass, half-full bottle of wine, an overflowing ashtray and a guttering candle in a jam jar.

'I was sitting out here, pretending I was in Madrid,' she said, putting a glass in front of him and pouring the wine. Oscar was incapable of the feat of the imagination required to transform a back yard in Bellhurst to a balcony in Spain and watched Agnes apprehensively as she tilted her chair back and leant against the scraggy jasmine that grew in a pot behind her.

She felt wonderfully powerful. Earlier on that evening when she'd gone to post an indignant letter demanding the overdue payment for the last of the *Charlie Chooch* artwork, she'd spotted his car standing outside the pub, its rear seat loaded with boxes covered by a pile of jackets on hangers. On a sudden hunch she had crossed the road, intending to go into the pub to see if he was there, but after having met him in the street had beetled back to the house, battling Seb to bed in a self-defeating hurry, waved goodbye to Phil, whose intended absence that evening she had not forgotten, washed her hair and changed her dress. She'd had to wait some time, but it had been worth it. He was there now, a captive lion before her and Bea could never say she had not pleaded his cause.

'Ssh.' She glanced up with an exaggerated grimace of mock dread and whispering, 'We must keep our voices down. Seb's bedroom window is just above us, and it's so hot I had to open it wide. I couldn't bear it if he woke up!' She removed the towel and shaking dark damp hair about her face, ran her fingers through it vigorously. There was a ripeness to Agnes that even in his distracted state Oscar found appealing.

'I've left Andrea,' he announced portentously.

'I wondered how long it would take for you to find out.'

'Find out what?'

'Ssh! That she's an alcoholic. When you first met her, she'd just come back from a drying-out session in a clinic. I met someone who'd been in the same clinic at the same time, only they were addicted to chocolate. It was Andrea's fourth time in there. That's why her husband pushed off.' Her look was open and sympathetic. 'I wouldn't bother, about Bea, if I were you. She's having a wonderful time.' Go carefully now, she thought, don't rub it in too much, just enough to have him feeling just a little indignant.

'But once she knows I've come home ... now things have changed, she'll see me, give me a chance to explain and try to make it up to her. I can't do that via solicitors.' He was trying to keep his voice down to a whisper. 'God, I feel so appallingly guilty – she must have been desperately miserable. Please, Agnes. Give me her phone number. That bloody Mrs Lewis refused point blank, only agreed to pass on a message. She seems to be a born-again artist, had some sort of awakening. I couldn't believe it was the same woman when she came to the door, all covered in oil paint and her face was all tarted up with bright red lipstick. She looked like an old ferret that had just gorged on a rabbit. I couldn't get through to her. Could you take a letter to Bea for me?'

'Of course I'll tell Bea. I can't give you her address – I promised. But don't, in any case, get your hopes up. She's been pretty adamant she doesn't want to see you again.' She leant forward and put her hand on his arm. 'Poor Oscar. She's become quite cool and unforgiving. Don't forget how well I know her. We were at school together, remember?' Agnes didn't remove her hand at once.

'You do understand, don't you? I simply can't break a confidence. It was a promise. But I'll see what I can do on your behalf. I promise that, too.' She gave his arm a tiny pat, beautifully timed, sensing the tense muscularity beneath the thin cotton of the shirt sleeve, and withdrew her hand slowly, so that it casually brushed his. Kind, sweet little person, he thought.

She's on my side. He felt a surge of optimism. Bea would surely listen to Agnes.

'I really am grateful, Agnes.'

'Mummy! Mummy? What are you doing? I've wet the bed.'

Seb leant out of the window above them, his face pale in the soft darkness and Agnes knocked over her glass.

Chapter Eight

'That was Mags on the phone. I'm just going to zap over and see her – I won't be long. Could you give Seb his supper, do you think?' Agnes stood before the glass by the front door, brushing her hair in smooth, unhurried strokes then bent over and shook it, ruffling it up again.

Phil watched her, intrigued by the apparently pointless ritual. Her eyes were very bright, even in the dark of the hall. 'OK. What's he to have for his supper? And what are we having? And why mess up your hair again just after you've brushed it?'

'Seb's having spag bol and an orange. I've already opened the tin and put it in the pan. I daresay you could manage to open an orange? We're having fish and chips, as we always do on Friday. I'll pick them up after I've seen Mags. And my hair is *meant* to look messed up.'

'Then why did you brush it in the first place?' He was really interested.

'For goodness' sake, Phil! I just wanted a different sort of mess, that's all.' She blew him a kiss, as if she didn't really know him. 'See you later.'

Phil padded back to the sitting room where Seb was sitting on the floor, close up to the television, watching a video. The room was stuffy. Phil made a few companionable noises, opened wide the window on to the street to let in some air, and settled down in the bulgy chair to read the newspaper. It seemed a very noisy video but he managed to concentrate until he heard terrible female screaming and looking up startled, saw Seb, fingers in ears, his head face down on a cushion. The screams came from a semi-nude woman being slowly and realistically chewed up by a giant beetle. He leapt up and turned it off.

'Calm down, Seb. There's a good chap. Whatever were you watching?' He cuddled the small tense body against his own broad shoulder and rocked him. The child was not much more than a baby – how dare Agnes let him see things like that? It was not surprising that he suffered nightmares. 'Look, we'll put on the old Disney one, *Bambi* is it?' He ejected the video and looked at the label on the box. It was rated for over-fifteens. Seb was now sobbing.

'But I don't want to watch *Bambi*. I want the other one back on. I liked it really, really I did.'

'Absolutely not. It's too old for you. Mummy must have got it by mistake.'

'I choosed it.'

'Then she can't have seen the label. Look. It says for people over fifteen and you're not five yet. I'll make your supper and then teach you how to play chess. How about that?' They were still engrossed in the game when Agnes returned.

'Good heavens! Why hasn't Daddy put you to bed? Phil, it's nine o'clock . . .' she stopped, realising she was about to shoot herself in the foot.

'Yes. It's nine o'clock. And he isn't in bed for a reason I'll tell you about after *you've* put him to bed. Let him finish the game first.' Seb, losing concentration with the interruption, was rushing a rook up and down the board, making car noises.

'He seems to have picked it up very quickly? Perhaps he'll be a grand master when he grows up.'

'You're a clever chap, aren't you Seb? He's had his supper, which is more than I have. Check.'

'Well hurry up, Seb darling. Why don't you cheat and then we'll get upstairs all the quicker?'

Phil looked up at her from the floor, the green eye piercing and she saw he was seriously angry. When she returned after putting Seb to bed, he was still fuming.

'So, where are the fish and chips you were going to bring back?'

'Oh shit! I forgot all about them. I . . . I had a bite at Mags's. But you could have gone to get them while I was putting Seb to bed, couldn't you? Mags and I were planning a trip to London, this weekend. There's an exhibition we both want to see at the Tate. That's why I was so long. Why don't you come too?' She was on safe ground here.

'No thanks. The last exhibition I saw with you was like an afternoon at playschool. If people want to put their navel fluff into little green bottles and label it "umbilical detritus – take two a day" that's fine. I just don't need to pay to see it. How could you be so careless with Seb's videos? Look what I found him watching.' He thrust the offensive object under her nose. His hand was shaking and his nose looked pinched.

'What's wrong with that?'

'It's a horror film, that's what. I think letting children watch that sort of thing amounts to child abuse.'

'Don't be ridiculous! Anyway, I didn't notice it was for over-fifteens. It's an awful mistake. I really enjoy being a bad mother. So, you don't want to come to the exhibition? Well, that's fine. I need to keep up with what's going on, get out of this dreary backwater occasionally.'

'I'm to look after Seb, I suppose?' He was furious.

'No, I rang Mum from Mags's. She says she'll have him for the whole weekend, so we thought we'd stay the night with an old art school friend of Mags's. Look, I'm sorry. I'll get the fish and chips now.'

'Don't bother, as you've already eaten. I'm going to the

Mummers. I need a drink. You seem to have drunk all the wine.'

That night they lay stiffly apart, avoiding each other's skin even in their sleep and were woken twice by Seb crying out with bad dreams; Agnes took Seb into bed between them, a useful barrier which made sleep easier for them all.

Bea was sweeping the painting-room floor, having a general tidy before starting on a fresh picture. It was near the end of June and she had got through her supplies of paint faster than intended. She checked the tubes of paint, noted down that more expensive cerulean blue was needed and thought how odd it was that Agnes hadn't been round for well over a week, nearly two in fact. As she contemplated the peace of the morning, the phone rang.

'I hope I'm not preventing the completion of another of your masterpieces,' said Agnes with an unusual sarcasm in her voice, 'but Seb has taken it into his head that he *must* visit the old lighthouse this morning. He's bored because there's no nursery school this week because both the play-leaders have mumps.' She sounded aggrieved. 'He's insisting you come too.'

'Heavens! I'm honoured. There's a sketch of a derelict boat, not far from the lighthouse, that I've not finished; if I came I could stay on afterwards and finish that.'

'Don't put yourself out. It's only a whim of Seb's.'

When Agnes arrived, she seemed distant and jumpy and was more than a little inclined to snap. Bea was not sure why she had bothered to come. 'She looks as if she hasn't been sleeping too well,' she thought, 'and it's odd how it always seems to be Agnes who determines how well we are going to get on on any particular occasion.' Bea collected her purse and outdoor painting bag and felt in her pocket for the keys. 'There are times when she seems able to manipulate me into a bad temper myself. Well I won't be, not today.'

They set off in their own transport as Agnes grumbled

she had to go back afterwards to lunch with her mother and didn't want to have to bring Bea all the way back to Little Rumm first.

It was a clear, hot day and Seb adored the lighthouse. Bea had never seen him so concentratedly delighted and felt his enthusiasm made up for Agnes's unnaturally crotchety and nervous behaviour. Bea pointed out a yellow light aeroplane looping the loop, the direction of his home far away inland behind the hills, the direction of France, the massive container ship in the distance barely moving across the crepe-paper sea.

'Look,' said Agnes, at last having got her breath back after all the stairs and ignoring the view, pointing down to the road, 'removal vans. See? Over there . . .'

'I see, in front of Nut's little house. But they're big enough to hold the house itself and he's not moving. I'd know and anyway he's away.' Far below a pair of black Levis hung stiffly abandoned on Nut's washing line and there was no sign of his blue truck. 'He's gone off for a few days to a conference in York. Three vans, and all those cars — perhaps it's a film crew?'

'How do you know he'd have told you? Are you sure it's a conference he's gone to? He might have gone off on a jolly with a beautiful scientist. He might even meet a sexy geographer there.'

'Of course I'm sure where he's gone to, Agnes. It's a conference on coastal erosion and he's giving a paper.'

'Sounds absolutely riveting. And are you still just good mates? Isn't he pining for a bit more? If you don't give him a break you'll lose him before you've even had him.'

'You said that last time too. He just isn't like that.' Ruffled, Bea turned round to Agnes and caught sight of a pouting bottom lip. She refused to be dampened down. 'He knows I'm still in chaos and need time. There are other sorts of relationships, you know.'

'It all sounds very vague to me — not what I'd call a very satisfactory relationship, without any sex. Ludmilla said my paths of sensory intelligence were all irritated due to lack of sex. Do you still think about Oscar?'

'Of course I do. But less and less. Irritated paths of sensory intelligence — isn't that just a fancy way of saying your nerves are on edge? Why don't you get her to cut the cackle and give you a good massage?' Bea had begun to wish she was somewhere else.

'I used to have massages sometimes, but when I rang up for one last month the receptionist said the aromatherapist I used to like so much had gone on an extended holiday to Dominica and she wasn't taking any more bookings for him, which is odd since I'm sure I saw him in The Body Shop in Parden soon after.' Agnes's tone was now markedly acid. 'I wouldn't bother to think about Oscar at all if I were you.'

'The last time I saw you, you were trying make me to feel sorry for him. What's up, Ag-bag?'

'Men,' she replied cryptically.

'Are you having trouble with Phil?'

'No, not more than usual.' Agnes sniffed and turned to start the long journey back to ground level.

They had a cup of tea in the little café nearby which was full of strangers. They were not the usual sightseers doing the round trip on the light railway from Hythe, but well-dressed-down London people who had pulled together two tables and sat with heads close in a group discussion, passing bits of paper about between them, noting things down on clipboards.

Agnes, who was introducing Seb to the thrills of rock cake dipped in tea, turned her chair a little so she could see them better, and they her. Seb dropped the second rock cake, in its entirety, into Bea's cup of tea.

'You're right, I think it is a film crew. I'll just go and get us some more tea,' said Agnes. 'Mine's got cake in it too, and I'll ask the woman at the counter if she knows what's happening.'

She returned and whispered loudly, 'It *is* a film, and they're starting today sometime.' She seemed to have had a swift change of mood and sat there uncomfortably sideways, her legs sliding out into the aisle between the tables with her skirt half way up her thighs, trying to hear what the film people were saying.

'Where's the tea?'

'Actually I forgot to get it. It's only a TV costume drama or something, called *Black Lace and Brandy*. Sounds like smuggling, doesn't it? An old-fashioned bodice-ripper of some sort? Perhaps I could get taken on as an extra? It's about time somebody paid me for the pleasure of ripping my bodice.'

'What's a bodice?' asked Seb, now biting open and squeezing little packets of salad cream that were placed temptingly, along with packets of brown sauce, in bowls on the Formica table.

'The top half of a woman's dress,' said Bea, attempting to fish out the disintegrating bun with a white plastic spike implement, intended to be used for stirring. It snapped beneath the sodden weight.

'Can I wear one? Why haven't I got any dresses?'

'Because boys don't wear them. Much. At the moment. Not unless they're dressing up.'

'I want to dress up. I want to wear a bodice. And I want knickers like Sylvie's got.' He giggled, unpleasantly knowingly, semi-aware even at four that there was something smutty-funny about women's underwear. 'Hers have lacy bits.'

'Who's Sylvie? One of your friends at nursery school?' asked Bea, fascinated.

'Yes! She showed me them! Why can't I have some like that?' He was now warming to his subject and half kneeling on his chair. His voice was piercing. He dragged a yellow plastic flower from the bunch sitting in a clean white yoghurt pot on the table, dismembered it and flung the petals into the air.

'Go on, Bea. Why can't he have some?' Agnes was proudly aware that the film people and the woman at the serving counter, had stopped to listen and was sure they were quite enraptured.

'Because you are a boy, and boys usually wear boys' knickers.

But if you ask Mummy,' she returned the ball to Agnes, 'I'm sure she'll buy you some, for dressing up perhaps.' She picked up the petals and tried to rearrange them on their green plastic stalk.

'Time to go home,' said Agnes firmly, 'or we'll be late for lunch with Granny.' She bent towards Seb hoping to avert the usual departure crisis. 'You can tell Granny all about climbing up inside the lighthouse, she'll love to hear about that.'

'No, she won't,' he protested, 'I'll tell her 'bout Sylvie's knickers. Ladies are more 'trested in that.'

'I'm sure she will be,' said Bea, helpless with laughter.

Agnes and Seb departed for their interesting lunch with Granny in Bellhurst and Bea fetched her khaki wide-awake hat and the canvas bag containing the tools of her trade from the truck, and set off for the boat.

The sun was high but there was a shady semi-derelict iron shed, open on the side facing the boat. Its roof was holed and it was half taken up with a skeletal and rusting Lister engine, pillaged for spare parts, and an ancient winch with the cable rusted solid, but there was room to rest against the small workbench and paint.

A fly discovered her and buzzed round her mouth annoyingly. She swiped it away. She ignored the sound of people walking nearby on the shingle, kept quiet and went on mixing colours, trying them out on a separate sheet, matching the many layered peelings of faded paintwork on the curving sweep of the boat's planked sides: scorched tangerine, jade green, flamingo pink.

'Pink, pink with a dab of yellow, salmon pink, peach silk Granny's knicker pink. Why should pink be a feminine colour? How long has it been a feminine colour? Which was the first scarlet-faced baby girl to be thrust into a pink bonnet? Which man first refused to wear pink underpants and vest? Who first felt silly in pink doublet and hose? And why does Seb want to wear Sylvie's knickers?' She supposed people not to be strictly male or female, only predominantly one or the other, most women having a few 'male' tendencies, and most men a few 'female' ones, without compromising their sex, since they wouldn't understand each other in any way at all if they did not.

The heat from the tin roof was drawing sweat from her palms. 'Odd though,' she mused, beginning to pack up her painting things, having finished the boat, 'how people who are without that sort of emotional cross-dressing in their being, the stereotypes from the extreme ends of the spectrum, are *the* most boring people on earth. The fatally "female" woman, from a traditional male point of view, with irrational and insatiable desires to both please and get things all her own way – one couldn't spend five minutes in her company without going mad with annoyance. Add a fluffy *pink* brain (I am, of course, thinking of Andreary) and it's hopeless trying to communicate with them, or the stereotype male, heavily muscled, dominant and unable to understand anything more emotionally complicated than a combustion engine. Baby-blue-brained. I wonder if stereotypes are attracted to stereotypes? Perhaps they are; then that would cancel out the boredom factor. They just wouldn't notice. Nature isn't bothered about people being bored, anyway, as long as they reproduce while they're being it.' Then she thought that Agnes seemed to be getting decidedly more pink-brained than she had been and perhaps the bad temper might be put down to volatile hormone levels, if hormones could be volatile. She imagined them more as moving upwards in a steady surge, whispering subtle innuendos along the way as they edged towards the brain to cram it full of unattainable and mind-bogglingly gymnastic demands. Her grasp of biology was weak. 'Time to stop. I'm going loony out here. Perhaps it's the heat.'

A wavering heat haze danced above the woodwork of the boat and the colours dried fast on the paper. She gulped down the last of the fresh water from the bottle and crunched off down to the shore to indulge in a cooling paddle. She hitched up her long skirt. It was very quiet and the sea was wonderfully calm, the waves barely rattling the gravel as they rolled back and forth, sucking softly at the larger stones, scouring gently between her toes and leaving trails of moonstone and opal bubbles on her skin. Turning to face inland, she was struck by the sloping expanse of gravel before her; a large canvas, just waiting to be marked.

Against the upper part of the steep angle she began to construct an eye; first a dark circle for a pupil, then the brown iris and this took a considerable time, since the brown stones were harder to find than most. Slithering about, using her green cotton skirt front as an apron for collecting stones for the white of the eye, then grey shading, then more dark for the outline, Bea was totally absorbed in her child's game and did not pause till the eye, like those painted on Mediterranean fishing boats, a four-foot long aversion of evil, guarded the shore. Exhausted by the effort, but determined to finish it she searched out one last white stone, and pushed it into the pupil whereupon the eye took on a wicked glint. The effect was intriguing, however short-lived; the next high tide would lap at least the lower lid, and probably erase it all. Her hands and forearms were a little pink with sunburn beneath their salty sparkle and she felt sleepy. Leaving the solitary and quizzical eye to stare out to sea, she headed back for the shady side of the boat, lay back against its wooden side, tilted the hat over her eyes and dozed.

'Excuse me for waking you, but would you mind moving a few yards back to that white marker over there? We're starting shooting, and although I don't think you'll be in view, we'd rather have the area clear for the next hour or so.' The polite voice came out of nowhere, out of the sun. Bea gazed up muzzily into a girl's dark face bending over her. 'I'm sorry,' the girl repeated, 'but I have to clear the area, get people out of shot.'

Bea yawned enormously, and staggered to her feet. 'What time is it, do you know?'

'Four o'clock. If you want to watch, there's a marker over there, if you stay the other side of it, you'll be OK.'

Things had been happening while she was asleep. A handful of sweating eighteenth-century soldiers, followed by a man on horseback wandered past her and two men in T-shirts, a large one whose extensive stomach bore the word 'Megabelly' across it, the other more sylph-like, with 'Minibum' printed on the back. From where she stood none of the shore itself was visible. The action must all be taking place below the shelf of shingle. She found a better vantage point out of the way, along the beach and settled down to watch.

A modern fishing boat came into view, towing a large wooden rowing boat behind it in which were actors dressed in period clothes. It was followed by a rubber boat filled with men in wet suits. One of the actors, a women in a dark-blue hooded cloak, leant over the side of the rowing boat and appeared to be being sick. This caused something of a hold up but the rowing boat was loosed, oars were raised and it was rowed ashore. There was suddenly shouting, megaphones and radios being used and a lot of rushing up and down the shingle. The scene appeared to be being filmed first from the sea where there was some passing back and forth of boats, of cutting engines and drifting about. The rowing boat was towed out a little way and then the oarsmen repeated their trip from sea to shore, less vigorously this time and the woman was sick again, which was obviously not allowed for in the script, since it caused a third performance. The oarsmen were quite definitely flagging. The attendant boats moved out of view and the scene was filmed from the beach. As the now exhausted oarsmen again leapt ashore to pull the boat up, the woman in the cloak was heaved out and set on her feet whereupon she immediately lay down and began to retch. She was made to sit, then stood up again, brought a glass of water brushed down and attended to by a frantic make-up girl.

Filming seemed to be a quite tedious process and not nearly as interesting as Bea'd expected it to be. She felt great sympathy for the seasick woman, but it all seemed to be taking forever. Her throat was dry and she was contemplating going home when the actress with re-pinked cheeks, having recovered herself sufficiently, weakly indicated that she was ready for another take. The filming started again and Bea didn't like to move past the marker. Just at that moment, a group of nuns in full flight, startlingly tall and closely followed by two men with camcorders came round the point at some speed. They wore shockingly bright pink habits and were shouting in deep voices and leaping balletically, paddling in the water and kicking up spray. The unfortunate man whom Bea took to be the director gave a wail of distress and squatted on the ground with his head between his hands. Having at first thought that the nuns were an intended post-modernist touch to the proceedings, it became apparent even to Bea that two separate films were in the process of being shot. There was further slithering about on the shingle and arguments between the less well-equipped pink nun faction and the bodice-rippers and a little temper and petty shoving.

The tide was steadily rising, eroding what little foreshore there was at that place, and the shadows were beginning to lengthen. Bea was thirsty and although she hadn't seen the soldiers and the man on the horse in action yet, it was time to leave. If they weren't actually shooting, she could avoid the markers and cut back across towards the pick-up. She overheard various bitter comments from the crew as she passed: 'Effing queens, they must have done it on purpose.' 'How's Marie-Christine? She going to throw up again, or wot?' 'The tide's coming in. Our Tel had better get a move on or the boat'll float off and the cast'll get drowned.' '... all I picked up was the sound of her ladyship vomiting.' 'She's never been in a boat before, didn't know she was going to be seasick.' 'Poor bitch. It's a flat calm. How can anyone feel seasick in that?'

Having settled the argument with the pink nuns, or monks, since they were definitely male, the director turned away and consulted with one of the crew. His voice hoarse with frustration, he called out to Bea.

'Hi there! Are you a local? I saw you in the café this morning. You don't happen to know when high tide is, do you?' He glanced reproachfully at the girl standing beside him, the one who had earlier on so politely woken Bea. 'We appear to have lost the tide tables and the phone link to the boats has packed up.' A tear rolled down the girl's cheek and dripped on her clipboard. The irritable speaker had a high, intelligent-looking forehead and a lot of thick brown hair and was dressed in khaki trousers and a crumpled cream linen jacket with bulging pockets that seemed too big for him; it was still quite hot and his sunburnt face was covered with a film of perspiration. Bea felt very sorry for them.

'It should be about five-thirty.'

'Oh Christ! It's nearly that now. Well, that does it then! We'll have to start again tomorrow. Go and get everything sorted, will you, Jane — and for God's sake, please stop weeping! I know it's not your fault.' He turned back to Bea, who still stood there, fair, slim and shyly intrigued; an apparition, a beautiful and somewhat scruffy sea goddess risen from the uncompromising English Channel, the hem of her trailing green cotton skirt tide-marked with salt. 'Thank you. Have you been watching? You won't believe what trouble we've been having.' He wiped his hands on a large green cotton handkerchief, then ran it round his face and neck. 'The first thing was that someone had drawn, built really, a massive great eye made of stones on the spot we'd marked out this morning for the landing.' He was staring with curiosity at Bea as he spoke. 'Of course we couldn't see it from this side, with the slope being so steep and it wasn't till the crew on the boat started shooting that it was spotted. Talk about the evil eye being cast in our direction!'

'That was me, I'm afraid. I did it earlier this afternoon. It took ages. I didn't know you were going to be filming at just that spot.'

'Good heavens, you might have warned us! Oh hell! It wasn't part of anything important was it, some project or something you were going to photograph? I'm afraid it's been destroyed. This was one of the few spots where we could film from the sea without getting anachronistic telegraph poles and houses in the shot. We had to catch the water level just right, in order to be able to pull the boat up.'

'Well, I didn't know that at the time. I only woke up when your production girl told me to move. Wouldn't it have been easier to film it on a sandy beach somewhere?'

'The script specified a steep shingle location and this was close to the others we had to use. You were asleep, on the beach?'

'Why not?'

'No reason at all, I suppose.' He rubbed his chin and held back a yawn. 'You wouldn't fancy a drink with some of us, I suppose, after we've packed up for the day. Do you know of a good pub, not too far away?' He sounded hopeful. In spite of his harrowing afternoon, he seemed still to have a certain amount of energy about him. 'We haven't discovered anywhere bearable in the area yet. We're all staying in Fingle, in various bed and breakfasts and a motel. It's always the way. By the time one's nosed out the best places it's time to be off somewhere else.' He thrust out his hand, 'Terence Moorbury.'

Terence Moorbury handed Bea an ominous glass of cider over the balding head of a moustachioed, wasted sixties' hippie slumped across the counter of the crowded bar of the Eeldyke Inn. The pub was already two-thirds full when she led in the film crew and the only available place to perch was on the sticky, glass-ringed mahogany lid of the piano. Terence took an appreciative gulp of his beer and smiled encouragingly at Bea whose eyes were wandering about the room, entranced by the shapes of the customers. Beer bellies bulged, breasts heaved, flesh tried to escape from clothing in all directions, or in some cases the opposite, where clothing hung limply on spindle shanks and flapped about narrow bony chests.

They had to shout to be heard above the engulfing waves of ten different conversations going on about them.

'How bizarre to meet up ... on the same floor at Queen Mary and Westfield ... do you remember? ... Well, I should try putting more oil into the mixture ... Hang Sok Joi got sent off for biting ... I'm not surprised, with a name like that it was surprising they let him on the pitch in the first place ... You were Cinematography and I was Social Sciences ... *endless* trouble with the gear box on that model ... Freedom from pregnancy, that's what we gained ... What do you call a dirty book for amphibians? ... the squirrel pie was wonderful, with toasted hazelnuts ... Frogsporn, ha, ha ... I can remember ploughing that field with horses ... No, the *pink* ones came from Kookai, these are from the Fingle PDSA ... George had a heart attack on one of the Countryside Marches and Auntie Meg inherited the lot and sold it to a developer ...'

'Tell me about *Black Lace and Brandy*.'

Terence looked puzzled. 'I'm sorry?'

'Isn't that the name of the film you're making?'

'Where did you get that from? It's *Patrick and Marguerite* we're filming, one of Connaught Marvel's nineteen-twenties' ghostie best-sellers. He's undergoing a revival at the moment, it seems.'

'Perhaps *Black Lace and Brandy* was what the pink nuns were filming,' said Bea, abashed at getting it wrong. 'I heard it second-hand from a friend who got it from the woman at the counter in the café this morning when we saw you all in there.'

'More likely *Black Lace and Randy*. In spite of the havoc they caused, it was very hard to keep a straight face.'

'I thought Connaught Marvel wrote travel books?'

'He did and they're wonderful, but he wrote these to finance his journeys abroad, hiding behind the nom-de-plume of A. C. Holliday. They're pretty good, I'm told, but I've only ever read this one, in the course of duty. This is for TV and an acquaintance of mine is working on a private life of Connaught Marvel, to go out nearer the time of showing but on a different channel. It's a pity I didn't find out about it earlier, we could have liaised.' He had to raise his voice still further to be heard above the prevailing racket.

'When's that going to be?'

'The end of January. A two-parter. Will you watch it?'

'I'll try to, although I haven't got a television at the moment and don't know where I'll be for the winter.'

'Why's that?'

She became evasive; friendly and approachable as he was, there didn't seem to be any need to give him the details of her current situation. 'I'm probably going to move and I'm not sure where to, yet.' At the other end of the piano a woman was complaining bitterly that she wasn't getting the same pay rise as a male member of staff in her company. 'I think it stinks! I thought we were supposed to have equal rights?' Terence glanced round at her then turned back to Bea with an encouraging smile, trying to draw her out.

'So, where do you stand, on equal rights? Have you got all you need?'

'Have I got enough of your sugar on my pancake, is that what you mean?' The cider had kicked in. She said it accusingly. 'Anyway, equality isn't the right word. I mean, it implies fair shares between two identical beings – we're as dissimilar as oranges and lemons.' She drew breath and caught a look of incredulous horror in the face of the underpaid woman behind Terence and grinned. He looked slightly taken aback himself.

'What I'm getting at is that we wanted for ourselves the rights men had, without realising that these rights were designed *by* men, *for* men, but now we've got them, it's as if we've been handed out men's clothes and are expected to be grateful. They don't fit. I'm thinking of returning some of mine and asking for a bigger size.'

He chuckled. 'What's the answer, then?'

'I don't think there is just one that won't make you choke with indignation at its apparent unfairness – how about the right to have a job, or children, or both and not be constantly criticised or financially penalised for whichever option we choose?' She gave a triumphant smile at the woman who had stopped talking to her friend and was listening warily, then she asked Terence if he could play the piano.

He could and did so without fussing that it was a little out of tune, beginning with a passable rendering of Fats Waller's 'I can't stand you 'cos your feet's too big'.

'Can you sing?' he asked, looking up with a grin and switching his playing confusingly to Kurt Weill.

'Yes,' she said at once, now fully unwound after her touchy morning with Agnes and unable to collect up any false modesty in time, since he was now playing 'Mack the Knife' and the coincidence was causing a strange recurrence of the physical agitation caused by Nut's closeness that other evening.

'You don't, by any strange stroke of luck, happen to know the words?' he asked, pushing back his hair and looking up at her hopefully.

'Yes,' she said again. It would be easy, there was a lot of noise and no one was really listening. This was something which she knew she was able to do and slightly better than him.

'Right then, off we go.'

Her voice was small, untrained, but warmly smoky and inviting and people nearby stopped talking to listen; Terence looked up, genuinely astonished.

'Good heavens! I thought you were a beach bum, or a wandering art student with a passion for rearranging the landscape. You could really do something with that voice.'

'I think I'd rather leave it as it is. Arranging the landscape is more interesting.'

He played a few more standards, then put down the lid and stood up.

'There's a party on Friday night, this Friday. Would you like to come?'

'Isn't this a party?'

'No, we can't stay long this evening. We've all got an early start tomorrow morning, to catch the water at the right height. I've been assured the weather forecast is good. We're going to dose Marie-Christine with anti-seasick pills with her coffee. So how about the party?'

The social life here was a definite improvement on that of Bellhurst. What a shame Nut was away.

'I'd love to come to a party. Where's it being held?'

'I'll give you the address, where is it, ah, here we are.' He pulled a large business card from his pocket and copied the address down, and Bea noticed with amusement the enormous black fountain pen he was using. Perhaps it was a sop to his ego, making up for a lack of inches, in height, she hoped for his sake; his other belongings, not just the jacket and pen, were perhaps also a size too large for him.

'Here you are. I hope you know where that is, because I don't – we're being taken by minibus, those that want to come of course. Some are heading back to the bright lights as fast as they can. We've been doing a lot of rural filming recently and it's beginning to get some of them down. The party's being given by the man who's doing the documentary on Connaught Marvel. It's a house-warming party and neatly coincides with the end of filming.'

The address, Blackshorne Court, Ragstone Street, St Rumwold-at-Cliffe, was written in larger than average schoolboy handwriting. She turned the card over: contrarily, 'Terence Moorbury, Mogalite Films' was printed in a neat minimalist format.

'I've met Connaught Marvel's grand-daughter. She lives somewhere near here. Do you think she'll be at the party? Saint Rumwold-at-Cliffe is about four miles away, that's all, along the inner edge of the marsh, on the top of the old cliff face. I've got footpath maps of that area at home; the house is probably marked on one of them. What time shall I come?'

'About nine-thirty? There's a band, and dancing. But on second thoughts, why don't we take you with us in the minibus? Then you can show us the way.'

Later that evening, occupied slightly dizzily in planning a painting of pink nuns dancing on the beach with Megabelly and Minibum, the telephone bleeped and an impossibly exigent Nest was there plunging about on the line.

'Darling, I'm worried about you. I felt I ought to warn you, you mustn't let anything, or anyone, come between you and your painting.'

Nest sounded breathless with urgency, but had in fact spent all week wondering how to broach the subject. Any hint of her protégée straying too far from the paintbrushes made her feel apprehensive and while they were potting up forty *Geranium* 'Kashmir White', Lucinda had dropped a little squib into one of her Molly Bloom monologues which had rattled her acute alarm system. '. . . Saw your Bea down at the beach a few days ago with Francis Nutmeg – he was helping her into a boat – one of the old derelicts pulled up on the shingle so they can't have been planning on sailing off to France, tee hee . . .'

'What are you talking about, Aunt Nest?'

'I'm talking about Blue's and your mutual friend. Nut, dear child. Nut. I've been thinking . . . Blue thinks, well I think he knows, he didn't actually say in so many words, that this Nut is seriously interested in you. I'm interfering, I know. But it would be out of the frying pan into the fire, wouldn't it, to get involved, if you are involved, with someone now you have your freedom? You shouldn't let anything come between you and your work.'

'Aunt Nest, I am not "involved", as you so politely call it.' She nearly shouted. It was intolerable that she should be discussed, that she should be told what to do, even if Nest did have a point ... 'Aunt Nest? Hello? Look, I'm in the middle of something ... in the middle of cleaning the oven.'

'That sounds very unlikely to me. No one else has ever bothered to clean it. Now I've made you cross. I'm sorry, darling. I shouldn't have rung up like this, poking my nose in.' Nest didn't sound remotely penitent. 'But do remember what I've said, won't you?' She paused and then repeated importantly, infuriatingly bossy, 'Your work must come first.'

'Good-bye, Aunt Nest.' Bea put the phone down, indignant and chewing a thumbnail. The strain of the workload under which she had put herself during the last weeks had been considerable and now she was being pushed further. Everyone was warning of involvement with someone they didn't even know and even Agnes had been discouraging, slotting uncomfortable ideas into her head. You could never tell; perhaps Nut did have a glamorous colleague with whom he was sharing the trip? Well, screw them all. It was ridiculous. She wasn't involved. Not yet. And she'd been working flat out while wading through friends and relatives, forcing herself into a spectator's role as other people came and went, had holidays and did interesting things. 'They're treating me like a teenager doing A Levels. I shall go to the ball. I will give dinner parties, get my eyebrows pierced even. No I won't – it sounds agonisingly painful but I will do what I damn well like. Too careful to have fun? Huh! I'll have some fun all right.'

Gently swearing, she stumped back up the staircase to the painting room and threw herself down on the scarlet bed, lying there her arms behind her head, worrying, whereupon a heat-seeking mosquito immediately homed in on her hot skin, searching for its blood meal.

As children, aged perhaps six and nine, she and Patrick had splatted mosquitoes lurking on the ceiling of one their bedrooms by the skilful aiming of tennis balls. It had been in the house near the river when their father was in his yacht-building phase.

The ceiling became decorated with a pin-chart of tiny splatters and they kept a pencilled scoreboard of the kills on the wall beside the light switch. Patrick had been most intrigued that the tiny splash of blood soaking in to the emulsioned ceiling after a direct hit was his own.

Aunt Nest could not be flattened with a tennis ball. Dear Nest had given the house for as long as it was needed. Nest, however importunate, wanted to be a part of what she was doing and it was owed to her not to be shut out. Bea rolled over on the bed and picked abstractedly at a piece of loose plaster. Something was missing; not the bland security of living with Oscar, so it was another something. Something was absent and she felt starving for it, as if having eaten a delicious but unfilling first course, she'd then been deprived of a chocolate pudding. It was, she had to admit, most probably sex. Other people went in for recreational sex. Agnes had, probably still did. But she couldn't contemplate allowing herself Nut, since he was a particular, special man, not until she'd painted herself out for the time being, till she was one hundred per cent certain that the growing ache for him wasn't caused by being on the rebound.

How very unpredictable and vaporous a thing a close friendship with a man was — one false move and it might brew up into something else entirely and what was there to be gained by it? An incubus munching away at one's edges, like the sea gnawing at the land, constantly eroding as it sought out a weakened place to seep or batter its way through . . . she laughed nervously. It was so still outside. Not a sound out there in the night. The moon was up and almost full and she got up and hung out of the window, listening and sniffing. There was the faint apple-waft from the rose, the smell of sheep, and saltiness. She could hear the sea murmuring in the distance but perhaps it was only the sound in her ears of her own blood flowing. Goose pimples prickled up her arms. 'I'm quite safe here; there's a solidity in the loneliness. Invulnerable, in my castle.' It was time to lock up the house and head for bed.

At about three in the morning the sound of revving engines, crashing gears, squealing brakes and voices woke her. Alert in a second, she peered out. Further up the lane, perhaps a hundred yards past Little Rumm, she could see the moonlight glinting on the roof of a car angled crossways and sharply downwards, as if it were half in the ditch, and another car was in the process of reversing. Automatically thinking there had been an accident, she was about to lean out of the window and call out offering help, when with a whoosh the crashed car was engulfed by flames, a figure ran across to the revving, waiting car and leapt into the passenger seat. It screeched back towards her with the doors hanging open, bouncing and crashing on the uneven track. There was a small explosion from the burning car as whatever petrol was left in the tank ignited. They were gone.

Jerry Rumm turned up on his bicycle before the police and fire brigade, come to check she was unharmed. A half brick had been hurled through the windscreen of his old Peugeot estate and he was puffing, his unshaven chin bristling with annoyance, the collar of a pink, blue-and-white-striped pyjama jacket flapping outside the neck of his green farm overalls.

'Joy-riders! My arse – excuse my French – criminals, that's what they are. Those lads come out from Parden in stolen cars and drive out here to disturb us, racing them up and down the lanes at night. They get low on petrol, dump the car in a dyke or set fire to it for kicks, see? Then they drive back to town in the other. It happens quite a bit here, in the summer. They chose the wrong lane here, didn't they just? No place for handbrake turns or racing. You all right, Mrs Mitty? You do look a bit shook up. You want to have a nice cup of tea and go back to bed.'

Alone again after a statement had been taken and the police had departed, she stood at the bedroom window, disturbed, listening again. An oystercatcher called mournfully, 'kee-eep, kee-eep.' All was quiet but the clean air was brutally contaminated with the stench of oily rubber smoke and petrol. Dawn was not far off.

Chapter Nine

On Friday morning Nut moved with practised caution about his hot and claustrophobic quarters beneath the eaves of the bed and breakfast in York, whistling as he sorted through papers. There had been a mix-up with the rooms at the University and not feeling much like socialising, having Bea seriously on his mind, he had been relieved to be sleeping out but he had not slept well. The guests in the room beneath had been up till late watching television and breathy, echoing voices accompanied by gunshots had penetrated the floorboards.

The landlady had looked doubtfully at him when he arrived, silently judging his height. Having expected a female Dr Frances Nutmeg she had him placed in the pretty rose-covered room in the attic of the house near the Shambles and not having any other rooms free, was forced to apologise for the shortness of the bed and the lack of height to the ceiling.

The centre of the awkward space was taken up by the splayed-out upper beams of a great king-post supporting the roof and by a forcemeat stuffing of unnecessary items intended to give a homelike air, things which tripped or bruised the occupant: fluffy green-and-pink bedside rugs – three; stools – two, their seats upholstered with needlepoint spaniels surrounded by white roses; ashtrays – three, two of them emblazoned with horned helmets and 'Welcome to Yorvik', the third decorated with shamrock leaves and with a model leprechaun seated, loathsomely perky, on the corner. An overhanging plethora of tiddly wrought-iron shelves bearing miniature jugs. A frilled glass vase of pansies and an electric copper kettle on a painted tin tray cluttered up the bedside table. A cut-glass bowl overflowing with infinitesimal packets of instant coffee and fiddly tublets of milk, designed to be opened only by the midget fingers of the repellent leprechaun.

Nut was not an urban man and was immensely pleased to be leaving. He preferred the fewness of things in the country to the many in the distracting jumble of cities with their itinerant populations of trooping tourists cluttering up the pavements. In what was left of the countryside, it seemed there was one person to look at at a time, to get to know, one particular dog or cat to befriend, house or barn to observe and the people and animals were proud of being well known and of their singularity. Joyfully tossing the majority of the papers, followed by his plastic name tag, into a painted tin waste-bin decorated with découpage carnations and chickens, he packed the remainder neatly in his briefcase.

He whistled while he shaved hunchbacked over the washbasin beneath the sloping roof, flushed away a faint tidemark of red whisker stubble, unplaited, combed and replaited his hair, stowed razor and toothbrush in his haversack and gave the room a cursory check for any remaining personal bits and pieces.

The little book on fossils which he had bought for Bea lay on the bedside table and he collapsed himself on the rumpled pink rose-printed polycotton sheets, as out of place as a large dog fox in a suburban flowerbed, and opened it, wondering what he should write as an inscription. He paused, then bravely wrote in a clear, italic hand: 'For beautiful, bewildered Bea – certainties to search for.' He stopped writing and crunched the end of the ballpoint pen between his tough white teeth, snapping the plastic, unsure whether to put 'with all my love' or just 'love from', and whether to call himself Nut, or Francie, which was what his parents called him, how he usually signed personal letters and which she didn't know about, or even plain Francis Nutmeg. He settled on 'with all my love, from Nut' and the date.

He'd been hopelessly distracted throughout the three-day conference by images of Bea, an enquiring gilt-bronze angel in indigo blue, untarnished by her husband's flit, who floated across his field of vision whenever his attention wandered from the current speaker. He'd felt so briefly close to her in the castle yard ... again he'd seen the thought fly through her mind, leapt to catch it as it raced through her body but he had again misjudged the opposing willpower. He didn't want to take temporary advantage of someone on the rebound, but what an everlasting ricochet it was turning out to be. He saw her, hopelessly romantically, both as a fugitive and as a gilded bullet with his name on it, always just grazing past when there he was with his tongue hanging out, shirt open and his chest waiting to receive the blow. He had been pursuing, mind, body and soul, as relentlessly and methodically as she single-mindedly pursued her painting and knew now that he was competing with a passion as serious as his own. Having reluctantly admitted to himself that he ought not to get in the way, he tucked the knowledge back on the shelf to re-read later when it was more convenient. He could not now do without her. Peace of mind depended on it.

He slipped the book into the rucksack and fastened the straps. Time to set off for London, breaking the journey back to Kent by having a meal and staying the night at the Nutmegs' tall terraced house in Lewisham. There was good news to impart; the offer of the university post which neatly dove-tailed with the end of his employment on the marsh. He was looking forward to seeing his plain-speaking mother and seeing her face crack into the smile which had the power to hoist the spirits of the sourest of personalities. She worked part-time for a wine importers and he wanted to collect two or three bottles of something special to set aside for an eventual celebration. The smaller the bubbles, she had told him, the better the quality of the champagne. She loved the job and living in London. What would she make of Bea? He could not imagine that his father wouldn't adore her too. The sight of her might stop him grumpily counting the days till retirement and getting back to Ireland. He didn't visit often enough in spite of living so close and it would be great to see them both again.

Now it was back to the marsh and back to tempting Bea. But who was tempting whom? Remembering once more the hot skin of her neck as he'd touched it, the frantic antelope agility with which she'd bounced away across the rubble at the castle, that one and only hug, he was once more incredulously impatient with the fleeting, tentative visits, the amicable wanderings about the marsh, like the young couples one still saw walking arm in arm round the stone-walled lanes at home in Ireland, trying to find a bit of peace away from the prying, giggling younger siblings. Courting, that's what it was, but why not? It was certainly an original idea. Was there a better way to get to know a person? He'd search her out again and again and *would*, eventually, take hold of the sheeny shoulders and melt her down. Metal, melting; wasn't it odd that all his images of her were metallic?

Contriving with a shiver to take a tougher grip on his imagination, he slipped on the rusty black jacket and once more thinking about the formation and deformation of the earth and its inhabitants, bent again to avoid cracking his head, bumped with bag and briefcase down the low twisting staircase, heading for the high-curving, vaulted Victorian elegance of York railway station and the intercity train to London.

The rebirthing of Geraldine O'Brien was not proceeding without its secondary labour pangs. On that same Friday morning she had started smoking again, comforting herself as she inhaled the first lung-heaving breath, that she did it merely as an aide-mémoire. She rummaged through the spring issue of *Modern Painters* in which she had spotted an advertisement for the Greensand Gallery and copied the telephone number onto a piece of card torn from the top of a tea-bag packet. She spent the remainder of that morning haunting the garden, flitting from plant to plant procrastinating, the piece of card so tensely clamped between her fingers that the numbers written on it became rubbed and faint. At last, going indoors, lighting a fifth cigarette and inhaling deeply, she sat down beside the telephone, only to delay things a little longer by opening that morning's post. There was only one missive, a promising fat envelope which disappointingly contained a thin booklet, with no covering letter, entitled *Pork Mince*. It seemed to contain, well, pork mince recipes. 'Why have I been sent this?' she wondered. 'Does someone think I look like a pork-mince eater? Does my address indicate I keep a black Berkshire pig secreted in the garden shed? How did a pork-mince seller get my address?' Like a goldfish bowl filled with tadpoles, her head had been swimming with small, developing black terrors, that Simon might have died, or had forgotten her, but the minced pork booklet made her smile. She threw it into the wastepaper basket and tapped out the digits, with a finger so tremulous that she had to re-dial twice.

'Simon Greensand Gallery,' said a young woman's voice, its American accent and languid tone so at variance with Geraldine's resurgent fright that it was oddly soothing. She could hear voices in the background and the echoing sound of someone walking heavily across a wooden floor in an open space. She forced the throttling quaver from her throat, sat up straight, stubbed out the cigarette and asked as casually as possible if she might speak to Simon Greensand himself.

'Simon! It's for you! the girl called out with what Geraldine felt to be a lack of deference, before she took in the fact that he was actually there. The languid voice returned to her as an afterthought: 'Who is this?'

'It's Geraldine O'Brien.' She restrained herself from explaining further who she was, or was not. There was a muffled exclamation as the information was relayed and further footsteps.

'Geraldine? Geraldine! What a most wonderful thing! How *are* you? *Where* are you?'

The conversation proceeded at first in jerks and tentative

tweakings of memories then settled to a steady exchange of facts, explanations, and delighted laughter. How stupidly easy it had been, after all. She was invited to London for lunch with Simon and his son and the son's wife tomorrow, that very Saturday, 1 July and she had accepted.

Crossing and recrossing the room in a daze, two things rose inconveniently in her mind as she passed the looking glass – hair and clothes. She telephoned Bea.

'... I'm in such a mess. But I have a few hours left in which to do something. Where do I start? What *should* I do, do you think?'

Bea could hear the indecisive agony in Geraldine's voice, imagining an older and down-at-heel self suddenly bravely rowing out from a rural backwater into the rushing mainstream; abandoning a juicy brushful of cadmium lemon, she rallied. She made a pleading phone call to Pauline, the hairdresser in Bellhurst who normally cut her own hair, managed to wangle an appointment for Geraldine at four o'clock that afternoon and galloped to the rescue.

Geraldine's lined, doubtful face, glazed between the diamond panes of the Wimple Coffee House, lightened as Bea, ready for an emergency shopping session and face flushed with enthusiasm, arrived to meet her as arranged three quarters of an hour later. Apart from the five charity shops, which were a last resort, there were only three clothes shops in Bellhurst. The first was male-oriented and contained merely heavy-duty farming clothes, moleskin trousers, ferretskin underwear and riding macs. There was improbable lingerie, pleated, printed silk dresses and pie-crust frilled blouses, not Geraldine at all, in the next; there being no time to drive all the way to Parden and desperate to discover something suitable they tried the boutique catering for the more fashion-conscious thirty-somethings. It was a hot and sultry day which made trying on clothes an ordeal for Geraldine, standing bony and vulnerable in her grubby white petticoat in the oven-like changing room. But Bea, taking the job seriously, guided her into a miraculously well-cut long black denim skirt with a decorous mid-shin slit that both suited and fitted Geraldine's tall body and a loose, saffron-yellow, Chinese-collared cotton jacket. Neither of these were expensive and while her lank and untidy hair was being transformed into a very becoming, straight silver-grey bob, Bea breathed easily again and hurried off to Boots to buy her a new lipstick as a present, a pale brownish rose-thorn pink. She was thrilled by the romantic aspects of the forthcoming lunch and much heartened by the sight of Geraldine in new clothes.

'I can't believe it was so easy. I won't be able to sleep tonight, I imagine, with excitement! I have so much to tell him. It's not too late for us to be friends. Did I tell you that his wife divorced him years ago and went to live in Venezuela?' Geraldine examined herself in the hand mirror with a touch of new found self-respect. 'I think I was pretty, once. I can't really remember. Thank you so much for the lipstick. I shall pitch the old gore-coloured one into the dustbin as soon as I get home!'

'I was wondering if you needed to borrow a little T-shirt or something to wear beneath the jacket?' Bea suggested as they left the hairdresser's and Geraldine was about to agree but suddenly changed her mind.

'No, dear Bea. I have just the thing at home, sleeveless black silk – old, but no one will see the little holes – I'll wear it back to front. Thank you for your help and time, and your quite extraordinary patience. I'd forgotten how to buy clothes and wouldn't have had the faintest idea what to do with my hair. I've interrupted your work long enough. You must trot off now and let me walk home and think about things. I'll ring you up and tell you how it went, as soon as I get back from London.' She leant forward and planted a grateful kiss on Bea's cheek.

Geraldine was thankful to have remembered Oscar's possible presence next door in time and turned Bea from the idea of escorting her home. It wouldn't do for her at all to discover the wretched husband had come back. If she had popped in to

Fleming Cottage to ferret out clothes she would have seen his belongings, might even have walked into him as he came back from work. What a dear girl she was! How could Oscar have left such a lovesome, toothsome, gladsome poppet? Then, wondering what it was that had made her use such antiquated adjectives in relation to Bea, she coaxed the skirt and jacket from the brilliant pink tissue paper and laid them out. The yellow jacket danced across the blue counterpane, a cut-out paper shape snipped by Matisse, and the flat black skirt bent at the knee in a reverence. With Piggy the cat's uncomprehending yellow gaze upon her, she took them up and tried them on again, struggling with the stiff new zip, the virgin buttonholes and twisted and turned before the long mirror, amazed at the sight. But she was not fooled – the apparently elegant old woman she saw was a weak, fumbling thing inside, with a heart as withered as her dried-apricot textured neck. It was sad when the clothes one wore became more interesting than what was inside them. There was a thread hanging from the sleeve of the jacket, and she nipped it off with her teeth. How badly finished modern clothes were, and how expensive. But she was not short of money, she reminded herself. She had spent nothing on herself for years.

It would of course be amusing, but also acutely painful, to meet Simon again after such a time but the central purpose of the visit was to tell him about Bea and see if he could be persuaded to offer her some help, even if only in the form of a second opinion, when she was ready for it. She hoped Bea would be pleased. She *had* asked for help in finding an outlet. Life was hard enough for artists and the offer of professional help, should it be forthcoming, was not to be swatted like some irritating midge. She carefully hung up the new jacket on an old padded silk hanger and laying the skirt across the back of her chair ready for the next day, went downstairs to pour herself a large Bloody Mary and went out into the front garden to inspect a rose.

*　　　*　　　*

Arriving earlier than expected on the Friday afternoon Patrick Kerepol had let himself into the house in the High Street with his old key and found it empty. His father was still busy with the ironmongery and his mother apparently out shopping for delicacies for the homecoming feast. He carried his bag up to his old room; the familiar smell of it grew elusively fainter with each leave and while retaining the trestle table, a green-painted bookcase full of his old books and a model pterodactyl still dangling dustily from a drawing pin in the ceiling, it had been reborn as his mother's office. Patrick shifted some papers on the table, searching for the name, *Agnes*, written several times in varying degrees of depth of desperation. He suffered a twinge of nostalgia on finding it, remembering the unlovely lust and fearsome longings of first love being swiftly followed by the pleasurably excruciating teenage pain of being jilted.

Assuring his father that he needed to stretch his legs after having been so cramped up on the train, he went out for a stroll in the late afternoon sunshine. Bellhurst High Street seemed to shrink in length and width each time he returned, the houses appeared to have become neater and smaller, the roses in the front gardens brighter and tighter. He was eager to visit his sister but understood from Tom that Jane wished for his undivided attention that evening and that they would probably not visit Bea in her hidey-hole until Saturday morning. He drank half a pint at the Mummers and then strolled up the narrow lane that led eventually to Bea's Cottage, partly to fill in time till Jane's return at six o'clock and partly because his legs just naturally led him there. How excessively tame it all was; how succulently green the neat front lawns, how glossy the front doors and windows.

Geraldine saw the tall young man ambling up the lane with his hands in his pockets and thought she had seen him before visiting Bea at some stage in the past. He smiled at her when he came level with the gate and as soon as he smiled she could see it must be the brother Patrick of whom Bea had spoken so fondly. She waved and spilled her drink.

'Mrs Lewis, isn't it? Hello.' He introduced himself. 'I'm back on leave and came out for a wander, killing time till the parents are back.' Having thought her to be a quiet recluse, he was a little surprised by the friendliness of the reception and the long cherry-printed cotton skirt.

'Well, why don't you come and kill a little more by having a drink with me? I've just spent the afternoon with your sister.'

He glanced across to Fleming Cottage. 'I'd love to. Bea wrote to me and said you were looking after the place. What's the news on that quarter?'

She bade him pick up a chair from the kitchen and bring it with him, leading him out to the back garden to sit in the thick shade of an apple tree beside the fence. She carefully lowered herself down onto the old steamer chair she set out each summer and leant back with a sigh of satisfaction.

'How good to be off my feet! I find shopping exhausting . . .' but before she could continue, they were disturbed by the slamming of the Mittys' back door and they heard raised voices. Oscar's they both recognised but the woman's, Geraldine thought, must be the woman he had gone off with, come back to beg him to return for they were indubitably arguing. Patrick recognised both voices and froze, looking agonised at Mrs Lewis and making as if to leave. She put a finger conspiratorially to her lips and hissed, 'Don't stand up, they'll see you!' and he obediently remained seated, feeling thoroughly uncomfortable.

'You're a shit, did you know that?' the woman said.

'For God's sake! The weekend was just a bit of fun. You said so yourself. I didn't know you were serious. It was entirely your idea.'

'Of course I was serious. I thought *you* were serious. You seemed pretty keen on it, too. We had a wonderful time, you know we did. We've always got on so well, anyway.'

'Yes, but that was it. It has to finish. You *know* it would be impossible to carry on like this, with Phil working for me. You never gave Bea my letter. I know you didn't. There were things in that letter that would have *made* her answer it.'

'I forgot to give it to her.'

'Bollocks! I bet you haven't even told her I've come back, either. Have you? *Have you?*' He was almost shouting. 'You're a deceitful little cat.'

'Talk about people in black houses calling glass pots! No, why the bloody hell should I have told her? She's much better off without you, I can see that now. You're a bastard and you're a louse in bed. No wonder Bea doesn't want you back!'

Geraldine was entirely riveted and Patrick entirely embarrassed. Geraldine thought the name of the woman he'd gone off with had been Andrea but couldn't remember and anyway it wasn't credible that she would be go-betweening for Oscar. She didn't care for the idea of eavesdropping but was determined to find out as much as possible on Bea's behalf. She smiled unashamedly and encouragingly at Patrick who became a trifle pink in the face as there came through the fence a screech of rage and the sound of someone getting their face slapped followed by a bit of grunting and squeaking as if there was a scuffle going on. Geraldine beckoned to him, took her chance and bending double, beetled back inside her house surprisingly speedily, drink slopping from her glass. He abandoned his vodka and reluctantly also hunched down and followed the bony print-clad behind across the grass. He had been listening to his brother-in-law fighting with Agnes and conflicting emotions washed about as he stood in Geraldine's kitchen while she dashed upstairs to see what was happening from the bedroom window.

Keeping her knees agonisingly bent, Geraldine poked her head above the sill. The woman was sitting on the grass crying angrily and Oscar was pacing up and down muttering and rubbing the back of his neck but she could no longer hear and didn't dare open the window. The girl got up and ran to the back door. She had seen that little person before, hundreds of times. It was Bea's friend Agnes, the one with the delinquent child, the one who wore her skirts so short you could see her knickers when she bent down to pick him up and her legs weren't quite up to the challenge either – a bit too short and plump around the thigh.

Geraldine had lost most of the Bloody Mary on the lawn and went downstairs again to pour another larger one and to inform the already enlightened and unhappy Patrick.

'Well, Patrick, that makes one or two things clearer, to me at least. Do you think Bea ought to be told? It might constitute interference, but this is not gossip. We both know what we heard quite clearly and there's no other interpretation one can put on it.' Geraldine thought it should at least make incredible any thoughts of Bea's reunification with the awful Oscar, if Bea had any lingering thoughts in that direction. Bea had mentioned Agnes occasionally, recently with a slightly guilty irritation. The girl was a two-timing egg-waster ... egg timer and two-waster ... the vodka was getting to her ... a two-timing time-waster. Bea deserved to be warned, but on the other hand, would the information upset her so much it put her off her stroke? It was not amusing to be the bearer of bad news, either.

'I didn't even know that Oscar had left the first woman, let alone started up something with Agnes,' said Patrick. 'What does Bea know about that?'

'Nothing, I imagine. I'm guilty of not letting her know that Oscar had returned to roost, but it was just as well, I see now. Are you going to tell her? She's in the middle of painting a most wonderful series of pictures and it would be sad if she were to be upset any further, just at the minute. However, I'm fairly sure she doesn't want to get back with him, so the effect of the news may be minimal. Except that it won't be too pleasing to find out that her friend has been mucking about with him. You must decide.'

Patrick's departure from Geraldine's house was delayed by the continuation of the altercation at Fleming Cottage. As he paused with Geraldine beneath the yellow roses at her front door, Oscar and Agnes burst out of theirs. Oscar seized Agnes, who appeared red in the face and hysterical, and shook her like a rat. Both appeared unaware of their rapt audience. Agnes expertly and sharply brought up a knee and caught Oscar in the goolies. Patrick winced, involuntarily sympathetic, imagining the excruciating pain of the impact. She raced down the path, leapt into an old red Citroën and roared off.

'Now really! Just what I would have expected of her,' said Geraldine, pretending to be shocked but chuckling with delight. 'Absolutely no manners whatsoever.'

'It's a bit exciting for Bellhurst, isn't it?' Patrick was bemused but the old lady seemed to have found it all rather invigorating. It was no time to wave to Oscar who, still oblivious of their presence, was on his knees holding on to the door jamb, clutching himself and swearing.

Patrick walked home puzzling over the various possible permutations of the scene. His adolescent love for Agnes had cooled to indulgent indifference many, many years ago and he'd gathered from Bea that Agnes was quite settled down with Phil Spring. He decided it could wait till he saw Bea the next day.

Bea had driven back to Little Rumm relieved by the success of the clothes-buying enterprise. She was determined to take a break, enjoy the party that night, forget advice, everything and everyone. She stood in front of the poppy water-colour gazing at the fanned out pre-Raphaelite red hair and without knowing she did so, ran hands through her own, mimicking the effect. In her mind's eye she again had her fingers in Nut's hair and shaking her head from side to side, she turned the painting face to the wall, ready for a few carefree hours on the outside.

It had proved impossible to work in a people-free vacuum as she'd expected when first arriving here. She'd been in such a tearing hurry, fearing that the money might run out before there was enough work got together. But what was enough? And got together for what purpose? She had not considered what might follow. Real difficulties would now begin and there was still the cottage to decide about and what would happen if Oscar did, or did not, return – but Oscar was no longer wanted, was he? She could no longer imagine that they could repair the damage. But should she try, if the occasion presented itself? Everyone should have a second chance. How would she earn a proper living once the money had run out? The bookshop wages were minimum, even if she were able to get the job back. She was untrained, useless, unemployable. She'd been a fool and would probably end up living at home again while taking evening classes in book-keeping or computer studies. Oh, Freda!

She put on an old Housemartins tape and danced about the room singing 'Happy-Hour Again' to drown out the panic-inducing practicality of her thoughts, to disassociate her mind from the swirling fog of worries and emotions. 'Too late, too late, too late,' she chanted, waving her arms about above her head. 'It's too late to stop now. Far, far, far too late! Party, party, party.' The course was set and she must find a new world and the price of an electricity bill.

Terence Moorbury was not quite able to believe his eyes when he jumped out of the bus that evening. It had halted, in order to have room to turn about, just short of Little Rumm Farm. The sun was setting overdramatically in a sumptuous whirl of orange rays and uplit clouds, turning the square white villa rose-pink, and casting himself a giant's long shadow across the turf where rose-gilded sheep, too many sheep and more sheep, quietly munched. It was not the outlandish flatness and impossibly romantic colouring of the scenery which stopped him in his tracks, he'd had quite enough of that during the last week, but the sight of the narrow column of the static woman in dark blue, standing outlined against the low horizon, apparently deep in conversation with a large black bird on her wrist. It was a painting by Odilon Redon.

'I'm not having that hen on board!' called out the driver. The place had been hard enough to find in spite of the instructions, the lane wasn't suitable for a tank, let alone his new minibus and he wasn't having a mucky bird travelling in it.

'I'm sure she's not going to bring it with her,' Terence called back and walked up to Bea who dragged her attention away from the bird and looked at him with rather vaguely as if not quite sure who he was.

'I don't know how to get him off my arm. He's very heavy. He's shat on my skirt, wiped his beak on my sleeve and if I stop scratching his neck, he tries to peck.' She spoke quietly and quickly, as if scared of hurting the bird's feelings.

'Well, what do you usually do, in order to get on with your life?'

'I don't usually *do* anything. It's never happened before. I mean, I've met him before, but he isn't my pet. I've not been instructed in getting rid of birds once they've outstayed their welcome. I'll try shaking my arm.'

Bea waved her arm about hopefully, but the crow hung on, rocking and balancing as if it was a game. Inside the bus the other members of the film crew hooted with merriment. Terence tried sharply clapping his hands but Budgie, who had arrived unexpectedly while Bea waited in the garden for her lift, struck out viciously, feinting at him with a fearsome meat-ripping beak and flapped and Bea let out a shriek as one of the great wings hit her on the nose.

'Suppose I come up from behind, and try to grab him? You could start scratching his neck again, to see if you can put him in a good mood,' Terence suggested, feeling rather ambivalent about this. He had never, that he could remember, touched a live bird. This one, he supposed it was a raven or something and obviously not a hen, seemed most unfrightened and was rather threatening. He advanced behind it and bravely grabbed, forcibly lifting the bird off, his hands cringing from the dry feel of dusty feathers, and jerkily launched him high into the air. A whoosh and flurry, a furious 'cra-ark, cra-ark' and the delinquent bird was airborne and circling with intent.

'Oh! thank you. What a relief – he was getting so heavy. Come in to the house.' He followed as she ran for cover and Budgie made a bombing run at him. Indoors, Bea scrubbed the mess from her skirt, examined her arms for scratches and then peered outside.

'I'm so sorry about this. I shouldn't have tried to get him to sit on my arm in the first place.' She looked at him again as if she couldn't quite remember why he was there. He wondered briefly if she was high on something. 'Of course, the bus is waiting. I'll try to distract him with a piece of bacon while we run for it. It seems all clear outside.' Their reappearance brought yells of encouragement and cries of 'Look behind you, look behind you!' from those on the bus, but Bea extravagantly tossed the rasher of best unsmoked back bacon to one side of the garden and they scrambled aboard the bus without any further attention from Budgie, who glided down from the roof of the house to inspect his danegeld.

Bea was flustered and pink. It wasn't quite the sort of impression she'd hoped to make.

'Well, tell us all about it. Is he a local crow, or has he just dropped in from the Underworld? Does he sit at the head of your bed and cry 'Nevermore!' at awkward moments to your lovers? *Hello*, is there anyone there or have you gone out to lunch?'

She jerked back to Terence who had passed his hands back and forth in front of her face.

'That was a raven that cried "Nevermore!" Budgie was hand-reared by a friend of mine and arrived while I was waiting for you. I stupidly thought it would be nice to see if I could get him to sit on my wrist, like a falcon – he was a bit reluctant at first. They've got such sharp toenails and very rough, hard feet. I scratched the back of his head which seemed to make him quite ecstatic, then he wouldn't leave. I'm sorry if I seem a bit distrait.'

'You looked like a sorceress with a familiar. Quite unearthly.'

'I suppose I must have done.' Terence was looking at her attentively. Finding him neither unpleasing nor wildly attractive, she felt easier in his company and relaxed, laughing a little. She hoped it didn't sound too false.

'How far did you say Blackshorne Court was, from here?' asked Terence, persevering.

'From here, about six miles, as the crow flies.'

'I hope to God he isn't flapping along behind us. There's something eerie about those birds. Harbingers of doom and confusion? Didn't the Vikings have a thing about crows?'

'Don't say things like that. You don't know how true that has been for me this evening.' Then suddenly she found she could not stop talking. 'Anyway, that was ravens again. Odin carried a pair about with him – Huginn and Munnin – Mind and Memory. It's just that all the crow family are scavengers, feed off dead things, road accidents and suchlike, that makes people think they are unlucky; that's why people salute magpies, to ward off the bad luck. Budgie doesn't seem to have brought dire happenings to the man who found him when he was a fledgling. I've never met anyone less doom-ridden and more cheerful.'

'I'm very ignorant about birds. That's the first one I've met socially. I was brought up in London and can only recognise pigeons, starlings and sparrows ... and swans and ducks, of course. I might even know a goose if I met one. Actually that's quite a good tally. I might even become a bird-watcher one day.'

Bea did not comment but tapped the driver on the shoulder, commanding, 'You need to turn right at the T junction just up here, and then first left after the Swan pub.' The driver, a Parden man, had earlier been reluctant to take directions. The minibus crossed a bridge over a dyke and carried on uphill, eventually coming to a halt at the junction. The driver pointed out exultantly that according to the signpost, St Rumwold-at-Cliffe was to the left, and seemed prepared to argue the point. He didn't like taking directions from women, he remarked aloud, since they never seemed to know left from right, waving wildly to one side while shouting out the other. He raised a cheap laugh among the other passengers.

'Ignore the signpost,' said Bea, firmly. 'It was blown round in a gale in the spring and no one's pushed it back. Ragstone Street is to the right, then first left.'

'You seem very confident. I thought you hadn't been here before?' asked Terence, peering out into the twilight dubiously.

'No,' whispered Bea, fearful of raising further irritation in the driver, 'but I memorised the way. I must admit I do get the words wrong when I'm poring over a map, just as the old misogynist in front complains. But once I've got the plan in my head, I never get lost, not even in all those mazy lanes we've come through. Look, there are the gates just up ahead.'

Ragstone Street, on the degraded cliff facing out over the marsh, was a Roman road. It petered out into a nettlesome farm track in a hamlet, in the centre of which stood Blackshorne Court, a miniature manor alternately augmented and destroyed over the ages so that now all that stood was the most ancient part, a tiny thirteenth-century chapel beside the central section of a Jacobean wing built of narrow red bricks, the old house from which it had sprung having been demolished by a Victorian coal merchant. They drove through the gates, past a lily-filled, semi-circular moat, in which a full and creamy rising moon was reflected. The sight caused the first murmurs of interest among the chattering crew, who craned their necks to see the top of the sole remaining turret behind which the moon sat fatly, as if pierced by the pinnacle and held captive atop like a crumpet on a toasting fork. The effect was decidedly magical and in near silence they disembarked among the other cars in the driveway and ascended the steps through a wide door, into a high-ceilinged, galleried hall, candlelit and already stuffed with guests.

Bea was herded through the throng towards their host by

the small and ever-attentive Terence, who had a firm grasp of her elbow and who began to remind her of a Border collie, a Ben, Pip, Bess, or Bel. The man, grey-haired although perhaps only in his late thirties, heron-tall and flaunting in a cream silk jacket, turned from the couple to whom he had been talking. Heron embraced sheepdog theatrically. 'Terence! How *won-der-ful!*' 'Justin! It's tremendous to see you again ... what a stunning place!' The couple to whom Justin had been speaking were Amelia and Edmund. Amelia let out a screech of surprise, 'Bea! How lovely!' and she was embraced by them both like a long-lost friend. Amelia was dressed in green, a sorceress's silver necklace round her neck, a thick hand-made chain hung like an old-fashioned charm bracelet with cast silver fish, shells and palms of seaweed, which chinked and tinkled when she moved. Justin released Terence from the bear hug.

'Now please introduce me to your *friend*, Terence.' He was staring down at Bea from his great height. 'Are you tired of being told you resemble Botticelli's Primavera, my dear? You are Simonetta Vespucci, to the life, and so appropriately dressed, in indigo blue.' Bea had not heard of Simonetta Vespucci; it sounded suspiciously like an Italian make of motorbike, but since it was obviously meant as a compliment, she was pleased by it. In the down-to-earth circles in which she had grown up, complimenting a pretty woman was considered to be not unlike taking beefburgers to McDonald's, it being assumed she must already know she was beautiful and therefore didn't need to have her head turned any further. She was about to thank the tall man and introduce herself but Terence spoke for her.

'This is Bea Kerepol, a painter. We've only recently met.'

Justin advanced upon her and bent to give her a light, almost butterfly-like brush on the cheek. 'Well, I'm very pleased you have come to the house-warming party. Now you must listen to *quite* an extraordinary story.' Justin's voice was resonant, and swooped up and down with unusual emphases upon unlikely words. It was perhaps a nervous tic of his, which distracted from the substance, scattering false clues about and making one wait for the unexpected pause or stress rather than hear what was said.

'I went to Edmund's beautiful *book shop* last autumn, when this *project* was still on the drawing-board, to enlist his help in collecting up Connaught Marvel's *out-of-print* oeuvres. We worked together for quite a while before, *lo* and behold! The most amazing coincidence – his partner, dear Amelia here, *is* Connaught Marvel's grand-daughter! She has been so helpful in telling me about his later life, and come up with some quite brilliant photographs of *him* and his mistress at their *farm* in Suffolk. I knew there was *a grand-daughter* of course, but had given up hope of tracing her,' he turned gracefully to Amelia, 'but it's your *story* my dear, why don't you tell this lovely Bea and pretty Terence all about it while I *discover* where all the *waiters* with the booze have hidden themselves. It's very trying having to do this all one one's own, when there *are* so many people I want to talk to.' He smiled benevolently at them and turned away, his eyes searching over the heads of the crowd for the errant waiters.

It transpired that Amelia's aunt, the wife of Connaught's son, had recently died gaga and intestate and the remaining copyright of his books had passed to Amelia. Only no one had told her of her aunt's death, the solicitors having been unable to trace her. Justin, whose researchers had only just managed to contact the aunt a few weeks before her death and found her sadly incomprehensible, was unable to get out of her the whereabouts of the niece, of whose existence Justin had been beginning to doubt. Then he had approached Edmund.

'And wonderful for Amelia that he did,' said Edmund, 'and as some of the A. C. Holliday novels are to be republished in paperback to coincide with the TV series and biography for the centenary of his birth, it's going to be financially rather pleasing. His travel books have often been reprinted before but Aunt Margaret seems to have had a stingy side and has been sitting on the royalties for years. Amelia and her daughter Josie are the old man's only living descendants.'

'Isn't *that* exciting?' said Justin reappearing with a wobbling trayfull of champagne, 'I was so happy to be the medium by which Amelia regained her rights. It is of course a fairy *story* and I felt quite smug to be the fairy godfather. So, on with the ball! The *music* in the marquee in the back courtyard should be starting up soon. I do hope you'll like the band, The Preachers. They specialise in Paul Butterfield-type Chicago blues, they tell me. Then by popular demand there's an Irish band for set-dancing or something; whatever it is I can't do it. I can only do Strip-the-Willow.'

He looked hopefully at Bea. 'I hope you enjoy dancing – I shall come and claim a shuffle and sway later on, but now I must go and prostitute myself by being charming to some rich businessmen and their wives whom I hope are going to be useful in relation to another project.' He gave an unlikely wink, the lid closing slowly like a blind over the penetrating bright blue eye then snapping up again and he stalked off. Affected and camp, but more intelligent than he let on, Bea decided.

'The last time we met Bea,' said Edmund, turning to Terence, 'was at an extraordinary midnight demonstration by a collective, no a coven, several covens of covens of witches down at the power station. We were all drawn there as if we'd been summoned. Quite odd really, but not without its farcical side. I expect Bea may have told you about it?'

'No, but that's also where we met. We were there for a couple of days shooting the final scenes of *Patrick and Marguerite*. We finished this morning, thankfully. The whole production has been dogged with troubles and we've all come up here to Justin's to let our hair down and relax. You say you met witches down there? Well, we became entangled with some rather raucous "nuns" in pink habits. That place seems to attract the bizarre. Have you read *Patrick and Marguerite* by any chance?'

'I have,' said Amelia, 'when I was about fourteen. I thought it was wildly romantic and quite frightening and totally missed the fact that it was a spoof.'

Terence looked puzzled, then awkward. 'What do you mean, a spoof?'

Bea was in need of the bathroom and excusing herself for a moment, left Terence to Amelia and headed for the wide staircase. Upstairs various dark doors opened off a wide corridor and she had to resort to testing them all to find the lavatory. The first opened on to a large bedroom where the lights were blazing, the walls hung with plain cream silk and was otherwise most unsybaritically bare, although what furnishings there were appeared to be in keeping with the period of the room. Her curious eye was trapped by a framed black-and-white photograph standing on a large oak table by the door; it was of a pussy-cat-faced woman with dark hair, looking as if she were about to open her mouth to complain and holding stiffly at a marked distance on her knee a very fat infant in long lacy christening robes. It was professionally done in the manner of royal photographs, the subjects posed on a vast sofa. Bea looked hard, twice to make certain, and then quickly shut the door again, heart pounding. The woman was unmistakably Andrea Bullingden.

'Are you searching for a bathroom, my dear?' said Justin, looming up behind her. 'It's the next one, on the left. I should have labelled them, I know, for the party. Are you all right? You look a little pale.'

'No, no, I'm fine. Thank you. I should have asked directions.'

When she reappeared, having recovered her calm, he was leaning on the banisters at the end of the passage by the staircase, apparently waiting for her, which she found rather embarrassing, but with an Edwardian courtesy he offered her his arm. She took it and they began the descent into the packed hall below.

'I can't resist walking downstairs with you like this in such a compromising fashion, although neither of us have been upstairs for long enough to have had a fuck.'

Bea became distinctly unamused and disengaged her arm.

'Oh God! I'm sorry, I didn't mean to upset you. I am a bit

pissed already, I fear. I do a lot of upsetting these days. Crude, bitter, horny old me.'

Bea stopped. He stopped too and looked down at her. The bright blue eyes were avuncular, apologetic.

'That photograph, on the table. Is that your wife?'

'*Was* my wife. I keep it so I can pull faces at her every morning. We were at last *divorced* this month – the party is not only a house-warming but an *un-marriage* party. We share my son fifty-fifty. A judgement of Solomon without the intelligent psychological insights.'

'My married name is Mitty. Is yours, your surname, Bullingden?'

'It is.'

'My husband Oscar left me, for your ex-wife.'

He did not speak for a moment, then put out a narrow, elegant hand and patted her cheek. 'How very nasty for *you* to have come upon her *face* to face like that! An unpleasant coincidence for you, but she is very attractive, on the surface, and it was quite likely that she would steal away *someone's* husband in the end. Whether she will be able to keep him long, I very much doubt. I also keep the photograph because it's the only one of my son as a baby, and it reminds me never, ever, to get married again. Yes, the name *tolls* a passing-bell in my head. Oscar Mitty, your husband. I remember seeing it on a solicitor's letter. How very strange.' He sighed. 'He does know, by now, that the hell-cat is an unredeemable alcoholic? I've spent a fortune, several fortunes, on getting her dried out. No, never mind all this. It's taking us an awful long time to come down these *stairs*. The band's getting going and Terence will be becoming fretful.'

'I only came tonight with Terence by coincidence,' she said, warming to Justin again as they came down the last flight of stairs into the great hall, 'and you won't mention this to the others, will you?' He shook his head understandingly. They rejoined Amelia and Edmund and the coincidental Terence. Amelia was laughing her head off and Terence was looking piqued.

'Well, it's hardly serious, is it?' Amelia was saying. 'At the end, when she's arriving by boat from France, to be reunited with her lover and they rush towards each other, knee deep in passion and shingle, and she is seasick in his lap on the beach.'

'That wasn't in the treatment, or the script! And when Marie-Christine Boulette, who's playing Marguerite, *was* actually physically seasick, we re-shot it, twice. We treated it as a straight ghost story; no one realised it was meant to be funny.' Terence sounded a little sulky, but began to see the silly side of it and rallied. 'Now I come to think of it, that bit where the ghost of her husband makes love to her in the French *auberge*, and she complains, in marvellously elliptical language, of having a cold fanny . . . what an opportunity wasted!'

'Poor Grandpapa! He'd have thought it hilarious, someone coming along and taking one of his jokey pot-boilers seriously. But it would have to be done straight in any case, in order to be funny – but it's a shame they've cut out the amusing bits.'

'I thought you said you'd read the book,' said Bea to Terence accusingly, delighted to have caught him out.

'Well, I didn't have time. Anyway, it's still a good story. Let's all go and listen to the band.' Justin had wandered off again to mingle. She could see him, head and shoulders above everyone else, moving through the crowd as if searching for someone.

The marquee was midnight blue and eccentrically fitted with circular panels of something transparent let into the roof round the central poles so that as one approached, beams of pale light from inside searched up into the sky. There was a sumptuous looking buffet laid out on miles of crisp white linen, the band was playing 'Blues with a Feelin'' and a great many very chic people were beginning to filter in and sit at the tables round the dance floor. The area was planted with flowerbeds of huge indigo-blue paper flowers. Bea became reckless, feckless and ready for any contingency, knocked back a third glass of champagne and took off for the dance floor, with Terence in sweaty pursuit.

Chapter Ten

Now small and riding coldly high, the moon cast a broad light across the waiting garden, light enough to guess the shade of pink of the newly opened apple-scented rose.

'Light enough to do some gardening,' she said aloud, fumbling the key into the lock.

'Moonlight gardening is out of the question,' said Terence firmly, behind her. 'What's that strange burnt smell?'

'Just a burnt-out car, up the track,' she said casually, then as if discussing a gas log fire, 'I love a good blaze, don't you?'

The minibus driver had first dropped the others in Fingle, apart from the obligatory missing member who had decided to take his chances with a pouting blond waiter and had disappeared just as they were leaving. The driver, complaining all the way, had then brought Bea home, accompanied by Terence, who had unexpectedly jumped out of the bus with her – just to say goodnight, she thought fuzzily, how sweet – but the bus had turned and driven away without him. Bea, happily full of poached salmon and bubbly, was unfazed and guessed that he just might have arranged this with the driver. Better to muck it up with a comparative stranger than with Nut, she thought, hazily irrational, better to have another breathing life in the house than be alone. She pushed open the door and let him follow her inside. Wild strangers had last night invaded her territory and she didn't want to sleep by herself.

She clattered the keys on the kitchen table and let out a cracking yawn, stretching long arms and witchy fingers up towards the ceiling and knocked the dangling lampshade, dislodging a dead moth. Terence's oak-apple brown, sheepdog eyes looked curiously inflamed at the sight of the red throat and white teeth, and he seized his chance and Bea about the waist. They tottered upstairs, Bea missing one step in three, and paused on the moonlit landing where she put her arms around his neck, sagging slightly at the knees. It was past two o'clock in the morning.

'Where to?' he asked, 'in here?' He put his hand out to the handle of the painting-room door, and she became alert, for a second.

'No, no! Not in there. This way.' He must not, they must not, sleep in the red bed. That was Nut's. She backed, still holding on to him and laughing, into the front bedroom, and they fell onto the bed.

'You do know what you're doing, don't you?' he asked, desperately trying to pull off his jacket with Bea still holding onto his neck.

''Course I do. Did you think I might scream "date rape" afterwards? I wish I could remember where I sowed the parsley,' she remarked incomprehensibly, laughed again and couldn't stop, and he was enveloped in the warmth of it and the salty taste of her skin and was immensely grateful for the lack of complication in the woman. Why couldn't it always be this simple?

She had not been able to stop herself from planning the next painting as he made love to her, or rather she'd made love to him. Only you couldn't really call it that. He had some funny ideas, which entailed her doing all the work. He was now tucked against her back, hotly asleep and snoring slightly, one hand still firmly anchored to the old iron bedrail with a long green silk scarf. Having slept for an hour or so she was wide awake again. It was difficult to sleep round the time of the full moon and even with the curtains so tightly drawn that not the finest needle of light penetrated, she felt its omnipresence, disconcertingly watchful, askance. 'So?' it seemed to query, 'SO?' and the O of the SO was itself. She had the strongest sensation of having made a very serious mistake.

A quarter to five in the morning. Moon-cooled air came in through the open window and she turned to look at the dark face deep in the crevasse between the pillows, sleep leaching sonorously out into the bedclothes. She crept from the bed, picked up jeans and shirt from the silvered chair beneath the window and tiptoed stealthily downstairs in the dawn. She would have to think of it as a practice run, inconsequential and yet again unsatisfying, even if in retrospect it had also been extremely funny. 'They say it's better to break a fast with a biscuit than a full meal,' she thought; her surmise about the giant fountain pen had been correct.

A blackbird fluted on the garden wall as she made a Marmite sandwich and a cup of coffee to chase away the cobweb wisps, taking great care not to rattle the kettle against the tap and to smother the clinks of knife against plate. There was no point in going back to bed now it was nearly light and further sleep would be impossible with the ridiculous Terence in her bed. Optimism seeped back into her with the first glimmers of sun to the east and she slowly drew the bolt, wincing at the scraping sound, slipping out into the garden with cup and sandwich. The flags were chill gravestones beneath her bare feet and she stood among the stock-still, tightly furled poppies by the wall, their dagged grey leaves thick with dew-bloom and filigree-trailed by little cream and brown humbug snails. One bud approached opening, flashing densely packed petals between the two halves of the splitting sepals. She stole a snail and held it on the warm palm of her hand, watching its painfully sensitive and tentative horns expanding, searching left and right, contracting from the harsh touch of a fingertip.

A magpie walked portentously across the field in white waistcoat and green-black tails, a self-conscious head waiter approaching to take an order in an empty restaurant. The air was milky soft, there was silence and mercifully no sign of Budgie. It would be beautiful down on the beach, but the noise of starting up the truck might waken Terence and it would be unkind, so early, and unforgivable to leave him to wake up alone with no means of transport. She would have to drive him back to Fingle after breakfast. It was Saturday, he was returning to London and that would be that. She left the morning to mind its own business and with rewarmed coffee and a humbug snail on a plate, to draw, slipped noiselessly upstairs to the painting room.

On that same Saturday morning, dressed in the new clothes, Geraldine nodded with satisfaction at the old-new self in the looking glass and then double-checked she had locked the back door, and that Piggy was shut outside and not in. Unused to being left alone for as much as a half day, he had taken to piddling in protest on the kitchen floor whenever she went out. Standing by the window, watching for the cab which would take her to Parden station and the train for London, she was soused in the unreality of the enterprise and checked again in her large black leather bag for the address of the gallery, although she had it by heart. In the bag were secreted two of Bea's sketch books, borrowed from the cottage before Oscar had returned, and Sylvia Plath's *Crossing the Water* to read on the journey. She thought it a flimsy lath-and-plaster name for such a turbulent poet, but guessed not much else might take her mind from the worry of seeing Simon Greensand again. It was a paperback bought just before she had started on the pills and had never read before her brain had turned to syllabub, unable then to concentrate for long enough to recall the beginning of a sentence before reaching its full stop.

She was catching an earlier train than was necessary in order to have time to look at shops and other galleries and not arrive in a hurry. She disliked to be fussed by arriving late. 'In Russian plays,' she reminded herself firmly, 'people all sit down for a moment before leaving on a journey, in order to gather their thoughts, remember if they've turned off the gas and to pray for a safe passage to wherever it is they're going. If I do the same, I will feel calmer and probably, as soon as I sit down, the cab will arrive — so it would be a good thing to do in any case.'

She sat in the middle of the faded sofa, bolt-upright so as not to crease the back of her jacket, bag on lap and neat feet together and immediately remembered she had not shut the bedroom window. By the time she was downstairs again, the driver was ringing the door bell.

The train itself was late in arriving at Charing Cross and was met by an outgoing rush of passengers on platform six, a group of poorly shepherded teenaged travellers were trying to enter the train before the incomers had left it; a kind young man, very tall and with red hair, gently held back with a long arm a shoving, baggy-trousered youth and smilingly offered her his hand as she descended. She was out of the station and into the Strand before remembering of whom he'd reminded her.

Simon was waiting in the sun at the door of the gallery as she approached, her heart fluttering. The once-loved, remembered shock of uncontrollable fair hair was now white, but still uncontrolled, and the inquisitive beaky nose was redder. Immaculate pale grey tailoring upholstered and retained a body that had thickened slightly but was not much changed. That, Geraldine noticed in spite of her interior agitation, was an extremely expensive suit. Simon had obviously done very well indeed.

Neither of them had clung to any illusions. Having recognised her immediately and apparently as undismayed by her ageing as she was by his, he beamed with pleasure as she walked slowly up to him. He took her hand and kissed her on both cheeks then drew her quite tenderly inside to meet the son James, one of the spoilt, beloved boys for whose sake he had sacrificed both their happinesses.

James was a gold-bespectacled version of his father, full-facedly prosperous and a little self-satisfied. He was dressed in a long black jacket and trousers and a collarless white shirt and Geraldine noticed premature little red spider veins crawling across his cheeks.

They lunched in a restaurant where one had to ring the doorbell to gain admittance, in the plain surroundings of a private eighteenth-century drawing room where the floorboards were bare and the service was neither obsequious nor patronising. It was pleasantly buzzing and the food was, to poor Geraldine, so much of a revelation that she definitely resented having to talk throughout the meal. She had only recently discovered pot-noodles and had been living on those for the last few days, being totally incapable of the mechanics of cookery.

Simon was explaining that he was now semi-retired, but that his opinion was still kindly sought and he still had command, courtesy of James, of one slot in the calendar of exhibitions. Geraldine pursued a piece of salmon dusted with parmesan and chopped rocket about her plate with the determination of someone who knew it was their last meal for a week. In November, Simon continued, he could put on a show of whomever he pleased. James looked proudly indulgent and poured more wine; his wife, May, half-English, half-Chinese, who had been waiting for them at the restaurant, was smiling with charmingly scrutable relief at the success of the reunion.

'Straight after your phone call I thought how a retrospective of your work would fit the bill. I did have a new young man booked, a bit of a wild card perhaps. Unfortunately he's taken a tumble off a motorbike and broken his wrist quite badly. He can't now complete the amount of work needed to make the show worthwhile. The poor fellow is so desperately disappointed. I've told him I'll keep the November slot open for him next year and perhaps we'll put one or two of his paintings in this year's group Christmas show, if James will allow it. Meanwhile, James agrees with me that your work would make a most intriguing show, stop-gap or not. What do you think?'

Geraldine, whose polished plate had now been replaced by a dish of succulent little rounds of venison with green beans, so fine they could pass through the eye of a needle, hauled her attention back to her host, put down her knife and fork and stared at Simon, eyes luminous with real food, wine and excitement. Was this a straightforward, genuine offer, or was it prompted by guilt? She did not care. Either would do.

'Simon! Where would we find all the work? I told you I virtually gave up after ... after Richard died. I've only just re-started and there are only about six presentable old works in the house.'

'And I also have four of my own, if you remember? I am still in contact with at least five other old patrons of yours. In fact I sat beneath one of your paintings at a dinner two weeks ago. There's also McNamara and Rob Gurgelfeldt in New York. As soon as you put the phone down yesterday, I started to think about this, and I've already been in touch with them and they think they can trace four or five more. Rob's coming over in September and could bring them with him. People like to lend their pictures – see their names up beside the artist's at the show. There are probably others I can contact if I go through our records. We have back sales invoices dating from the nineteen fifties,' he leant back and looked fondly at her, 'and your last solo show with us was in November, nineteen sixty-eight. I didn't have to look that up; I remembered it very well.'

'Your gallery is huge, two vast rooms, and most of my work is on the small side.' Geraldine thought it the perfect moment to broach the subject of Bea. She blotted her mouth with a thick linen napkin and sat up importantly.

'I have an idea to put to you which will entail you coming to me at Bellhurst and visiting a certain young woman, Bea Kerepol. She is my own discovery and I'm very proud of her. She was the reason I came off those wretched carnivorous, life-digesting tranquillisers – they should come with a government health warning.' She had a swig of Perrier and making an effort not to be side-tracked by her own regrets, recovered the thread, conscious that she was dangerously putting a label on Bea, that such a label might possibly deter as much as attract.

'Bea is a one-off. She has spent her life until now – she is thirty, I think – drawing and painting. Teaching herself to draw, teaching herself to paint. Her imagination is frightening and she doesn't know it but is astonishingly strong-minded. Her work is figurative, modern, funny and yet there is a neo-romantic undercurrent. Insofar as they belong in any particular type, I would suggest an unlikely parentage, by Stanley Spencer out of Leonora Carrington. You *have* to see them. Once you have, if your views concur with mine, then perhaps she could be approached to fill up the other room? You could then have my retrospective and her launching together? I don't know why I'm addressing myself only to you, Simon. James, she'll interest you too. Now, I've been rather underhand and stolen something from her to whet your appetites.' She bent down and from the black bag elatedly produced the two sketch-books. 'This one is what she was doing as a child. Look, it's dated. She would have been ten or eleven? It's quite extraordinary. And this one is last year's.' She passed the child's one to James and the other to Simon and managed at last to get a piece of the melting venison into her mouth. Oh, bliss!

'Go on and have a look. But when you come to see her, if you come, you must not under any circumstances mention these – she would be furious with me. Oh my goodness, this venison is just too delicious! I know I said she's quite tough but there's a tender plant behind the front of hawthorn hedging, apparently most tiresomely lacking in confidence in her own abilities. I thought it might be a form of attention-seeking at first, but now I believe it to be genuine reticence.'

Geraldine was enjoying herself, hearing her own confident sales pitch. All three of them had ceased to eat and were listening attentively. How much easier it is, she thought, to make men *really* listen when one is older and they are no longer distracted by one's face or body. James was leafing through, turning the book this way and that, showing his wife, intent and amused. Simon's jaw had dropped slightly. He was looking at a water-colour of Agnes sitting half-naked in the dappled shade of an apple tree drinking a gin and tonic, while overhead a massively suggestive boa constrictor coiled itself about the branches, watching. It was drawn from the viewpoint of just above the boa and was both ridiculous and suggestively tense.

'Normally we'd like to be sent slides first, and CVs,' said Simon, 'but under the circumstances, I think I'll come.'

'Me too,' said his son, adding carefully, 'but I'll leave the decision to you, Dad.' He knocked back his wine, refilled his glass and turned politely to Geraldine, knowing that his father's apparent altruism was usually based on sound judgement. 'I grew up with your paintings on our walls, Geraldine, and continue to love and admire them. I'll trust your judgement.' He thought Bea's juvenilia very interesting and although not quite his scene, the more recent sketch-book showed promise of considerable commercial potential; he thought it would be tasteless to mention the latter in front of another artist. May, delicately scenting the promise of getting first to an interesting discovery said she would like to make a visit to this Bea Kerepol.

'May,' said James, gobbling down his halibut, 'is a freelance arts journalist,' he raised his arm to attract the attention of a waiter and ordered another bottle of wine, 'which as you can imagine, can be discreetly useful to the gallery at times.'

Geraldine became hypnotised by the food as the meal progressed through walnut-and-ginger steamed puddings and cheeses and became quite silent till they returned to the gallery for coffee. She went with Simon to look through the racks of paintings of the gallery's stable of artists in the basement storeroom. One or two she did not comprehend at all, another made her cackle with laughter: 'Good God! Is that old fraud still at it?' More often she was most interested in what she saw, and thoughtful. It was always best to start at the top end of the market when selling something. Yes, she could see Bea Kerepol fitting in with these, outshining quite a few of them with honesty and ease. But then, she knew she was so very biased.

'So,' said the old man behind her, putting his hand on her arm as she eased a painting back into its upright stack, 'you've forgiven me?'

'There's nothing to forgive. You were right, in the long term, although I couldn't accept it then. You suffered from Bea's problem. Too nervous of other people's opinions, perhaps?'

'I didn't want to lose the boys. I couldn't have borne it.'

'No, it would have been an atrocious decision to have to make. I do understand, but I also want you to know, Simon, what happened to me after Richard found out about us. I was virtually imprisoned — trussed up with yards of his stringy insecurity. I didn't survive, or rather the painting did not survive it.'

'My dear Geraldine, I am so terribly sorry. I felt too guilty to contact you after Marjorie buggered off. I felt sure you wouldn't want to know. I was a coward.' There was a stricken look in his eyes but Geraldine, wiser and now feeling no more than a gentle affection, and some power, did not quite relent.

'Yes, you were. And so was I, later on. You owe me, perhaps, just a little more . . . I obviously won't press you about Bea if you are disappointed by her work, but I know I'm right. Anyway, I have too little of my own to sell, most of it will be on loan, and perhaps Bea might do even better than I think and ensure the gallery doesn't have a complete loss of income for a month! Simon, it *is* wonderful to see you again.'

*　　*　　*

The breakfast, the full kippers-scrambled-egg-bacon and sausages of it, had been a bit much after the massive homecoming supper of the night before and Patrick sat back from the table and let his belt out a couple of holes. He had not dared give the food less than his whole attention. Ecstatic to see her beloved boy home again, Jane sat among the eggy breakfast plates and scattered yellow croissant crumbs and between demanding to know further details of the state of his health, love-life, teeth, career, plans and politics, was explaining to him the tribulations of rewriting an eighteenth-century cookery book. Tom had relapsed into silence. To him, the breakfast was imperfect without Bea. Tom wanted his family complete around him and wistfully asked Jane if she'd tried to call Bea to invite her over for breakfast.

'You know I did. Several times. But she'd switched the phone off again.' She turned to Patrick. 'I hope you can talk some sense into her when you see her, if she allows you anywhere near, that is. We worry so about her living in that damp hut of Nest's. She just daubs away all day and probably all night, quite alone.' Jane's voice rose a fraction, irritably. 'She's impatient with us if we visit. One can see her longing for us to leave as soon as we arrive. I think the shock has temporarily unhinged her – poor child. I hate to think of her grieving alone like that, unable to share her troubles.'

'I remember going there for a picnic in the garden with Aunt Nest when I was about thirteen. It wasn't a damp hut – rather a solid little house and very sunny. It must have been so difficult after Oscar left, quite desperate for her. She always hated sympathy because she always tends to think things are her own fault. It's hardly surprising she wants some time on her own.' Defensive of his sister, Patrick tilted back on his chair and reached for the phone on the dresser. Bea found it difficult to accept help and that had always frustrated Jane.

'I'll try her again myself. If it's switched off, we'll just go round unannounced, on the off-chance. You'll drive me over, won't you Dad? If she's not in we'll leave a note asking her to lunch and go for a walk on the beach.'

Bea's phone was still switched off.

'I *told* you so,' said Jane dramatically, pouring Patrick another cup of coffee. 'She could have become a Moonie and not told us. We only wanted to help her sort out the practical, legal side of her separation. We're having nettle soup and poached chicken for lunch.' Patrick chortled; Jane's vivid, strong-flavoured nettle soup delivered a blood-cleansing punch that usually brought Bea out in spots. He looked at his watch.

'It's half past ten already and she's an early riser.' He thanked his mother for the emperor's breakfast and gave her a kiss. 'Are you sure you won't come with us? No? You go on ahead then, Dad, I've just got to run upstairs for something.'

He delved in his suitcase among neatly folded shirts for the two-inch square miniature brown paper parcel, tied with cream thread and red sealing wax seals the diameter of a pencil. Buying the contents had taken three minutes but wrapping it had taken half an hour. With a fine-point pen he addressed it, in minute handwriting, 'To Mrs R. Crusoe, Nest's Hut.'

'Hello? Bea?'

The smell of burnt toast drifted through the open front door and Nut had knocked and entered without pausing, following his nose fast into the kitchen, so eager to see her, calling out as he came.

How rare she looked to Francis Nutmeg as she sat there in a long white cotton dress at the kitchen table, shining amid the matt sheets of grey Formica. There was alarm in her face, an unflattering astonishment as she looked up from the kitchen table, caught spreading butter on toast, her hand with the knife in midair, hair swinging round her face. At the table also sat a bare-footed man in a dishevelled state of unbuttoned unbrushedness, who also looked up at him, his features first registering an iced surprise, followed by the unmistakable creakings of antagonism.

There was silence in the room, encompassing perhaps five seconds – a long five seconds. Nut snapped it, not by speaking but by crashing the book on fossils down upon the table, so hard it rattled the china. A half-open poppy, broken off short and placed in a glass of water, dropped one of its iced-jade sepals with a soft plop and the shutter clicked, the still was taken. Swinging round on his heel – they felt the air moving as he turned – he strode out of the house, a red ruffling breeze that became a hurricane as he drove off down the track in the blue van.

Terence, relieved, picked up another piece of toast.

'Who was that?' He gave an uncertain little chuckle. 'He didn't look too pleased to see me.'

Bea was still staring after Nut, shocked.

'No.' She closed her eyes for a second. 'He wouldn't have been. Though, for all he knew you could have been my brother ...' Her cheeks were flaming. 'Oh God! It's this weekend that he's due on leave – I'd forgotten.' She still held the buttery knife in one hand and the toast in the other and was thinking rapidly what to do. She felt very bad indeed, powerless, roughly shaken in his wake.

'That was a friend of mine, a close friend ... he's been away these last few days.' She wished desperately he hadn't discovered her with Terence. But he had no reason to be quite so angry. Of course he had; she had led him to believe she might ... Terence curtly interrupted her.

'Oh, I see. I'm just an interim passion, am I?' Now he was annoyed.

'Who said anything about passion?' she snapped, swinging round on the unfortunate man and a nobbet of butter flew off the knife and landed in his coffee. He scooped it out with a spoon, eyebrows raised but his mouth stretched tight and turned a little down at the corners in a disappointed smile. He'd awoken that sunny morning in a mood of delighted optimism; now things were no longer as they had appeared, were drifting out of his control.

'You seemed quite certain about it last night.'

'That was last night,' then she added, with a hopefully disarming smile, 'Today we are . . . well, friends. Won't that do?'

'Oh, I see, just like you and the departed Viking. Well, I'm usually better friends with the women I don't sleep with. You're a lunatic, did you know that?' The skin on his face was taut, but then softened a fraction. 'OK. You've made a mistake. I don't think I have.' He stood up in an attempted graciousness, fighting back disappointment and tucking his shirt into his trousers. He looked small and disproportionately furious. He looked, she thought, as she fought back tears, exactly like Seb.

'I'll get the rest of my clothes and leave you in peace – but I'm not walking all the way back to Fingle. You'll have to drive me.'

'Of course I'll drive you. Please, please don't get cross, there's no need.' She was aware now that he was hurt. She had assumed that a one-night stand was what he'd been expecting and had not allowed for him wanting more than that. There was the sound of a vehicle drawing up outside and Terence became vigilant for a moment, half-expecting the return of Nut, armed this time not with a book on fossils but with a double-headed axe. Doors slammed and another male voice called out.

'Bea? Where are you?'

In burst a tall, sunburnt young man who swept past Terence and gathered up Bea in a hug so tight that she squeaked in protest. Another lover or the brother she'd mentioned? He was followed by yet another man, older, grey-haired with a black eye-patch. Brother, Terence decided, thankfully noting the physical resemblances, and Daddy. They were all too damned tall and the one-eyed old man was peering at him in a most unfriendly manner. Terence was marginalised, a member of an ethnic minority.

Bea sat down again, shakily putting aside her panic about Nut till she had dealt with poor Terence and her family. A blush was spreading. She tried to shift her mind from Nut's obvious distress at finding her breakfasting with someone else, deferred thinking of explanations and managed to introduce Terence to her relations, in what she hoped was neither an offhand nor too overtly affectionate way, telling them that she would be taking Terence back to Fingle fairly soon and that if they helped themselves to coffee, she would return in a moment.

'All right, Bea. Don't worry. Only mind how you go – the farmers round here seem to have a death wish – we were nearly forced into a dyke by a red-haired lunatic on the way here.' Tom glowered again at the discomfited Terence as if it was his fault.

Terence would have liked to re-shoot the morning and give it a different ending; that being impossible he wished to be rapidly removed from this increasingly undignified farce. He smiled tersely good-bye to brother and father, collected his jacket and shoes and followed the impossibly distanced Bea outside into the sunshine, vibrating with annoyance.

'Sorry about all that,' Bea said, inserting herself into the driver's seat of the truck, white skirt tucked up over brown knees, long brown hand wrestling with the gear stick, 'but I haven't seen Patrick for over six months. He's in the Navy, you see.'

Terence couldn't care less which branch of the armed forces her brother was in. He felt in his pocket for the little camera he always carried. He'd taken photographs of her dancing with Justin the night before, like two beautiful cranes circling each other, and of some of the paintings he had discovered in that other entrancing room full of dreams while she had been making breakfast. He had let his imagination run amok. He didn't want to drive to Fingle in silence and he wasn't going to give up, not yet. As if nothing had occurred between them and their peaceful post-party breakfast had not been rudely interrupted by a succession of giants, he forced a return to attentive politeness.

'You're quite a painter, aren't you?'

'You went into the painting room?' Her voice was not encouraging.

'And what did I see? Not what I expected, I admit. I expected tender little water-colours of sheep and barns, I don't know why. Nothing quite so feisty, or so magical. Where do you exhibit?'

'I haven't shown my work anywhere yet, although I've been painting for a long time, ever since I could hold a pencil or a paintbrush – look, this is no good. I'm sorry, so sorry. I'm a bit distraught. If I've led you up the garden path, I didn't mean to. Your friend Justin, my husband Oscar ...' He looked startled so she hurried on, 'I found out last night that the woman who Oscar ran off with, Andrea, was Justin's ex-wife.'

'So it was revenge of some sort, your sleeping with me?

'No, it was hardly revenge,' she said tiredly, 'that all happened months ago. Finding out brought it all back, that's all. Then there were the car-burners the night before. I didn't want to be alone, needed to go to bed with you. I thought that was all you wanted?' She sounded genuinely puzzled.

Terence was unable to deny it, but also found that it was no longer the complete story. Having seized an opportunity last night, expecting to leave the next morning without any entanglement, he now contrarily wished to continue the relationship; but she seemed to hold all the cards and the Viking was certainly an impediment. He turned and stared at her profile as she drove, the gently rounded chin with the merest hint of a cleft in it and felt despair.

'You're unique. Quite unique. Thank you for last night.'

She drew up outside his lodgings. 'I am not an unicorn, really I am not,' she said imploringly, 'and I am sorry, I really am. If Nut hadn't turned up like that, and then my family, we'd have parted company without all this fuss, wouldn't we?'

He had to suppose that was the truth and wondered if it was

merely the Viking's appearance and violent departure that had unearthed his competitive spirit. She smelt of the honey she had eaten for breakfast and he was about to try to kiss her good-bye but a plump child in a tightly-stretched acid green T-shirt, wobbling up and down the pavement on rollerblades, seemed to be taking too keen an interest in them and put him off.

After Tom's departure, Bea and Patrick lurked in the thin shade of the tamarisk bushes and Bea, too hot, tired and miserable to protest, submitted to Patrick's tactfully intrusive interrogations. He steered the conversation away from his own doings and enquired casually about Terence. Lying flat on her back with a straw hat over her face, she gave muffled explanations of her feelings about Nut.

'And have you see much of Agnes since you've been here?'

'Have I seen Agnes! She practically lived here for a while, or so it felt. There were times when I thought she was going to ask if she and Seb could move in, but she's recently become oddly distant and rather bad-tempered. I haven't seen her a few days for which I am supremely thankful.'

'I witnessed a rather strange scene between her and Oscar yesterday evening, that's all. It was quite crudely embarrassing since I was having a drink with your Mrs Lewis in the back garden and they didn't know we were there. She's been having an affair with Oscar and they were rowing. She kneed him.'

'What?' Bea removed her hat. '*Agnes* and Oscar? *Oscar* and Agnes?' Bizarre, unthought-of things rushed into her mind. 'Did it look as if ... What *did* it look like?'

Patrick recounted the tender scene. 'You don't get that physical with someone, for no reason.' He looked at Bea anxiously. 'Oh God. She is impossible! She's just not happy unless she's mucking someone about or causing a scene. I never told you, anyone, but Agnes was my first.'

Bea sat up so suddenly she nearly ricked her neck.

'You are joking? When?'

'Well, I was fifteen. During the summer holidays, after O levels. I was desperately in love with her for at least six months, but after a couple of little notes from her when I went back to school in September, she lost interest. I was longing for the Christmas holidays but by then, she'd gone off with someone older than me. I was devastated!'

'Oh, Agnes!' Bea lay down, put the hat over her face again and laughed till she wept and Patrick patted her hand as the sun pierced the tightly woven straw in little prismatic pin-pricks, shifting and changing as she breathed, star-blurring as tears came into her eyes. She was overwhelmed by the gentle, brotherly concern.

'Poor, poor Patrick. I didn't mean to laugh. It's just that everything has come like three courses of a badly cooked dinner served all at once ... Do you know something? I don't give a damn about either of them any more. At least I now know that there's no *way* Oscar and I could make a go of it again. Agnes has been miserably underhand. It all suddenly makes sense. She's been forever keen to find out what my intentions were, should he come back. Perhaps he's been back for ages and lying low and Ag-bag just sank her little teeth into him. But I'm narrowing my interests for sanity's sake. Painting and Nut. Nut had no *right* to be so upset. We aren't lovers ... Although I think I love him ... I know I love him and he knows I know; it's just that I gave the impression that I didn't want to get involved with anyone at all, not sexually anyway, at the moment; he jumped to the right, wrong conclusion this morning.' She wailed. 'All I need at the moment is to paint – it's an imperative thing – but people won't let me alone and the motives for everything I do are beginning to be suspect even to me.'

'Can I look at your pictures?'

'Of course you can. Everyone else seems to have looked at them, whether they've been invited or not. Leave me here for a bit and go upstairs and see what you think, or is it think what you see? Although I don't know that I want to hear what you thought you saw, afterwards. I am dreadfully, dreadfully tired.'

She heard his grunt as he got to his feet and his footsteps receding across the flagstones towards the house. There was the distant roar of some antique lumbering hulk, bravely vibrating its way through the sky to a flypast at some far off Saturday airshow. The closer soft pulsing of Jerry Rumm's generator. The minute scraping of an insect beneath a leaf, just by her ear. A lark shouting its head off overhead. A penetrating whistling as shepherd directed dogs and the indignant baa'ing of newly shorn sheep a few fields away. The thud of explosives at the firing ranges. The creaking of swans as they flew overhead. Although blinded by the hat, she could see the swans in her mind's eye. 'How sad one should get used to seeing swans fly. It seems such a miracle they could get off the ground.'

Picking at a mosquito bite, she wondered if she could cope with a family lunch, for that had been the plan when Tom left them. Then, Agnes, who'd never shown signs of the sort of concentration required for serious plotting. Was there any man left in the Bellhurst area that Agnes hadn't had at one time or another? She liked to spread herself around generously, like Marmite on toast. She was a sportswoman who had 'stalk, catch and kill' in her vocabulary, but not 'keep' since her prey always turned out to be inedible. Then Nut's agonised, incredulous face returned to Bea and she began to chat to Freda as she had not done since she was a child distressed; a conversational prayer for guidance around the minds of men, as it had forever been.

'"From ghosties and ghoulies and long-leggitty beasties,"' said Patrick, '"and things that go bump in the night, Good Lord deliver us." What were you muttering about?'

'In confabulation with Freda, or me, since we are obviously the same thing, about Nut. I've started talking aloud to myself rather a lot.'

'My God! Is Freda still in residence? I thought you'd lost touch with her when you were ten.'

'She visits occasionally. I am not mad. I will not go mad. I have never been mad.'

'Of course you aren't. Won't. Weren't. I've made you something cool to drink. Look, orange juice and lots of ice. Your feet are getting sunburnt.'

'Well, what did you think of them?' She pushed off the hat and sat up, squinting in the brightness, strands of hair sticking damply to her forehead. She looked very forlorn.

'I thought you didn't care to know what I thought.'

'Well, I do care. Very much.'

'I'm a bit astounded still. They are so much bigger than anything you've done before. I think they're absolutely brilliant. I need time to think about them. This is what you've been building up to, ever since you were a child, isn't it? All this time you've been a thunderstorm brewing, and none of us noticed.' He sat down again beside her while she gratefully sipped the orange juice. 'I'm not joking when I say I'm stunned. They look so utterly different to what I'd imagined.'

'That's the second time someone has said that today. Do I look like an aged spinster indulging herself with water-colours of oast-houses and cherry blossom?' She sounded sharply cross.

'No. Not much.'

'Oh, good.' She made a decision at last. To attend a happy family lunch would be a torture, but it might enforce a temporary order among the thousand threads of Nut-anxiety, at least until the afternoon. A respite of sorts. Dealing with events. Doing them. Living them. Confrontations, arguments, assessments, assignations, encroachments, a thick, black molasses of impossibilities to be rendered into fine flowing golden syrup.

'I've left a little present on the chair in your painting room, something to while away your evening,' Patrick said later that morning as they were leaving for lunch in Bellhurst. 'Don't forget to go and look for it when you get back. Mum's going to be very relieved to find you haven't become an anchorite and she'd relax even further if you tell her

what you told me about last night's amazing navy-blue party.'

'Yes, she understands parties.'

'But not much else, you mean?'

'I don't think that's fair, but at times it seems so. We expect
too much from our parents, don't we? She works so hard.
Anyway, I'll tell her *everything*; apart from Terence, obviously,
and not about Agnes and Oscar, and you're not to tell her
about Nut either, although it's possible that Nest has passed
that one on already.'

'It's going to be a quiet lunch then.'

'I have to visit Nest after lunch. She's owed an apology since
I was a bit cross on the telephone and she's been so excellent,
allowing me stay at Little Rumm.'

'I thought Mum and Nest didn't see each other much.'

'They don't. Mum's always been jealous of Nest's education,
and is secretly appalled by Blue, and Nest thinks Mum is
bird-brained, which she isn't, and wasting her time with all this
foodie thing. Fetishist, she calls it. Her food writing certainly
seems to be bringing in the cash – I can't think the ironmongery
makes enough to live on. They love and disapprove of each other,
but you never know. I don't want Mum charging down here
insisting on meeting Nut, particularly now he's evaporated.'

'He looked a bit steamed up as he passed us this morning.
A fiery fellow, obviously. Come on. Let's get going, or we'll be
late for lunch and it's your favourite thing. Nettle soup.'

'Ugh! We'll both wake up tomorrow morning covered in
whiteheads.'

The fiery fellow was standing hands in pockets, cooling his
heels in the English Channel. Pewter-coloured clouds were
brewing far away to the west and the afternoon air was stifling.
Nut's sweeping eyebrows were drawn fearsomely together as he
proceeded through the useless litany common to those who

have reacted incautiously to an unpleasant surprise. Had he been sensible he would have waited to be introduced, at least found out the identity and intent of the stranger and then he would not now be suffering. Shit, shit, shit! Was it Bea or himself who had transgressed? It *could* have been her brother sitting at the table – she'd mentioned a naval brother; but he hadn't the look of a brother, so short and dark, but then it was possible. Anything was possible and it was the anything that frightened him. His expectations had obscured the facts. The sea was nagging at the bottoms of his rolled-up jeans and he kicked at the water hopelessly. He was hatless and the sunlight's flicker on the water gave him the beginning of a headache and began pitilessly to scorch the bridge of his nose. His eyes suddenly filled with ridiculous tears and he stood facing out to sea, struggling unsuccessfully to contain them; after a while he became interested in the phenomenon of their steady drip from cheek into the sea: salt to salt, water to water. Disgustedly he dragged his great waterlogged feet out of the shallows and set off home.

On arriving at the railway carriage, as hot inside as a biscuit tin left in the sun, he tried to work for the rest of the afternoon, reassessing the findings, both sedimentological and microfaunal, for the supposed course of a tidal inlet. He laid out photocopies of ancient maps and plotted routes but his mind was elsewhere, fretting and hoping Bea might ring, but she did not. He tried to call her to apologise but there was no answer. There was no reason for her to explain herself and he was miserable and sick to the stomach in the way of a small boy who has broken a longed-for Christmas present within five minutes of unwrapping it.

Switching on the radio he caught the tail end of a severe weather warning on the local station. A freaky hundred mile-wide front of thunderstorms was fast approaching from the south-west with high winds and heavy rain imminent. The radio was crackling furiously. Better batten down. He saved the afternoon's pathetic vacillations on the computer and unplugged it, fetched a tin bucket to place beneath a persistent leak in roof of the lean-to conservatory, went outside again to wind up the windows of the van and stood astonished, watching the approaching storm. The sky faded from metallic cobalt to an eerie liverish yellow, lit by flashes of lightning of a dangerous electric blue. The landscape of sunny sand-coloured shingle turned to olive green as the clouds piled up, boiling black. A wave of hot air tumbled over him, vacuuming up dancing bits of litter. As the glaring sun was engulfed the first great raindrops slapped across his face. He stood there till his shirt was sodden, daring the lightning to strike him, then went indoors and lay flat on the bed, listening to the rising wind and the creakings of the flimsy house. Whatever strength the storm reached, it would not be sufficient to match his mood.

Struggling with the key, hair blown into blinding seaweed tangles and soaked in the short dash from the truck to her house, Bea burst in and fought the door shut against the wind. She retrieved the fossil book from the kitchen table and stumbled upstairs, dripping white dress dark against her skin, to find dry clothes and search for Patrick's present. Once dried and sitting safe on the bed in the painting room, she admired its meticulous wrapping and with a penknife carefully slipped beneath the tiny seals — she was reluctant to break them — unwrapped it and stared at the contents in her lap: a minuscule tinfoil package of cannabis, a packet of Rizlas and a pinch or two of tobacco. She let out a screech of laughter. Dear, dear Patrick. It was too dark to work, although only five o'clock, and the power was off. The storm seemed to be growing in strength and there was nothing else to do. It might stop her crying over Nut.

With clumsy fingers she heated then crumbled a piece of resin, as she had watched Oscar do in the days before they had grown out of it, had less and less time to spare. She rolled up a little spliff and lay smoking and smiling idiotically, pictures forming and dissolving on the canvas of the cracked white ceiling, as uncatchable as drifting petals. Her body sank heavily into the scarlet sheet as she analysed the depths of each tearing crack of thunder, followed the dwindling, rumbling timbre into the distance till the storm abated some two hours later. The wind blew an oboe-like note through the letter box. At one time she considered the addition of a circular patch of viridian to the two-thirds-finished picture leant against the wall, but mercifully became aware in time that perception of colour, perspective and her rationality were still quite hopelessly distorted. She turned to the fossil book and became visually entangled in the segments of a trilobite, enjoying the tranquillity of a non-functional brain.

At seven-thirty the storm blew itself out and yawning, she sat up, not quite able to dismiss the idea that she had been wasting time. The problems were still there – but were they really problems? Problems emerged or rose up, challenges were thrown down. Nut had thrown down the little book on the table at breakfast, that morning which now seemed so far away as to be over the horizon. She could no longer defer the knowledge of being not in control and deeply to blame.

In the newest painting, Freda had sprouted wide, carved and painted wings and loomed across the sky; she had put on weight and appeared to be moving at some speed, a vast and streamlined angel above a little group of people on the ground all looking up and pointing. Better not work on it tonight, but tomorrow she must get on with it. No work done since lunch time yesterday. Geraldine. Geraldine O'Brien's London lunch! What had transpired as the two elderly lovers met again? Her foot crunched unpleasantly on something on the floorboards as she went to fetch the unloved mobile phone and switched it on. It bleeped instantly.

'Please, Freda, let it be Nut. It must be Nut!' flashed through her head, but Geraldine had connected with her previous thought. Rapidly dragging ragged thoughts together, her own voice sounding like a ponderous echo in her skull, she enquired:

'So, how did it go? Was he bowled over by the splendour of your Chinese yellow jacket?'

Geraldine chuckled — a new laugh.

'He did admire it, and yes, it all went well, very well in fact. I've just got in, and what a storm that was, so exhilarating driving through it from Parden in the cab! But I'll save the details of the lunch for a minute, there's something I want to sort out first. The thing is that Simon is coming to lunch with me in a couple of weeks. His son is coming too, and perhaps the son's wife, who is a journalist. That's the sixteenth of July, Sunday, I think. Now take a deep breath and don't immediately panic and start thinking up excuses.' Bea had stiffened automatically, and then did as she was bid and uncurled. 'I want to bring them to your house,' continued Geraldine firmly, 'perhaps for tea, so you can show them your paintings. Simon wants to see them. Now, transport. They are coming by train, since the son, James, appears to have had his driving licence taken away and his wife doesn't drive at all. Simon refuses to drive more than ten miles. They're getting a taxi at Parden. You'd have to come and fetch us from Bellhurst and drive us back here afterwards? Please Bea, you must not pass up this opportunity out of misplaced shyness.'

'Oh! Yes!' Bea was astounded by the simplicity of agreeing and the resulting sense of euphoria.

'Yes?' Oh, I am so relieved. Well done, my dear. I know how difficult you find it. You won't regret it, whatever happens, I promise you. Astoundingly, I've been offered a show myself, a retrospective! But he is a very rich man, and very kind, and can afford to indulge himself occasionally. Now, shall I tell you how it went, the lunch?'

*　　*　　*

Bea went back to the bed, still with the phone clenched in her hand. She could no longer telephone Agnes and give her the good news, nor could she get through to Nut. On the floor was the squashed shell of the humbug snail. The heightened introspection brought on by the cannabis caused her to wonder if it was a warning, that the snail was a future self squashed by fate for being too adventurous in new places or whether it was a sign that the drawing in of horns leads one unsafely to nowhere, and she silently began to shake with hopeless giggles. Of course it all meant nothing of the sort, nothing at all. It was a meaningless accident, except for the unfortunate snail. The storm had passed on its way along the coast and the evening sun was patterning the wall with pink light.

She spent the rest of that tiresomely revelatory evening moving pictures needlessly about, worrying at them, shifting them into groups, fretfully rearranging them into further sub-divisions. She inspected her face for signs of emergent nettle spots then went outside to the cooled, wet garden and desultorily weeded goose-grass seedlings from between the flagstones. She ate a carrot. In between she repeatedly tried to raise Nut on the telephone, making little bargains with Fate/Freda of the 'if he answers then I'll do all the washing by hand for the rest of my life' variety, but she eventually dozed off on the red bed before it was quite dark, evading thoughts of Simon Greensand's impending visit, angry with herself for having stamped on Terence's feelings, since she liked him, futilely wondering *why* Agnes had gone after Oscar behind her back, despairing that she had damaged for ever her relationship with Nut.

If she couldn't see Nut she would see no one else and come what may, the angel picture must be completed during the next two weeks.

Chapter Eleven

Agnes Spring was unused to things going so embarrassingly wrong. She had allowed herself to think of Oscar as an escape route but chutzpah and flamboyance had both deserted her in the three days since the confrontation with him; however the indignity of the outcome had been a little reduced each time she recalled the satisfying, invigorating feeling of the *slap* as the palm of her hand connected with his face and his look of shock as the knee had driven home. She had come to believe, as she frequently did, that it was she who had come off best in the encounter.

The delicate little black eyebrows were twitched together across the china-doll face and the grey eyes were still a couple of tones deeper with discontent. She sat in a huddle over the drawing board, tussling with a further commission for the grand gardening magazine who had accepted her previous page-headings with an unflattering lack of appreciation. This was a delicate rococo water-colour of misty blues and sepias to illustrate an article on garden furniture. A chinoiserie summer house with matching benches and pergola with a drift of wisteria tumbling down elegant steps. To punish them for their lack of interest, and late payment, she was bloody-mindedly painting in a tiny garden gnome, peeing fully-frontal into an antique watering can, just to the side of the summerhouse, melding in nicely with the climbing plants. 'I bet a hundred to one that they don't notice it. It'll be interesting to see if I can get away with a gnome and a penis in such a precious mag.' She laid her brush down and shaking back her hair, half closed her eyes and inspected her work. 'Too good for them.' This effrontery gave rise to a resurgence of good humour and she gleefully set about making out the invoice.

If Oscar was out of the question, she was most definitely out for a good time. It had, after all, been quite ludicrously simple to overcome his pretended eagerness to get back to Bea and he'd rolled over on his back like a pussy cat. Not much of a challenge after all. The really hard work had gone into it when he was still with Andreary. At first he'd seemed so very interested in her dreadful life with Phil, the lack of mental stimulation, of understanding and of her need for appreciation and excitement. It was incomprehensible to her why he should want to break it up after their weekend away and she had felt used and put upon. At least Bea didn't know about it and there was no way she would find out. Oscar wouldn't tell her, that at least was certain. Why was it Bea seemed to collect all the attention without ever actually *doing* anything?

She looked at her watch. Two o'clock. Her mother had collected Seb from nursery school and was baby-sitting him all afternoon so that she could finish her work. Well, it was finished now so she could go out and buy a new pair of sandals, or go and visit Mary, or Mags. Or . . . she might drive over and see if the most interesting Nut was at home. They'd got along so well when they'd met that Bea had got pleasingly near to being annoyed. Well, she deserved a little competition. Bea and Nut weren't exactly together, an item, were they? In fact Bea showed a strong disinclination to get any closer to him; trust Bea to go one better and find someone with the full complement of green eyes. To Agnes their relationship was inexplicable and she had felt waspish towards Bea since being manoeuvred away from seeing the paintings. What strange imaginings were being concocted up there in that painting room week after week and why shouldn't she see them? Bea suddenly appeared to her like a sailing boat on a pond, forever gracefully circling. She had the sudden urge to call up a storm and sink her.

Nut, returning from a trip to Canterbury, saw Agnes from the road as he parked his van. She was peering through the window of his house, nose close up to the glass and shading her eye with her hand. He could not for a second place her and was momentarily annoyed by the peering.

'Hello, Nut, remember me? We met at the Eeldyke Inn a few weeks ago? Bea told me where you lived and as I was down here doing some drawing – I am an artist too, you know – I thought I'd drop by. I was sure I heard a noise inside, that someone was in.'

Nut was perplexed. What could he do but ask her in for a cup of tea?

'So, have you seen Bea today at all?' he asked hopefully.

'Oh, no. I hate to bother her when I know she's working so hard. She takes her work so seriously – no time for anyone else! I haven't seen her for ages.' He put the kettle on and unpacked his briefcase and Agnes sat down heavily on the crisp pages of a report that he had printed out that morning and leaning back in the chair, beamed at him.

'Could I ask you to move for a moment, while I rescue those papers?'

She didn't actually get up, but mischievously wriggled aside so he had to put his hand beneath her to remove them, was forced to touch the warm flesh of the plump thigh.

'So where do you live then, Agnes?'

'In Bellhurst – that's where Bea and I met – we were at school together. But she's changed so much, you wouldn't believe, since her husband left her.'

'Have you met her brother? The one in the Navy? Patrick,

is it?' He was looking at her with what she interpreted as rapt interest.

'Good Lord, yes! We're very old friends. But we don't see him often.'

'So he's not on leave, paying a visit at the moment? I thought she mentioned something about him coming this month.'

'Oh, well I wouldn't know. She never tells me anything any more . . .' she insinuated deep regret, 'I'd love to see him again. We had quite a thing going when we were teenagers.' Again, a touch of delicate sadness crept into her voice. 'I think Bea tries to keep him away from me, when he's on leave. She broke it up in the first place, you know. I think she was a little jealous. They look so alike, almost twinnish. Almost unhealthily close.'

She watched him voraciously as he made the mugs of tea. She had never had sex with a redhead.

She stayed and chatted for too long till Nut, tired and miserable, made 'I have some work to do' noises and she left, threatening to make a return visit one day when he wasn't so tied up.

So, it had not been Bea's brother, sitting at the table.

In the late afternoon of the following Tuesday, Bea put the final touches to the angel painting and lay flat down on the floorboards and cried with relief. She was mentally worn out but there was something she could do about it. She washed her hair and rinsed it in a tea made from chamomile flowers. She made up her eyes and with a water-colour of a fat ewe and lamb in a little folder as a present and every hope in the world, she set out to make amends.

The crude juxtaposition of Nut and Agnes was to Bea's eyes so unexpected that for a second her vision fogged. When she looked again it was still there, only this time instead of frantic movement there was a stillness. The front door had been ajar. As she had stood uncertainly in the doorway she had seen straight down the tunnel centre of the railway carriage, through the kitchen, into the bedroom and there was Agnes, wrestling with Nut on the bed. Nut's cry, 'Bea! Help!' sounded to her as an admission of guilt on being discovered rather than the cry for assistance that it was.

With a shout of near murderous hate, Bea flew towards them and dragging Agnes to her feet by her hair, knocked her sideways with a left hook. She then turned and fled. As she got in through her own safe front door in a moither of misery, Agnes's mother phoned.

'Ah, Bea dear. How are you? Agnes is with you, isn't she? Can I speak to her please? It's just that Seb has been violently sick and I wondered when she was coming home.'

Bea's anger was terrible.

'No, you can't speak to Agnes. She isn't here and hasn't been here at all. At the moment she is screwing somebody. My somebody, my man. I hope she burns in hell!'

Later Geraldine telephoned.

'I just wondered how the work was going, Bea. Bea, Bea? Dear girl, whatever is the matter?' Bea was sobbing heartbreakingly down the line; all self-restraint had vanished with that blow to Agnes's face and out came the sad story.

'That girl's a malicious little bitch, but *ce n'est pas le fin du monde!* Why don't you ask your Aunt Nest if she'll come over to keep you company. I think, for once, that you don't want to be alone? Or you could come and stay with me for the night? I've got some wonderful blue vodka.'

'I don't think I could drive, Geraldine. I'm all shaky. But you're right. I don't want to be alone and I will ring Nest. The angel painting is finished. I'm all geared up for the Greensands' visit next Sunday, really I am.'

'Good. That sounds nice and positive. Now ring Nest.'

*　　*　　*

Blue dropped Nest at Little Rumm at eight o'clock and told her to give Bea his love since he couldn't come in because he had to visit a man about a fishing trip and would pick up Nest later.

Nest poured her unhappy niece a glass of burgundy, in fact several glasses of burgundy, for she had been certain that it would be a two-bottle occasion and had come prepared, together with a chunk of duck-liver pâté and a packet of oatcakes. She was deeply worried but also pleased that Bea had so unusually confided in her. She listened, sitting with Bea on the front steps in the twilight till they were driven indoors by midges and then listened some more, sitting by candlelight since there was a power cut caused, the electricity board said, by a swan flying into a power cable. She was unusually quiet, only interjecting the occasional word of comfort but when Bea had eventually dried up and was looking across the table at her somewhat muzzily, she tightly clasped Bea's shaking hands and admitted she was partly to blame.

'I've pushed and nagged you, Bea. I am so sorry. And this Geraldine friend of yours, she has too, hasn't she? And you've been driving yourself in order to escape from the past, so determined to succeed and worrying about what the gallery people will think of the paintings? And this Nut fellow – he's been after you too? Oh poor darling – you must have felt quite hounded! But you really do love him, do you?'

'I'm afraid I do. Absolutely. Oh, Nest! If I hadn't been so sanctimonious about my work, none of this would have happened ... And whatever possessed me to go to bed with Terence?'

'Darling, don't get things so out of proportion! That's a very minor misdemeanour, surely?'

'Then, I'm supposed to take finding him screwing Agnes as a minor misdemeanour ...? I can't ... I can't! Particularly because it was Agnes.'

'You are certain you didn't misinterpret it?'

'How do you misinterpret finding someone astride the man you love, in the process of removing her dress? She didn't have anything on underneath, either. And her bottom's all flabby.'

'Did you hit her very hard?' Nest looked a bit worried.

'Not as hard as I meant to. She sort of jerked backwards. And my hand only hurts a little.'

'Bea, I can't believe I'm sitting here discussing you and violence in the same breath!'

'It seems to be all over the place – everyone knocking about everyone else. I think I just picked it up, like a verruca. I felt, felt sort of *diminished*, afterwards. I think we've all gone mad. I will recover, won't I?' In the flickering, moth-infested candlelight Nest stared across at Bea's face with its pathetic shadows beneath the eyes. 'I don't believe she knows how beautiful she is,' thought Nest. 'None of us, certainly, has ever told her. She has no more defences, no more energy and needs calm, to be loved and cossetted. She needs the wretched Nutmeg ...' An extraordinary thought crossed Nest's mind and once implanted, refused to be removed. She was all for trying things out. And if the ridiculous little plot that was burgeoning in her mind didn't work, she would have to send in the heavies, Blue in particular, to speak to Nut.

She was unaware at that moment that Blue was half heaving, half supporting a drunken and near speechless Nut back across the shingle to his house. He held up the great height of the staggering man and somehow or other got him into the house and managed to roll him on to his bed and remove his boots.

'Goo' man, Blue. I'm uspshet. My girl's uspshet too. My fault. Fuckin' muddle. It's all shite. Don't know what to do ... Hrmph. She'sh a goo' ... She'sh a dangerous hitter. Southpaw.'

Nest interrogated Blue later that night about Nut.

'So he says it was accidental – that she jumped on him? Hm.

I've heard that before, sometime, still ... You must tell him that he's not to bother Bea for the next few days – if they see each other now, they'll only fight. The dust needs to settle. She's seriously overwrought and needs lots of rest. I have a plan.'

'I can't tell him what to do, Cuckoo! We don't talk about our private lives.' Nest looked eerily like Bea, but the expression was not one he'd ever seen on Bea's face. Crafty.

'You will ring him tomorrow when he's sober and tell him,' continued Nest. 'What *do* you talk about during those hours drinking then, if you don't talk private lives? Just evade the gaskets and mackerel for once and tell him. As I said I have a plan.' She was on the telephone to unknown acquaintances for a long time, till Blue called from the top of the stairs, was he never going to get his story that night?

On Wednesday evening two women came to call on Bea. They introduced themselves as friends of Nest's and said they had a proposition to put to her. Thinking it was something to do with painting, she invited them in and there still remaining half a bottle of burgundy on the dresser in the kitchen, glumly offered them a drink. There was something covert about their attitude which reminded her of something, but in spite of being in a highly suggestible state of mind, she was completely taken aback by what they had to say and just sat there looking at them with her mouth open. They smiled charmingly, further explained that they believed the unnecessary stress caused by modern living was a form of psychic pollution and were prepared to help, and waited patiently.

What could rational, well-educated Nest have been thinking of? Why had Nest told these complete strangers, these two members of an apparently elect inner circle of the Daughters of Nature, about her private life? But they hadn't mentioned what they knew at all, they had merely said they understood she was in trouble. It was all so completely removed from her adult existence that she had to force her mind back to childhood, to the discovery of Freda, before she could comprehend what it was they were about. Then, past rational argument, she thought, 'What the hell! Why not? My life is in ruins. It can't make it any worse.'

The elder of the two women produced a mobile phone and spoke to someone, very briefly. 'Bell? It's on. And not a minute too soon. Yes. Very, very strained and unhappy. No, only a little resistant. We'll see you shortly.' 'What very up-to-date witches they are,' thought Bea, 'and how practical.'

They seated Bea in her favourite blue chair in the centre of the room facing the fireplace. They drew the yellow curtains, lit candles on either side of Nut's portrait and lit one in an old blue enamel chamberstick and placed it on a stool before her where it guttered in the draw from the chimney. They turned off the phone and checked that all the light switches were off and were generally so thorough in their efforts to ensure that they would not be interrupted that she had to stifle the urge to giggle hysterically and twiddle her thumbs. Whatever had she let herself in for? It was monstrously ridiculous. But she would co-operate.

There was a soft tap-tappit on the door and one of the women crossed to the little hall and Bea could hear muttering, like someone negotiating with carol singers, then: 'Yes, we're all in place. Off you go.' It was like having an operation, Bea thought. 'Any minute now they'll approach with hypodermics and offer me a pre-med.'

The two women locked back and front doors and instructed her to watch the candle flame and think only of her dearest wish. 'Just like a fairy story,' thought Bea, 'only they're short-changing me. I should have three dearest wishes.' Resigned to making a fool of herself and remembering Nest's motto 'Try everything once, except murder and incest,' she submitted. It was all so weirdly commonplace, so excitingly banal.

They took up positions standing behind her chair which at

first felt uncomfortable, since she'd rather have liked to keep an eye on them. Outside in the warm dark a soft chanting began, so soft that she was unsure if she was imagining it and strained to hear. It rose and fell and her invigilators seemed to slink gradually away into the background, the whole dark room slowly sinking away from the chair and she was suspended in space and could not take her eyes away for one second from the aching brightness of the candle flame for fear of falling, nor turn her cheeks away from its heat. Her dearest wish was definitely Nut.

She awoke the next morning with a crick in her neck and with the sunlight pouring in through the window behind the collection of blue glass bottles and bowls. She stretched cautiously and blew out the candle. Something fell to the floor from her lap. It was Nut's fossil sea-urchin. She had fallen asleep, evidently, while the women were still there and they had gone away disappointed at her lack of appreciation. Well, no harm was done and she did feel very clear-headed and comfortable for someone who'd slept the night in a chair. Her hair was a bird's nest, there was a wine stain on her T-shirt and her skirt had a spatter of candle grease across the front.

She couldn't remember the women's faces at all, other than that they had been heavily made up, like stage make-up, mask-like faces now she came to think of it and that their voices had been soft, reasonable and insistent. Even that small amount of recall seemed to fade as the morning drew on and she got on with washing clothes. The washing machine had long since expired and as she scrubbed the collar of a white shirt with a nail-brush she remembered someone saying, at some stage last night: 'Allow three clear days.' The events of the night before didn't hold her thoughts for long. She'd gone along with it to please Nest – knew only that she had not dreamt it, had been in some fashion hypnotised, that painting was for the time being finished, that she had survived and was now quick and awake. She opened the back door and took the washing out to the sunshine.

There were spots of candle wax on the paving stones and the long feathery grasses around the door had been trodden down.

Had she blown out a candle when she woke up? How could it have stayed alight all that time? In spite of the brightness of the day, a shiver ran down her spine.

On the morning of the Greensand visit she pottered about the misty garden in her nightdress, refreshed and wakeful with a piece of toast and honey in her hand, inspecting the poppies. She had been sleeping well since Candle-Wednesday, curled up cat-like and dead to the world with her tail around her nose.

The morning promised heat. The smaller flowers, the strange greyish violets, soft dusty pinks and whites of the *Papaver rhoeas*, were flowering now. Very pretty, she thought, but they couldn't compete with the *paeoniflorums*, blackberry purple with tightly scrunched petals doubled and quadrupled around the powdery cream anthers. A decadent *fin de siècle* rustling petticoat of a flower. There were other lovely marvels in the mixture which she and Nest had sown together; in particular a singleton, a wicked looking plant fit for a sorcerer, a sinister mediaeval popinjay. The petals were perfect cockleshells of purple pleated silk, darkening to black at the base, flame scarlet towards the dagged and snipped fringing of the upper edge. She went indoors again to fetch paintbox and water-colour paper.

The painting room was prepared for the aliens' landing that afternoon and, over-tidied, looked uncomfortable. The paintings still stood with their faces to the wall except the latest one since sections of the paint were still tacky, particularly round Freda's head. Freda was no longer a stone figure about the face and upper body; a blushing hint of blood was running in the marble veins and her enigmatic lips were a definitely predatory pink. Bea cast a considering eye around the room; a stack of preparatory drawings and a pile of water-colours were laid out upon the bed. She had no idea at all what

Simon Greensand might be like, could not picture Geraldine's reluctant lover.

'Well, there it all is – can't change anything. But I can think "take it or leave it" now. After driving them back to Bellhurst, I might just have to go Nut-gathering. I can't take-or-leave him. Whatever he was up to with Agnes – pretty obvious what he was up to, actually – it couldn't have been serious. I know it was just revenge for finding me with Terence. The distress, my distress, was deserved. It matches his. Every time I think of him, there's this mewling in my stomach, demanding to be fed. Someone's got to make the first move and if we don't meet soon, I'll wither away.' After all the past agonising, she was surprisingly certain that he would want to see her.

Outside again and sitting on a kitchen chair painting the popinjay flower, she found her hand was trembling slightly and she had to get up again, walk about, shaking it to loosen the wrist. Jerry Rumm, ambling past the house on his snorting, rusty tractor, caught a startling glimpse from his high seat of a phantom woman in white, walking up and down wringing her hands in distress; but the ghost turned and waved at him and he saw it was Bea in her nightie, waved back and drove on, an unlikely grin spreading the sombre foldings of his dark weather-beaten face. That was quite some strange party she'd had round there on Wednesday night.

By mid morning, Bea, on her seventh painted poppy, decided it was time to get dressed and start preparing for the afternoon's ordeal. She put on black jeans and T-shirt and the long-abandoned watch; her wedding ring still lay half-hidden, embedded in the rush seat of the chair on which it had been discarded months before. No, it was not an ordeal, more of an examination. Think, she told herself, of taking an exam. You know the syllabus, you've an inkling of the questions; for goodness sake, be more positive. She began to work out an explanation, moulding it into a manageable formulaic sentence, trying to sound as if she knew what she was doing. 'I'm working on a series on growing up,' sounds inane, she thought as she scrubbed out the lavatory. She was thirty-one in a couple of weeks. 'Rites of Passage' sounded a little more intelligent and feasible and was not far from the truth. Shaking a rush mat outside the back door, she thought that there was a new rite of passage now, slotting into life between the births, marriages and deaths – divorce. A second leaving of home and certainties. She wondered why the Church of England, now it more or less accepted divorce and in some cases even remarried divorced people, or at least blessed their unions, had not jumped on the bandwagon and instituted some sort of memorial un-blessing service to mark divorces. The participants could wear scarlet and black clothes, perhaps with bows of sackcloth to signify remorse. 'I, Beatrice Jane, renounce thee, Oscar George, from this day forward . . .' The idea was really quite attractive. Guests might even be invited to jump forwards at the appropriate moment and declare impediments to their being put asunder. The congregation could hopefully sing 'Abide with Me'. There was another painting there, somewhere.

She had truly meant her marriage vows when they had married that windy autumn afternoon in Bellhurst parish church. She had wanted to get married in a registry office, but Oscar's family had been scandalised at the idea (his uncle being a vicar) and she wished to keep them happy. It didn't matter much to her where the ceremony took place or under whose auspices, civil or religious. Vows were vows. The reception had been held in a flapping red-and-white striped marquee, on the lawn of the house belonging to the organist, adjacent to the church. Agnes had danced on a table. She had made a small painting of Agnes's dancing. The idea of divorce had always been distasteful – but she could not stay tied forever to someone who wasn't there. Time to cut the legal string, or even the ribbon – like opening a new supermarket, pull the cord unveiling both a memorial and the future. When tunnel-visioned by a sense of besotted rightness and very young, she had been utterly convinced that

Oscar was the only man she'd ever love. Wrong, but she had weathered the disappointment rather well; it would soon be time to speak to Oscar but now it was time to eat.

A tap on the door disturbed her as she was breaking an egg into the pan.

Nut stood there, but a strange Nut. She became cold as ice with fright and it took a heart-thumping second or two to focus on the nature of the change. He'd cut his hair and relieved from the weight of the scraped back plait, it surged out round his head in a simmering halo painted by William Blake.

'Hello,' he said, his face pinched with anxiety. He held out a hand tentatively, to take hers, or just to touch? 'If I'm not welcome now, tell me at once.'

'Your hair!' she squeaked. It was hacked off roughly, at just below ear-level.

'I've come to apologise for bursting in like that the other morning, and for what you think you saw the other day.'

'There's no need, really. I understand you wanted to get back at me ... But your hair ...' She at last took the outstretched hand in both of hers.

'I didn't want to get back at you, not at all. It was, you see, I'd come to think, then, that we ...'

'Stop! *Why* have you cut your hair off?'

'Don't you like it shorter? I'm sorry I jumped to conclusions – it was, is, none of my business ... Agnes ...'

'But why? I ... I loved it long.'

'It was none of my business who you choose to break-fast with.'

'I'd rather have been breakfasting with you,' she admitted.

'Ah ha! So why didn't you wait ...'

'As you said, it's not your business.'

'But I want it to be.'

She knew he knew. 'Well, I'm sorry. I was breakfasting with a friend who stayed the night. He left that morning. We won't meet again. End of story.' Not a lie, but thrifty cut-work. 'Your turn.' Her eyes gleamed sapphire at him.

'Agnes attacked me. I am not joking. It was the second time she'd been round. She came for tea the first time and for me the second, it appeared. Perhaps I didn't give her enough biscuits first time around. I was nearly suffocating by the time you got there. I'd given up and thought my days were numbered. Didn't you hear me call for help? The hair will grow again, you know.' His eyes were brilliant with release. 'I went to the bedroom to fetch a notebook and she followed and jumped on me as I bent over to get the book from the other side of the bed. You know how small that room is. Mind you, I don't know how long I'd have been able to resist — she's very strong and a few minutes later it might have been a different story.' True, but embroidered with silk thread.

Bea hooted at the image of a man of Nut's size unable to subdue the sexual onslaught of tiny Agnes and a warm relief flushed through her. It would be all right. 'We won't talk about breakfasts any more, or Agnes again, ever. I don't want to know. Who cut your hair?'

He had intended to tell her it was self-inflicted but decided ruefully on the shaming truth. 'I'm afraid we'll have to talk Agnes again. It can only have been her.'

Bea gaped at him and anger rose up in her throat.

'How, how could she? Without your knowing?'

'She flounced off pretty quickly after you interrupted her attempt on my virtue. I remember seeing a little wallet left on the desk, beside where she'd sat in the living room. Everything got exaggerated in my head and looked blacker and blacker and I'm afraid I got a bit pissed with Blue that evening and he couldn't lock the door behind him when he left; he had to put me to bed. I had my hair when I went to the pub and when I got back at about ten o'clock. In the morning, no hair, no wallet and the dressmaking scissors I'd borrowed from Millie next door, to cut up a map, they weren't where I'd left them on the desk either, but were on the front step. It wasn't Blue, that's certain and I couldn't even stand up, let alone wield a pair of shears. Perhaps she wanted it as a trophy. She's probably tied it to the radio aerial of her car.' He ran an exploratory hand over his hair, still missing the weight of it. 'What are you doing for lunch?' He didn't look too worried about the hair but Bea was still furious.

'Oh Nut! I'm so sorry. It must have been her – she did it once before, at school. She's unbelievable, a monster. You could sue her for assault! Was it a little red wallet, with a flower on it? Would you like me to re-cut it? It looks a bit raggedy.'

'Oh please, Bea, yes, and yes, it had a daisy on it. It's a bit weird though, to think she was wandering around in my house when I was asleep. She must have been hanging around down there, out on the shingle all evening, then, waiting? Is she mad? What does she do with that tiresome child, when she's out on the razzle? What is that awful smell?'

'Oh shit! My egg!'

The offensive smell of scorching albumen was dire enough for Bea to agree to go for a pint of prawns a little later and she threw open all the windows, explaining the impending invasion of Geraldine and the gallery people. There had been no destructive arguments, no recriminations. She was being offered a meal, a respite, a hand and knew it was not deserved.

'You're very cool about this deputation of art dealers,' said Nut, who appeared to have somehow sneaked an arm across her shoulders and it was all she could do not to bury her head in his chest. 'Are you not frightened any more?' He was sunnily smug with the outcome of the foray. Earlier that morning he'd ingenuously come to believe that the change in his appearance might just be beneficial, give him a few seconds' advantage in a conversation with her, a shock tactic to stop her from slamming the door in his face which was a contingency that he'd been unable to get out of his head. They were talking again and that was all that mattered.

'No, not scared at all anymore.' said Bea. 'There's no point. A bit worried perhaps, but I'm dying to ring up Nest and tell her all about it once it's over, even if it goes badly. She's good at mending people who've been carelessly dropped, or who've chipped themselves . . . What did you do all this time?' she asked, gently removing his arm and searching for a comb, taking the scissors from the red wicker sewing basket on the windowsill.

'I'm afraid I moped a bit, but there was a lot of work to do and I polished off an article for an extremely prestigious journal in between mopes. I'm not usually so forthcoming about my emotions, you know. By the way, the gentleman who calculated the age of the earth from the Bible – his name was James Ussher and he was the Archbishop of Armagh. What did you do?'

'I worked. I've not seen anyone since I saw you. Except Nest that night, and,' she stopped for a second but decided to tell, even if he laughed, 'some rather odd women who came to see me. Nest sent the Comforters Division of the Daughters of Nature round to hex me out of my miseries after I'd come upon you and Agnes – I'd got everything out of focus, I think. She was worried.'

'You mean you consulted *witches*! You are joking? No, you're not. Am *I* enchanted then? You haven't put the black spot in Agnes's hand have you? You don't *believe* in all that stuff, surely? Did they arrive on ecologically sound electrically-driven broomsticks, come in red cloaks? What did they do with you?'

'No, they were just two ordinary women in ordinary clothes, with extraordinary presence. All they did was light candles and sing me to sleep, I think. It was odd.' Just how odd, she could not explain. 'They locked the doors and shut the windows. It was very hot. They didn't seem to mind I wasn't taking it seriously. They were very persuasive. Someone ought to employ them selling double-glazing. There were more of them, I think, circling outside the house, chanting, sort of, in harmony . . . I can't remember anything more. I was terribly tired and never saw them go. I knew you'd laugh.'

'So they didn't ask you to whip out your chequebook and make a huge donation?'

'No. They just came, sang, and left. I woke up feeling much better and with the painting all done for the moment, I spent the last three days just doing blissfully mundane things, like cleaning the windows, making a skirt and lying in the shade with a book. I've even finished *Gulliver's Travels*.'

'Is that the skirt? It's very pretty. Did you know you could see through it, against the light? Can you cook and sing and spin as well? You are extraordinary. A lunatic. You think you brought me over here by witchcraft? It wasn't you that cut my hair? I'm joking, I'm joking.'

'Oh, Nut! No. I was going to come over to you myself. Isn't it funny, I'm sure they said it would take three days.'

'Blue told me, from Nest, that I was to keep away for three days, under threat of bastinado. It's all the power of suggestion.'

She fetched a wheelback kitchen chair and seated him on it outside in the sun, threw a blue-and-white checked tea towel about his shoulders and started to snip and shape around the bent and vulnerable neck. She'd often barbered Oscar's hair; pale, straight, slippery hair. Nut's hair sprang forcefully from his head, glossy, alive and slightly curling, each lock a trail of sparks between her fingers. A tiny far-fetched thought came uncomfortably to her concerning the whereabouts of Nut's thick plait. Something to do with red cloaks. No, it was too silly. It *must* have been Agnes.

'There – head up – don't fidget, the blades are close to your ear – that's better. A bit choirboy for someone of your great age, but that's what your hair seems to want to do.' Snip, snip.

'I'll trust you.' The smile was devastating as he peered slyly up at her and she caught the briefest glimpse of the ten-year-old Francis Nutmeg.

'Well, you shouldn't.' Snip, snip. 'Are you a Catholic or a Proddy?'

'Neither. Well, I suppose I'm a Catholic. I was baptised one, but after first communion my father lost interest and my mother took over. At one point they gave me the choice but I couldn't bear to offend either of them. Primary school was Catholic, Secondary was Protestant. I got bullied at both which makes for atheism. That's all there is to it. Now, you'll tell me about Freda?'

'Freda is a concatenation. There's a word for one of your Conclusions! It happened when we were visiting Canterbury, to see my mother's Aunt Maude when I was five or six and went into the cathedral and saw the Saint Eustace wall paintings – or rather copies of them. I was never taught to say bed-time prayers and I'd barely been into a church then, let alone a High Anglican cathedral smelling of incense. Then we went down into the crypt to the Chapel of Our Lady Undercroft where there is a ceiling painted with a starry pattern and a gilded bronze statue of the Virgin and Child, and candles, and a very heavy sense of mystery, of depth, both mental and physical, deep down in the bowels of the earth. That was before the days when it became overcrowded with giggling Japanese and screeching French teenagers on coach tours. I was allowed to light a candle and make a wish or say a prayer, whatever you will. It all seemed immensely powerful. The candles, I could feel the heat from the candles ... Then we went back and had tea in the garden with Great Aunt Maude. She left this house to Aunt Nest – move your head a little this way, there, almost finished – she had a statue in the garden, a Ceres, with a garland of wheat and a cornucopia. It was pretty. The statue became wonderfully confused with the Virgin Mary I'd seen in the Cathedral. I asked Aunt Maude what the statue's name was and she said Freda. So that was it. For years all desires and secrets and a certain amount of adoration were bestowed on a transmogrified female deity. It was a naturally occurring religious urge, albeit pagan. So, there it is.'

'I've heard of children having imaginary friends and pets, but never one with a tame goddess. As a child I had a magic bone.'

'Tell me? What were its powers?' Snip.

'It was a cow's leg bone I found in a field. I cut a Viking pattern on it; it was more of a wishing bone – I wish that Kevin McGee would fall in the lake and drown himself – I wish that Siobhan O'Brien would hold my hand, that sort of thing. It didn't actually work, of course. I buried it when we left Ireland thinking it would be nice for someone else to find. I'd stopped loving it when I was ten but it hung around in my bedroom for a while, breathing out irrationality. Have you finished, now?' He did not mention the small sister who in spite of all the bone-wishing, had died of meningitis when she was five.

The sudden, unexpected but wished-for, easy intimacy of holding his head between her hands was overwhelming, and she became contrarily crisp and matter-of-fact.

'We'll have to make it an early lunch. I have to be at Geraldine's at three. You know, I think her hair was red too, when she was young, though I imagine it to have been more fine-cut orange marmalade, not such depth of colour as yours.' She finished the personal journey round his face and neck, softly blew away the feathered clumps and tufts that decorated his shoulders.

They went to the Bell and Hatchet for lunch and sat outside at a table in the hazy sunshine, ate and covertly watched each other eating. Nut's appetite, which had all but deserted him during the past week, vigorously returned. He rolled his shirt sleeves up and set to, snapping off the prawns' pink heads, and without removing the shells and legs crunched up the bodies with relish, devouring not only his own lettuce and bread and butter, but seeing she hadn't touched hers, with permission ate most of that as well. He watched her lingering over her share, squeezing a little pool of lemon juice onto her plate, frowningly de-whiskering and peeling them with extraordinary spiky fingers, examining the little segmented bodies and dipping them in lemon before popping them into her mouth. She looked preoccupied in spite of what she'd said about not being scared, as if a child's pre-school fear still lurked inside her. She watched his hands busy with the food, the long curving line from point of elbow to wrist bone and was suddenly aghast at having to leave him that afternoon.

'What's the matter, Queen Bea?'

She tried to drag herself back to the business fast approaching. 'I'm trying not to worry. Little worries, but they refuse to drown. They never give one quite enough lemon, do they?' Then, becoming obscure, 'Do you think trilobites were edible?'

'What can I do? Come with you, perhaps? Lighten up, my love, it'll soon be done with. I'm still hungry.' Grinning, with fishy fingers held out, 'Can I give you a crustacean kiss?'

A camper van cruised by, engorged with disorientated, gawping Belgian tourists. Big-boned Susie came out to collect their plates, chuckled and retreated. A dusty collie who had previously been asleep in the shade of the newspaper shop doorway ambled over to investigate who was eating whom. Somewhere, in a back garden close by, throaty chickens clucked and murmured thoughtfully. His breath blew through her like a breeze in a flute.

'Have we time to go back to ...'

'No, we haven't. I *must* leave in ten minutes.'

'What a strong woman you are! But you're right as usual, I suspect. It'd be a shame to rush things. You'll call me, as soon as it's all over, whatever happens? No, don't call. Come round to me? I'll have a fatted calf ready, although God knows where I'll find one, on a Sunday.' His eyes had narrowed into green slits in the sunlight and she leant her hopeful, prawn-filled person against his shoulder, knew she was sinking deeper and deeper in and couldn't bear to leave. It was nearly time to give in — abandon Freda, take on the Promethean Nut.

'I will. I'll be there between seven and eight. Would you like me to hang a flag from the car, black or white to signal disaster or success as I drive down the road?'

'Yes. I'll be waiting.'

They had to stand up together, all of a single piece, propping each other up and unable to let go.

'I must go, now.'

'Yes, you mustn't be late. Let go my arm then.'

'You let go first.'

'There. I think I'd better sit here a little while behind the table till there's a sign of subsidence.'

She glanced at him furtively, and then drowned him with warm and wicked laughter.

Chapter Twelve

Bea parked out of habit outside her house rather than Geraldine's. Neither Oscar's car nor his bike were in evidence. The strip of grass that ran alongside the brick path had been mown, but the flowerbed beneath the sitting-room window was knee-high with weeds through which poked two or three stunted cornflowers, the sole survivors of seeds sown in March. When she returned the Greensands later that afternoon and if he still did not appear to be in residence, she'd go inside, make decisions. She hung back a minute or two, hugging the memory of Nut's parting embrace, before swinging down from the pick-up, pushing hot hair back from her face and opening Geraldine's creaking iron gate. She strode up the path, appearing as bold as brass to Geraldine, watching for her from the open sitting-room window.

'The door's open, Bea. Come in, my pet, come in!'

In spite of the heat Geraldine had resumed the green cardigan, but emphasised the parrot theme with an orange silk scarf and the new black skirt. She looked dazed.

'I've been being interviewed, Bea, and I didn't even know it was happening!' Her eyes were wide and she sounded as if she had expected a tooth extraction, but had been pleasantly surprised by the skill of the dentist.

The guests turned, expectant and inquisitive as Bea walked in. Her eyes had trouble for a second adjusting to the shade after the brightness of the light outside, the room being all reflected greens from the trees and shrubs beside the window, a sub-marine flickering dancing across the faces of Simon and his son as they put down their coffee cups, got to their feet and extended hands; Simon's was cool and dry-papery, his son's slightly moist and over-firm, his face flushed and he was brandy-breathed. The daughter-in-law, May, a chic small person in black trousers and blue denim shirt, had a near-circular face, the features as neatly painted on the surface as a pattern on a plate. Her smile was small, confined, and her Chinese eyes were sharp and noticing. Bea automatically felt lumbering and large. Beside May on the worn pomegranate sofa was a professional-looking camera, discarded film boxes and a black file. She saw Bea's glance.

'We have been photographing the reluctant Geraldine. I like to take my own pictures to illustrate the profiles. I'm proposing to do an article on her for a magazine.'

'A review you mean, of the retrospective in November?'

'No, I write biographical pieces rather than reviews, although it will obviously contain an appreciation of her work. This is a pre-show piece, an appetiser, to remind those who've not seen her paintings for some time and to inform those who have never seen them. I have been interviewing her over lunch.' She sounded very business-like.

Geraldine closed the window firmly. 'Now, I think it's time we made a move, don't you? I have blankets and cushions, Bea, for the men to sit on in the back.' They had arrived as instructed, very much townies dressed for the country. James had had visions of struggling through deep mud and rushes and wore a khaki bush shirt and trousers tucked into expensive-looking, stout new walking boots. Bea wondered if Geraldine's and Simon's intertwining past had been unearthed during May's interviewing, and what James thought about it.

There was only the faintest smell of burnt egg still hanging about when she led them in to Little Rumm. Simon and James

were windblown breathless after their jolting up the track, and
speechless with amazement that anyone could live alone in such
a desolate place. James was regretting the half-full glass of brandy
he'd left at Geraldine's.

'Shall I take you up now, to see the paintings?' asked Bea,
eager to get the thing over with. During the drive, in order to
turn aside Fate's beady eye, she'd managed to convince herself
they'd hate them.

'By all means,' said Simon, recovered from his hellish
shaking. He had brushed the worst of the dust from his trousers
and was even now rehearsing the telling of the ordeal to his
London friends. 'Lead on. Are you coming too, Geraldine?'

'No, there won't be room up there. I'll put on Bea's hat and
go and sit in the garden while you contemplate and rummage.'
Geraldine was as tense as Bea.

It had been a useful idea, turning the other paintings to the
wall. As the Greensands entered the sunny white room, they
were faced, undistracted, by the angel picture.

'Wow!' said the perspiring James, who darted forwards, past
discomforts forgotten. Simon was silent for a while, then said
merely, 'Right! Now let's see the others, one by one.' They
spent an hour in the painting room in the heat of the afternoon,
questioning, examining, considering. They delved among the
sketches and water-colours, asked ever more apparently irrelevant
questions till Bea felt ready to explode with nervous tension.
Moon-faced Mini-May was moving silently but obtrusively
about in her tiny black espadrilles, taking photographs of her
talking to James, of her with one of the paintings and again alone
by the window. Bea was not expecting an unqualified approval
but her mouth had gone dry with apprehension.

Simon produced a red notebook and a pen, and said: 'Now
let's see, there are four of the "Freda" paintings completed, and
those three large preparatory sketches which are very interesting,
worth framing up and showing in their own right. Of course
you have the rest of the summer to work? Good, then we'll have

another look later and select a few more, say in late September? I'd also like the four smaller oils, particularly the one of the wedding. Could you bring it out again and put it on the chair, there?' This was the painting crowded with figures in a dark marquee, their faces blurred with movement, all except one of whom were leaning suffocatingly in towards the tall central mound of bride, groom and cake. The light was diffused through red striped canvas walls, but came strongly through the opening in the tent, shining on the flaunting exception who was Agnes, dancing on a table.

'Mm. Yes. Yes.' He went and stood by the window, considering as he stared out over the shimmering fields for what seemed like aeons.

'Well, shall we go downstairs, and start organising things? I will of course be writing to you to confirm the details, but Geraldine says you haven't shown before, so I expect there are things you'd like to discuss?'

James and May were still sorting through the water-colours, putting some aside. Bea was witlessly staring at Simon.

'Is something the matter, my dear?'

'No, I mean, I don't know. Have you just offered me a show?'

He looked quizzically at her, then threw back his dishevelled mane of white hair and laughed. Having at first thought him a bit wimpish, Bea began to like him.

'I think I have,' he said, and held out his crisp hand again, to shake on the deal.

They drank tea out of Nest's thick bird-watcher's cups and made lists, wrote notes, discussed which paintings needed to be framed and how, prices (which Bea, starry-eyed, thought veered into the realms of fantasy but she was brought sharply back to earth by taking in the fact that the Gallery's commission was fifty per cent) and Geraldine, quite beside herself with delight, wouldn't stop chattering.

'I told her, you know, but she wouldn't believe me. Bea,

where's the painting of your sleeping friend? Has Simon seen it? James, don't you think that the one of the Freda-angel is otherwordly? And that dark water-colour portrait of her father outside the ironmonger's shop window with the sun setting, isn't it exciting? I do love water-colours used like that, full strength. You'll need a photograph, Bea, of yourself, for the exhibition card, won't she, Simon?'

'May's taken care of that while we were upstairs. Now, Bea. I need a brief autobiography, since you have no relevant CV. I think its important to include some of the smaller water-colours too, since they appear to be studies for the larger paintings.'

'I *am* dreaming this,' thought Bea, pink with embarrassment at the approval and little warning bells jangling guiltily as she began to discover the rare pleasure in being approved of. 'There must be some mistake. I mustn't float away on a cloud. This is happening because of Geraldine – he wants so badly to indulge her,' she started to write out the requested list of titles, sizes and mediums used, 'but I must get them out of here; they're driving me insane.'

Chattering and even squabbling a little they were manoeuvred back into the truck. Bea drove back again to Bellhurst silently bubbling with joy and almost beside herself with excitement. She was intent now on the next move and was muttering a Monopoly mantra: 'Pass GO, Collect £200, grab your get-out-of-jail free card and get back to Nut.'

Oscar's car, she noticed, had acquired a new dent. It was parked outside the cottage, which seemed so normal that it was a second or two before it dawned upon her. The day was filled with sticky complications. She might have to face him. A shadow crossed the glorious afternoon. Involuntarily she checked the time, five-thirty. No, not now, she couldn't. It would spoil everything.

Geraldine almost danced up the path, forcing Simon to bend stiffly and sniff the chocolate-scented *Cosmos* and insisting that Bea come in with them to have a sherry, collect the badger's skull and see the painting of it. Bea agreed, needing time to think. What would it be like to see Oscar after three months apart? Knowing that he had also had a fling with Agnes? Disquieted, she followed them in to collect the skull, politely refused a drink, truthfully admired the painting, and thanking Simon gratefully for his time and the offer, said good-byes and promised a London visit soon to see the gallery and the space which would be hers. She hugged Geraldine in gratefulness and backed out into the garden, waving. Geraldine threw open the sitting-room window and leant out, orange silk scarf catching on the yellow rose bush, calling out:

'You see, it wasn't impossible, was it?' She disentangled the scarf with an impatient jerk. 'Good-bye, my dear, and watch out! I've become a boldy oldie!'

There was the summer smell of grass cuttings, of some sweet lemony scented rose which covered the dead apple tree in the garden. She was startled by the opening of the front door of Fleming Cottage and the incautious appearance of Agnes, hand in hand with Oscar. At that point Bea was hidden from their view by the apple tree. Her inclination was to run for the truck and get the hell out of it but it was the hand in hand bit which floored her. Stunned, she stared as they came down the path. Agnes halted as she noticed Bea's truck first, then let out a squawk of panic as she saw Bea herself, standing both indignant and irresolute on the path of the house next door. Agnes skidded on the bricks in her pretty sandals and dropped her little bag. Oscar, in the middle of a sentence, went scarlet, then paled, pale as his hair, which Bea noticed had been cut much shorter. He was wearing a pink shirt which she hadn't seen before and was considerably plumper. Her heart lurched in such a violent fashion that she felt herself turn sick and shaky. Their own shocked surprise made things suddenly quite clear to her. They had been laughing. So, he had forgiven Agnes for kicking him in the balls. They had made up their differences. Nut, Nut had definitely been to Agnes what Terence had so deftly described as an interim passion.

To their great discomfort Bea now laughed, all the way on jelly legs, a long way – a mile at least it seemed – from Geraldine's front garden to the truck. She climbed up into the hot cab, still grinning viciously, placed the badger's skull carefully on the meltingly hot plastic seat beside her, and started up the engine. Agnes was instantly at the window, saying things at first placatory, then, as usual, defiant. '. . . but you didn't want him, you said you didn't . . .'

'Piss off, you cow!' shouted Bea suddenly, making Agnes jump. She put the truck into reverse and shouted some more. It felt pretty good, shouting. 'I don't give a damn about Oscar. Oscar's second-hand, third-hand, junk-shop stuff. I don't care now how many little slappers he stuffs. You knew he'd left Andreary, had come back, and didn't tell me because you wanted him yourself! You've always been after him. Am I right? It's you having a go at Nut that I care about, more than anything. How could you? How could you cut off his lovely hair?'

She stopped and stared straight into Agnes's shocked wet-slate eyes, noticing the small bruise on the cheekbone, and saw that Nut's suspicions were proven. Then she spoke more quietly, although it was still audible to Oscar. 'How much did you enjoy making me look a fool? Not much – it must have been too easy. Did you ever think at all? What the fuck did you think you were doing? You terrified the wits out of Nut and nearly ruined our lives.' She jerked backwards in the truck, regained control of herself and executed a perfect three-point turn. Then she leant out of the window and said to Oscar, still whitely gaping at the gate: 'You've got obscenely fat.' Agnes, crying now and suddenly impassioned, called out, 'Well at least I can give Oscar what he wants! I'm pregnant, Bea, I'm pregnant!'

'Poor old Oscar,' called out Bea, 'I didn't know you had it in you! I'll give you sixteen to one it's not yours.'

The Greensands, their taxi to the station due at six, were crowded round Geraldine's window unashamedly watching and listening, fascinated. They now gave her a round of applause. She waved cheerily to them and roared off. Geraldine would explain.

Agnes's eyes were brimming as she and Oscar hurriedly retreated to the cottage for shelter and recriminations. She thought she heard Mrs Lewis's husky, mocking laughter as the heel of her sandal detached itself and flapped awkwardly as they scurried back up the path to shut the door again behind them. There was a lot of explaining to do and Agnes wasn't sure her imagination was up to it. She had tried to seduce Nut out of sheer devilry. It had just seemed an interesting idea at the time. She could see now his alarm, his intended rejection ... No, of course he wouldn't have rejected her, it was only that Bea had burst in and he'd felt guilty. Oh well, that was just a little mistake, now she had Oscar back in line. Fight. She would fight for Oscar, and the pretty cottage and garden. She'd gone to the doctors pretty smartly though, when she was two weeks late and it had taken a panicky few days patching up with Oscar, but Bea might now have screwed up that a bit ...

Oscar paced up and down in the sitting room, wonderingly running through the convolutions of the scene. Bea had looked amazing, just slightly tanned and shiningly healthy, hair much longer. He was wondering how to cope without Phil at the ironworks – he had never forgotten that blow to the nose. The weekend with Agnes in London and the few odd evenings afterwards had been a spur-of-the-moment thing; he'd left the practicalities of it to her, never imagining she would actually be able to extricate herself from her family for a whole weekend and had been a little nervous when she'd phoned to say it was all arranged. Despondently alone after the debacle of Andrea and in the face of Bea's apparent indifference, there had been Agnes panting for him, most flatteringly adoring. His efforts to break off the affair had caused an appalling scene. Yet today, today she'd brought him the test results from the surgery and he was so exhilarated by the idea of a child that he'd almost forgotten about Phil, almost forgotten how she'd cheated on him by not delivering his letter; it sounded as though it would have had little effect anyway ...

'It's going to be a real bore to have to find someone else at such short notice,' he said, a little petulantly.

'What do you mean, find someone else?' She was staring at him, horror-struck. He hadn't thought she could be so daft.

'Don't be ridiculous Agnes. Phil and I can't go on working together after this. He'll resign. When are you going to tell him? Who is Nut? And who's collecting Seb from your mother's?'

'Poor, poor Phil,' thought Bea. She was driving automatically, thinking furiously. 'Agnes always lets people down.' It had been a shock, to see them holding hands like children. That's what they were, children, in which case they deserved each other and should get on famously. Bitch-child Agnes.

The heat was shimmering on the road, causing wavering watery mirages on the hot tarmac ahead. The marsh was smothered in a hovering heat haze and fields of wheat, just turned to dusty gold, hemmed her in on either side, bowing as she rattled past unseeing.

'I just wish that if she was so unhappy with Phil, she could have bothered to look a little further for a replacement. Replace-ments.' Bea corrected herself. 'Right on her own doorstep. How lazy. Oh hell! It doesn't matter how it came about. I knew, I knew the whole thing was over between us, before Oscar even left, and wouldn't let myself believe it. But why, why did she go for Nut? Just for fun, to see if she could pull him? Or did she really want to hurt me? Why? I must have done something to get up her nose so badly. And there's poor, monstrous little Seb, who thinks Phil is his Daddy. Will she drag him off to live with Oscar, or stay and battle it out with Phil? Which would be worse for him?'

By now she'd reached the track without remembering having driven there at all. Time to celebrate with Nut. The saga of Nut, and the paintings (she had a feeling it would be a saga and not a fairy story – there'd been quite enough fairy stories) had just begun. She'd be so bold even Geraldine would be shocked.

Bea indulged in a ritual bath to cleanse away the day, ex-husband, ex-friend and the sweat of fear of unknown people. She lay there twiddling toes and chin on chest, looked down her own length, thinking how funny her breasts looked from that angle, rising up out of the deep steamy water like white islands with small coral castles on the top. She shaved her legs and sang a snatch of 'Pirate Jenny', thinking serious sex with Nut and knowing that even if it were no better than with Oscar or poor Terence, she would still want him. Oscar had been a destination, a full stop, when she was seventeen. Nut was a destiny she'd been trying to dodge. One must keep trying. The bath water swirled away with all her stale young past, as if sucked down by a thirsty biographer.

Dressed in the now fading indigo skirt and shirt and digging hurriedly about in a drawer, she found a white halter-neck top that Agnes had once lent her and went outside to fix it to the bent and useless aerial of the truck: a white flag of success. She was startled by a strange hiss from the back and went round to investigate. Geraldine, in her concern for Simon's aged behind, had kindly placed a folded tartan rug on the floor of the truck just behind the cab, and on it was now encamped a white farmyard goose.

There was no end to these birds! Had someone put it there in the half hour or so she'd been indoors? She suspected a Nut joke and walked cautiously round the house to make sure no one was hiding. Perhaps it was injured. She couldn't go to Nut's place accompanied by a goose! Letting the tailboard down and hitching up her skirt, she climbed up but it resisted shooing and arched its neck, put its weaving head down level with the floor and hissed again, the mad blue eyes warning. She bravely put her arms around its body and tried pinning the suddenly thrashing wings to its sides, making a quick grab for the snaking neck but it hissed more ferociously than ever, jabbed and nipped her with its horny orange beak and she lost her nerve and jumped out in a hurry and re-fixed the tailboard. It stared at her, ruffling its snowy feathers. It obviously thought the rug was a nest. It was seven o'clock and Nut would have started his vigil. Since he had a way with birds, he could damn well deal with it! She fetched a blanket and slung it over the vituperative bird which thus extinguished, fell immediately silent.

Broad-shouldered, whippet-hipped, Francis Nutmeg leant against a telegraph pole at the side of the empty road, long hand shading eyes against the slanting sun, watching for her as she slowly approached along the pot-holed tarmac. His house was ready, tidied and scrubbed, flowers in a milk jug, food cooking in the oven. He spotted the white pennant, waved ecstatically and punched the air, leapt to open the cab door and handed her down.

'There! I nearly didn't bother to look, I was so certain it would be white not black. I'm quite relieved. If it had been black I thought you might want me to throw myself in the sea like King Aegeus.' She was almost smothered by his hot embrace and struggled loose, still perturbed by the problem of the truck's cargo.

'Nut, there's a goose in the back of the truck!'

He looked startled. 'But you shouldn't have bothered, my Bea. I have a little leg of lamb roasting in the oven! And the best of new potatoes, all waxy and yellow ...'

'No, not to eat! The goose is alive, and terribly cross. It won't get out and I don't know how it got there.'

Nut also walked round the back, swung aboard athletically, and removed the blanket. There was a further frenzied hissing.

He jumped down again. His way with birds did not apparently extend to domesticated members of the *Anserinae* family and besides, his mind was on other things.

'Come on, we've better things to do than worry about mad geese. We'll leave it alone and perhaps it'll take itself off.'

'Perhaps it's going to lay an egg?'

'Too late in the year. Now let's *leave* it.'

'Yes, of course. Do you think she might like a bowl of water?'

'We'll bring one out later.' Dear God, he was thinking, am I never going to have her whole attention? She became aware that she had all his and took his arm, distancing herself from goose, and the whole hot cauldron of the day.

Nut produced a bottle of champagne with a flourish from the midget fridge in the kitchen and picking up a couple of glasses, led her through the sunroom out to the wooden deck where he'd placed two chairs and laid a white cloth on a sea-bleached wooden table.

'It seemed a pity to waste another fine evening and supper won't be ready for half an hour. Now sit down, just there, at a proper distance from me, so I can look at you while you tell the story.'

She recounted the stages of the afternoon, the Greensands' offer, Geraldine's overexcitement, but deleted Oscar and Agnes from the script. His eyes never left her face but for once she wasn't self-conscious, her own being similarly engaged. While she spoke and sipped the champagne, children called to each other in the distance, pastel washing flapped on the next door railway-carriage's line, a black-and-white collie dog picked its way across the shingle, a stick in its mouth and a long shadow in front of it. Gulls cruised past, the early evening sun shining through their transparent wing-tip feathers. The power station hummed in the background and the lamb sizzled in the oven. An unlikely and ridiculous place in which to be drinking champagne; but no such place exists.

'It's a beautiful soft evening, isn't it? You've got the sun in your eyes. Turn around a bit, and I'll go and carve.'

The lamb was pink and tender, the potatoes just as he said they would be and he'd tossed up a sharp green salad with dandelion leaves and borage flowers. His legs were firmly clamped on either side of hers as they ate, as if to prevent her from escaping. He could cook. It was definitely love.

'In this light, you look as if you'd been lightly coated all over with cream,' he said, stroking her shoulder and seeing in the half-veiled blue eyes staring at him in the early twilight an expression combining delighted surprise, smugness and not a little cunning, a lottery winner at last. He reached forward and with a cool hand stroked back the tangle of hair from her forehead. Her entire interior from scalp to toes had been transformed to honey.

'That's what it feels like. I didn't know it could be like that,' she stammered, a little shy of what she was about to say. 'I mean I knew it could be better, if I could get there, but I never did, quite, before.'

'You're joking!' He sat up, disbelieving, shocked. 'You *never* had an orgasm?'

'No, I'm *not* joking! And no, not like now.'

'But you were with your husband ... how long?'

'Twelve years.'

'What a good thing you're shot of him! Oh Bea, what a waste, and what fun! And it's barely dark. The whole night's ahead of us. I think there's some cream in the fridge.'

'And how did you sleep, Bountiful Bea?'

'Oh! pretty well, considering ...' She rolled over lazily, insolently exultant eyes peering at him through tangled hair. She was back inside her skin – a comfortable skin – warm, loved, melted. 'We used to play a game with our grandmother, Patrick and I, called 'I love my love with an A . . .'

'Because they're anxious, awkward, argumentative, amorous, agnostic, archaic,' he rattled them out, ticking them off on his fingers and then found more '. . . amicable, amusing, arrogant, aggravating, anatomically perfect . . . Yes, I played that in the waiting room before the dentist . . . Where are you off to? Oh I see. Here, wrap this about you. We're not like you, living in the wilderness, we have neighbours here and I don't see why they should get the benefit of the sight of you through a window when I've had to wait so long.'

He knelt up on the bed and wrapped a length of blue-and-green printed cotton around her as she stood, rolling over the top like a sarong.

'There, that's my dressing gown. I didn't think myself a jealous man till That Morning. Now I'm disgustingly jealous and hate to let you out of my sight. But I will, though. I was quite fearful that you would disappear last night, between the roast lamb and the bedroom. I'll trust you not to dissolve into a pool of sea water or slip off with a seal while I make us tea?'

'I wasn't jealous either, till That Afternoon,' she called out. Almost loth to wash away the night, Bea stood turning herself beneath the shower then dried with Nut's green towel, surveying the extent of his personal things lying there in the prismed sunlight from the patterned frosted glass, and greedily knew that even his belongings were now a part of her. The green toothbrush and black razor lying on the edge of the basin, the twisted toothpaste tube squeezed from the middle and wearing a collar of dried paste (they wouldn't have rows about that, at least, she thought, grinning, an offender herself). She even sniffed the soap and felt a personal fondness for his balding shaving brush. Already missing his presence, she tied the sarong about her again, went and stood in the doorway of the little dark kitchen, watching his dark shape framed against the brightness of the tiny window, unable to get enough of looking at him, destroyed by the tall grace of his body, completely and utterly at ease with it and for once, with her own.

'*You* don't seem worried that the neighbours might walk past the windows?'

'They could only see me from the waist up.'

'Nut! We've forgotten the goose! She might be lying there, dead in the back of the truck!' She leapt for the door, stopping long enough to slip her feet into Nut's Herculean boots and shuffle clumsily across the hot shingle to the roadway. Nut followed, swearing, struggling into his trousers as he hurried after her. An old boy passing on a bicycle wobbled lethally across the road. Was he witnessing an attack? Should he pedal furiously for the nearest telephone box? But he knew Nut by sight and remembering the night of the witches, decided that nudity was now the fashion in the area and pedalled on, glancing back, shaking his head and clucking as he saw that the hopping, red haired chap had now managed to get both legs into his jeans and now decently buttoned up, was tentatively barefooting after the girl. He'd not catch her at that speed anyway and the girl was turning about, calling to him, from the back of a truck. Nothing to worry about, though from what he'd seen, you'd need a fire extinguisher to put that man out once he was taken with a passion. That was flaming red hair, and no mistake.

'Nut, she's gone! Do you think someone stole her, or that she went off on her own?'

'I guess she managed by herself. I've stepped in a goose turd. Perhaps she's a sea-going bird.'

'I was quite looking forward to keeping a goose.'

'Never mind. Can I have my boots back, please? I think I've trodden on some broken glass as well. I'll give you a piggy-back.' He bent and she mounted, clutching at the slithering sarong. 'Hey up, off we go. I was thinking of taking the morning off. You don't have a pressing reason for going back to Little Rumm, do you?'

'No. Of course I'm carrying on with the painting, but the

pressure's over. It's been a little bit like being on a pilgrimage, a static pilgrimage, more of a retreat perhaps.'

'Then here's a cockleshell for you to prove it. You'll have to sew that on your hatband, like the pilgrims to Santiago de Compostella.' He stooped to pick it up and she shrieked and clung, almost catapulted over his head. She slid down from his back at the door.

'What's this bird's-nest stuff on the ground here?' She bent to examine a mound of tangled, reddish threads weaving through a ground-hugging, wind-dwarfed clump of broom.

'That's dodder. It's parasitic, like mistletoe. Its leaves are too small to see, but look, it's got minute pink flowers dotted about it.' He crouched down to show her. The expanse of naked shoulders, the bloom on the fair skin, the slim line of the spine, dividing the two sets of muscles, diving below the back of the old salt-water-stained black jeans had a marvellously erotic effect; she became supremely uninterested at that moment in either the goose or little pink flowers.

Half an hour later they heard the overfamiliar sounds of a police car but did not allow it to interrupt them.

They were unaware then that Agnes, having found that Oscar was a little too interested in the paternity of her forth-coming child to be comfortable, had driven down to the sea, bought a ticket for visiting the old lighthouse and was now at the top of it, clutching at the railing and threatening to dash herself to the ground below if Oscar refused to believe her. She was rather cross about having to buy a ticket, since she felt that attempted suicide was one of those missions that should have made her eligible for at least some sort of discount, if not free entry. Oscar was sent for and panted up the one hundred and sixty-nine steps in a sweating, panic-driven fury, the policewoman attending the emergency having been unsympathetic both to his pleas of innocence and his rather querulous and vague shouts to Agnes from the safety of the ground. Out of embarrassment and genuine fear for her safety, he promised all manner of things which he later would have preferred to forget, and took her back to Fleming Cottage.

A couple of days later, when things had calmed down a little and Bea and Nut could support the idea of sharing a moment of their Olympian hours together with mere mortals, Bea rang first Geraldine and then Nest, who responded exultantly to the news of the promised exhibition.

'Darling! I always knew you'd pull it off! What an excitement though, a London show straight off! Can Blue and I come and see at last what you've been up to?'

'Of course you can, Aunt Nest. That's why I'm telephoning, to thank you for all your help, particularly the curiously sedative couple of occult envoys, who worked so well. How about a celebratory supper at Little Rumm, Thursday night? Geraldine's coming. I knew about it on Sunday, but made myself wait for written confirmation, in case it was just a nice dream. It came this morning. There's something else. I want you to meet Nut. He's very eager to meet you.' Nut stood behind her, his sharp nose buried in her neck, stroking a shoulder, sliding his other hand around her hip and downwards, distracting.

Nest's pride in the rightness of her convictions knew no bounds — she was the instigator, a thaumaturge, a Svengali! She raced off to find Blue and discovered him in the little office behind the long greenhouse, his feet on the desk, reading a tattered copy of *Memoirs of a Midget*. A muddy finger was passing slowly along the lines and his lips were moving. That was another of her successes, having taught him to read.

One late August morning Oscar stood impatiently in the drought-stricken front garden of Fleming Cottage, waiting for Bea to put in an appearance. It was an unbearably sticky day and both weeds and herbaceous plants had suffered that summer — the flowerbeds were a tangled mane of fawn and tawny seedpods and cracks had appeared in the dried-out little patch of lawn.

The agent's sign in the dusty hedge now had SOLD slapped across it and in two days' time the new owners would move in. It was over.

Bea drew up in her truck. It was the apocalyptic day when they met to split the remainder of their possessions; they had already discussed settlements at the end of July and The Divorce was now on its stealthy journey. She imagined it passing through letter boxes and across solicitors' desks, in and out of IN and OUT trays, being tapped out on word-processors, dated, sealed, stamped, preserved, laminated, set in concrete and tied up in pink ribbon.

She looked very good, Oscar thought unguardedly as the blooming, polished Bea approached up the brick path, a little plumper and smoother in neat black jeans and T-shirt, smiling pleasantly (she could not help smiling since she was, as everyone had been telling him for some time now, perfectly happy), her thick hair twisted up into a large golden knot, striped further by the sun and escaping wildly in all directions.

'Isn't it a relief it's gone so quickly?' she said, nodding at the agent's board. 'Shall we go in and start at once? It needn't take long. I know what's yours – you know what's mine. We could toss a coin for the rest.'

He followed her. She had a little heart-shaped patch of sweat between her shoulder-blades. He was unable quite to believe that he had lost forever that lithe body. But it had happened. He had made it happen. And now he had Agnes, and his child to come although he still had doubts. They sorted through the remaining books: SAS and motorcycle manuals in one box, everything else in the other.

'The baby's due in March,' he said casually, evaluating the depth of the circular ripples of thought floating out across her face.

'Jolly good for you!' she said, as if he'd scored a century in a school cricket First XI, smiling up at him, brow shining. She brushed a dangling piece of hair aside and carried on packing.

'That's my school Bible, the Coleridge and the Penguins and the Revision notes on *Othello*, that's your *Fungus the Bogeyman* — is the RHS *Vegetable Gardening* yours or mine? Yours? OK. Shall we do the china next?' She could be discomfited by nothing.

On the kitchen table was a box of odds and ends which Agnes had brought with her only a few weeks before, on the sadly ill-founded assumption that she and Seb would be moving permanently into Fleming Cottage with Oscar. Oscar was unable to raise the amount needed to buy Bea out without borrowing exorbitantly and so the cottage had to be sold; they were now domiciled, or rather incarcerated, in a rented flat on the far side of Bellhurst, with no garden at all for poor Seb to play in.

Bea began piling china out on to the table. 'Look, I remember these plates came from your mother . . . and these are mine, Aunt Maude's. I'm sure there were *two* vegetable dishes?' She looked up, querying.

'Seb . . .' began Oscar, but Bea swiftly interrupted him.

'Say no more. And this pile is wedding presents. Oscar, do pay attention or we'll never be finished. You pack these away in your box. Have you got a coin in your pocket? Right, give it to me. Heads or tails for the silver saltcellars. Heads? Tails. I seem to have got them. Now you spin it and I call for the toast-rack. Actually I don't want it anyway. Now for the teaspoons . . .' here her voice trembled. She had not expected to have to take charge so completely, while Oscar stayed mum, staring desperately at her, his throat working. Her lack of sentimentality had always thrown him.

'Oscar?'

'Yes?' His voice, diminished to no more than a croak, came from miles away.

'We can't change anything, now. I don't want to, never really wanted to, I'm afraid. I told you, even if Agnes and Geraldine had passed on your messages, it would have been far too late. I don't feel any animosity towards either of them for not doing so, since I might have felt I ought to give it another try,' she looked squarely at him, at the fair hair sticking to his forehead in the heat, 'and I know now that it would have been utterly wrong for both of us, and it's very miserable of you to try and make *me* feel guilty. It's quite obviously your turn to look after Agnes. Everybody else has tried it and failed.'

Oscar swallowed, did as he was told and they spun and spun the twopenny piece till the things had all been fairly divided and tucked away in their respective boxes.

Civilised to the last, together they carried out and packed into the truck the small amount of furniture and boxes. Neither of them desired the bed. The curtains and rush matting went with the house.

'How will you manage on your own, at the other end?'

'I have Nut, waiting to help.' She looked at him a trifle anxiously. 'We're getting married, after the show in November.'

Oscar looked sharply at her. 'What show?'

'Of course. You haven't been told. I'm being given a show at the Greensand Gallery in London. Geraldine has one half of the gallery for a retrospective and I get the other.'

Oscar felt dazed. Bea reached out a hand and put it on his upper arm to balance herself and leant forwards from a distance, planting a cool kiss on his cheek. Oscar sensed the chasm between their bodies with an interior sob of self-pity.

'I'm going in to see Geraldine now. We'll be in touch. 'Bye.' She half turned, then came back to him. 'Is Agnes at the flat this afternoon?' Oscar, looking down and playing with his key ring, said she probably was.

'What's the flat like?'

'Not too bad. It looks out over an orchard – it's quite pretty. But they're cutting it down soon to build executive homes.'

Poor Agnes, Bea thought. She'd love an 'executive home'.

Geraldine O'Brien, painting *molto furioso* in her sitting room, on glancing up from her easel saw them by the truck, standing so very much apart and gave an almost vulpine grin and waved, a little wildly, as Bea came up to the door. The pointer measuring her state of mind over the course of the summer had gone from 'deep sleep', passed 'calm' at some speed, and was now quivering nervously somewhere between 'excitable' and 'manic'.

'Won't you be glad when this hot spell is over? I can't wait for one of those cool mornings, when one can see all the spiders' webs laid out in the grass covered in dew, and smell decay. I'm old and decaying and now take an even greater interest in the process. It's nearly mushroom time. You do look wonderful. Are you pregnant yet?' She vigorously cleaned a brush and looked at Bea with interest.

'Oh, I shouldn't think so for a moment.'

'So, it's all sorted out is it, Bea? There were no confrontations about who has the salt spoon and who the saltcellar? Well done! Now what do you think of this picture? Hold on a minute, I've some iced coffee ready in the kitchen. You must be parched after all the emotionals.'

Bea watched her with affectionate amusement as she spun about the kitchen, fussing through the drawers for spoons and hunting among the geraniums on the windowsill for sugar. She was moving very fast these days. Bea wondered if perhaps she been prescribed tranquillisers for other reasons than distress, had been a little overexcitable even before her breakdown.

'There's no hurry, Geraldine!'

'No, of course not. I seem to be whizzing about these days. There's still so much to do before this exhibition. Now, there we are. Come into the sitting room and tell me what you think.'

The painting was of flowers – just the flowers, no stalks or leaves, and they were crushed together to cover the entire small canvas; loosely painted in some areas, more sharply focused in others, glowing, slightly sinister. Roses, their faded silk velvet petals insect-nibbled. Bent-petalled daisies, dying lilies, withered irises ... from a distance it was a pretty Victorian posy – from close-up, something else entirely. Bea wanted it quite badly.

'It's incredibly decadent. I love it.'

'The idea came from all those unfortunate flowers dying in the sun in their silvery paper pokes; cut, chopped and suffocated when the Princess of Wales died. I'm planning to paint rotting pumpkins in the winter. The moulds that grow on them are stunning. Putrescence can be so intensely colourful. Simon's coming down again next week to have his final pick and to see which of our new ones can fit in, so he can get the catalogue printed, I suppose. Are you excited? I am. No stage-fright at all. See?' She held out a remarkably unsteady hand.

'Bea, do you never have periods?' Nut leant up on an elbow, a mug of tea in his hand, watching Bea speculatively as she lay reading one of the multifarious sections of the welter of Sunday newspapers, cosily propped up on the pillows in the bedroom at Little Rumm. Bea was startled and glanced at him slightly apprehensively.

'Oh, yes, occasionally. Normally only about three or four times a year ... I thought it was great, getting off so lightly ... is that what you're on about? I did warn you there's little chance of me becoming pregnant.'

'And why didn't you find out what was wrong? Didn't you want children?'

'Nut, I lived in dreamtime, then. Nothing mattered much except keeping Oscar at bay and as happy as possible so there was time to draw. I wasn't bothered since I never felt anything was wrong. The idea of intervention was frightening.'

She folded up the newspaper in a great untidy rustling mess and ruffled about searching for the colour magazine, then looked up at him again, anxiously. 'Do you mind about not having children? Because if you do, I'll find out if it can be solved, immediately.' She sighed. 'Now Agnes is in pod, it looks as if it probably was my fault, all along.' She put the paper down and looked at the foxy length of him, his cheek pushed up with his fist and the sea-water eye above it narrowed, shining like a pale green tourmaline.

'No, I'm easy. You get your career going. It would be nice to have a daughter though, don't you think? I'd like to have a copy of you, if at all.'

Nut could imagine, almost touch, a little giggling thing, golden or red-haired, in a green cotton dress, running up and down the sand while he chased her, caught her and lifted her up close to his heart. The vision was clear enough to be quite disturbing. His eyebrows were twitched together for an instant and a shadow lay across his face.

'I just wondered,' he continued, carefully picking his words, 'if you might perhaps be pregnant and were hiding it from me till you were certain sure. You'd tell me, wouldn't you, if you were? You've got rounder all over, more curvy. Your behind is sumptuous. A juicy-lucy bum.' He left it at that most wisely, and cowered since she was threatening to beat him to a pulp with the rolled-up lifestyle section.

'I'd know if I was pregnant! One feels sick in the morning, and goes off coffee, all that sort of thing. I feel absolutely wonderful and I've loads of energy.'

Three weeks later, driving back from Parden Station after a visit to the Greensands in London, Bea's eyes became unfocused, and she was forced to pull up sharply in a field gateway. With singing-ringing noises in her ears and the sickening sensation of being whirled away down a darkening circular corridor, she fainted. She did not know for how long but on coming round, she had to sit there for a while attempting to regain her equilibrium before shakily continuing on her way back to Nut's house.

She told him about the incident, but because she now felt infinitely better and wonderfully hungry, she made light of it. Nut was cooking smoked sprats for supper and she went down to the shore, feeling suddenly that she needed to be alone for a few minutes. She stood invoking Freda while the cooling September sea made little hissing rushes at her feet and dashed against her shins and along with it came the certainty that she too was pregnant.

She was astonished and a little piqued that it could have happened without her knowing, but this soon gave way to an absolute and tense excitement. Apart from the fact that there was the faintest but agonising possibility that the child might be Terence Moorbury's. Terence had been true to form and taken Extra Large precautions, which she seemed to remember had not been entirely satisfactory. She'd been so certain of her infertility. The child *must* be, *was*, Nut's. This conviction took quite a while to take root, but in the short term she achieved it. The companion seedling fear was temporarily crushed.

The fact was later confirmed and the surprised and congratulatory doctor mentioned spontaneous ovulation as a possibility. Hmph! she thought. If any spontaneous ovulation had occurred, it had definitely not been procured by Terence's doings. During the following months, she never confessed the fear to Nut; her whole being was caught up in the experience of being both impregnable in the mental sense and pregnant in the physical.

If Nut briefly remembered the stranger at the breakfast table he had put the thought aside, preferring to indulge the euphoria waiting in the wings. It was a memory he did not mention to Bea, willing himself to be convinced by the strength of her own apparent certainty. Women, he told himself, firmly disregarding all past biological evidence, know these things. He still did not know if she had slept with Terence or not and no longer cared. He was happy to see Bea apparently so very contented and in his eyes she was as hopelessly seductive and interesting as before; the minutely thickening waist, the swelling breasts made her resemble more and more some secretive renaissance beauty. He was a brave man and a loving man and decided to bite the bullet and not enquire any further – he was besotted and would in any case have taken her on with an army of other men's children.

Geraldine was already at the gallery when Nut arrived with Bea for the private view. Bea could see her through the glass door, wearing a green silk jacket that they'd bought together in Canterbury. She was talking to Amelia and Edmund, gesticulating with her glass of wine as was now her wont, erratically. A niggling November wind nipped their cheeks as they lingered together outside in the London street, looking in at the brightly lit interior and the early-comers wandering about with catalogues in hand, examining the pictures. In the window on the right side of the central plate-glass door hung one of Geraldine's darkly glowing paintings of vegetable decomposition, suspended by invisible nylon thread, and on the left side hung Bea's wedding painting, likewise suspended in mid air. The names Bea Kerepol and Geraldine O'Brien were displayed on the glass window in three inch high white letters.

'Take a deep breath, Bea,' said Nut, sensing her sudden panic, taking hold of her hand and squeezing it before pushing open the door and holding it for her to pass through from the dark evening into the warm, light interior. Once in he stood protectively behind her for a moment, hands comfortingly on her shoulders before propelling her forward. 'Go on, my darling, it's you they want to meet. I can look after myself.'

The strange thing was that she felt completely disassociated from the paintings. 'Good heavens! Did I do that?' was the only thought that occurred as she travelled with Simon round the wall space, admiring how they had been displayed and trying not to notice parts of them which could have been handled better. The rooms filled up rapidly and she was soon whirled away from friendly well-known faces to be introduced to (and interviewed by) terrifying potential clients. Phil came, solid, strong and bitter but so obviously pleased to see her that her heart went out to him.

'I miss Seb dreadfully and I never thought I would. I keep finding little toy cars under cushions. She lets me take him to the playground, now and then . . .'

Mary Dunnock arrived with her husband and only two of their offspring, followed by Justin Bullingden who already appeared to know four fifths of the other guests.

'Ah Bea! Before I go and look at the pictures, Terence asked me to give you this.' He handed her an envelope which contained a blown-up photograph of the eye she had made from stones on the beach that unpropitious day in the summer. It had been taken by a crew member on board the boat. On the back was tactfully written: 'Heard about the show from Justin. Congratulations and hope it's a sell-out. Terence' Justin stooped and whispered in her ear. 'He says to tell you he has no hard feelings and sent the picture for good luck.' The reminder of Terence sent an unwelcome frisson to her stomach but she was instantly distracted by the arrival of Aunt Nest, stunning in violet velvet, with an astonishingly washed and manicured Blue.

Nut moved about the rooms on his own while Bea was being busied about, eavesdropping on the private viewers' reactions to her pictures with growing pride, wondering how it was that a person so susceptible to fears and forebodings had achieved work of such astounding self-confidence. He discovered Jane standing predictably bemused before the boat-launching picture.

'*What* is this about? I'm afraid I don't understand it at all. Why is that giantess pulling those people out to sea in a boat? And who are all these robed people, waving? Is it a nursery rhyme? And what does it mean?'

'I wouldn't worry about what it means, Mrs Kerepol. You know Bea. Always abstruse . . . That girl is putting a red sticker on its label. Does that mean it's been bought, do you suppose?'

'How exciting. Why do you think they want it?' Nut looked

again at the now familiar picture; Bea, softening in her attitude to the past summer's incursions by family and friends, had been altering various parts of it since he'd first seen it in the painting room. In the prow of the boat standing like a pair of smug figureheads were himself and Bea. The robed figures were Jane and Tom, Oscar, Agnes, and others whom he did not recognise, including, he'd been told, the art teacher from Bellhurst Grammar. Bea'd explained that it appeared less intolerant for her and him to be seen sailing away helped by Freda. To have her parents and acquaintances apparently dragged out and possibly dumped at sea would not be conducive to family stability, however much that had been the prickly original intention. Mercifully Jane had not identified herself.

'Have you seen the portrait of your husband, Mrs Kerepol?'

'Yes, but it doesn't look in the least bit like him, does it? So very dark-skinned and with all those pinky splotches down the side of his face. Makes him look as if he had a skin disease.'

Tom had found his portrait and was most impressed with the finished article. He spent some time standing close by it, hoping someone would remark on the likeness; it was hard not to, with the eyepatch so satisfyingly identifying the subject. He was bursting with pleasure in his daughter's achievement and indulged in mutual congratulations with Nest.

Blue sauntered about and finally made himself known to James's secretary who, proving susceptible to both his particular brand of rough-trade charm and the gap between his front teeth, briefly disappeared with him downstairs into the stock room to demonstrate the difference between an etching and a lithograph.

Nut was detailed by James Greensand to ensure that Geraldine did not hit the bottle and become uncontrollable.

'I'd be so grateful if you could go and engage her in a bit of banter for a while, make sure she eats some nibbly things,' pleaded James, refilling Nut's glass. 'I don't want to stop her enjoying herself, but if you could just keep her down for another half hour, then it doesn't matter if she kicks off her shoes and dances a can-can like any other nineteen-fifties bohemian. I must say Bea's being most helpfully lucid this evening. I'd thought that she was something of a shy flower but she's quite overpowered Mrs Gurgelfeldt – the one over there, the old American leather lady all in black, yes, that one with the grey number two haircut – it was like witnessing a confrontation between a seraph and a bat. Oh! Goodie! I can hear the rustle of a chequebook.'

Bea was sweating after her encounter with Mrs Gurgelfeldt, and had hidden in a corner of the gallery where she encountered Patrick bending to look at a set of four early charcoal drawings which had been included in a little section showing the development of her work. These drawings had been done at the age of sixteen and were of Patrick mending a lawn mower.

'I've bought that one, Bea. I thought it ought to stay in the family!'

'Then I'll give you its companion piece as a present.'

'Which one is that?'

'Oh, it isn't here. It's back at home. It's of you at about the same age, smoking secretly behind the hornbeam hedge in that field we used to go to, to get away from all the cooking, if you remember. We used to sit in the wet grass coughing, with clouds of blue smoke drifting up, thinking how adult we were.'

'Of course I remember. You are absolutely grown up now, aren't you, Bea? This show sort of puts the seal on it. Professional. Are you all right? You look a bit over-rosy.'

The room was very warm, and smelly – to Bea's over-sensitive nose a synthetic cacophony of the competing scents, a bouillabaisse of the talcum powders, soaps and aftershaves of the well-groomed private viewers. It was a shame, Bea thought, that they didn't co-ordinate themselves before leaving home, that the particular smell to be worn should be printed on the invitation – 'Gardenia tonight, please' or, 'Only Ylang-Ylang will gain you admittance' and already she longed for a salty sniff of sea. She murmured to Patrick that she was fine and was fanning herself with an exhibition card when Simon came up to her and whispered, 'Go and take a peep in the other room. You'll see red stickers on three of the big Freda paintings, and several of the little ones. You're doing really well . . . that piece by May in the *Daily Telegraph* about you and Geraldine aroused a lot of interest. We're very pleased. You look a bit pink — are you all right?'

Preoccupied, Bea was staring at Simon as if she had not heard. A delicate but self-important fluttering sensation had just run across her interior like a mouse, making her gasp and clutch at her stomach. She was wearing a long lace jacket which hid any hint of bulge beneath her straight dress; very few people had been let in on the secret.

'Now you've gone quite white,' said Patrick anxiously, 'are you all right?'

'No, yes, I'm . . . I'm absolutely stunned, Simon. Where's Nut? Have you seen him? I've got to tell him at once.' He was standing by the drinks table, his arm firmly clasping Geraldine's while telling Amelia a tall story, making them both rock with laughter.

'Nut, just a second, I must speak to you,' she whispered and drew him away, quivering with excitement.

'Are you sure? It's quickened?' Eager and solicitous, he slipped his arm round her waist, spreading fingers out over her stomach. 'I can't feel a thing.'

'No, it came and went so quickly — but I'm certain.'

He was grinning like a Cheshire cat, but she felt a mixture of thrill and fear. Closer, closer came the time. Five months more and it would all be clear. There was nothing to worry about. Of course it was Nut's. He looked wonderfully elegant that evening, in a new dark blue jacket and cream shirt. She loved him so fiercely she felt almost sick, a physical manifestation that Oscar had never managed to engender.

The evening wore on and on and the small talk grazed past her ears like bullets but as she was never sure if it was Geraldine's or her own work which was the target or something else entirely, she took little notice, but continued to shake hands and smile.

'... A secular spirituality ... perverse degeneration ... Peter's girl is doing very well at Leeds ... inspiring ... magical ... nine hundred pounds ... prostate trouble ... I must say, Geraldine's aged incredibly ... How much was it? Speak up m'dear, I'm deafened by this racket ... What? No, Caroline's had hers lifted, twice, *and* implants ... wind-tunnel effect ... that one has a tenderness and an authority ... wildly idiosyncratic ... Carla's very good at ball-room dancing – she did a lot of it in Zimbabwe ... what draughtsmanship, so rare in the young ... it was Henrietta who kept the de Kooning.'

'Right, Bea. Are you feeling all right? Have you done your duty and chatted up all the customers? Might we go to supper soon? Geraldine's sold her three new pictures and just tipped back another drink. She's trying to entice James into taking her on to some pub called the French, in Soho, with a lot of old reprobates who've come along to support her! One of her old haunts apparently. Was she really a shy old lady when you first met her? She's not now, is she? She's just felt my bum and Simon's hiding in the other room in case she tells everyone they once were lovers.'

'Did she tell you that?' Bea asked.

'She did, and told Amelia and Edmund who, incidentally, have just bought one of your mad water-colours of fat angels eating poppies. And your Heron Man, Justin. He's bought two drawings.'

'Oh, that *is* flattering! I still can't quite believe it's all happened. It *wouldn't* have happened without my three lifeboats: Nest, Geraldine and you. We should be allowed to go now, it's nearly nine and it was supposed to end at eight and I'm starving again. Should we stay and help Simon with Geraldine, perhaps? She's staying the night with him.'

'Jesus! No! Let's leave him to it. They've got years' worth of making-up to do.'

'Right, I'll just go and say good-bye and thanks to Geraldine and Simon and then round up the family.'

Chapter Twelve and A Half

Bea had at first been reluctant, then cautiously agreed as Agnes pleaded and they met, still with suspicions on Bea's part, at the recreation ground in Bellhurst on a June afternoon. Seb, released from primary school, hung upside down by his knees from a climbing frame and hooted like an owl. Sitting on the bench beneath the fresh green leaves of a lime tree, they inspected the wriggling contents of each other's baby-baskets.

Agnes peered at Bea's fairy changeling lying there in the dappled shade. It appeared to grin at her, delicate little wrists and minute hands circling and waving as if enticing, wreaking enchantments.

'What have you called her?'

'Freda Mary.'

'Good lord! That sounds a bit heavy. Sort of Lawrentian. Freda! Is it a family name?'

'No, it just came to me. It means peace – which of course was asking for trouble.'

'Well, at least there aren't any doubts about whose it is. I've never seen a baby with so much red hair.'

Bea glanced nervously at her, as if expecting her to produce some scissors, and did not mention that her great Aunt Maude had been a red head, as her mother had pointed out loudly in the hospital, in front of Nut. She hastily turned to inspect

Agnes's little boy, bending over him for an uncomfortably long space of time and when she looked up, she could barely keep a straight face.

'God! Agnes! But the chances of this happening are astronomical. I didn't think it was something that could be inherited?'

The kitten blue mist had faded from the baby's eyes and Bea had seen that the blond, plump, rose-cheeked William's eyes were of different colours: one slate, one green. Agnes looked away into the distance, disconsolate.

'Well, it's happened, astronomical or not. Oscar noticed, went all white and quiet and after muttering about deceit and other things I won't go into, has left. I got a letter this morning from his solicitor, demanding blood tests.'

'This is Phil's son, then? Have you told him?'

'It looks like it, doesn't it?' Agnes replied crossly; little lines were beginning to etch themselves about her mouth. 'I can't think how it happened. I must have been drunk. And he was three weeks earlier than expected. Just as well, he weighed nine and a half pounds. Anyway, even if it's just a freak chance and the tests prove whose it isn't, I don't want to go back to either of them. Oscar's a pompous prat and Phil's a sanctimonious grouch. And Seb's being horrid to William. As soon as my back's turned he pinches him.'

'Agnes, he's probably terribly jealous, poor lamb. And as far as Seb's concerned, Phil is his father. Phil would be devastated if he knew this one might be his.'

'It's not fair, Bea.' Agnes's voice wobbled. 'Why does everything always go wrong for me and right for you?'

Unfathomable, except by Freda.

Under Construction
PAMELA JOHNSON

Everyone says it's crazy: renovating a dilapidated house in North London is no job for a young widow with teenage daughters. But it's three years since Greg died, Amy needs a new start. A team of builders tears the house apart around her. As they rebuild it, Amy develops an intimacy with Conor the Irish joiner. Where in her new life can she accommodate a relationship with a married man, father of four young children?

Conor and Amy can exist only in the pockets of time and space they slip into, unnoticed: London cafés, windswept Dungeness, the West coast of Ireland, and the infinite space of Amy's imagination. In reconstructing her life, Amy treads a fine line between creating something and destroying it.

This poetic first novel explores the intimate spaces one woman constructs as she recovers herself.

'Irresistibly readable, with a striking storyline. Pamela Johnson writes with great feeling and wit'
HELEN DUNMORE

'The slow, yet dizzying slide into love makes for a compelling read'
JAMES FRIEL

Pamela Johnson writes, lectures and broadcasts on contemporary visual arts; she also publishes poetry. She lives in London with her husband, son and daughter.

∫

SCEPTRE

A selection of bestsellers from
Hodder and Stoughton

Under Construction	Pamela Johnson	0 340 71798 X	£6.99	☐
Defrosting Edmund	Nina Dufort	0 340 71682 7	£6.99	☐
In the Heart of the Garden	Helene Wiggin	0 340 69571 4	£6.99	☐
That was Then	Sarah Harrison	0 340 70731 3	£6.99	☐
The Trespassers	Pam Rhodes	0 340 71236 8	£5.99	☐
Kinvara	Christine Marion Fraser	0 340 70714 3	£5.99	☐
The Bobbin Girls	Freda Lightfoot	0 340 67438 5	£5.99	☐
A Promise Given	Meg Hutchinson	0 340 69684 2	£5.99	☐

All Hodder & Stoughton books are available at your local bookshop or newsagent, or can be ordered direct from the publisher. Just tick the titles you want and fill in the form below. Prices and availability subject to change without notice.

Hodder & Stoughton Books, Cash Sales Department, Bookpoint, 39 Milton Park, Abingdon, OXON, OX14 4TD, UK. E-mail address: order@bookpoint.co.uk. If you have a credit card you may order by telephone – (01235) 400414.

Please enclose a cheque or postal order made payable to Bookpoint Ltd to the value of the cover price and allow the following for postage and packing:
UK & BFPO – £1.00 for the first book, 50p for the second book, and 30p for each additional book ordered up to a maximum charge of £3.00.
OVERSEAS & EIRE – £2.00 for the first book, £1.00 for the second book, and 50p for each additional book.

Name _____

Address_____

_____

_____

If you would prefer to pay by credit card, please complete:
Please debit my Visa/Access/Diner's Card/American Express (delete as applicable) card no:

Signature _____

Expiry Date_____

If you would NOT like to receive further information on our products please tick the box. ☐